Michelle Smart's love affair with books started when she was a baby and would cuddle them in her cot. A voracious reader of all genres, she found her love of romance established when she stumbled across her first Mills & Boon book at the age of twelve. She's been reading them—and writing them—ever since. Michelle lives in Northamptonshire, England, with her husband and two young Smarties.

USA TODAY bestselling author **Heidi Rice** lives in London, England. She is married with two teenage sons—which gives her rather too much of an insight into the male psyche—and also works as a film journalist. She adores her job, which involves getting swept up in a world of high emotion, sensual excitement, funny and feisty women, sexy and tortured men and glamorous locations where laundry doesn't exist. Once she turns off her computer she often does chores—usually involving laundry!

Also by Michelle Smart

Spaniard's Shock Heirs

Greek Rivals miniseries

Forgotten Greek Proposal
His Pregnant Enemy Bride
Greek Boss to Hate

Also by Heidi Rice

Billionaire's Wedlocked Wife

Claimed by a Greek miniseries

The Heir Affair

Greek's Kidnapped Princess

Discover more at millsandboon.co.uk.

THE WEDDING CONTRACT

MICHELLE SMART

HEIDI RICE

MILLS & BOON

All rights reserved including the right of reproduction in whole or in part in any form. This edition is published by arrangement with Harlequin Enterprises ULC.

This is a work of fiction. Names, characters, places, locations and incidents are purely fictional and bear no relationship to any real life individuals, living or dead, or to any actual places, business establishments, locations, events or incidents. Any resemblance is entirely coincidental.

Without limiting the exclusive rights of any author, contributor or the publisher of this publication, any unauthorised use of this publication to train generative artificial intelligence (AI) technologies is expressly prohibited. HarperCollins also exercise their rights under Article 4(3) of the Digital Single Market Directive 2019/790 and expressly reserve this publication from the text and data mining exception.

® and TM are trademarks owned and used by the trademark owner and/or its licensee. Trademarks marked with ® are registered with the United Kingdom Patent Office and/or the Office for Harmonisation in the Internal Market and in other countries.

First published in Great Britain 2026
by Mills & Boon, an imprint of HarperCollins*Publishers* Ltd,
1 London Bridge Street, London, SE1 9GF

www.harpercollins.co.uk

HarperCollins*Publishers*, Macken House, 39/40 Mayor Street Upper, Dublin 1, D01 C9W8, Ireland

The Wedding Contract © 2026 Harlequin Enterprises ULC

Marriage Made in Revenge © 2026 Michelle Smart

Boss's Bride Price © 2026 Heidi Rice

ISBN: 978-0-263-41821-7

03/26

Printed and Bound in the UK using 100% Renewable Electricity at CPI Group (UK) Ltd, Croydon, CR0 4YY

MARRIAGE MADE IN REVENGE

MICHELLE SMART

MILLS & BOON

CHAPTER ONE

BETH GRANGER PULLED up outside the magnificent villa she hadn't set foot in since she was nineteen years old. All around her, people dressed in black were getting out of their cars and embracing each other as if they hadn't already spent the day embracing and pretending to mourn.

Through her rearview mirror, she watched the large black SUV with the tinted windows make its way through the gates, and closed her eyes.

Her heart was thumping hard enough for the ripples to make her motion-sick.

She didn't know if she could do this. All she wanted was to drive back to the airport and take the first flight home to England.

The day had been a million times harder than she'd anticipated. Beth hadn't been close to her grandfather, but he was her last biological link to her mother. For that fact alone, he deserved better than to have his only living relative spend his funeral with her mind and emotions concentrated on someone else.

She'd genuinely believed she was over Xavi. She'd seen him a number of times since their break-up at parties that had been held during duty visits to her grandfather. Those occasions had always been emotionally difficult, but sheer bloody-minded pride had forbidden her from letting Xavi see just how difficult it was for her to be under the same roof as him. She'd taken *fake it until you make it* to professional levels; so much so that the bastard genuinely thought they were on friendly terms.

The last thing she'd wanted or expected was to walk into the chapel of rest eight years after their ending and for her senses to pick him out of the vast crowd like she was *still* some kind of Xavi-homing pigeon. Luckily, so many people had gathered to pay their respects to Beth's grandfather that there hadn't been the time or opportunity for them to do more than nod an acknowledgement of greeting to each other. She'd done herself proud with that smile, making sure it was just the right side of solemn—it was a funeral after all—and friendly. Oh yes, she'd mastered the art of being friendly to the bastard.

She'd done herself even prouder when she'd sensed his stare on her throughout the service. She hadn't reacted to it at all. Not externally. She was less proud that she'd had to fight herself not to look back at him. She'd *ached* to look at him. Worse, she'd ached for him to come and sit with her and hold her to him.

She could only assume her grandfather's death had triggered something in her because it felt like she'd returned to the days when she'd struggled to even get out of bed. The urge to reverse out of the driveway, fly home and bury herself in bed with a large tub of chocolate ice cream was close to irresistible.

Her grandfather, for all his many faults, deserved better, and Xavi de la Rosa was not worth all the calories that came from comfort eating.

It was nearly over. All she had to do was get through the wake. One hour of small talk and then *adios*, Spain. Forever.

Pulling her compact out of her bag, she was disconcerted to find her hands trembling. She took a deep breath. The vain, prideful side of her nature would never allow Xavi to see her looking anything other than her best, so she reapplied her lip gloss and touched up her eyeliner as best she could before climbing out of the car. After straightening her dress, she blew her fringe out of her eyes, tucked a lock of hair behind an ear, elongated her neck and then put her best foot forward towards the villa she'd last been in the day Xavi had smashed her heart into pieces.

From his vantage point in the main open-plan living area of his family's villa, Xavi de la Rosa watched the curvy redhead swish through the reception room, stunningly understated in a calf-length flowing black shirt dress cinched at the waist with a thick black belt, and long, heeled black boots.

As always happened, his heart juddered in an echo of the first time he'd set eyes on her.

Eight years and she'd hardly changed at all. Every time he saw her, he marvelled at how well she'd matured into full-blown womanhood. Her long, thick red hair still shone gold under the sunlight, and she still had the same narrow face, crystal-clear green eyes, apple cheekbones and slightly square chin. Same snub nose and pixie ears, too. Her generous curves were more voluptuous, her hourglass figure one that people always took a second admiring look at.

The Beth Xavi had fallen for all those years ago had been a fun-loving eighteen-year-old who'd mesmerised him from the very first glance. She'd been quick-tempered but also quick to smile and even quicker to laugh, a hugger who was affectionate with everyone. It was a trait she'd never lost, and he watched her embrace everyone who approached her as if they were old friends when she only distantly knew a few of the hundreds of people gathered there. Those who'd never met her were naturally curious about Raul Belmonte's only living heir. Once the news broke about her inheritance, the whole of Spain would be curious about her, too.

She stepped away from an embrace with the flamboyant artistic director of an Italian fashion house, and for the first time since entering the de la Rosa villa, her stare glanced Xavi's. She smiled at him, and for a moment, barely the beat of a second, the connection between them was strong enough to touch. The beat broke when his mother pulled Beth into a tight embrace.

It was time to make his move.

The hairs on the nape of Beth's neck lifted. Her chest tightened.

He was heading towards her. She could feel it as she always did, and tightened her hold on her handbag.

'It's so lovely seeing you again,' she said to Mireia, Xavi's mother, in her best Spanish. 'Thank you for—' she couldn't think of the words to say, 'making all the arrangements,' and so settled for '—all this.' Meaning the funeral.

As her grandfather's only living relative, Beth should have been the one to arrange the funeral, but living in a different country and not knowing the first thing about Spanish funeral customs, she'd gratefully accepted Mireia's offer of organising everything, right down to opening her home for the wake. The de la Rosas had known Beth's grandfather a million times better than she had.

Beth hadn't even known of his existence until her eighteenth birthday.

'Hello, Beth.'

Even though she'd braced herself for it, hearing that perfect English delivered in that rich, deep voice made her heart flip.

Keeping her features composed took more strength and concentration than all the other times she'd seen him since he broke her heart. Turning to face him, keeping that hard-fought composure drew reserves she hadn't known existed.

'Hello, Xavi,' she replied lightly, meeting the dark chocolate brown stare. 'You're looking well.'

The young man who'd swept her off her feet was now thirty-two and much changed. The cropped hair, almost the same dark chocolate colour of his eyes, was longer than he'd worn it when they were together, the gorgeous smooth face covered in a neat, dark beard. The changes suited him, as did the faint lines around his eyes and on his forehead. Even the black suit he wore looked effortlessly elegant on his tall, wiry frame. The bastard.

His wide, sensuous lips made the ghost of a smile before his large hands clasped her shoulders, and he leaned down to press a kiss to both of her cheeks.

There was no time for her to prepare herself or hold her breath before sensation zinged over her skin and she was engulfed in a scent so familiar and loved that everything inside her contracted.

Keeping his hands on her shoulders, he stepped back and studied her with a widening smile. 'You look incredible.'

Somehow, she managed a playful wiggle of her head. 'One does one's best... So, how are things? I imagine the last few days have been difficult for you.' Her grandfather had retired from the luxury brand conglomerate he'd founded with Xavi's grandfather three years ago. She'd attended his retirement party, had been there when he'd publicly entrusted his share of the company in Xavi's hands and expressed his full confidence in him to achieve great things for the Rosbel Group. She'd applauded like everyone else in attendance and congratulated Xavi with a smile and an embrace. She'd even kissed his cheek and resisted disinfecting her mouth until she was alone in a bathroom.

He'd been running the company single-handedly since, just as the bastard had always wanted. Her grandfather's death had made international news, the press descending on the Rosbel Group's headquarters in a frenzied determination to know what Raul Belmonte's death meant for the company.

His smile became rueful. 'Nothing I can't handle.'

'I'm sure.' It was only human emotions Xavi couldn't cope with.

'How about you? Are you keeping well in yourself?'

'Very much so.'

'That's good to hear.' The smile around his mouth faded, but the sparkle in his eyes didn't diminish at all. 'Can you spare me a few minutes of your time? There is something I need to discuss with you.'

Her stomach plummeting, she made a point of looking at her watch. 'I've got a flight to catch, so you'll have to make it quick.'

'I'll be as quick as I can, but it is best we speak in private.'

Her plummeting stomach now quivering, she raised an intrigued eyebrow. 'That sounds ominous.'

The lines around his eyes crinkled. 'Nothing ominous, I promise. It's to do with your grandfather's estate and the legacy he's left you.'

They were words to make her pause. 'What legacy?'

'That is what we need to discuss.'

'Shouldn't the lawyers be the ones to discuss it with me?'

'Trust me, it is better you hear it from me first.'

How she didn't punch him in the face for that she would never know.

Trust the man who'd promised to love her forever?

Trust the man who'd been her earth and her sun, and then broken her?

But Beth hadn't spent eight years carefully curating social media posts—Xavi had never stopped following her on them, his frequent 'likes' and comments proving he kept an eye on them—and turning Photoshop into her best friend for nothing, and she made another point of looking at her watch. 'I can give you ten minutes, and then I'm really sorry but I'll need to make a move.' She didn't need to make a move anywhere. Her flight home didn't take off for another six hours.

It was Xavi she wanted to escape; Xavi and this villa and all the memories tying together, memories making the past feel like she could touch it, and if she could touch it then she could feel it, and God help her if she ever had to feel any of that again.

'I'll be as concise as I can,' he promised in his shamefully excellent English. 'Walk in the garden with me?'

'I don't have sunscreen on,' she lied as a strong memory of falling asleep on the sprawling de la Rosa lawn beneath the shade of an olive tree and being woken by a kiss smashed through her. The de la Rosas had been having a family summer party, and Beth had got all sleepy after too much sangria. With voices floating in the distance, Xavi had woken her with a kiss and then silently brought her to orgasm with nothing but his hand.

It had tortured her imagining him doing that with the women who had come after her. Her third trip to Madrid after their break-up had been to celebrate the New Year with her grandfather. He'd taken her to a party thrown by one of Spain's leading art dealers, and the first person Beth had seen when they'd walked into the villa had been Xavi with a blonde bombshell attached to his arm. Beth had made a point of going over to them, throwing her arms around Xavi as if they were long-lost best friends and befriending the appendage. She'd kept her happy face going the whole night, dancing, drinking and making merry like everyone else. The next day she'd flown back to England, detoured to a supermarket on her way home, then sat in bed eating her weight in chocolate ice cream. It had taken her months to recover from the painful shock of seeing him so clearly happy with someone else. It was a shock Beth had never understood as she knew damned well he'd replaced her with that Ellen bitch days after breaking off his relationship with her.

'Let's talk in the study,' she suggested. That was one room they'd never done anything dirty in.

In their time together, they'd made love in every room of this sprawling villa. It had been a game to them, their own playful version of sex bingo. Only the occupied bedrooms had been off-limits. The only room they'd failed to christen and so get a full house in before Xavi had dumped her was the study, so at least there wouldn't be any sex memories to slap her around the face in it.

As soon as she crossed its threshold, though, and the

door closed them inside the intimate space, Beth knew she'd made a mistake and cursed herself for lying about the sunscreen. They could have talked at the front of the villa by her hired car, and then she could have driven off, 'accidentally' screeching the wheels so he got a face full of gravel in the process.

Determined to give away nothing of her inner turmoil and to continue projecting the carefree image she so carefully curated on her social media feeds, she hitched her ample backside onto the highly polished mahogany desk and folded her arms loosely across her stomach rather than wrapping them in the tight hug she so desperately needed to hold herself with. She looked him in the eye with a smile. 'Well?'

Instead of telling her about her mysterious legacy, he strode to a cabinet, looked through its contents and pulled out a bottle of whisky and two crystal glasses. 'Drink? Or shall I have one of the staff make up a strawberry daiquiri for you?'

Beth's cocktail of choice. Her social media posts showed her enjoying them at regular intervals.

'Thank you, but I'm driving.'

'Very responsible,' he said drily, filling a glass for himself to the brim.

'Practising to be an alcoholic?' she asked with a grin she only managed by imagining herself throwing the whisky all over his ultra-expensive hand-tailored suit.

He raised the glass to her and drank half the contents. 'Dutch courage.'

'You are full of intrigue, *Señor de la Rosa*, but I've got a flight to catch so tell me about this legacy. Has he left me one of his paintings? Or maybe a car?' A thought made her blanch. 'Not Diego? I'm not allowed pets.' Not in her apartment building. And she had no garden. *Surely*, he wouldn't have left his Spanish Water Dog in her care? Surely, he'd have left him in his housekeeper Salma's care?

'He's left you the lot.'

She blinked, unsure of what she'd heard. 'He's left me a *pot*?'

'*The lot*. Everything. The villa and all its contents. All his cars and holiday homes. His personal helicopter and his shares in the business. Diego. Everything. It's all yours.'

She studied his serious face a long moment before bursting into laughter. 'That's a good one. You nearly had me going for a minute. Go on, tell me, what's he really left me?'

Not a flicker of amusement crossed his face. 'Your grandfather has left you everything, Beth.'

Still grinning widely, she shook her head. 'Not a chance. He took great delight in reminding me of his intentions for his estate every time I visited him—he was leaving his Rosbel Group shares to your family and everything else to charity.'

'He kept saying that in the hope it would entice you into changing your mind about working for the company. He never seriously intended to disinherit you—it was just a threat, a ploy for you to give in and comply with his wishes. You were his only living heir, and that meant everything to him.'

She laughed to cover how unsettled she was with the whole situation and jumped off the desk. Snatching the glass from Xavi's hand, she tipped the remaining whisky down her throat.

Beth hated whisky, but right then she needed something to cut through the effect of being in an enclosed space with Xavi and the shock of what he'd just told her. The hefty measure burning her throat wasn't enough, and she refilled the glass and drank it in three swallows.

'I thought you were driving,' Xavi said, eyebrow risen.

'Stuff it, I'll get a taxi. After all, you've just told me I'm rich.' And with that, she burst into another peal of laughter.

Rich? Possibly the biggest understatement in the world.

Beth's mother, Lorena, had died in childbirth. Beth had been raised by her father and her grandparents. Her childhood had been happy. She'd missed having a mother, but in a very abstract, curious way. She couldn't miss her as a mother because she'd never known her, but she'd been filled with curiosity about her. Everything she'd learned about her had painted a picture of a fierce but happy, loving Spanish woman who loved to dance and run barefoot. A free spirit, much like Beth.

One thing, though, that Beth had never been told about was her mother's family. The impression she'd been given growing up was that her mother didn't have any family.

This impression had been a lie engineered by her father. She'd only learned the truth on her eighteenth birthday when an elderly Spanish man knocked on their door and introduced himself as her grandfather.

Lorena, it transpired, had been estranged from her father since her late teens. Her own mother had left him when Lorena was only twelve. When Lorena had moved to England, she'd never seen either of her parents again.

Beth's father had respected his dead wife's feelings and had refused to let her father have any involvement in their daughter's life until she was eighteen and old enough to make her own judgement about him.

Learning of her Spanish grandfather's existence had come as a huge shock. A lifetime of barely satisfied curiosity about her mother, and all along she'd had a grandfather? To then learn her Spanish grandmother had died only two years earlier…

That had been a huge blow, but she'd swallowed her hurt and anger at the lies of omission from her father because he was her father and she loved him, and even through her hurt, she'd known he'd acted for what he thought was the best. Her English grandparents had felt compelled to go along with his decision on the matter.

The second shock Beth had received that fateful day was learning her grandfather was rich.

Not just rich but stupendously rich. Raul Belmonte was co-owner of the Rosbel Group, one of the wealthiest companies in Europe, making Beth's grandfather one of the richest men in Europe.

His wealth, though, had meant nothing to her, not when she was gazing at the face of the only living biological link to the mother she'd never known. Her desire to know him had been strong, but she'd known before she agreed to spend a summer with him that he wasn't the fluffy, kindly old man he was trying to portray himself to her as. After all, her mother had been estranged from him for a reason, and just because he'd not been allowed to see her didn't mean he couldn't have helped her father out financially or put some money aside for her.

Those thoughts weren't motivated by greed but by comparing him to her paternal grandparents, who'd taken their son and his motherless newborn baby into their small home and helped raise their grandchild. On the day her super-rich grandfather presented himself to her like a long-lost unicorn, they'd presented her with a bank statement worth four thousand pounds. It was money they'd invested over the years in a child-saver bank account for her, money they'd hoped would be useful as she stepped into adulthood. Her grandfather probably earned that amount—if not more—in interest on an hourly basis.

The months she'd spent with her grandfather in Madrid confirmed her worst fears as to the kind of man he was. If not for the gorgeous Spaniard who'd swept her off her feet, Beth would have flown back to England within days.

The *ifs* were many. If her grandfather hadn't decided to invite his business partner, Ferdinand de la Rosa, and Ferdinand's family to a dinner party to show off his granddaughter on her second night in his home, Beth would never have met Xavi. If Ferdinand hadn't been grooming his grandson to take over the running of the Rosbel Group, and Raul determined to teach Beth everything about the business, too, Beth and Xavi wouldn't have spent so much time together.

By the end of her first week in Madrid, she'd been smitten, and so she'd stayed. By the time autumn morphed into winter, she was back in England with a broken heart and shattered dreams.

'Do you understand what this means, Beth?'

She blinked herself back to the present and to the man responsible for her broken heart. 'Yes. It means I have a dog.'

Diego had been her grandfather's only real redeeming feature. He'd doted on the soppy Spanish Water Dog.

'It means you and I are now business partners. As you know, my grandfather retired five years ago and put the de la Rosa shares under my control—I've since bought my family out, so the shares are mine alone. When your grandfather retired, he entrusted his shares into my safekeeping and gave me the power to act and vote on his behalf. His death means those shares are now yours to do with as you wish. We each own thirty per cent of the company.'

Beth thought about the glamorous Rosbel Group headquarters in the heart of Madrid's business district and all the luxury brands under its control and the stonking value of it all. Thought, too, of all her grandfather's other assets, and shook her head in growing disbelief.

She'd never believed for a second he would leave her any of it. In the months Beth had spent working for the company, it had been like a war zone between them, ending in a screaming match when Beth had taken one too many long lunches for her grandfather's liking. Her grandfather had shouted that if she wasn't prepared to take the business seriously and learn her way around it and take her rightful place within it, he would leave his shares to the de la Rosas and everything else to charity. She'd shouted at him to go ahead and then refused to set foot in the headquarters again.

That was another of those *ifs*. If she hadn't been head over heels in love with Xavi, she would have flown straight home and probably never seen her grandfather again. Instead, she'd continued living with him, and slowly they'd thawed and forgiven each other.

She hadn't wanted his money or to be groomed to run an empire and would never have agreed to spend the summer with him if she'd known that had been his end game. She'd wanted a grandfather, something he'd come to accept, even if he didn't have a clue how to be a grandfather, but he'd been the last link to her mother, and that had been enough for Beth to learn to forgive the sense that he was hiding something fundamental about himself from her and his many, many flaws. She thought it had been the same for him, too.

'If we combine our shares like our grandfathers did, we retain control of the Rosbel Group,' Xavi said, pulling her out of yet another reverie.

She met his dark brown stare. It seemed impossible that the man who exuded such warmth could be so cold and cruel and so careless with another's heart. 'I take it you want me to entrust my shares with you like my grandfather did?' As if she'd trust him with *anything*.

'Whoever has the majority holding has the controlling interest. I've already fought off one hostile takeover—an American corporation with a fifteen per cent stake. I hear its ringleader's in financial trouble now, but I have no doubt that your grandfather's death means they or others like them will be on manoeuvres again soon.'

She downed the last of the whisky. 'So you *do* want me to entrust my shares with you.'

'In a fashion.' He refilled her glass and filled a glass for himself.

'What kind of fashion? Do you want to buy them?' He could want all he liked. Hell would freeze over before she handed him a single share of the business he'd chosen over her.

'Only if you refuse my proposition.'

'Which is?'

A hint of caution came into his voice. 'I want you to promise to hear my reasoning.'

She shrugged. 'That's fine.'

He studied her long enough for her skin to prickle and her heart to pound harder. 'Just hear me out and then take the time to think about it before giving me your answer. Take all the time you need.'

The prickles on her skin were growing, a sense of dread and anticipation uncoiling in her stomach. She took another drink to calm it and nodded. 'I can do that.'

He leaned back against the cabinet, drank some whisky and said, 'I want us to marry.'

CHAPTER TWO

Xavi watched Beth's reaction closely. Other than the slightest twitching of her lips, she gave nothing away... not unless you counted the sudden loss of colour on her face. Although the knuckles of the fingers holding her glass had whitened, too, nothing suggested she was about to throw the glass at him.

He would never forget the sound of shattering glass in the moments before he'd kicked open the door of the bathroom she'd locked herself in. He'd found the tiled floor covered with shards of glass and clumps of wax from the scented candles she'd thrown on it, but his fear that she'd been hurting herself went unrealised. By the time he'd smashed the door in, all the emotions driving her to destroy his bathroom had worked their way out of her system.

Beautiful face red and blotchy through crying, she'd looked him in the eye, apologised for the mess she'd made, and with quiet dignity walked out of his life.

Two years passed before he next saw her in the flesh at her grandfather's eightieth birthday. She'd embraced him warmly and even made a joke about the state she'd left his bathroom in. He'd been relieved, but also strangely disconcerted. It wasn't that he'd wanted histrionics or a glass of water thrown in his face, but to find he'd meant so little to her that she could treat their break-up like a joke had thrown him.

The tendons of her neck stretching, she jerked her head, indicating for him to explain his reasoning.

'I appreciate my proposition must come as a surprise.'

Her face scrunched up, and she matter-of-factly said, 'Just a tiny bit considering we once spent a whole evening discussing the kind of wedding we wanted, and then weeks later you dumped me.'

Chest and stomach wincing simultaneously, he inclined his head in agreement. 'I never did apologise for the way I ended things with you, did I.'

She waved an airy hand and rolled her eyes. 'Xavi, it was eight years ago.'

Eight years and yet he still remembered their time together so vividly that it could have been days ago. He doubted it was the same for her. For all her words of love, Beth had got over him pretty damned quickly, something he knew he had no right to resent. He had no right, either, to feel jealousy whenever she posted photos on social media of her raising a glass with a group of friends that usually had equal numbers of men and women. Whenever he made the occasional comment to her posts, she always reacted, whether with a thumbs-up or a heart or with a witty remark that made his mouth smile and his heart hurt.

He made his mouth smile now. 'I'm just saying that I appreciate my clumsy way of ending things will make it harder for you to take my proposal seriously.'

She smiled. He'd always loved Beth's smile. Her top lip was just the slightest bit fuller than the bottom one, and when she smiled her mouth formed an upside-down heart. 'Forget the past and tell me your reasoning. If nothing else, I'm curious.'

'For one, it better protects the business and both our interests in it,' he answered steadily. For all her smiles, there was a sharpness in Beth's stare that told him she would detect any hint of bullshit.

'How?'

'Your grandfather's death has already increased speculation and scrutiny of the business, and it will encourage the sharks to start circling again. Marriage will allow us to pool our shares the same way our grandfathers did and allow me to continue running the Rosbel Group without outside interference and make us both a lot of money—profits have increased significantly since I took control. Us marrying gives certainty to the tens of thousands of people we employ around the world and gives certainty to the financial markets, too.'

'Wow, you really know how to make a girl feel special with *that* reasoning for marriage.'

Refusing to allow himself to remember how he'd woken one morning to find her already awake and gazing at him and how he'd said, 'We *are* going to marry, aren't we?' he pulled a rueful smile. 'You could entrust them to me or I could buy the shares from you, and the effect would be the same, but marrying me protects you, too.'

Her eyes narrowed. 'Hmm…how have you worked that out?'

'You're a very wealthy woman now, Beth. The sharks won't just circle the business, they'll be out circling you, too.'

'Why would the sharks know about me?'

'It will soon be public knowledge that Raul left everything to you.'

'Not if no one tells them.'

Xavi knew she wasn't naive enough to believe that.

'Your grandfather was one of the richest men in Europe. Whoever he left his wealth to would make the news—that he's left everything to the granddaughter who didn't want it adds to the story. That his granddaughter is beautiful by anyone's standards will have the press salivating. Every shark and chancer in the western hemisphere will want to take their chances with you. Once the news breaks, you will find yourself unable to trust anyone you don't already know. I can help you navigate this world.'

'That doesn't require marriage.'

'Agreed. But it will make it easier for me to protect you.'

She laughed and pulled a face. 'I don't need protecting.'

'You will, very soon, and you are not prepared for it.'

'Again, protection doesn't require marriage. I can buy an army to keep me safe.'

'Beth, you will never be able to trust another man again. That is your new reality. Always you will wonder if it's you they want or your money, and those suspicions will not go away if you have the children you always wanted with them.'

For the first time, he detected a flash of emotion in the crystal-clear green eyes. 'But you expect me to trust you?'

He dragged his fingers through his hair and forced air into his lungs. This was do or die. If Beth refused to marry him, the business would never be safe from the predators. 'I have always hated myself for hurting you, but if I had to make that choice again, I would make it without hesitation because the business has to come first. I lost sight of that when I was with you. I lost my focus and made some stupid but dangerous errors that would have cost the business dearly if our grandfathers hadn't picked up on them. It dented their confidence in me and made me see how close I'd come to destroying everything they'd built. My life and focus had been all on you when it should have been on the business, and I needed to switch it around and prove their confidence in my abilities to run the Rosbel Group wasn't misplaced.'

Pretty lips trembled as she looked him up and down before they pulled into a tight smile. 'That's a lot of words to reiterate that you chose the business over me.'

A statement he could not and would not deny. 'Beth, since my father died, all I've wanted is to step into the shoes he was unable to fill and take over the running of the Rosbel Group—you know this. My grandfather wanted to retire twenty years ago, but he couldn't have predicted his only son would die at such a young age.' Xavi's father had died when he was fourteen. Not even billions in wealth could stop cancer's advance. 'That's why our grandfathers' bond remained so strong—they both lost a child. They both lost the heirs they expected to take the company forward.'

'My grandfather lost his daughter long before she died.'

'Yes, which is why it was so important that I stepped up to the mark. I always knew it had to be me. I was the only family member left from either side of the partnership with the aptitude and willingness to do it.'

Like Beth's mother, Xavi's father had been an only child. Xavi's sisters had never had any interest in the business, one growing up to be an archaeologist, the other a human rights lawyer.

As a child, he'd happily imagined himself working with his father, whom he'd hero-worshipped. His father would take over the running of the Rosbel Group, and then one day, Xavi would step into his father's shoes.

He'd had no idea fate had such a cruel trick planned for his family.

'I know I ended things abruptly with you,' he continued, 'but I saw it like ripping off a plaster—once I knew I had to end it, I knew it was better to make a clean break.'

Pressing her crystal glass to her breasts, she arched an eyebrow. 'Better for whom?'

He would not look at her breasts. 'For both of us. I was too young for marriage back then. We both were. Hell, I was twenty-four and fresh from six years of back-to-back university degrees, and you'd only just turned nineteen. What were we thinking, talking about marriage and children when we were barely adults ourselves?'

'I completely agree.'

'You do?'

'Absolutely. I was young and foolish and believed in love at first sight, whereas what we had, if we're thinking logically, was more of an instant lust thing than love.' She gave another smile. 'If it meant what we both believed it to mean while we were living it, neither of us would have moved on so quickly.'

'For sure.' He would not allow himself to remember the sensation of his heart ripping when he'd seen a post of Beth beaming widely with her cheek pressed to another man's at a New Year's Eve party months after he'd ended their relationship. 'And now we both have eight years more experience of life and the world at large. We're ready to take that step now. You're the only woman I've ever trusted—what I said about sharks and chancers circling you comes from experience. You're the only woman I've been with that I had complete certainty was with me for me and not for my money and connections, and you can have that same trust and certainty with me. We were good together, Beth, and there is no reason to suppose we can't be good together again, and this time we're old enough and mature enough to make it work.'

There was a flash in the green eyes that had been studying him so intently. 'You say all that about trust... if it wasn't for the shares now being mine, would you be asking me to marry you?'

He returned the intensity of the stare. 'I've never stopped caring about you.'

'That isn't what I asked.'

'I know, but if I didn't care, I wouldn't be suggesting it. I couldn't marry someone I feel nothing for. I'm ready for marriage now and ready for children, and who better to do all that with than the other half of the Rosbel Group? Marry me and you will have the confidence that your fortune is safe because I will only ever do what's best for the business, and I will keep you safe, too, and always act in your best interests. It is a perfectly logical move for both of us... Unless you are already in a relationship you haven't gone public with?'

Her pretty little nose lifted into the air. 'I'm not officially attached to anyone at the moment if that's what you mean.'

His heart thumped at this confirmation. 'And neither am I.'

She took a step closer to him and lifted her chin, the clear eyes ringed with sweeping, thickly mascaraed lashes studying him even harder. 'I always assumed you would end up with Ellen.'

His head reared back in surprise. 'I wouldn't marry that bunny boiler.'

Ellen had been a part of Xavi's old social circle, a hanger-on who'd wormed her way into his group of friends during his years studying in England. She'd been the most predatory woman he'd ever had the misfortune to know. She'd made no bones about her attraction to Xavi—an attraction in no way reciprocated—and when Beth had come on the scene had been so snide and nasty to her that he'd taken to avoiding gatherings she'd be at to protect Beth from her.

'So she didn't finally lure you into her bed after we split?'

For the first time in their exchange, he hesitated before answering, remembering the time Ellen had sent him unsolicited nude selfies with the message: *Look what you're missing out on.* Up to that point, Beth had felt quite sorry for her, arguing that she must be lonely and insecure to be so bitchy and behave so outrageously. One look at those pictures and the message, and she'd wanted to storm to Ellen's home and rip her hair out. 'No.'

There was another flickering in the green depths, her lips making the faintest of twitches. 'Okay,' she eventually said, tilting her head as she drained the last of her whisky. 'I'll think about marrying you.'

'You will consider it seriously?'

'Yes.' She stretched her arm to put her empty glass on the cabinet. 'But before I start thinking about it, I think we need to establish something first.'

'Which is?'

'This.' Without any warning, she'd closed the gap between them, risen onto her toes to wrap her arms around his neck and pull him closer, and then her soft lips captured his.

Since Xavi had been given the news of Raul's death,

his thoughts had been consumed twofold: with retaining his control of the business and with the certain knowledge that he would be seeing Beth again. It wasn't until he'd woken that morning, though, that the two strains of his thoughts had converged and the big picture had made itself clear.

Everything he'd told her of his reasoning for marriage had been the truth. The biggest truth was that the Rosbel Group was *his* and he would do anything to protect it and protect his control of it, and so he'd concentrated all his energies on what he needed to say, instinct telling him this was his one shot at getting Beth's agreement, and clamped down on all the physical reactions being in her presence had unleashed. He'd suppressed the zing flowing through his veins, blocked his senses to the heady scent of her perfume, refused to allow his mind to strip her naked or remember the weight of her breasts in his hands...

One press of her lips to his, and the eight years they'd spent apart melted away along with all thoughts of the Rosbel Group.

There was no hesitation in her kiss. Her fingers scraped through his hair and her tongue slipped into his mouth, and then she was devouring him with a hungry boldness that sent his senses reeling under a blizzard of sensation.

Dios, he'd forgotten how much he'd missed her. Missed *this*. Missed the magic that he'd singularly failed to replicate with anyone else.

Revelling in the softness of Beth's lips and the warm silkiness of her tongue, Xavi set the glass in his hand onto the cabinet and then wrapped his arms tightly around her, kissing her back with matching hunger. *Dios*, she tasted even better than he remembered, and he deepened the kiss until her breasts were crushed against his chest and they were nothing but two tightly locked bodies and fused faces.

It was Beth who pulled away first.

Keeping her hands linked around his neck, she drew back to gaze at him with dilated pupils. Her cheeks were flush and there was a breathless quality to her voice as she murmured, 'Well, that's answered my question.'

'What question was that?' he asked huskily.

'Whether the chemistry is still there...' She brought her mouth back to his. 'Let's do that again.'

Lips and bodies crashing back together, the thrills that raged through him were strong enough to melt bone.

This was why there had been no magic with anyone since Beth. Xavi didn't feel his desire for her just in his loins but in the whole of his being. Theirs was a chemical formula impossible to replicate.

Squeezing the succulent bottom that was as soft and pillowy as her glorious breasts, he gathered the skirt of her dress; would have steered her to the desk and lifted her onto it if she hadn't broken the kiss again and gently pushed at his chest in an unspoken gesture to say their chemical experiment was over.

His breaths as heavy as the thumps of his heart and the weight of his erection, he gazed into Beth's desire-laden eyes and didn't know whether to laugh or groan when she blew her fringe out of her eyes, staggered to the desk to grab her bag and then staggered to the door.

Arousal coursed so strongly through him that it took a moment to speak. 'Where are you going?'

The breathless quality in her voice deepened. 'Somewhere to think.' She turned back to face him and lifted her chin. 'I'll let you know of my decision soon.'

'How soon?'

After gathering her gorgeous autumn-leaved hair onto the top of her head, she let it fall as she smiled knowingly. 'As soon as I've made it.'

Another knowing smile, and she slipped out of the study, shutting the door quietly behind her.

Xavi stared at the closed door for an age and then shook his head and laughed, more with relief than anything else.

Considering he'd half anticipated a punch in the face, he'd say that had gone damned well.

Beth had given him a fair hearing, which, despite the friendly nature of their relationship since their split, was more than he'd expected. More than he deserved if he was being honest with himself. She hadn't thrown anything at him. And she'd kissed him... *Dios*, how she had kissed him.

He wondered how many other men she'd kissed with such boldness, then cut the thought off at the knees with much-practised precision. He'd been Beth's first, and if he had his way, he would be her last, a thought that was almost as satisfying as securing his control of the Rosbel Group.

All the years spent apart from her had been with the hovering thought that one day the time would be right to bring Beth back into his life. Now was that time. All the things that had driven him to end things the first time no longer existed; the dangerous power Beth had had over him that had driven him to forget his responsibilities to the business now muted.

If she agreed to marry him, he had full confidence he could keep her compartmentalised in the way he'd never succeeded before.

Draining the last of his whisky, he came close to allowing himself the luxury of imagining Beth giving her agreement. But only close.

The only thing predictable about Beth Granger was her unpredictability.

Beth waited at the de la Rosas electric gates for her taxi and searched on her phone for a hotel. She'd sort out her hire car later. There were other things to do first. Things that had to take priority.

By the time her taxi turned up, she'd booked herself into a reasonably priced, superbly located hotel with decent reviews. Twenty minutes later, she was striding into its reception and being given the key to her room.

The room itself was clean, the bed large and comfortable. Most importantly, it had a multitude of pillows. She unzipped her boots, yanked them off and chucked them onto the floor, then crawled under the duvet, put her face on one of the pillows and pulled another two over her head, sandwiching herself in them.

Only then, knowing her screams would be muffled, did she open her vocal cords.

She screamed and raged until her throat was raw, and then she sat up, grabbed another pillow, got on her knees and started battering it with her fists. Imagining it was Xavi's face, she punched the pillow so hard and for so long that her knuckles stung.

She wished she could cry; would give anything to cauterise her pain with the release of tears. Not that tears cauterised anything, but they allowed emotions to be purged, even if only for a short while.

Beth hadn't been able to cry since the ocean of tears that had fallen when she'd miscarried her baby.

Xavi's baby.

The baby she had desperately wanted and loved with the whole of her being from the moment the pregnancy test had confirmed she was carrying his child.

She'd waited until he'd gone on a five-day work trip to Milan—their grandfathers had forbidden Beth from going with him—before taking the pregnancy test. She'd only been a couple of days late for her period and hadn't wanted to build Xavi's hopes up for nothing.

The rush of joy at the positive sign was like nothing she'd felt in her life, and she'd hugged her secret tightly to herself until he'd returned. She'd wanted to tell him to his face and see the joy on it.

Already practically living in the de la Rosa villa with him, she'd been waiting in his bedroom for his return from his trip, too excited about what was to come to think too hard that he'd been too busy that week for anything but short conversations and that he'd barely messaged her.

He'd stepped into the bedroom. One look at his face and the spring in her legs to bound over to him and tell him their wonderful news had turned to lead.

Xavi had thought taking the ripping-a-plaster-off approach the best way to end it? Well, he should have tried being the human that plaster had been ripped off of.

After six months of bliss, Xavi had run his fingers through his hair and curtly delivered his obviously prepared words. 'I'm sorry, Beth, but we need to end things. Neither of us is ready for marriage and I've been neglecting my responsibilities with the business when you know it has to be my priority. We've gone too far too fast and now we need to put the brakes on it.'

She'd never known such naked fear existed until she heard those words.

At her blank, open-mouthed stare, he'd jammed his

hands into his pockets and ruefully added, 'It doesn't have to be forever. I hope we can part as friends because I'll always care for you and will always be there if you need me, but as things stand, I need to concentrate on the business. I owe my father and our grandfathers that.'

There had been an implacability to him, an emotional switch-off that had made him seem like a stranger, and she'd gazed at him in a strange state of petrified confusion and perfect understanding.

Xavi was an all-or-nothing man. He threw himself into whatever he set his mind to, and when he made up his mind about something, nothing could change it. He'd thrown himself into his love for her, but now the switch had been turned off. If he wanted Beth out of his life, nothing would change that.

That hadn't stopped her from trying when the shell shock gave way to hysteria, but the more she'd pleaded with him to change his mind, the more intractable he'd become. Hysteria had given way to pain-fuelled rage, and she'd locked herself in the bathroom and smashed anything she could get her hands on until the rage had given way to fear that if she didn't get a grip on herself, she would harm their baby.

It was thoughts of their baby that had made foolish hope spring alive and fill her. She just needed to wait for him to come to his senses because there was no way he meant it. Sure, Xavi never changed his mind when on a set course, but wasn't he changing the set course of their relationship? He was having cold feet or something like it, but in a few days or weeks he'd realise what a terrible mistake he'd made and beg her to come back to him, and then she'd forgive him and tell him about the baby and they'd all live happily ever after.

She'd gone back to her grandfather's full of misplaced hope. Five days later she'd sobbed her heart out for the final time in her bathroom, crippled with the pain of missing Xavi and crippled with abdominal pains she wouldn't wish on her worst enemy, not even that Ellen bitch.

That Ellen bitch who'd sent Beth a photo of Xavi sleeping in Ellen's bed just three days after Xavi had ended their relationship. She'd even location and time-stamped it for good measure.

Xavi had kicked Beth out of his life and days later jumped into the bed of the woman who'd spent their entire relationship practically stalking him and doing everything she could to lure him away from her, and barely two hours ago the bastard had barefaced lied about it. She'd have thought more of him—going from a base of zero, that wouldn't take much—if he'd admitted it.

And now he seriously thought she would agree to marry him and have his babies? Was he really so arrogant that he believed she'd forgiven him for so coldly throwing her away for the business? Did he really believe her friendliness the few times they'd seen each other and her breezy replies to his messages over the years were signs of her moving on rather than her pride demanding she pick herself up and prove she could live a good, fulfilling life without him just so he'd never know the depth of the agony he'd put her through?

She'd believed in him so strongly. Believed he was fundamentally good and true.

She should have known better. Hadn't her own father proved even the best of men could lie when he'd let her spend the first eighteen years of her life believing her mother had no living relatives? She should have known better than to expect more of Xavi, so more fool her. And more fool her for having a heart and body that hadn't learned their lessons well enough and still filled with longing for him.

She could still taste him on her tongue and feel the sensation in her breasts where they'd crushed against his chest. She could still feel the essence of Xavi flowing through her bloodstream, and she *despised* him for it.

Her kiss had been calculated. She'd wanted—needed—to prove to him that he wasn't the one in control and prove to herself that she'd matured enough to control her desires and not just be a slave to Xavi's.

By the time she'd pulled away the second time, her control had hung by a thread.

The chemistry between them had always been strong, one of the reasons why his abrupt ending of their relationship had hit her so hard. The night before his trip to Milan, he'd made love to her the whole night through.

Sometimes she looked back and wondered how she'd survived it all.

After swallowing hard, she pulled air into her lungs and stopped battering the poor, blameless pillow. The path she needed to take, half formulated in Xavi's office, had come more sharply into focus.

Throwing herself backwards, Beth spread her arms across the mattress, gazed up at the ceiling and concentrated all her thoughts and emotions.

She would accept the arrogant bastard's proposal. Yes, she would marry him and let him use her shares to continue his role as chairman and CEO uncontested, and while he was merrily running the precious business that meant much more to him than she ever had, she would sell off her grandfather's villa and other assets and use the proceeds to buy up the other shares until *she* became the majority shareholder. She might even go into cahoots with the American sharks who'd already attempted a hostile takeover.

Whatever she did, *she* would be the one to oust him from his precious business and destroy his dreams the way he'd destroyed hers, and then she would eject him from her life once and for all.

And then maybe, just maybe, she'd be able to move on from the invisible hold Xavi had kept her trapped in these past eight years and find a man deserving of her love.

CHAPTER THREE

XAVI'S EYES SNAPPED open to pitch black. His phone was ringing. He groped his bedside table until his hand fell on it.

Bringing it to his face, his heart slammed into his ribs and all sleepiness fell away when he saw the name on the screen.

'This is an unexpected pleasure,' he murmured. He'd thought she would make him wait a minimum of a week just to play with his mind.

'I'll marry you.'

He expelled a long breath and smiled. 'That is the best news a man could be woken to at two in the morning. I assume you timed it deliberately?'

'Naturally.'

'You always knew how to keep me on my toes.' And always in a good way. One particular memory stuck in his mind of Beth flopping onto her back after making love and deciding she wanted to go for a drive. It had been three in the morning. Thinking she just wanted to take it for a spin, he'd thrown some clothes on, indulgently given her the keys to his sports car and jumped in the passenger seat beside her. She'd put the soft top down, turned the music up and hit the accelerator. Three hours later, they'd been sat on La Malvarrosa beach eating churros and watching the sun rise.

Their impulsive trip had resulted in him missing a board meeting and being on the receiving end of his grandfather's anger and disapproval for the first time.

There was a long pause. 'Xavi, are you sure you want to do this? I'm not the Beth you remember. I haven't spent eight years in a silo. Things have happened that have shaped me.'

'What things?'

'Things I will tell you about when the time is right. I just need to be certain you understand that you won't be marrying the Beth of old.'

He laughed. 'You're still Beth, but I already know you're not the Beth of old, and I know we're going to have to get to know each other again, but *mi vida*, that kiss we shared proved the spark that was always there still lives.'

There was another long silence before she murmured, 'Okay, on your head be it. Don't say I didn't try to warn you.'

He laughed again. *Dios*, it felt good to laugh. It felt even better to know he'd soon have Beth back in his bed. The buzz in his veins since their kiss wasn't even close to abating. Just to imagine her head on the pillow next to his and her gorgeous red hair fanned over it made the buzz tighten and thicken in anticipation. 'Where are you? I'll send my driver for you.'

'Let him sleep,' she dismissed lightly. 'I need to go home and sort things out in England, but if you meet me at my grandfather's villa after breakfast, we can get the ball rolling for our wedding before I leave.'

He sighed and then grinned at his impatience. Just five minutes ago, he'd been asleep and expecting to wait days longer for her answer. If she'd said no, he'd have been back to fighting wars to retain his control of the Rosbel Group. Beth's agreement meant that fight was won *and* he had her back in his life.

Dios, all he'd thought about since their kiss was how good the sex had been between them. All their years apart, he'd forbidden himself from thinking about it, but now he was free to let the memories unleash and remember how incredible it had been between them. To break apart from her, he'd needed those days in Milan without her sexy, distracting presence to enable him to think clearly, had needed to block the receptors in his brain from switching on once he was back in his bedroom delivering the words he knew would break her heart.

The blocked receptors were back in full working order, and very soon, once she'd wrapped up her affairs in England, she'd be back in his bed permanently, and they could make up for all the lost time between them.

'I will get my team on it… How long are you going to make me wait to be my wife?'

She laughed, that old infectious, joyful sound that had never failed to bring a smile to his face. 'I'm happy to marry as soon as it can be arranged.'

'That makes me very happy.'

The tone of her voice changed slightly. 'I do need to ask a favour of you.'

'Anything.'

'Would you mind sorting out all the taxes and stuff on my grandfather's estate? I know it's all different to how it works in England and I wouldn't have a clue where to start.'

'Your grandfather named me as his executor, so consider it done.'

'Thank you.'
'*De nada.* What time tomorrow?'
'Nine?'
'That works for me.'
'Great. I'll see you then.'
'Sweet dreams, *mi vida.*'

Beth threw her phone across the hotel room floor and grabbed furiously at her hair.

The lying bastard! How dare he call her by that endearment?

Mi vida? My life? More like my *expendable* life.

Well, now it was Xavi who was expendable; Xavi who was going to learn how it felt to lose the most important thing in his life and for his life and dreams to be ripped apart.

By the time Beth was finished with Xavi de la Rosa, he would hate her every bit as much as she hated him.

It was hard to feel hate for someone when you walked into a villa and found them sitting around a dining room table looking all sexy in a dapper navy blue suit, pale blue shirt and thick checked silver tie, and with a large brown Spanish Water Dog on their lap, gazing at them adoringly whilst having the undersides of their ears rubbed.

Beth supposed it proved that dogs could be as stupid as humans. She'd once been as big a sucker for affection from Xavi as Diego. Still, it gave her perverse pleasure when Diego took one look at her from beneath the shaggy mane of curly hair on his head and jumped off Xavi's lap to charge over and run around her like she was his personal maypole.

'He likes you,' Xavi observed.

'He likes everyone.'

'Yes, but he *really* likes you. He clearly has excellent taste.'

'Clearly,' she agreed, laughing lightly, biting back the comment that if Diego really did have excellent taste, he wouldn't have given affection to Xavi. She would make sure to give the dog a stern warning of the danger of showing affection to Xavi when she was next alone with him.

To buy herself time to compose herself from all the memories that had started slamming into her before she'd even walked through the villa's front door and the slamming of her heart at the first glimpse of Xavi, she crouched down to cuddle Diego, taking much-needed comfort from his soft warmth.

This was the home the mother she'd never known had grown up in, the villa Beth had first walked into as an unworldly eighteen-year-old hoping to forge a relationship with the grandfather she'd never known. The villa she'd met Xavi in. The villa they'd made love in every room of except her grandfather's bedroom.

Even this dining room came prefilled with memories. Xavi had lifted her onto the sideboard dancing in her eye line, and taken her with such exquisiteness that she'd had to bite into his shoulder to stop her cries of ecstasy sounding through to the other rooms.

The room directly above this dining room was the bathroom she'd sobbed in when she'd miscarried their baby.

Still fussing over Diego, she forced herself to meet Xavi's warm brown stare and willed her racing pulses to settle. 'You know he's going to have to live with us?'

His lips curved. She imagined he'd carried that smug, self-satisfied smile since she'd agreed to his proposal.

He thought he had his future mapped out to his exact specifications. Let him enjoy the delusion while it lasted.

'I'd assumed as much.'

'I hope your home's not got too many valuables at low heights. Diego still behaves like a puppy at times.'

He stretched his long legs out and hooked his ankles together. 'I will get my staff to Diego-proof it.'

'Where do you live now? I assume you don't live in the family home anymore?' When she'd met him, he'd not long returned to Madrid after six years studying in England. Back then, it had thrilled her to think he'd lived only forty miles from her home in the heart of England.

There was the slightest hesitation. 'In Salamanca.'

She only just managed to stop herself from visibly blanching.

Xavi had once taken her shopping in Madrid's Salamanca district. The nineteenth-century neighbourhood oozed charm, glamour and beauty, and for Beth it had been love at first sight. So smitten had she been that when Xavi suggested buying a home for them there, she'd thrown her arms around his neck and kissed his face off.

'Oh, right,' she said as if she hadn't just had another knife plunged into her heart, and tried desperately to think of something light-hearted to add to cover the coldness of her shock.

When they'd been together, Xavi had been making plans to buy a place of his own. *Their* own. She was supposed to have moved into that place with him. In Salamanca. Moved into it and made a family of their own in it.

'What about your sisters?' she ended up plumping for. 'The last time I spoke to Carlota, she was still living at home…when she's not off on one of her archaeological digs, that is, but I haven't spoken to Blanca in years.'

Blanca was the human rights lawyer sister. Beth liked her very much, but had found her a little too earnest. She'd much preferred Carlota's company, Carlota being of a similar age and temperament to Beth. The two young women had delighted in ganging up on Xavi and teasing him mercilessly, teasing he'd always taken in the spirit it was given. The two women had kept in touch over the years, meeting up if Carlota was in Spain when Beth visited her grandfather and when Carlota visited England. By unspoken agreement, Carlota's bastard brother was never mentioned.

'She moved to Brussels a few months ago but uses home as her base whenever she's in the country.'

There was a tap on the dining room door, and then Salma came in with a tray of coffee, followed by three men and two women in suits: lawyers who most definitely did not concern themselves with human rights.

Their presence allowed Beth to compose herself properly, push aside all the memories assaulting her and shake off the tendrils of tension the mention of Salamanca had unfurled between her and Xavi.

Getting to her feet, she shook the lawyers' hands then positioned herself at the table facing Xavi, figuring she'd rather have him in her eye line than sit beside him and suffer his nearness.

It was a decision she soon regretted. The lawyers had given her folios and a heap of paperwork on the workings of the Rosbel Group so she could refamiliarise herself with it all, but instead of diving into the shareholder information, her eyes kept seeking Xavi.

The more she looked at him, the more her pulses kept

racing into a canter and the more she was forced to concede just how well his longer, floppier haircut and trim beard suited him. How much sexier they made him, giving him an almost piratical edge.

Really, she should be glad she still found him so sexy, as it would make it easier to play the game of marriage until she took everything from him. Beth had tried to fake desire a few times in the years without him, but it had always ended in such a hopeless mess, she'd lost the will to even try.

He ended the call he was on and smiled triumphantly. 'Two weeks on Saturday.'

Sixteen days? She came within a whisker of gulping. 'At the Almudena?'

His triumph grew. 'I told you they would fit us in.'

'Fit *you* in,' she commented drily. Her throat felt as dry as her tone. Plans for a wedding that twenty-four hours ago hadn't even been a thing were suddenly steamrolling ahead. Beth had suggested the Almudena Cathedral on a whim, an impossible challenge for Xavi to fail at, never expecting they'd be able to fit them in on such short notice.

She'd forgotten the sheer clout Xavi held in Spanish society, a clout that could only have grown in their eight years apart.

'You will courier your birth certificate and the other documents we spoke of?' one of the lawyers asked.

She smiled brightly. 'It will be my top priority.'

One of the lawyers who'd disappeared into Xavi's office returned with an armful of documents.

Soon, everything that needed to be signed was signed, hands were shaken and the small army of lawyers bustled out. Beth had politely declined the offer of lunch with the excuse—a truthful one this time—of having a plane to catch.

'I'll drive you to the airport,' Xavi said once she'd arranged for Salma to stay on and care for Diego until they returned from their honeymoon.

'I'm sure you must need to get to work, so don't worry about that. I can get a taxi.'

'I insist.'

She managed not to clench her jaw. She'd be marrying him in sixteen days. She needed to learn how to cope with being alone with him. 'Thank you.'

The summer sun was high in the late-morning air when they stepped outside. Protecting her eyes with her shades, Beth strode to the convertible car that had to cost more than her grandparents' house.

It was incredible to believe that soon she would have the money to buy her grandparents and her father a swanky new home each and make the equivalent dent in her bank account as buying herself a new jumper currently made in it.

'Still don't like being driven around?' she asked lightly once she'd strapped herself in and Xavi had lowered the roof, something for which she was grateful as it meant she didn't have to breathe in such heavy doses of his gorgeous scent. His scent was something else she hated him for. Why couldn't he smell like a sewer?

He put his shades on and grinned. 'No, I still don't like being driven around, but the relentlessness of my schedule means I'm reliant on my driver more than I would wish to be.'

'The downside of being the boss?'

'The perks make up for it.'

'And what are the perks?'

'Not being answerable to anyone.' He pulled out and joined the crawling traffic. 'As we're talking of jobs, what do you intend to do about yours?'

'I'll have to resign. It's too hands-on for remote working, plus it would be weird to stay when I'm going to be a major shareholder of the Rosbel Group. We consider loads of your brands to be our rivals.'

'*Our* brands,' he corrected, flashing a quick grin at her. 'Miss Amore is now *our* rival.'

'Another thing for me to get my head around.' She shook her overloaded head.

'Are you still a fashion buyer there?'

'I am indeed.' It was a job she loved and one she was damned good at.

'I imagine you're excellent in the role. As I remember, you were always more animated about the fashion side of the business than the corporate side.'

He was referring to the three months she'd spent shadowing Xavi and their grandfathers within the Rosbel Group before she'd had that final spectacular fallout with her grandfather.

He wasn't wrong. She'd found the whole process of turning the designs created into finished products fascinating, from identifying the next big fashion trend to sourcing the materials and accessories and getting the best price for them. Her vague life plan to do a degree in English Literature and then find a career she could use it for had bitten the dust. Beth had found her path.

'I considered training to be a designer, but then I remembered that I can't draw for toffee.'

He laughed. It was the deep, spontaneous sound she used to love, but now landed like nails on a chalkboard.

'I take it you didn't consider using your connections for a similar role within the Rosbel Group?'

'You know I didn't want to work for my grandfather.' He'd been insufferable to work for, a control freak who wouldn't have looked out of place in a spy movie cast as the baddie set on world domination.

She'd never grown to love him like she did her other grandparents, but they'd developed their own unique way of handling each other and making the grandfather-granddaughter relationship work. To Beth's mind, that had only been possible through her steadfast refusal to ever work for him again.

However much she'd not wanted to work for her grandfather was nothing to how she'd felt about Xavi. She'd rather have eaten worms than work, however indirectly, for him. The fashion world, though, had found its way into her blood, and she'd been grateful for it. She'd used the knowledge she'd gained from her grandfather and Xavi to blag herself an internship at a growing hip fashion chain based in Manchester and never looked back. Her job—the work itself and the fun, creative people who worked there—had saved her, had made her see she could live a happy and fulfilling life without Xavi de la Rosa.

When she'd taken her revenge and her marriage was over, she'd buy Miss Amore, she decided, and give everyone a pay raise.

She felt Xavi's gaze glance her. 'He never stopped hoping you would change your mind and join us.'

She smiled sadly. 'I know, but it was for the best that I didn't. We clashed too much to work together.'

'I remember.' A smile resounded in his voice as the traffic came to a stop. 'At times, it was like dealing with two rutting bulls.'

About to make a quip back at him, Beth's tongue froze, her senses soaring to high alert a beat before Xavi slid a hand onto her thigh and gently squeezed. 'You cannot know how good it feels to have you back in my life.'

There was no time to react to his touch or his words as the traffic started moving again and Xavi moved his hand to put the car back in gear.

She blew out the breath she'd sucked in and tried to relax.

Theirs had always been an affectionate and physical relationship, and the kiss she'd instigated in the study had led him to believe that it was a side of their relationship she was willing—keen even—to resume. And she *was* keen, but only insofar that she would be using it as a weapon to destroy him with. His affectionately delivered words just then meant nothing to her, not after all his lies, but if she could resurrect even a fraction of Xavi's old feelings for her, it would make his fall when she pulled the rug out from under him taste that much sweeter. And the way to Xavi's heart was through his cock. If she kept him happy in the bedroom, he'd have no reason to believe she was plotting his downfall behind his back.

But she wanted to be in control of it. Fully, completely, entirely in control, and that one squeeze of her thigh had proved how easy it would be for her to lose it. It was disconcerting how quickly her senses had retuned themselves to his frequency to the extent her body had anticipated his touch before her mind had. She'd only been back in his orbit for a day!

'What about you?' he asked.

She hated that his voice still acted like nectar to her ears. 'What about me?'

'How do you feel about having me back in your life?'

'I don't know.' That, at least, contained a nugget of truth. Beth had been racked with such a tumult of emotions since her return to Spain that to narrow it all into one concise sentence was impossible. 'I'm still trying to wrap my head around everything.'

'You must feel something for me to have agreed to my proposal.'

With this, she was able to look at him, and with complete truthfulness say, 'Xavi, my feelings for you are as strong as they have ever been.'

'Good strong or bad strong?'

Time had dimmed how perceptive he could be.

She laughed and looked out at the other vehicles fighting the same fight through the traffic as they were. 'Let's just leave it at strong, okay?'

Although she wasn't looking at him, she felt his smile before she heard it in his voice. 'Strong feelings I can work with. Indifference would be a different matter.'

She wondered if he'd feel so positive about her strong feelings for him if those strong feelings manifested in her throwing vases at his head.

If only she did feel indifference for him. She might have been able to move on in her personal life. 'Indifference is one thing I don't think I could ever feel for you.'

'Good... Music?'

'Sure.'

Using voice commands, he selected an album of the rock band he'd flown her to Germany to watch perform live.

Glad she had her sunglasses on, Beth closed her eyes and worked at not letting her inner feelings show on her face.

Mercifully, the traffic thinned out, and soon they were

out of the city itself and homing in on the airport. Only the blasted music of the band she'd spent eight years avoiding listening to stopped her chest from lightening with relief, and when he pulled up at the express drop-off point, it took everything she had not to throw herself out of the car. It took even more to face him.

He was already looking at her, his shades removed. Wordlessly, he removed her sunglasses, too, and for a long moment simply gazed at her.

Bringing his face close to hers, he gently stroked her cheek. 'I know you still have doubts about me,' he said quietly, 'but I promise you will not regret your decision.'

The surge of emotion that rose so powerfully in her almost shocked Beth into silence. That Xavi could still read her so well despite all her efforts to conceal her true feelings was almost as frightening as the longing to believe him and the depth of her need to cover his hand and press it tighter to her cheek.

Gazing into eyes that were like melted dark chocolate, she whispered, 'Aren't you worried that you might regret it, too?'

His gaze didn't so much as flicker as he brought his face closer to hers. 'No, I'm not.'

Her lips were tingling with anticipation before she felt his breath on her lips and the tickle of his beard, and then she was filled with the glorious sensation of his tender caress on her lips.

He drew back with the ghost of a smile. 'You should go.'

Wishing she wasn't already craving more of his mouth on hers, she nodded.

He clasped the back of her head and nuzzled his nose to hers. 'Let me know when you've landed?'

Unable to resist, she pressed her mouth to his for one last kiss and murmured, 'I promise.'

When Beth strode into the airport on legs that felt all wobbly, she didn't have to look back to know he was watching her.

When Beth was out of his sight, Xavi turned the engine back on and drove away, resisting the temptation to abandon his car and follow her back to England.

He'd long wondered what her apartment, or *flat*, as she referred to it on social media, looked like. All she'd revealed were snippets; nothing that would allow a follower to identify the location or make an educated guess to it.

Her job, though, he knew a lot about, not just because of what she'd told him the few times they'd seen each other over the years or through what she'd posted, but because he owned the company.

Miss Amore was the first fashion chain he'd bought as a personal investment. He hadn't put it under the Rosbel Group umbrella, and only expert journalistic levels of digging would find his name as the owner.

He'd bought it on a Beth-like whim when she'd posted about starting an internship there. He'd experienced a lot of guilt in those days. Beth had only been expected to spend the summer in Madrid. It was because of Xavi that she'd given up her place at university to stay past the summer, and so when he'd learned that she'd decided to join the fashion world after all, he'd felt he owed it to her to smooth her path into it. It had been at his behind-the-scenes insistence that her internship had become a full-time position. Everything else she'd achieved had been through her own hard work.

She'd excelled without him. Thrived without him, personally and professionally.

Whereas he…

Xavi didn't like to remember the days when he'd had to bury himself in work just to get through the days without her.

CHAPTER FOUR

THE AIRPORT WAS BUSY, but Beth got through security with minimal queuing. After buying a coffee, she found herself a spot at the departure gate near a large, rowdy stag party. She knew it would be more prudent to wait until she was home before making this call, but with Xavi's kisses still fresh on her lips, she was fired up, almost buzzing with the desperate need to purge the tempest of emotion coursing through her. With her fellow travellers giving the stag party a wide berth, no one would be close enough to hear her side of the conversation.

She dialled the number, put the phone to one ear and a finger to the other to drown out the background noise.

A male American voice answered. 'Paul Haldron.'

'Hi, Paul, it's Beth Granger.'

A beat of silence.

'Do you know who I am?'

'I'm familiar with the name.'

'I'm Raul Belmonte's granddaughter.'

Another beat of silence.

'I'm his sole heir. Once probate's dealt with, I'll be the joint majority shareholder of the Rosbel Group.'

'I did wonder if that would be the case,' he said slowly. 'What can I do for you, Miss Granger?'

'Call me Beth, and it's not so much what you can do for me but what I can do for you. I understand you spearheaded the recent attempt at a hostile takeover.'

More silence and then a cautious, 'That's in the past. Xavi de la Rosa fought it and won.'

'He won because he had my grandfather's shares in his pocket. Those shares now belong to me…well, they will once probate's been granted. In a matter of months, they will be mine to do as I please, as will the rest of his estate, which I'm sure you must know is worth a *lot* of money.'

'Okay…?'

'How amenable would you be to selling your shares to me?'

He laughed.

'Paul…may I call you Paul?'

He laughed again. 'Sure.'

'Paul, Xavi will never relinquish his control of the Rosbel Group. You can try again, as many times as you like, but you won't win. He will never let you win.' And neither would she. The Rosbel Group belonged to the de la Rosas and Belmontes. She might not have her grandfather's name, but she was the only Belmonte left. Her grandfather and Ferdinand had built the company from nothing, and, having forced herself to think about it with rationality rather than emotion, she knew she couldn't destroy their legacy and put it in the hands of strangers. The only thing she wanted to destroy was Xavi.

'Cut to the chase, Miss Granger.'

'Beth,' she corrected. 'You can't beat him, but I can. Name your price.'

'I beg your pardon?'

'Your shares. I want them, and I'm prepared to pay any price for them.'

The silence this time went on for so long that she thought he'd hung up on her.

'You're preparing your own takeover?'

She ignored the question. 'You bought the shares as an investment fourteen years ago. Your investment has increased twelvefold. I'm prepared to pay more than the market price for them—I'm prepared to pay *any* price. You're a businessman, Paul. You invested in the Rosbel Group to make money. Now's the time to recoup that investment and make some serious money. Name your price.'

'I'll need to speak to my business partners,' he said slowly.

Beth smiled. Fired up with hurt and pain after her 2 a.m. call with Xavi, she'd thrown herself into researching Paul Haldron. His efforts to take over the Rosbel Group had cost him financially, and his other investments were performing poorly. He couldn't mount another hostile takeover attempt even if he wanted to. 'You do that. Get back to me with a price—I trust you will approach this with discretion?'

'Mom's the word.'

'Good, because for this to happen, not a word about it can leak.'

'Understood.'

The call over, she blew out a long breath. The buzz that had taken her through that phone call—she'd channelled one of her favourite on-screen kick-ass female characters to get through it—was already plummeting, and she fought valiantly to recapture it.

Paul was interested, of that she was certain.

The first step towards Xavi's destruction had been taken.

* * *

Four days later, Beth read Xavi's message that had just pinged into her phone:

No budget. I'm in Paris and extremely busy. Please direct all messages during working hours that concern the wedding to Fenella. I will call you this evening when I've finished working to catch up. X

Her mouth tightened at his brush-off. The working day was done already. All she'd asked was the budget for her wedding dress.

She looked at all the boxes piled in her living room. Xavi had sent a team over to assist in packing up her life. If she wanted, she could fly back to Madrid right now. Her boss had taken her resignation well—too well, really. Beth had half expected pleas for her to change her mind, but *nada*. As soon as she'd told him the date for the wedding, he'd told her not to worry about working her full contracted notice. She had the feeling he'd have let her leave without working any of it, which was odd considering they didn't have an obvious candidate to take her role. He probably didn't want to miss out on his wedding invitation. She'd invited everyone she worked with. Let them enjoy the wedding of the century. After all, Xavi was paying for it all.

Oh yes, Xavi was paying for *everything*, and he was not holding back in the lavishing of his money. It was only his time he refused to lavish. He'd got her agreement to marry him, and now he was laying his marker and making sure to emphasise that their marriage would be nothing like their relationship of old. The kiss at the end of his message had been a sop, a marker of intent that quelled much of the guilt that kept nibbling at her.

She was reading the message a third time when her phone rang in her hand.

'Hey, Beth, Paul Haldron. I have good news for you.'

His next few words were lost in the sensation of white light flickering behind her eyes.

Forcing a long breath from her lungs, she casually said, 'And the price you require?'

It was as outrageous and greedy as she'd anticipated, but she was in no mood to barter. She wanted this done. 'Deal.'

'I did wonder if the news about your marriage would mean a change of heart.'

So news of their marriage had reached America. Xavi had put out a press release the day before. Any moment and the press would discover her location and descend on her. Anticipating this, Xavi had already sent a team of ex-special forces to keep watch over her and keep her safe.

Her answer was a clipped, 'Not at all.'

He gave a low chuckle. 'Lady, you must *really* hate him to be playing him for such a sucker.'

'My reasons are none of your business,' she informed him coldly. 'I'll be in England for another week or so, and I want an agreement in principle before I return to Madrid for my wedding. I imagine I'll be in a position to complete the purchase within three months, and I want things arranged so the moment I give the go-ahead, the transfer is made immediately.'

His laughter had a touch of patronising indulgence to it. 'Do you know how the transfer of shares works, lady?'

'I'm learning, but I do know how the power of money works, and if you want any of mine, you'll keep your mouth shut about this conversation—if Xavi hears even a whisper of our plans before the transfer takes place, the deal will be off and your march to bankruptcy will carry on at the pace it's currently travelling.'

She ended the conversation without saying goodbye.

Her heart was racing manically.

The ball was now well and truly rolling. Very soon, she would roll it some more to hoover up enough of the smaller shares to make her the majority shareholder of the Rosbel Group.

She had another read of Xavi's message and willed her heart to harden. Any feelings he held for her were secondary to his devotion to the business. He would dump her again in a heartbeat if he felt their relationship threatened his control of it in any way. She must never forget that.

Two weeks after she'd returned to England to pack up her life, Beth stepped out of Xavi's private plane and strode through late-afternoon air so thick with heat it shimmered.

The driver and passenger of the familiar black SUV waiting for her both got out before she reached them. The former started loading all her suitcases into the boot. The latter, in faded jeans, brown boots and a snug white T-shirt that emphasised the muscularity of his impossibly tall, wiry physique, simply gazed at her from behind his shades.

Making no attempt to kiss or embrace her, his firm lips curved into a lazy smile. '*Hola, mi vida.* Good flight?'

Just to hear his voice was to make her heart, racing with anticipation at seeing him again from the moment she'd woken, thump harder.

The longer she'd spent away from him, the more fully

he'd invaded her mind. The wonderful memories of their six months together had fought with the awful memories of their sudden break-up and its aftermath, her resolve at what she was planning for him wrestling with guilt and doubt. So exhausted had the constant thoughts and heightened emotions left her that she'd kept falling asleep hours earlier than she normally would, only for vivid dreams to keep springing her awake.

The dreams had all centred around him. The worst one had been just last night when she'd dreamed of walking into his old bedroom while he was sleeping. Ellen had sat up beside him, naked just as she'd been in those vile nude pics she'd sent him all those years ago, smiling triumphantly at her, and Beth had realised it wasn't Xavi's bedroom but Ellen's bedroom, not their bed he slept naked in but Ellen's bed. And then Ellen had morphed into the woman from the New Year's party.

It had been her own whimpers that had pulled her awake from that one. Her chest had been icy cold ever since. If she could have delayed her return again, she would have done.

There would be no more delays. Xavi's mother was throwing a pre-wedding dinner party for a select number of family and friends that evening. As much as Beth would have preferred to stay away from Madrid until the wedding itself, she couldn't do that to Mireia. Xavi's mother had shown her nothing but love and had sent her the most wonderful message saying how delighted she was at the news that, finally, Beth would be marrying into her family.

However cold she felt inside, she wouldn't let Xavi see it. Beth's pride had dragged her out of bed in the early days of their break-up, had made her smile widely and embrace him the few times she'd seen him over the years and had made her pull herself together every time her heart stopped when he liked one of her posts or left a comment.

If not for her pride, she would never have recovered from any of it and if she was going to get through the next however long of marriage to him, she would have to cling to it tightly because the one thing she would never allow herself to do would be to fall apart in front of him. She would never give him the power to break her again. In the future, she would be the one with the power to break *him*.

Producing an easy-going smile, she said, 'I'd forgotten how convenient flying private is over economy.' The entertainment on her flight to England from Madrid had come courtesy of the rowdy stag party. She imagined they were still fighting off their hangovers.

Beth had thought about the stag party a lot during her return flight on Xavi's private jet. Thought, too, about the corresponding hen party. If the hen was as happy to be marrying as the drunken stag who'd got to his feet approximately every ten minutes to yell out, 'I'm getting *married*!' for all the plane to hear, then she thought they would have a good chance of making their marriage work.

Eight years ago, Beth would have been the happiest hen in the world.

His lips curved. 'More leg room, too.'

'How would you know? You consider first class to be slumming it,' she teased. Xavi's first holiday had been to his family's private Caribbean island when he'd been three months old, every whim catered to by a fleet of staff. Beth's first holiday had been to a decrepit British holiday resort when she'd been six as part of a newspaper cut-price deal. Her bed had been little bigger than a cot, which had been better than what her poor grandparents had had to deal with—the moment they'd climbed into their bed, it had collapsed beneath them. It had rained the whole week, too.

The curved lips widened into a grin. 'Can I help that I've been raised to have rarified tastes?'

'You've been spoiled your whole life.'

He laughed and swept an arm to the car. 'Come on, let's get you to your new home.'

The car's cabin was wonderfully cool, a relief after that short blast of Spanish heat that had warmed even her ice-cold chest a little. At least, Beth told herself, it was the heat that had warmed it, not being back in Xavi's orbit. If only the years had lessened his sex appeal by even an iota instead of enhancing it.

'Are your family and friends ready for tomorrow?' he asked once the car started moving.

Breathing through her mouth to stop the potency of Xavi's scent doing too much damage to her senses, she nestled against the door and twisted around so she was facing him. First thing in the morning, the eight members of her English family, her five closest friends and fifteen of her colleagues were being collected from their homes to be driven to their closest airports, then flying first class to Madrid and being put up in Madrid's finest hotel, all expenses paid, courtesy of Xavi. 'Yes. Everyone's very excited, especially my dad and my nan. Fenella and the rest of your staff have done a fabulous job getting it all arranged, so thank you for that.'

'They were happy to do it.'

She kicked her heels off and casually asked, 'How's everything going with my grandfather's estate?'

They'd spoken every evening in her absence, but they'd been short conversations. Xavi had been far too busy getting his affairs in order to take time off for their wedding and five-day honeymoon to hold a conversation that involved more than checking in with her. She hadn't needed to pester him to know his crack team of lawyers would be pulling out all the stops to get probate done swiftly. After all, it was in Xavi's interest for it to be completed as speedily as possible.

'The grant of probate should be ready within the next couple of weeks.'

'That soon?' She'd assumed it would take a few months at the least, even factoring in Xavi's diligence.

'Your grandfather was a meticulous man who left his affairs in exemplary order.'

That he had been, although *control freak* probably described him better. Domestically, he'd been fastidious about everything, from the correct way to hang a towel to demanding Beth straighten the cushions when getting up from a sofa. He'd been far worse within the workplace.

By the time he'd died, Beth had become so used to the control-freakery that she barely noticed it, let alone let herself get riled up about it. It was just the way he was, and she liked to think that if her mother had lived, she, too, would have learned to ignore the infuriating aspects of his nature... Or maybe not. Beth hadn't been raised by him or married to him. She'd only known him in his twilight years and then only sporadically. It wasn't just her mother who'd left him, but her grandmother, too.

As Beth had eventually learned from her father—her grandfather had adamantly refused to discuss the subject—Marta had been much younger than Raul. When she'd left him, she'd been so desperate to get away from him that she'd agreed to leave their only child with him. She'd taken the payoff and lived her life in quiet solitude, passing away ten years earlier. A part of Beth wished she'd known about her before she'd died so she could have tried to reach out to her, but another part was glad she hadn't. Beth's mother had given her life so Beth could live. Beth's grandmother had left her twelve-year-old daughter with the husband she despised. While Beth had suspicions as to why, she doubted she would ever know the truth. The dead couldn't speak. Beth was the only one of the bloodline still alive.

'That you are his only legitimate heir helps, too,' Xavi added, unwittingly tapping into her thoughts. 'There will be a hefty inheritance tax bill to be paid, but your grandfather made provisions for that. There is no reason to believe everything can't be signed over to you when we get back from our honeymoon.'

Her smile at this needed no practice. Whenever her conscience gnawed a little too deeply at the wheels she'd set in motion, all she had to do was bring up Ellen's time-stamped photo of Xavi asleep in her bed three days after he'd kicked Beth from his bed and remember his barefaced lie for resolve to steel her spine.

Their whole relationship had been a lie. Beth would have chosen to live the rest of her life in a grotty bedsit than live without Xavi. He'd not even given her the chance to make adjustments to their relationship so he could devote more of his time to the business, just off the bat dumped her like she was an unwanted plaster that needed ripping off his skin.

She *had* distracted him from his work, that had been

true, but he'd let her. They'd had sex in his office more times than she could remember, and he'd been more than happy to go along with her impulsive, often madcap whims, whether that was deciding at three in the afternoon on a Friday to drive to Barcelona for a long weekend or gatecrashing a party because the music pumping from the house had been so enticing—that had been a brilliant night—or whisking him off to Ibiza with zero notice to visit its hippy market she'd just read about.

If he'd ever said no to her she would probably have pouted, but would have accepted it. If he'd said she had to confine her impulses to outside working hours or do them without him, she would have accepted that, too. Instead, he'd severed their relationship without discussion. Whether he'd always planned to bed Ellen or if Ellen had just been a perk of being single again, Beth didn't know nor care to know. It didn't make any difference. Ellen had just been a huge dose of salt rubbed into a wound that had never healed.

It would heal soon, though, when she took the Rosbel Group from him. With probate only weeks from being granted, she could be in a position to take it from him sooner than she'd hoped. She had an agreement in principle with Paul Haldron for the shares he controlled. Once they were in her name, she would own 45 per cent of the Rosbel Group. She was already sounding out wizards of the financial world to act on her behalf in hoovering up the smaller shares until she reached the magic 51 per cent for it.

Xavi was a barefaced liar who'd stolen her dreams and her future and broken her heart beyond repair, and now she was returning the favour.

There was nothing to feel guilty about.

CHAPTER FIVE

A SHORT WHILE LATER, and Beth had to work to maintain her smile when they drove through the wide, open arch of a stunning white-and-red Baroque building with turrets on its roof and came to a stop in an immaculate courtyard that edged sprawling lawns ringed with enormously high trees and a pond so big she wasn't sure if it shouldn't be called a lake.

It was exactly the kind of home she'd once dreamed of them living in, and she was glad she couldn't cry because knowing Xavi had gone ahead and bought their dream home without her filled her with emotions it was hard to breathe through.

Luckily, the time it took for him to whisk her to the top floor in a private elevator that needed his fingerprint to operate gave her time to compose herself.

Inside, the vastness of the high-ceilinged open spaces came as no surprise—Beth's months of living in Spanish opulence had inured her to what incredible wealth could buy you—but the tastefulness of it all did. Neutral walls were enlivened with an eclectic mix of artwork, the mass of dark leather seating richly inviting.

Hating to imagine Xavi consulting with a lover—Ellen? Appendage lady?—over the interior, she stepped out onto the living room's balcony to breathe in the warm air, and soaked in the grounds from this new perspective.

It was hard not to sigh with wonder at it all, and just incredible to believe something like this existed in the heart of Madrid.

'This place must have cost you a fortune,' she commented when Xavi stood beside her at the balustrade.

'It's my most expensive piece of real estate, but worth every cent.' She felt his gaze turn to her. 'What do you think? Can you be happy here?'

She tightened her grip on the iron railing and fought her throat from closing.

Eight years ago, she would have been ecstatic. As amenable as the de la Rosas had been to her practically living with them, Beth had longed for her and Xavi to have a place of their own. As much as they'd spoken of buying a place just like this, she'd have been happy anywhere so long as it was with Xavi.

Eight years ago, she'd been a naive fool.

She brought a smile to her face and said, 'Waking up to this view every day will make me happy.'

The glass door opened, and his housekeeper stepped out carrying a tray of coffee for them.

Taking a seat at the balcony table, Beth tried not to wonder how many other women had taken this very seat.

'Is the whole top floor yours?' she asked once the coffee had been poured and they were alone again.

'The whole building is mine,' he said. 'I rent the other apartments out.'

'You bought the *whole building*?' If she were judging it by London standards, she would estimate it could be divided into homes for a minimum of ten families, all living in plentiful space and luxury. By Manchester standards, twenty families.

A muscular shoulder lifted. 'Why own a part of something when you can own the entire thing?'

'You do have a thing about owning the entirety of things, don't you?' At his raised eyebrows, she added, 'The primary reason you're marrying me is so you can keep control of the entirety of the Rosbel Group.'

His shaded stare stayed steady on her. 'Yes, keeping control of the company is my primary reason for marrying you, but that doesn't make my other reasons redundant, and it doesn't change that you're the only woman I've ever wanted to marry.'

Rather than throw her coffee over him, she laughed and fixed her gaze back on the distant lake-size pond. Figures she thought looked small enough to be children were paddling in it. If their child had lived, it could have been one of those children. It would have just turned seven, and it never failed to hurt her heart that it hadn't lived long enough for her to know its sex.

'I mean it, Beth. No one else has come close to you.'

'Gosh, I am *honoured*.' She would not give him the satisfaction of saying no one had come close to him, either…not that she believed him. Xavi would say whatever needed saying and do whatever needed doing until he had his ring on her finger.

'You don't believe me?'

She shrugged. 'Does it matter when we're getting married in two days?'

'It matters to me.'

'Regaining my trust in you is going to take time.' Until the end of days and then some.

An edge came into his voice. 'If you don't trust me, why agree to marry me?'

So I can destroy you.

'Because you made such a convincing pitch for it?' She laughed again and shook her head, wondering why she couldn't just outright lie to him. 'Xavi, let's not pretend that everything's going to be chocolate sprinkles straight away. We need to get to know each other again.' She removed her sunglasses to look more directly at him. 'Just remember, if I didn't hold such strong feelings for you, I would never have agreed to marry you. I'm uprooting myself from my life, all of it. Everything I've built for myself these last eight years. I'm leaving my family and friends behind and walking away from the job I love for you.'

Removing his shades, too, Xavi studied Beth with the same intensity he'd studied her at her grandfather's wake.

Beth had warned him that she'd changed from the young woman he'd been in love with all those years ago, but he'd already known that before proposing. He wouldn't have contemplated taking this path if he'd thought they were the same people as they'd been eight years ago, but the changes to Beth weren't just in general maturity; there was something else, too, something that had been gnawing at his gut since she'd returned to England and had grown stronger with each excuse to delay her return to him.

The Beth he remembered had fed on emotion. This Beth fed on logic and rationality. The passionate fire and zest for life that burned so bright in her had muted, and he couldn't shake the feeling she was smothering it deliberately, just like he'd been unable to shake the voice nagging in his head that something else was going on with her.

He pulled in a deep breath through his nose and reminded himself that she was here and that in two days she would be his wife. After eight years apart, he couldn't expect things to be *chocolate sprinkles* immediately—he needed to find some patience, a trait he was forced to admit was not on his list of attributes. Beth was right that he was spoiled, and being spoiled with women counted in that, too. Xavi had grown used to women pretending that the sun shone out of his backside and could see how easy it was for men in his position to believe it actually did. Not every man of his position had a younger sister called Carlota primed to bring him back down to earth at every given opportunity.

Beth had never treated him as if the sun shone out of his backside. She'd treated him as if he *were* her sun, but his family's wealth and standing had meant nothing to her. She'd loved him for him, and that had been as intoxicating as the sex between them, and now she was back in his life, marrying him and entrusting her shares to him and so securing his position within the Rosbel Group. She'd entrusted her grandfather's estate into his care, too; trusted him with billions in the form of assets, cash and shares. She trusted him where it most mattered; that was the important thing.

The second most important thing was that Beth was the only woman he'd ever wanted to marry, the only woman he'd envisaged having children with. That had never changed, and there was nothing to make him think they couldn't make it work. They still shared a humour, and the spark was still there between them, too.

A lot of marriages survived with less than spark and humour. He didn't think his parents' marriage had been miserable, but he couldn't remember it being particularly happy, either. That hadn't stopped his mother's utter devastation at his father's death. She'd wandered the rooms of their home like a wraith for months, unable to settle, unable to concentrate, incapable of caring for her three grieving children.

'You need to step up now, Xavi,' his grandfather, grieving the loss of his only son, had told him privately the night his father had taken his final breath. 'It is time for you to become a man. Your mother and your sisters need you. *I* need you.'

And so he'd stepped up to the mark his grandfather had set for him and become the man his family needed. He'd channelled the grief that had threatened to choke him and taken control of the household, from directing the domestic staff to ensuring his sisters did their homework and that Carlota, then only nine, brushed her teeth. He'd held everything together until his mother came out of her fugue, and then devoted his time to the studies he'd neglected for the sake of his family. Knowing his grandfather's retirement plans had been put on ice, he'd worked hard and earned his place at Oxford on merit, and completed back-to-back degrees. His studies done, he'd joined the Rosbel Group, ready, willing and able to be groomed into taking over from the two aging men who were both more than ready to devote their lives to their local golf course; and then within months, Beth Granger had appeared in his life, and for six months derailed him from everything that was important in his life.

Reaching across the small table, he took hold of her dainty hand and brought the tips of her fingers to his lips. 'I will make all your sacrifices worthwhile, I promise.'

Something flashed in her eyes before she leaned closer and clasped her fingers around his, her lips stretching into the upside-down heart he so loved. 'If I didn't know it would be worth it, I wouldn't be here.'

Their lips brushed together across the table. Closing his eyes, Xavi breathed her in. The heat from the sun enhanced the soft scent of her skin, which was a smell like nothing else on this earth. If its uniqueness could be captured, he'd get his perfumers to bottle it. They would make a fortune. But it couldn't be captured, and so it was a scent that belonged only to him, and in two days, Beth would belong only to him, too.

After pulling his mouth away, he gently tucked a lock of her English autumn-coloured hair behind one of her pixie ears. He'd longed to touch her since she'd stepped off the plane, but had resisted. Beth's kisses were just too potent for sensibility. He could still feel the effect of the kiss they'd shared in the study, had carried her taste on his tongue since she'd left to pack up her life in England. 'We need to get ready for my mother's dinner party.'

Those incredible crystal-clear eyes pulsed. 'Is this where we go to the bedroom?'

He kissed her again, a longer, deeper fusion. Rubbing his cheek to hers, he murmured, 'Patience, *mi vida*. We need to leave soon.'

Her hand clasped the back of his head, her lips parting, her tongue darting into his mouth to dance with his. 'You're going to make me wait?'

'You've made me wait for two weeks. Consider this payback.'

'I thought we were all mature now,' she teased seductively before sliding her tongue back into his mouth.

He returned the kiss... *Dios*, she tasted so damn good...and threaded his fingers deeper into her hair. 'Only until you kiss me, and then I am twenty-four again.'

And when he was twenty-four, he'd been insatiable. The six months he'd spent with Beth had been the most hedonistic months of his life. He'd wanted her constantly.

He would not allow himself to fall back into that lust-blinded state again. This time, he would keep firm control of his libido and create clear demarcations between his work and his home, lines that had blurred beyond recognition when they'd first been together. Professionalism and propriety had gone out the window. Eight years on, and Xavi was still unable to look at the left side boardroom window without remembering how Beth had sat on its ledge with her skirt hitched up to her waist and her legs wrapped around him as he'd pounded into her. They'd barely straightened their clothes before his grandfather's executive assistant had strolled in with pastries for the imminent meeting.

Beth had stripped him of his self-control and professionalism, and the result had been the near destruction of everything. He'd spent years waking with cold sweats from dreams of his father shaking his head and sorrowfully saying, 'You promised to step up, Xavi.'

The first time that dream had struck him had been his first night in Milan after the meal where his grandfather and Raul had driven home how badly he'd taken his eye off the ball and screwed up. He'd woken in his hotel bed with a chest like ice and his skin clammy cold, and known there was no alternative. He had to end things with Beth.

When Xavi threw himself into something, it took all his attention. His feelings for Beth had consumed him and stolen his attention from the business and imperilled it. If he wanted to fulfil the destiny fate had set for him and step into the legacy his father had never been able to fulfil, it would have to be without her.

'If you were twenty-four again, you'd have screwed me in the back of the car on the drive here,' she said into his mouth. 'You didn't even try to kiss me.'

'That was deliberate. You, *mi vida*, are irresistible. One kiss is never enough. I didn't want our first screw in eight years to be a quickie in the car…'

'You screwed me nearly as many times in a car as you did in a bed.'

'That was then.' And he would never be that man again. The intervening years had taught Xavi the needed art of separation. 'When we make love again, we're going to do it properly. When I take you, you will be naked in my bed.'

'I can get naked now, if you want?' she breathed.

Desire a heavy thrum in his veins, he groaned into her wet, hot, pliant mouth. *Dios*, he wanted to slide his hand beneath her plain cream top and cup the breasts that were anything but plain, lower his head and take a pale pink nipple into his mouth.

Her fingers dipped beneath the neck of his T-shirt. Her touch scorched his skin. 'Are you only kissing me now because there's a table between us?'

'Damned right.' Summoning all his control, he wrenched his mouth away and hauled himself to his feet.

One look at Beth's flushed cheeks was enough to make him suppress another groan. 'I'm going to take a cold shower in a guest room. Isabel will have unpacked your clothes by now—she will show you around our bedroom suite. Anything you need, she will provide it. We leave in an hour.'

Beth stood beneath the waterfall shower of the most stunning bathroom she'd ever been in and lathered herself with the gel Xavi's staff had unpacked for her, trying to breathe normally rather than just inhale tight, shallow snatches of air. Her heart was still thumping manically, her skin still so fevered it was hot to the touch. There was a pulsing ache between her legs she'd not felt in eight years. The closest had been two weeks ago in the de la Rosa study. Before that, she might as well have been dead from the waist down for all the sensation she'd felt there.

She wondered what Xavi would do if she were to seek out the guest room he'd hidden himself away in and stand before him naked. In their first incarnation, he'd never resisted an opportunity for sex. He'd been her slave for sex as much as she'd been his, but just as she was different from the Beth of old, he was different from the Xavi of old. She knew he still wanted her—she'd seen the hunger in his eyes and tasted his desire in his kisses—but in their first incarnation, he'd never hidden from it, had let his desires control him. The Xavi of today was a man who never relinquished control of himself.

Ellen's beautiful, spiteful face flashed into her vision. Ellen, who'd enjoyed Xavi's incredible lovemaking while Beth was still pregnant with his baby.

How many women had come after Ellen? Obviously, the appendage lady had, but how many others that she didn't know about? A handful? A baker's dozen? A score? Two score? More?

Beth had long ago learned not to torture herself with these nausea-inducing thoughts, but as she dried herself off, she refused to push them away. Tonight she would share Xavi's bed. They would have sex. Her heart would be at its most vulnerable. She needed to shield it. She needed to shield it through all the nights she would share his bed.

The bed they would be sharing was enormous and sinfully inviting. The bedroom itself, with its high ceiling, abundance of mirrors, seductive artwork and blue velvet soft furnishings, was sinfully inviting, and she forced herself to wonder how many other women had been invited into it. How many other women had made use of the shared dressing room? How many other women had sat at this dressing table and applied their makeup?

How many of those women had he lost control with?

By the time she was dressed, her hair dried and smoky eye makeup done, Beth's stomach churned so badly with self-inflicted nausea she doubted she'd be able to eat anything that evening.

Breathing as slowly and as deeply as she could, she took stock of her reflection.

When she came back to this room later that evening, she would enjoy Xavi's gorgeous body and let him enjoy hers. She would let him take her as many times as he wanted…and he always wanted more. As the weeks of their marriage passed, she would shamelessly use sex as her weapon of choice to break his defences and drive him wilder and wilder until she was buried as deeply in his head and heart as he was buried in hers, but through it all she would be full in control of herself with her heart shielded. The only control that would be broken would be Xavi's.

And then she would destroy him.

When Beth joined him with two minutes to spare in the living room, Xavi's heart doubled in size with just one beat.

Glass of whisky in hand, he got to his feet and drank in the stunning, colourful vision before him.

Wearing a floral sleeveless maxi dress that cinched at the waist and emphasised her voluptuous feminine curves, its autumn colours perfectly complemented her long red hair, loose and gleaming under the last rays of the setting sun penetrating through the windows. The dark tan of her wedged sandals perfectly matched the handbag slung over her shoulder.

As confident in her skin as a catwalk model, she strode towards him with a wide smile. 'You look *good*!'

Before he could respond, her arms hooked around his neck, and he was engulfed in a cloud of freshly showered and perfumed Beth.

'This is where you tell me that I look beautiful,' she reminded him brightly, her face straining up to his for a kiss.

'You always look beautiful,' he assured her truthfully before pressing his mouth to hers. He allowed himself only the smallest taste before breaking the kiss and removing her hands from his neck. He took a step back and laughed at her pout. 'Later, *mi vida*.'

She tilted her head and pouted again, but her eyes were dancing with a knowing that made his veins thicken and loins tighten, and when the crystal glass was prised from his hand and she tipped the remaining liquid down her throat and wiped her mouth with the back of her hand with a flourish, he shook his head and laughed. *Dios*, Beth made even the stealing of his drink sexy.

Diving his fingers into her glorious hair, he gazed into her eyes. 'I take it back—you haven't changed at all. You're still fabulously crazy.' Crazy in the best way. He'd never suffered a moment of boredom with Beth.

Her lips formed their upside-down heart. 'Only to a degree. I've learned to control the crazy…to a point.'

He rubbed his nose to hers and inhaled her skin. 'Good. You wouldn't be you without it. Now, let's get out of here before we're forced to call the wedding off on account of my mother killing me for being late to her dinner party.'

'How many people are going to be there?' Beth asked as their driver navigated the busy early-evening Madrid streets filled with tourists and locals alike heading out for meals and drinks and whatever else people did when the working day was done.

Xavi rarely did anything when the working day was done, mainly because his working day was never done. The grandfathers had split the running of the Rosbel Group, Xavi's grandfather controlling the financial side, Raul controlling the creative side. Xavi controlled all of it, and with Beth's shares he could maintain that control until the day came that *he* chose to cede it. If fortune were in his favour, that control would be ceded to one or more of his and Beth's children.

'She said it was only close family and friends.'

'So half of Madrid, then?'

He met her eye and grinned. 'You know my mother.'

She smiled in agreement.

It seemed incredible to him that he could still read her smiles.

'Is Blanca going to be there?' she said. 'I meant to message Carlota earlier and ask.'

'She flew in a couple of hours before you landed.'

'How does she feel about us marrying?'

'I haven't spoken to her about it, but I don't imagine she has any negative thoughts. She always liked you.'

'I always liked her, too... Is she still very serious?'

'Blanca was born serious. I think our father's death solidified that aspect of her nature.'

Her smile turned into one of sympathy, and she slid her hand across the small but deliberate divide he'd created between them to squeeze his. 'Is she seeing anyone?'

'If she is, she hasn't mentioned it.'

'What about Carlota? Is she still seeing that archaeologist?'

'What archaeologist?'

She shook her head and chided, 'Do you actually know *anything* about your sisters?'

He tried not to feel defensive at a subtle rebuke similar to ones his mother often made. 'I know they're both getting on well in their careers. Their personal lives are none of my business unless they choose to make it my business.'

'If I had siblings, I'd make their business my business. I'd want to know everything about their lives.'

'Why?'

'I like knowing the minutiae of my friends' lives, so I imagine my nosiness would be even stronger with a sibling.'

Beth, Xavi remembered, had always wanted siblings. He'd often thought one of his attractions for her had been the female-dominant contingent of his household. She hadn't just loved him, she'd loved his mother and sisters, too, especially Carlota. Although Carlota never spoke of it, he knew they'd stayed in touch over the years. He'd been glad of it; another tenuous way of keeping Beth in the periphery of his life.

Sure enough, when they reached the villa and got out of the car, Carlota was straight out the front door to greet them. With a squeal that made his ears hurt, she bounded down the marble steps to throw her arms around Beth, an embrace that was enthusiastically returned.

Inside, the villa overflowed with people. One glance around the open-plan reception and Xavi figured every single aunt and uncle—his father had been an only child, but his mother was one of six—cousin and second cousin was there. Entertaining, he'd long ago realised, had been his mother's way of coping with the loss of her husband. Once she'd pulled herself out of the worst of her grief, she'd taken to throwing parties of all shapes and sizes for any given reason, and had the space and money to feed whole armies if she so wished. Tonight was her way of celebrating her eldest child marrying before the press turned the nuptials into a circus.

Soon, everyone piled around the tables in the garden to drink whatever the hell they pleased and feast on a variety of tapas before the chefs brought out pans of traditional paella.

One of the things Xavi had always so loved about Beth was her unashamed love of food. There was none of the nibbling at dishes the way his mother and sisters did or the few women he'd dated over the years did: She attacked it the way she did everything else in life, with gusto and relish. It was sexy. Watching her expertly peel the shell off a langoustine was sexy. Watching her screw up her expert shell peeling and splatter her cheek with paella juice and burst into laughter as she dabbed at it with a napkin was sexy, and it came to him, really came to him, that in two days he'd be marrying her. After eight years of emptiness, the time was finally right for them.

Seated directly opposite him, Beth's stare caught his. His heart caught in his throat.

She raised her glass of white wine to him.

He lifted his bottle of beer to her.

Carlota, seated to Beth's right in complete disregard of their mother's table plan, whispered something in her ear that made her laugh again and take a large drink of her wine, which she promptly spilt down her chin to even greater peals of laughter.

'I'm glad she's giving you a second chance,' Blanca said softly from the seat beside him.

His eyes still on Beth, he nodded. 'So am I.'

'You're a lucky man. Not many women would forgive what you did to her.'

His defensive hackles immediately rose. 'All I did was end a relationship that wasn't working for me, nothing that people haven't been doing since the dawn of humanity.'

'It was the way you ended it. You forget I was there. I saw her before you got home. It was the happiest and most excited I'd ever seen her, which is a high bar for Beth, and then I heard her pleas and her sobs. We all heard her, and we all saw the state she was in when she left. You broke her, Xavi.'

'That was a lifetime ago,' he dismissed. 'And I didn't break her. She was upset at the time, I don't deny that, but she got over it quickly. She understands why I ended it the way I did, and she agrees I was right to do so. Neither of us was ready for what we had then.'

'Sure about that, are you?'

'Yes,' he said, his tone brusque and with a hint of irritation enough to tell his sister he would listen to no more on the subject.

Beth's musical laughter cut through the tense air that had formed between Xavi and Blanca, and he shrugged off the irritation and strange discomfort his sister's unwanted probing had set off in him and focused his attention back on the woman about to retake her place as the most important person in his life.

In two days, this fabulously crazy, vivacious woman with a zest for life was finally going to be his wife. Tonight, though…

Tonight he would make her his again, and this time she would be his forever.

CHAPTER SIX

'You looked like you enjoyed yourself,' Xavi commented as they drove out of the de la Rosa estate.

'I had a great time.' Beth smiled wistfully. 'It was lovely seeing everyone—I'd forgotten how big your mother's side of the family is.' The first time Beth had seen the whole family together, she'd felt incredibly intimidated, a state of affairs that lasted only seconds as everyone had made her so welcome. She'd had no qualms about seeing them all again, and she left with a lovely warmth in her chest, which made a wonderful change from the ice that had been in it since she'd wrenched herself out of that horrible dream.

Her cheeks had received more kisses in one night than the whole of her face had received in eight years.

'It was a shame your grandfather couldn't be there,' she added. She'd managed only a few short words with Ferdinand at the funeral.

'He will be at the wedding.'

'Good.' She tried to sound like she meant it. She liked Ferdinand as much as she liked the rest of Xavi's family, and it had struck her that evening that they would all be there at the wedding, would all hear them exchange their vows and believe Beth meant hers. Guilt was already trying to scratch at her over this. When she took the Rosbel

Group from Xavi, they would all wonder if she'd been playing them, too. She could only hope they all, Mireia, Carlota and Blanca especially, found it in their hearts to forgive her. None of the women cared about the business, not in the way Xavi did, and had no financial stake in it anymore, but she didn't want to hurt them. If she could stay married to the family without having to stay married to the man, then she'd take it in a heartbeat.

She had to stop thinking like this and keep her focus on her revenge. Her professional life had gone forward in leaps and bounds these past eight years, but her personal life had been stuck in stasis. She'd tried to move on, but it had proved impossible. Xavi had ruined her for every other man. Until she eradicated him from her life once and for all, she would never have the family she had once so craved. She wouldn't be capable.

They would already have a family if he hadn't put his precious business above his feelings for her. There was no way of knowing if their child would have survived if they'd stayed together, but Xavi would have been there for her through the loss, and they would surely have tried again.

Knowing from the tightening in her stomach and chest that she was on the cusp of falling into melancholy, she breached the deliberate distance he'd once again created between them and leaned into him. For her revenge to have maximum impact, she needed to keep focused.

'Are you nervous for Saturday?' she asked softly, resting her hand on his lap.

In the old days, he would have covered her hand and slid it up to his groin. This time, he covered it and squeezed. 'I don't do nerves, *mi vida*.'

And neither would she. Nor guilt.

Twisting her bottom, she draped her leg over his lap and tugged her hand out of his hold to press it to his chest.

He gripped the thigh lying on him, but made no effort to slide his hand up the skirt of her dress.

'What are you doing?' he asked with husky bemusement when she undid a shirt button and slipped her hand through the gap to place her palm on his naked skin. Her heart trembled at the familiar warmth of his smooth skin and the softness of the hair covering it, and then trembled more violently to feel the strength of his heart beating beneath it.

In their old life, Beth had spent hours with her head on his chest while he slept, listening to the rhythmic beat that kept him alive while he was unconscious. Death was something Beth had always had a strong respect for, a respect that verged on fear. As a child, she'd often woken in the night and slipped into her father and grandparents' bedrooms to check they were all still breathing. With her family, that check had been enough for her to go back to sleep. With Xavi, she'd woken regularly through the night, that switch in her brain pinging her awake just to check he hadn't slipped beyond the veil.

Every morning, without fail, she messaged her father and grandmother with two words: Good morning. She never felt settled in her skin until she heard back from them, and now, with the weight of Xavi's heart thumping so strongly against the palm of her hand, she wondered for the first time if she'd become such a prolific social media poster because the likes and comments Xavi gave them were the proof her subconscious needed that his heart was still beating.

So frightening was this thought that instead of answering with something flirty and seductive as she'd intended, her whispered, 'I just need to touch you,' came from her trembling heart.

His grip on her thigh tightened.

By the time the driver had dropped them off and they were taking the elevator back up to the apartment, Beth had shaken off most of the strange thoughts that had almost caused her to reevaluate the meaning behind her social media content.

She'd never lied to herself about Xavi always being at the forefront of her thoughts whenever she pressed the post button, but that had always been because she knew he kept an eye out for her posts, and she wanted him to see what a fabulous life she was living without him. To think it had meant more than that…

Nope. Not possible. All she felt for Xavi was hate. In fact, she might just pluck some of his body hairs out while he slept and make a voodoo doll with them. Obviously, she'd need to do an internet search on DIY voodoo dolls, but she was creative and could follow instructions. It would be easy. She'd just have to learn where to poke the pins in so it only maimed him rather than anything serious, because if she…

There was a lurch in her stomach and heart that made her reflexively squeeze the warm fingers laced through hers.

'Are you okay?'

She met the concerned dark brown eyes and nodded.

His forehead furrowed. 'You've lost colour on your face. Are you sure you're okay?'

She forced another nod and, because she couldn't tell him the truth, said the first thing that popped into her head. 'Someone just walked on my grave, that's all.'

'Is that one of those English sayings?'

This time, she managed to dredge a smile with her nod. 'You know that sensation when a shiver runs through you with no warning or apparent reason? That's what the saying refers to.'

Right, so voodoo dolls were out. She might be working to destroy him, but she didn't want to *hurt* him.

She didn't just not want to hurt him, she *couldn't* hurt him. Her brain wouldn't even let her think of it, not even as a macabre joke.

The elevator door opened. Instead of stepping out, Xavi cupped her cheek and brought his face down to hers and murmured, 'Very soon, *mi vida*, the only shivers you will experience will be the shivers of pleasure.'

Just to feel his breath on her face was to send shivers of sensation racing through her and remind her that hate wasn't the only emotion she felt for him. It wasn't even the strongest.

There was the lightest touch of his mouth to hers before his eyes gleamed, and he turned to lead her into the apartment.

Her heart beating erratically, Beth kept her hand in his firm grip and concentrated on breathing as they walked closer and closer to the bedroom.

It had been many years since Xavi had sat propped against a headboard in a bed with such heavy anticipation coiling through his veins and with the beats of his heart feeling so weighty. Even his skin felt like it had come to life; electrical tingles charging through his atoms.

He'd finished in his section of the bathroom first. He'd showered, heavily aware of Beth showering on the other side of the divide. There was no door separating them, just the marble wall that divided his side from hers. If he'd wanted to, he could have walked around the end of the divide and joined her.

The Xavi of old would have knocked the wall down to join her if it had saved seconds walking.

He wasn't that Xavi anymore. He was no longer driven by his desire for Beth. He controlled his desire, not the other way round. He would have taken her without thinking in the study that day of the funeral, but only because he'd not been prepared for her 'chemistry test.'

He was prepared now. Prepared for the rest of his life. He could delay his gratification as he'd proved numerous times that day. Showering with a full-on erection just to imagine Beth lathering herself naked only feet from him was but one of the many tests to his control. He could have taken her in the car on the way from the airport and the drive to and from his family villa. He could have taken her before they'd left for the dinner. He could have taken a casual walk to the hidden spot at the bottom of the de la Rosa garden and taken her there as he'd done a dozen times before.

He'd never had to think about delaying gratification in the intervening years. His control had never come close to being compromised…well, except in those early days after he'd ended things with her, but that had been a different form of control he'd struggled to keep hold of.

The bathroom door opened.

Even before she emerged into the dimly lit room, his arousal throbbed and hardened into rock.

His chest filled, and his throat ran dry.

He'd expected her to emerge naked. Instead, she wore a skimpy translucent black negligee that both covered and revealed her most intimate, feminine parts and showcased the spectacular curves that had always driven him so wild.

Long hair loose around her shoulders, full, weighty breasts gently swaying, she stepped slowly to him.

He swallowed for breath as he took in the wide hips and shapely legs, the softly rounded belly that cinched in at the waist, the slender arms…

She reached the foot of the bed and stopped.

Crystal-clear green eyes locked on his, she pinched the hem of the negligee with both hands and slowly hitched it up, past the juncture of her thighs and the soft, trimmed red bush he'd once shaved until they decided they both preferred it in its natural form. Higher it rose, over her navel, her breasts and pale pink nipples rising and stretching as she lifted it over them, and then it was travelling the length of her slender throat and briefly over her face before it was dropped onto the floor and the hair captured in it was tumbling back down and Beth was staring at him with such naked desire it was all he could do not to launch himself at her, throw her onto the bed and plunge deep inside her.

She climbed onto the bed and crawled towards him like a lioness hunting her prey.

Beth's heart was hammering so hard and fast it had become an indistinct burr. The bedroom's dim, romantic lighting perfectly accentuated the piratical darkness of Xavi's features and turned his body into light and shade. The only movement of his features and body was the flaring of his nostrils and the pulsing of his hooded eyes.

She fought for breath as she took in the changes time had made to his glorious body. So much was the same, but so much was different, too. He'd filled out more than his clothing had revealed, his wiry body far more muscular than it used to be. She didn't need to touch his washboard stomach to know it was harder than it had been when she'd been the most important person in his world, and she squashed the swell of misery that rose to wonder how many other women had already enjoyed this version of him.

She couldn't think about them. Mustn't. Not here in this bed. Not when the one thing that hadn't changed about him was standing proudly to attention, the tip practically touching his belly button.

Before Xavi, she'd always imagined she would find a real-life penis disgusting. Raised in a culture where pornography was rife and the boys of her school thought it hilarious to send dick pics to unwitting girls—a practice eventually stamped out by a determined headmistress and police liaison officers—she'd felt so violated and grossed-out at the unwanted pictures sent to her phone that she'd been in no rush to get intimate with anyone, certainly in no rush to see a male naked in the flesh.

That had all changed with Xavi. Oh, he'd been as horny as the male dogs in her school, but he'd been horny for *her*. He'd wanted Beth, not her vagina. She hadn't been the port in any storm to him. *She'd* been his port. He'd wanted to know *her*, all of her. He'd made her feel beautiful and sexy, and his delight in her body had banished any hang-ups she'd had about the size of her hips and backside. His penis, huge though it was, was something she'd learned to love and not fear. When they'd made love the first time, he'd taken such care of her that there had been hardly any discomfort, let alone pain.

She would have walked on burning coal laced with

glass for him, and it killed her to know there was a tiny part of her that still would.

The texture of his skin was another thing that hadn't changed, and she trailed her fingers up his legs, marvelling and despairing that she remembered it so perfectly. Marvelled and despaired, too, that she was burning up to taste and touch him and to feel the exquisite joy of his possession.

He crooked a finger. Heat was blazing from the hooded eyes locked so tightly on hers. 'Come here,' he said thickly.

Suddenly furious with herself for letting her thoughts take control of her when she was on the first stage of her mission to take control of *him*, she ignored his beckoning finger and took hold of his cock.

'Beth...' His protest cut off when she closed her lips around it.

She could have cried. It even tasted of the same Xavi cleanliness as she remembered. It felt the same, too, a hard, almost glassy-smooth warmth on her tongue. She'd never been able to take it all in her mouth, but that had never mattered; she'd learned to drive him insane using her hands, too, even masturbating him between her breasts. She'd been shameless and wanton in her need to give him pleasure, and as she began to pleasure him now, his reactions fed the burn inside her, turning her on as effectively as if he'd been the one bestowing pleasure on her.

Fingers dove into her hair, his stomach brushing her forehead as he cradled her bobbing head with low groans until he gently lifted her face and gazed down at her.

Meeting his stare, her heart punched hard into her ribs, and the part of her that still loved him wanted to punch him as hard as she could for the way he was looking at her, as if she were his dream come to life and not the dream he'd only picked back up off the reject pile because she had something he wanted.

She was barely aware of being pushed onto her back until she was flat on the mattress and he was lying over her, still gazing at her in the way that made her heart sing and cry all at the same time.

Gently, he smoothed her fringe out of her eyes and then with her name a whisper on his tongue, he kissed her.

Although she'd spent so much of the evening aching to feel Xavi's lips back on hers, the crying part of her heart instinctively resisted his kiss. She wanted to make love to him, not the other way round. She wanted...*needed*... to control all of this, just as she'd controlled the intimacy that had brought them to this point.

His face lifted off her, his concerned stare locking back onto hers. 'What's wrong?'

To her utter horror, the tear ducts she'd spent eight years believing had run dry filled, the pressure that had been missing all these years burning the back of her eyes. The terror that they would spill out and he would see her cry and so see all the things she'd sworn to never let him see again was even stronger than the terror of losing herself in the pleasure of Xavi, and she speared the back of his head to pull his face back down to hers.

Their mouths fused, and in an instant she was close to being lost in the hunger of his kiss. Lips moving in a lusty, possessive dance, their tongues entwined, and Beth was helpless to do anything but cradle his head and drag her fingers through the soft, dark hair she'd once spent hours of her life stroking.

His weight lowered onto her, and then it wasn't just

her mouth being crushed but her breasts and her stomach, sensation burning like a greedy flame through her as they became a tangle of entwined limbs.

'*Dios*, I have missed you,' he muttered into her mouth, words to make her want to cry and want to smash her fists into him, but then his lips dragged over her cheek and down her throat, and she fell back into her Xavi bliss.

The softness of his beard scraped her sensitised skin, a brand-new sensation that heightened the thrills, and when he took the hard peak of her breast in his mouth, her cries came from a place she had no control over.

Xavi had never considered himself a breast man until Beth had come into his life. He still didn't. It was *Beth's* breasts that turned him on so much, not just the weight and fullness of them but the way she writhed and moaned at his slavering worship of them. They were like marshmallow-filled pillows and tasted even sweeter, and he would gladly take his last breath suffocated in them.

He would gladly take his last breath anywhere so long as it was with her. Making love to Beth was like making love to a hedonistic heaven condensed into soft, womanly form.

He would never forget the first time they'd made love. He'd never known himself capable of exerting such control, and he would need similar control to draw strength from to stop himself falling back into the Beth spell that had once captured him so completely.

Breaking that spell had taken such focus and strength that he'd broken a part of himself in the process, a side effect of breaking her heart he'd always accepted.

All the years spent without her had been lived with the hazy thought far in the back of his mind that when the time was right, he would bring her back into his life.

That time was now, but this time, he would not allow her spell to capture the whole of him again.

Here and now, she was exactly where he wanted her, in his bed and in his arms, and he closed his mind of all thoughts and sank back into the heaven of Beth.

He kissed and licked every glorious inch of her flesh, sinking his fingers into the buttery soft skin, letting her cries and moans soak into his senses and feed his arousal. When he buried his face between her legs, he found her swollen and ready and radiating the soft, musky scent of her desire, a scent and taste that had lost none of the potency of old and darted straight into his burning loins.

Time had dulled the potency of the effect of Xavi's lovemaking. It must have done because *this*… He'd barely opened her up to him and pressed his tongue to her throbbing nub before Beth was riding a climax she'd been barely aware of forming under the weight of sensation ravaging the entirety of her being, a climax she was still riding when he kissed his way back up to her mouth.

Throbbing with desperation for his possession, she cupped his face tightly as their mouths and tongues entwined and lifted her thighs to wrap her legs around him. She could hardly breathe for anticipation, could hear nothing over the roar of her heart and the groans coming from Xavi's throat.

His hand skimmed her belly and her pubis as he reached for the weighty arousal straining against the top of her thigh, and she adjusted herself as he took hold of himself to press the tip right in the place they both needed it.

He filled her with one deep thrust.

The pleasure was so intense that she cried into his mouth, cries repeated as he began to move. With kisses as deep as his penetration, he drove into her with his hips, gripping her thighs to push them farther back and shrinking the world so it contained only them.

Lost in the paradise of Xavi's possession, Beth closed her eyes and sank into the swell of sensation. She was no more ready for her climax than she'd been for her first, and when it came, she could no more stop it than she could stop her heart from beating. It rippled out of her like a crescendo from deep within her, wave upon wave of pulsating rapture. So powerful were the ripples that she was barely conscious of Xavi's fingers biting into her thighs or the fevered drive of his thrusts, his deepening groans a distant echo until he came into sharp focus with a roar as he bucked into her one last, violent time, catching the swell of her abating climax and driving her back into a state of bliss that carried her off into another dimension.

CHAPTER SEVEN

Xavi splashed cold water on his face and took stock of his reflection. He expelled a long breath of relief to find it was the usual face staring back at him. The sensation that something had changed within him had been a delusion born from incredible sex.

Dios, incredible hardly did it justice.

Patting himself dry, he took another moment to compose himself and let his heart rate settle. One last look in the mirror to double-check it really was his face reflecting at him, and then he strolled back into the bedroom.

Beth was propped against the headboard in almost the same pose he'd waited for her in earlier. The difference was that she'd covered herself in the bedsheets.

'Hello, lover,' she said softly. There was a gleam in her eye that was so unexpectedly familiar, his throat caught. It was a gleam that only appeared after making love.

Breathing through the tightness, he padded to the bed. She pulled the sheets off with deliberate seduction, exposing her breasts as she welcomed him back.

He'd climbed off her only minutes ago. He shouldn't be feeling fresh twinges in loins that were still fizzing from the strength of his orgasm. Shouldn't be, but Beth wasn't a normal woman. She was a goddess, and her breasts were manna from heaven.

What the hell. He wasn't losing anything by allowing her to tempt him into taking the manna into his mouth. This was their bedroom, and what they did in it had no effect on his working life or his self-control.

She sighed with pleasure at his sucking of her breast, and arched her back. 'God, that feels good.'

'*You* feel good.' He licked around the peak before gently biting it. 'Give me a little time, *mi vida*. I'm not twenty-four anymore.'

Her grin was sinfully wicked. 'Define *a little time*.'

Laughter rose, and he trailed his tongue up her throat and kissed her with a growl before flopping onto his back beside her. Wriggling down, she curled into him with her cheek on his chest.

For the longest time, they just lay there, Xavi stroking her back, Beth's fingers making circular motions around his nipple.

'How many men have you been with since we broke up?' he asked casually. It was a question he'd wondered virtually every day they'd spent apart.

Her fingers stilled. 'Why do you want to know?'

'Curiosity.' All the nights he'd had to drive away images of Beth sharing her goddess body with a faceless man. The times she posted a photo of herself out drinking with men… Those nights had been the worst for him.

'Curiosity killed the cat.'

'Is that another English saying?'

'Yep. Let's just say I've spent the intervening years enjoying my life and leave it at that.'

Beth would rather boil her head than tell him the truth.

'What if I don't want to leave it at that?'

'Then tough. I don't want to know about all the women

you've been with.' Bad enough torturing herself with guesses. Having it confirmed…

'There haven't been many.'

Feeling like she'd been punched, she sat up and tightly said, 'I just said I don't want to know. I had no claim over you, and you had no claim over me, and I don't ever want to hear about or know which women you've shared this bed with.'

He gave a half smile and cupped her cheek. 'Only you.'

She went to slap his hand away, but ended up clasping it tightly. '*Liar!*'

'Beth, this place was our dream home. I couldn't bring another woman here. It would have felt wrong.'

Oh, why was he saying such things? 'You expect me to believe that?'

'Why not?' His eyes didn't even flicker. 'We've always been honest with each other. I bought this place with you in mind.'

She could do nothing to stop her burst of cynical laughter. 'Sure you did.'

'I think I always knew we'd end up back together.'

'Well, *I* didn't, so it's just as well I've been too career-focused to let another man sweep me off my feet, isn't it? Fully off my feet, that is,' she hastened to add. She would never let him even guess at the truth, and she was angry with herself for letting her jealousy at his other women seep out. 'Otherwise, you'd have bought this place for nothing and your wish to keep control of the Rosbel Group would have been screwed.'

He grinned. 'When you put it like that, I consider myself a fortunate man.'

How she *hated* his grin. Hated that it made her pelvis melt. Hated that it made her mouth want to reciprocate into a wide smile of its own. 'So you should. Who knows what I'd do with the shares if I were already married? I might feel obliged to sell them to one of those sharks to stop my husband being jealous about our history.'

He lifted his head, his grin widening. 'You wouldn't do that.'

'Wouldn't I?'

He palmed the underside of her breast and stretched his thumb to her nipple. 'You've changed in some respects but not in the ways that really matter. You're not someone who would do anything she didn't want to do and you would *never* screw another person over.'

'Maybe you don't know me as well as you think.' Oh, *why* did she keep trying to give him these damned cryptic warnings?

Holding her waist, he sat up and bowed his head to take her nipple into his mouth. 'I don't care how many men you've been with since me,' he said between licks and sucks. 'I know you better and more intimately than anyone.'

Sensation was filling her again, the heat in her pelvis bubbling back to life, and when he trailed a hand down her side to her thigh, she let him gently coax it over his lap so she was straddling him.

This was what she'd wanted when she'd agreed to marry him. Sex. Lots of sex. Not pointless pillow talk that hurt her heart.

What she must not do was allow herself to believe his lies, even if her heart ached for his words to be true. Xavi hadn't bought this gorgeous baroque building with her in mind. He was just saying what he thought needed saying to protect his interests.

He moved his attention to her other breast. She clasped

the back of his head and raised her bottom so she straddled his arousal.

He gazed up at her with glazed eyes. 'No one could ever compare to you, *mi vida*. No one.'

Blocking his words out, she sank down on him with a long moan of pleasure.

'Does this place have a swimming pool?' Beth asked. Despite making love twice, she was still wide-awake, too many thoughts crowding her head to allow sleep to snake its way into her. Too many thoughts she did *not* want to let loose.

'You want to go swimming, *now*?'

Her cheek on his chest, the beats of his heart a steady, comforting—too comforting—sound, he didn't see her wistful smile that he still knew her well enough to know that when she asked a question like that, it generally meant she wanted to do it right away, not at some future date.

'Yes.' She lifted her chin to gaze into his eyes, and seductively added, 'But I don't have a swimming costume to hand so it'll have to be skinny-dipping.'

He made a groan-like laugh and shook his head before flashing his perfect teeth at her. 'What the hell. Come on. Let me show you my swimming pool.'

Her nudity wrapped in her silk kimono, Beth happily let Xavi, who'd slung a pair of shorts on, lead her out of the bedroom to a flight of stairs at the end of the corridor.

She climbed them and stepped out into the heady scent of night-blooming jasmine and twilight heat. Enough of the city was asleep for the black sky above them to glitter with stars, a sight that had her gaping—she couldn't remember seeing a star in the Madrid night sky before.

And then she lowered her gaze and gaped even harder, taking a long moment to soak in all she was seeing. 'How on earth did you get permission to do this?'

This being the most gloriously spectacular roof terrace. Its perimeter aglow with soft night-lights, its central pièce de résistance was an enormous swimming pool with a gorgeous mosaiced bottom of dolphins at play. Around it, plentiful plush seating for sunbathing and dining alike, along with a Caribbean-themed bar and an outdoor cooking area.

It was the panoramic view, though, that really took her breath away. It felt like the city went on forever. The pond-lake at the rear glistened under the lights of the stars like a private oasis of tranquillity, the trees surrounding it dark shadows melting into the night.

Standing behind her, Xavi put his hands on her hips and brushed his lips against her neck. 'Money and power talk.'

Surprise and disappointment lashed her even as shivers of excitement coiled up her spine. 'Bribes?'

'No, *mi vida*.' His hands were working on the sash of her robe. 'There is no need for bribes when you pay for the restoration of many of your home city's historical monuments and fund numerous shelters and rehabilitation units.'

Relieved, although why she didn't know, supposed it was that she didn't want to think the Xavi of old who'd always taken pride in the Rosbel Group being built on honest endeavour could have changed *that* much, she closed her eyes and leaned back into his strength. 'You've become a philanthropist?' Philanthropy made much more sense.

'Don't sound too impressed—it is all for the sake of my soul. I'm following in the footsteps of my father and grandfather. They taught me that with great wealth comes great responsibility.' As he spoke, he cupped her breasts and squeezed them in the way she so liked. 'Also, Blanca is always keen to remind me of the biblical quote about it being easier for a camel to go through the eye of a needle than for a rich man to enter the kingdom of heaven, and on the off chance that she's right, I prefer not to take any chances.'

She laughed and wriggled her bottom provocatively against his arousal. 'And how much of her personal wealth has Blanca given away?'

Still squeezing a breast, he slipped his other hand down her belly, bending her forward a little. 'At least half of it to various human rights charities. Carlota uses hers to fund the archaeological digs she goes on—her work benefits people in a very different way, but as she is always keen to tell Blanca, humans need to know where they come from and the journey that took us to where we are today.'

'To think they could both just sit on their backsides and live off their trust funds...mind you, that applies to you, too.' The de la Rosa family's fortune had been secured when Xavi's father was a child. Their vast portfolio, even outside the business, meant none of them or future generations ever needed to work.

Xavi could have married her eight years ago and spent his life doing exactly what he was doing to her now with barely a dent to his wealth.

'My father had such a strong work ethic that he would turn in his grave if we sat around doing nothing all day.'

'You've all got way too much energy to sit around doing nothing, even if you wanted to,' she conceded, closing her eyes as his fingers dipped between her legs. 'I admire your sisters so much. I don't think I would've progressed as far and as quickly as I did at Miss Amore without their attitudes to inspire me—honestly, the number of times and situations where I've doubted myself is ridiculous, and all it needed to snap me out of it was to imagine Blanca strutting around a courtroom like a dog with an ankle in its teeth or think of Carlota spending hour after hour patiently brushing away at millennia-year-old soil to find a fragment of pottery.'

He nipped at her ear and slipped a finger inside her heat. 'No more family talk. I don't want to think about my sisters when I'm seducing you.'

'Is *that* what you're doing?' she asked huskily, even as the pleasure of what he was doing to her was filling her with heated sensation and had her wriggling her bottom against his rock-hard arousal again.

He growled and moved his hand off her breast to pull his shorts down and release his erection.

'*Excuse* me,' she said primly, pulling his pleasuring hand away and darting out of his orbit. 'But I thought you brought me out here so I could swim?'

Shrugging off her kimono, she threw him a wicked grin over her shoulder and then ran, naked, to the swimming pool and jumped in.

The water was wonderfully refreshing, but there was no time to consider this for Xavi dived in beside her, grabbed her legs and pulled her under. Spluttering and laughing, she resurfaced, only to be enveloped in his arms. A moment later, he had her pinned to the side of the pool. They were both still laughing as he dived into *her*.

Movement woke Beth from a deep, sated sleep. Or was it sound that had woken her? The room was dark, but the bed was empty.

She sat up and strained her ears. The shower was running.

Reaching for her phone, she checked the time. Five a.m. What was he showering for at this unholy hour? He could have had only a couple of hours' sleep.

She must have dozed off again because when she next opened her eyes, Xavi was sat on the edge of the bed, fully dressed in a suit and tie.

'You're working today?' she asked sleepily as she tried to blink herself back into full consciousness.

'Back-to-back meetings.'

She shuffled over and put her head on his lap. 'I didn't think you were working again until after the honeymoon.'

He ran his fingers through her mussed hair. 'I'm taking six days off for the wedding and honeymoon. I can't take any more, not with the buyout of the Grimaldi brand.'

She tried not to let resentment stab her. It shouldn't bother her that Xavi was only carving out five days in his schedule for their honeymoon on his family's Caribbean island. She had the feeling he thought she should be grateful for that! He'd mentioned a couple of times about the Grimaldi buyout and how it had dragged on longer than anyone had anticipated. At some point in their near future, he'd be flying out to New York to oversee its push over the line.

What she *was* grateful for was the reminder of where she lay in his priorities: as a vessel to sate himself with in the evenings when the working day was done, a state of affairs she was determined to change.

She nuzzled her cheek farther up his thigh to his groin, then nuzzled her face between his legs, smiling at his arousal.

Lifting her face, she worked at his trousers button,

only to be foiled from opening it by his hand covering hers and moving it away. 'Later. I don't have time now.'

She rolled onto her back and pulled the sheets off her breasts. 'There won't be a later. I'm staying at the hotel tonight.' At the same hotel as her friends and family for one last send-off to the single life.

There was a flash of hunger in his stare, and then the switch turned off.

It was the same switch he'd turned off when he'd ended them.

'We have our whole lives to make love, *mi vida*,' he said reasonably but with an edge to his voice that demanded no argument. He pressed a firm kiss to her mouth, unceremoniously removed the arm she hooked around his neck and got to his feet. Looking down at her, his tone gentled. 'We're not kids anymore, Beth. I have responsibilities, but when we go away…' His gaze dipped down to her exposed breasts and then roved back to meet her stare. 'I promise you will have *all* my attention.'

She never got the chance to reply for he strolled to the door, only looking back once he'd opened it. He gazed at her with an expression that made her heart catch. 'Until tomorrow.'

'Until tomorrow,' she echoed.

He pressed his fingers to his lips and then walked out of the bedroom.

When the door closed, Beth swallowed a breath and closed her eyes, willing the burning tears back.

She shouldn't let him hurt her. He'd already set his markers out and made it clear their relationship would be different to how it had been before. Just because he'd made love to her in such a carefree way on the roof terrace didn't mean his thoughts on the matter had changed.

Just because she'd seen the young man she'd fallen in love with all those years ago reemerge for a brief moment in time didn't mean he would be prepared to let him out again.

For a brief moment in time, she'd felt like she was eighteen again.

She pinched the bridge of her nose and took a deep breath.

All these years of being unable to cry, and in the space of twelve hours her tear ducts had proved they'd only been in hibernation.

She wouldn't let the tears fall. Not for him. Not again.

That afternoon, Beth had barely left Xavi's driveway when her phone rang. It was Paul Haldron, now listed in her contacts under the name of Arsehole. It was a moniker he'd earned and more than deserved. She checked the intercom between her and the driver was switched off, and took a deep breath before answering with a cool, 'Hi, Paul.'

'Beth!' he exclaimed as if they were old friends. 'Just checking in to see if there's been any movement.'

'Nothing since we last spoke.' She saw no reason to tell him things were likely to proceed quicker than anticipated, mainly because his voice made her skin crawl and so she wanted him out of her ear as soon as possible. Everything was in hand as she'd demanded. The granting of probate would release investments and cash assets that would comfortably cover the agreed price. The remainder would more than comfortably cover the other shares she'd already instructed her legal and finance team to vacuum up as soon as funds allowed. Even after her share-buying spree, she would still have more money than she'd know what to do with.

'Okay, well, keep me updated, yes?'

'Sure.'

'I'm travelling to Europe on business next month. Let me take you out for dinner?'

'Considering my emphasis on discretion, I don't think that's appropriate, do you?' His chuckle made her lips twist in distaste. 'I'm getting married tomorrow, Paul. Don't make any further contact until you hear from me or my people.'

She ended the call and closed her eyes.

This time tomorrow, she would be a married woman. Married to Xavi. Sunday morning, they would fly to his family's Caribbean island where they would make love like rabbits on heat.

Everything was proceeding exactly as planned.

She just wished her heart didn't feel so heavy, and when her phone buzzed with a message, wished it didn't leap with hope that it would be from Xavi.

It was from her father, letting her know they'd landed. She messaged him back saying she'd meet him at the hotel. A moment later, it buzzed again. Again, it wasn't a message from the man who'd spent the night making love to her.

It would never be from him. Not in working hours. He'd set out his markers, and he would stick to them until she broke his defences and control. Five days in the Caribbean should do the trick. If he took his laptop with them, she'd 'accidentally' throw it in the sea.

It was her own control she was having concerns about. She kept replaying their night together and chastising herself. She should have played it like a cucumber when he'd spoken about his past lovers, but she'd been powerless to stop her jealousy seeping out. When she took the company from him, she wanted to be as controlled as him. She wanted to look him in the eye and not display a flicker of emotion. She wanted him to look in her eyes and know he'd been played and that she felt nothing for him.

She only wished it could be the truth.

CHAPTER EIGHT

XAVI RUBBED HIS exhausted eyes and closed his laptop. That was it. The Grimaldi buyout would be finalised the week after his return from the Caribbean. All business was done for the next six days. He would be contactable in the event of an emergency, of course, and he had a couple of video conferences lined up, but they couldn't be helped. His father had worked during family holidays. Xavi and his sisters hadn't thought twice about it...although he seemed to remember his mother pursing her lips when he was late joining them for a meal or activity because of it.

His father had been on the verge of stepping into the role Xavi now held. The Rosbel Group founders had been preparing to embrace retirement when he'd received his diagnosis. Overnight, everything had changed. Retirement plans were put on ice as a miracle that never came was sought.

Strange how prominent his father had become in his thoughts in recent weeks. He was always in his heart, of course, but since Raul's death, he'd pushed himself to the very edge of Xavi's consciousness; a spectre watching his every move.

He'd been five, maybe six, the first time his father had taken him to the Rosbel Group headquarters. As young as he'd been, he'd recognised the respect and deference all the many, many people who worked there had shown him. Xavi remembered how his chest had puffed up with pride that Javier de la Rosa was *his* father, and hoped that if his father was watching and looking over him, that he felt an ounce of that same pride.

He would give anything for him to be there to witness his wedding.

Xavi waited until he was being driven home before calling Beth. It disturbed him how he'd had to stop himself calling her numerous times that day. It had been hard enough putting her from his mind to concentrate on his work while she'd been back in England, but knowing she was here, in his city, and with the thrills from their lovemaking still alive in his veins… *Dios*, he could still hear her laughter as she'd climaxed in the swimming pool.

He'd forgotten how much fun sex with Beth could be. Forgotten how intoxicating that could be.

Putting her from his mind had been close to impossible.

The Xavi of old would have locked his office and video called her.

Just to hear her cheerful, 'Hi, Xavi,' was enough to ease the tightness he'd barely been aware of forming in his chest.

'How are things?' There was a lot of background noise on her side.

'Bonkers. I didn't realise you'd booked the entire hotel for our wedding. My grandmother, who considers more than half a glass of wine with her Sunday dinner as binge drinking, is currently doing shots with Benoît Blanchet.'

'The creative director of Kovoski?' Xavi had steered the buyout of the Kovoski brand a year earlier and paid a small fortune to the hugely flamboyant and hugely talented Benoît to extend his contract with them.

'The one and only... And Gustav Blanc's just joined their party. Oh, dear. The bar staff are pouring them what looks like flaming sambucas.'

He grinned. He'd only met Beth's grandmother once, when Beth had impulsively whisked him off to England for a long weekend to meet her family. Her grandmother could have come from the central casting version of what a grandmother should be. To imagine her drinking shots with the temperamental Benoît and the normally ice-cold fashion editor Gustav Blanc was beyond his imagination, which reminded him that Gustav's birthday party was coming up soon, and being hosted in Madrid. Xavi disliked Gustav, but the man was powerful in the fashion world and needed to be courted. 'Is everyone else behaving themselves?'

'Only my father. He's gone to bed. He's terrified he's going to screw up our walk down the aisle and thinks lots of sleep will stop that happening.'

'And you? What are you doing?'

'Drinking wine with friends and keeping an eye on my grandmother.'

He came within a whisker of asking if those friends included men. He'd seen the guest list she'd provided and was certain a number of the men on it were men she'd posted pictures of herself drinking with.

Xavi had told Beth he didn't care about the men she'd been with while they'd been apart, but it had been a lie. He knew he shouldn't care. Knew he had no right to care. But he did. He always had.

'How are things your end?' she asked. The background noise had diminished. He guessed she'd moved somewhere quieter. 'Finished working yet?'

'All done and on my way home.'

'Good. You work too hard.'

'For the next six days, I belong only to you.'

'I'm going to hold you to that.'

He laughed. 'I wouldn't have it any other way.'

'You won't be given a choice. I'm not taking any clothes with me on our honeymoon. Only bikinis.'

He groaned softly at the memory of Beth in a bikini. 'I'm tempted to say let's skip the wedding and go straight to the honeymoon.'

'But then I'll miss the pleasure of seeing your reaction to my wedding lingerie.'

'Is it sexy?'

'*Very* sexy.' She lowered her voice. 'I'm still debating whether to bother with the knickers.'

His groan was louder.

'And with that thought, I shall bid you good-night.'

'You're saying goodbye to me now, when you've just made me hard?'

'Have I?' she asked innocently.

'You know you have, you tease.'

Her voice lowered even further. 'Remember how we used to have video sex?'

'You're trying to kill me.'

She laughed huskily. '*Beunas noches*, Xavi. Sweet dreams.'

'*Beunas noches, mi vida.* Dream of me.'

There was a long passage of silence before she softly said, 'Always.'

She disconnected the call.

His heart as swollen as his cock, Xavi threw his head back and laughed.

Beth put her phone back in her bag, rested her hand against her thumping heart and willed the burn between her legs to ease enough to enable her to walk back into the hotel bar without anyone wondering what was wrong with her.

For a few beautiful moments, it had felt like she'd slipped back in time to an age when her love and desire for Xavi had been the purest emotions on this earth.

'Beth!'

She looked at her grandmother, who was half hanging off her stool. Her grandfather was hovering protectively close by. His bemused yet indulgent expression suggested this wasn't the first time he'd seen his wife let her hair down like this, and she felt such a wave of tenderness for them it was almost a physical pain. In their quiet way, they'd taken real, loving care of her when she'd returned to England after Xavi and the baby. They hadn't asked her any questions, just given her the unconditional support and love she'd needed to pick herself up. Her father had been the same, and it was this loving support that had allowed her to put his lies about her mother's family behind her. All three of them had rallied around, and when she'd announced she was moving to Manchester, they'd rallied again to help her.

Their lack of surprise at her sudden announcement years later that she would be marrying Xavi was something she chose not to think about.

What was harder not to think about was the growing ache in her heart for their marriage to be real.

The ache was a ghost from her past, a ghost of the young woman who'd loved him with the whole of her heart and had been loved back with what she'd believed to be the whole of Xavi's heart.

Xavi had to hold himself still. He wanted to pace the cathedral, preferably by the entrance so he could assure himself of his bride's arrival.

The cathedral was packed. Outside, the press had gathered en masse. The wedding of the century was minutes away. All they needed was the bride.

He checked his watch again. She was now officially late.

'Your grandmother was fifteen minutes late for our wedding,' his grandfather said with quiet knowing.

'Yes, you said… You're sure you have the rings?'

His grandfather patted his top pocket.

Not until he'd been deciding on a best man for himself had Xavi considered that he didn't have a single close friend. He had friends. Lots of them. He received regular invitations to parties and nights out, some of which he accepted. But close friends? Not in years.

When had he let his social group slip away from him and become so solitary that he could think of no one to act as a natural fit to the role of best man? He'd briefly flirted with asking Carlota or Blanca to take the role but hadn't wanted to deal with the inevitable fallout from the one not asked.

The natural fit had been right in front of him. Who better than his grandfather, one of the original halves of the Rosbel Group, to hand over the rings as the de la Rosas and Belmontes became more than friends and business partners and became family?

He liked to think it was a decision—and a wedding—his father and Raul would approve of.

It was the change in atmosphere that alerted him to the bride's arrival.

Holding her father's arm, she emerged bathed…shimmering…in light.

All the breath left his body.

Clutching a posy of pink and white flowers, her glimmering white lace dress clung to and accentuated her curves. Strapless, it fitted like a heart-shaped hourglass to her thighs before spreading out like a mermaid's tail, trailing gently behind her. Her auburn hair, swept over her left shoulder in soft waves, shone and sparkled, and as she walked slowly towards him, a lock of her fringe fell into her eyes. Without tearing her gaze from his, she blew it away before her lips formed their dazzling upside-down heart.

Only the roar of blood in his ears told Xavi his heart was still beating.

Beth had never had to consciously think about walking, but with her legs like jelly, it was taking all her concentration to put one foot in front of the other. There was a tempest of nerves in her stomach, the racing of her heart enough to put a hummingbird's to shame.

Only her father's steady presence beside her kept her vaguely rooted in reality. This didn't feel real. She'd spent the morning feeling like she was in a waking dream and, walking through this magnificent cathedral with its impossibly high frescoed ceiling and with the light flowing through the stained-glass windows bathing everything and everyone in colour, that dreamlike sensation only grew stronger.

It wasn't until she was ten paces from Xavi, darkly gorgeous in a light grey three-piece wedding suit, that the dream veil lifted.

Her hummingbird heart sighed and wrenched in a single motion, and in the next beat, the tempest in her belly churned with such violence she feared she was going to be sick.

She was on the cusp of marrying Xavi.

She was about to wilfully pledge her life to him knowing her pledge was a lie, and as all her thoughts and emotions collided, the impulse to turn on her tail and run away was almost stronger than she could bear.

Her heart wrenched again. She wanted it to be real. This wedding. Their marriage. The old dream of spending her life with him... She was about to touch it. Touch that dream and then step into it. If she could only forgive the devastation he'd wrought on her, she could step into it and embrace it.

Did it really matter that Xavi's reasons for marrying her now were so different to when they'd made their plans for marriage and a family all those years ago? He would be hers, just as he'd once sworn he would always be. Why should she care that he wasn't marrying her for love? He wanted her and desired her; that hadn't changed. Why couldn't it be enough for her when the truth was she'd never felt a moment of real, true happiness without him?

She barely felt her father release her arm or the kiss he placed on her cheek. Her hand had been enveloped in Xavi's, and he was all she could see and feel.

The dreamlike sensation cloaking her again, she gazed into his dark brown eyes and felt the warmth and desire blazing from them warm her skin as effectively as his touch.

The two of them saturated with the colourful light filtering through the stained-glass windows, Beth watched Xavi's lips move as he spoke his vows, but her heart was pounding too hard to hear the words as more than a distant whisper.

And then it was her turn, and Xavi's dark gaze held hers as intently as she'd held his.

Squeezing his fingers tightly, she repeated the Spanish vows, flooded with emotions strong enough to burn her eyes with tears that didn't fall, and yet her voice didn't falter…*she* didn't falter. 'I promise to love, cherish and be faithful, in good times and in bad, all the days of my life.'

When the time came to seal their vows, they gazed into each other's eyes one long, last moment before their mouths came together in a tender, lingering caress that sealed what her heart already knew.

The vows she'd just made…she would never be able to break them.

'Are you happy, *mi vida*?' Xavi whispered into his bride's ear as he moved her around the floor for their first dance.

She turned her cheek from where it was pressed against his chest and lifted her gaze to him. 'I feel like I'm in a dream.'

He smiled and bowed his head to kiss her.

Truth was he felt like he was in a dream, too.

When they'd exchanged their vows, he'd felt something touch him, something that had felt almost holy, which was a strange sensation for a man who rarely attended mass and would have been happy marrying in the grounds of this hotel.

They'd been married only eight hours, but he felt different. He'd felt different since he'd walked Beth back down the aisle as his wife. He hadn't expected that. What was marriage but a piece of paper? It had meant more to him when he'd been young and crazed on lust, and it had felt imperative that he tie Beth to him forever. That young man had let his head be turned for six months into believing in fairy tales and magic. Beth's magic. It had possessed him.

He could feel her spell weaving around him again now, but that was okay. This was their wedding day. She'd made the same vows as he had, to love and be faithful for all their days. Powerful words that contained a magic of their own.

Had he ever stopped loving her? He couldn't say. He couldn't even say if what he felt for her *was* love, and it was dangerous to even think in such terms, a certain path to the madness that had subsumed him before.

He knew better than to let Beth's spell weave too deeply into him.

Tonight he would make love to her all night long, and then tomorrow, they would fly to the Caribbean and make love whenever and wherever they liked, and then they would come home and settle into their new lives together with the boundaries he'd put in place carefully adhered to.

But for tonight and the next five days, he would honour his promise and be entirely hers.

Beth lifted her hair so Xavi could unclasp the tiny button at the top of her dress, and shivered with pleasure as he slowly pulled the hidden zip down to the base of her spine.

She released her tresses as the dress fell into a puddle around her feet.

He buried his nose into her hair and gripped her hips, pressing his arousal against her back. Thickly, he said, 'All day I have wondered…'

Naked except for white silk stockings, Beth turned around and wrapped her arms around his neck. Gazing into his eyes, she whispered, 'Make love to me, husband.'

His molten stare held hers. 'For all my days, *esposa*.'

Her heart, incapable of beating properly the whole of that magical day, ballooned. *Esposa*. Wife. Xavi's wife.

Gathering her into his arms as if she were as light as a small child, he carried her to the honeymoon bed of the honeymoon suite and laid her down.

Their mouths fused.

There was no hot desperation in their lovemaking. Not that night.

Together, they unhurriedly stripped Xavi out of his wedding suit until they were skin to skin. Hands roaming and exploring each other's naked flesh, their tender yet passionate kisses came from the same dream that had carried Beth through the day.

It had been a beautiful day, and she wasn't ready to let it go and for reality to seep back into her psyche.

Let her have this one day and night of believing their marriage was what her heart so wished. One day and night before she pushed the illusion of feeling loved aside and accepted reality back into her heart.

His dark stare locked on hers, he drove into her slowly, then captured her mouth for another deeply passionate kiss.

Limbs tightly entwined and enveloped in a blissful dream of heady emotion, Beth let the pleasure of Xavi's lovemaking saturate her, heart, body and soul, and when she came, consciousness drifted away until it was only them left in the world.

The dream cloaking Beth was still in no hurry to lift itself. She was still in no hurry to shake it off. The de la Rosas' private island was a picture-perfect paradise. Situated between the Bahamas and Turks and Caicos, they'd flown to the former, then speed-sailed on Xavi's new catamaran to the island itself. Barely six miles square, it was thick with greenery and spectacular wildlife and ringed with the finest, softest light golden sand. The shallow turquoise water surrounding it was clear enough for her to swim out and marvel at the colourful fish who'd escaped the coral reefs farther out swimming around her. Even the villa was a delight, in part because it was no villa but a hamlet of Balinese-style lodgings dotted around a main house that had all the facilities of a luxury hotel.

She would have loved her time there no matter the company, but sharing it with Xavi sealed its perfection.

These had been the best days of her life.

'When can we come back?' she murmured on their last evening as they lazed in bed after making love. Her cheek lay on his chest. The comforting rhythmic beat of his heart lay beneath her ear. The French windows of their suite facing the sea were open, a delicious, gentle breeze cooling their skin.

His fingers continued their lazy circular motions on her back as he said, 'As soon as I can carve out more than a few days in my schedule.'

She kissed his chest to stop her mouth from protesting. The dreamlike state she was living in was too wonderful to spoil with words that could wait until they returned to their real life. 'Can we try for the New Year?'

'That should be doable.'

She sighed her happiness and nuzzled her cheek over the fine dark hairs of his deeply tanned chest. A veritable sun magnet, their days there, few though they'd been, had deepened Xavi's olive skin by several shades. By contrast, Beth's pale skin had gained a few extra freckles. She supposed slathering factor fifty sunscreen on every couple of hours didn't help the tanning process, but with her complexion, she wasn't taking any chances. The upside was that Xavi had insisted on being her personal sunscreen slatherer.

'I have to admit, I thought you would find it boring here,' he commented.

'You're kidding? This place is heaven!'

He chuckled softly. 'You're like a bee, always busy, busy flying from flower to flower in search of your next dose of pollen. And you're impulsive. When you get an idea to do something, you jump in with both feet. There's not much scope for impulsivity here.'

She considered this. 'I suppose it depends on where I am and what I'm doing. If something takes my fancy and it's doable, then yes, I'll just go ahead and do it because why hold back? Life is short—we both know that—and so I guess I just want to live it while I can because who knows when it will be over for me?'

He was silent for a long time. 'I can't be like that, Beth. I don't think I'm built to be like that. I have to have lines and boundaries on my time, otherwise everything blurs.'

Her happiness ebbed at the reminder. 'Is this your way of reminding me that our marriage is just a business deal with benefits?' she whispered sadly.

He'd rolled her onto her back before she could snatch a breath; had pinned her wrists to the sides of her head before she felt his fingers wrap around them. 'That isn't what this marriage is,' he said tightly. 'I wanted to marry *you*, Beth. I want to father your children and have a family with *you*.'

Her heart swelled with a combination of hope and sadness, and for the first time since they'd been on their honeymoon, Beth was unable to stop herself thinking about the child they'd lost. The child Xavi had never known existed. Another swell bloomed inside her, a swell of sudden yearning to tell him the truth that he'd already fathered a child with her, but how could she? She'd never spoken the words to a soul and didn't know if she could do it now, and even if she could, what purpose would it serve other than to hurt him?

To hurt him would be to hurt herself.

Xavi was right that she was impulsive. She'd agreed to marry him thinking she was going to embark on a wrecking project to destroy him the way he'd destroyed her, and then jumped in with both impulsive feet on her plan of action to pull it off.

He'd never wanted to hurt her. She was certain of it. Not deliberately. He'd behaved terribly to her, but she needed to find a way to forgive him for that because one thing she was certain of was that she was in this marriage for keeps. She loved him. She'd always loved him. She would always love him. She had no more choice in her love than she had over her natural hair colour and freckles.

The past was the past, and she had to find a way to live with it and find a way to embrace their future together. Find a way to embrace Xavi for who he was and not hate him for no longer being the young man who'd put her first, second and third in his life.

She had no idea how long they spent positioned like that, with Xavi pinning her down, his gorgeous face glaring at her, his arousal slowly springing to life at the base of her pubis.

And she had no idea what he was thinking. The face she'd once read like a book was closed to her of everything but what he wanted her to see.

Without saying a word or yanking her wrists from his hold, she held his stare and tilted her hips so his arousal was positioned at the entrance of her heat.

Neither spoke nor reacted facially as he slid inside her. Neither moved their gaze from the other as he brought them both to orgasm.

CHAPTER NINE

BETH OPENED HER eyes to dusky early-morning light and the weight of Xavi's arm over her belly and the delicious feel of his chest and thighs spooned into her.

She smiled sleepily to herself and wriggled her backside, ready to tempt him into waking and making love to her again before he left her for the office and she collected Diego from Salma. After five magical days away together, reality could wait a little longer.

His arm tightened around her stomach. His mouth nestled into her hair. She wriggled again, luxuriating in the wakening of his arousal against her buttocks, and she turned her head to seek his kiss, only to find the movement hurt her head…and now she realised her head was aching, she realised the weight of Xavi's arm over her belly was constricting and hurting her.

She sat bolt upright without even thinking about it. 'I'm going to be sick.' The words came out with no thought, either, and it was without thought that she scrambled off the bed and threw herself into the bathroom.

She only just made it in time.

Xavi, propped against the headboard, stroked his sleeping beauty's fevered forehead and closed his eyes.

He'd never known Beth to be sick before. Sure, she

suffered menstrual pains—at least, she used to—but that was it. He couldn't remember her even having a sniffle, and it enraged him all over again to remember his doctor's refusal to say whether she was suffering from food poisoning or a stomach bug. He hadn't paid him an extortionate amount of money to drag himself to his apartment at eight in the morning and diagnose his new wife to be rebuffed with *likely this* or *likely that*. He was the doctor. Make the bloody diagnosis and then give her something to make her better, not all this, *either way, it needs to work its way out of her system* crap. Xavi was no doctor, but an internet search had given him a better bloody diagnosis than the so-called bloody expert. If it was food poisoning then Xavi would be suffering from it, too. They'd last eaten on the plane home, both eating the same meal. If it was a stomach bug—much more likely, especially now that she'd developed a fever, too—then that meant some bastard had passed their germs to her. When he found out who it was, he would kill them.

His phone rang.

It was his executive assistant. The head of his cabin crew had just informed her that two of the crew had been struck down with a virulent stomach bug and wanted to warn Xavi in case he was struck down with it, too.

He swore very loudly in his head. He couldn't even take delight in seeking revenge in his imagination, not when the perpetrators were his hardworking crew.

He did, however, get his revenge on Doctor Do-Nothing by calling him and insisting he pay house visits to both his stricken crew. 'Wear a mask,' he said icily when Doctor Do-Nothing tried to protest.

Beth's eyes opened. 'You're still here,' she mumbled.

'Where else would I be?'

'In back-to-back meetings?'

He smiled at her feeble attempt at a joke. 'I'm staying right here until you're better.' Screw the meetings he had racked up for the day. Some things were more important than work.

He didn't let himself think about the video calls he'd cancelled on their honeymoon. That was a different matter entirely. He'd cancelled one because Beth had wanted to go snorkelling, the other because he'd gone three hours without having sex with her.

'I'm fine. Go to the office.'

'You're not fine. You look like a corpse.'

'You're so romantic.'

'It's a gift.'

She gave a wan smile. 'Honestly, I'm fine. I've not been sick for ages.'

He looked at his watch. 'It's been twenty-six minutes.'

She blinked her surprise. 'Is that all?'

'See, now you're delirious.'

'Now you're a comedian.'

'Another gift.'

'Aren't you afraid you'll catch it?'

'Germs are afraid of me.' And even if they weren't, there was no way on earth he was going to leave Beth alone in this state. Isabel had offered to watch over her but, even though he trusted his housekeeper with every aspect of his domestic life, he was damned if he would trust her or anyone else to look after Beth properly. Besides, Beth was too unpredictable to guess what kind of patient she would make. So far, she'd been obedient, but it had only been six hours of illness.

'I wish they were afraid of me,' she said forlornly.

He smoothed her hair off her forehead. 'I wish they

were, too. Now, close your eyes and go back to sleep. When you're feeling stronger, I'll have some plain food brought to you.'

Her smile this time was soft. 'Thank—' The smile dropped. Her head lifted off the pillow, and, covering her mouth, she staggered back to the bathroom.

On Beth's third morning back in Madrid after their honeymoon, she woke feeling much better. She'd made it the whole night without using the bathroom, and the only ache in her stomach was the ache of hunger. Since falling ill, she'd eaten a couple of bananas and three slices of toast in total, and that was just to shut Xavi up.

She didn't have to check his heart was beating. He was cuddled into her, his breaths of sleep dancing into her hair, his warm hand on her hip. She had a moment of wondering whether to wriggle her bottom to wake him, but then thought she didn't want to push her luck. She'd never been that ill in her life. Lord knew how Xavi had dodged catching it. Maybe he was right that germs were afraid of him.

Besides, she must stink. She hadn't showered in days. Or brushed her teeth.

Creeping out of bed, she dragged her weak legs to the bathroom, scrubbed her teeth to within an inch of their lives, and stripped off her pyjama shorts and T-shirt. She smiled to remember Xavi's insistence that she wear them. 'I'm not sleeping without you, *mi vida*, and I am not going to risk accidentally making love to you while you're ill and defenceless, so let me put them on you.'

How he could *accidentally* make love to her was a conundrum to be mulled over when her brain was fully functioning again. For now, the only thing she wanted to think about was how well he'd taken care of her. He'd given up two full days of his precious work to watch over her. Yes, she was aware he'd worked on his laptop while she'd slept and had often heard his low voice holding conversations, but he hadn't left her. He'd even eaten his meals in the room and insisted they be plain, bland food in case strong scents set her tender stomach off.

Lathering herself, she thought that he did care for her, and though she hardly dared allow herself to think it, that he'd put her over the Rosbel Group must mean she meant more to him than the company did. Or at least put her on a par with it.

'What are you doing?' the voice she so adored chided from behind her.

She turned slowly, her smile forming much quicker than her legs were working, and was thrilled to find Xavi in all his naked glory. 'Destinking myself.'

He stood beneath the pouring water, closed the gap between them and, his hands firm on her hips, bowed his head to kiss her gently. He grinned. 'Much better.' The grin quickly faded. 'But you should be taking it easy. Are you all clean now?'

'I need to wash my hair.'

'I will do it for you.'

Reaching for the shampoo, he stood behind her and massaged a good dollop into her hair. The sensations in her still-tender head felt heavenly. After rinsing it out, he reached for the conditioner. His erection stabbed into her back the whole way through, but he didn't even mention it, let alone attempt to seduce her. Once the conditioner was rinsed out, he turned the shower off and enveloped her in a huge, fluffy Egyptian cotton bath towel.

'Back to bed,' he ordered firmly, even though his erection was now trying to stab her stomach.

'My hair's still wet.' It was still dripping.

Guiding her to the bathroom chair, he patiently and gently towel-dried her hair as best he could before nodding. 'That will do. Now back to bed. I will have food brought up for you.'

'Can I have scrambled eggs and toast?' she asked once she was settled and Xavi had propped a load of pillows behind her back and head.

'Can you manage it?'

'I think so...but I will only try if you go to work.' It was Sunday but she knew he had lots of stuff to catch up with, stuff he'd neglected while looking after her.

He pulled the stern face she'd become so accustomed to these past few days.

'I'm better,' she insisted. 'I just need to build my strength back up, and then I'll be as right as rain.'

He pursed his lips. 'One more day,' he decided. 'If you hold down the food you eat today, I'll go back to work tomorrow.'

She smiled. Her heart came close to exploding. 'You have a deal.'

Beth managed to eat most of her breakfast *and* keep it down. Even better, Xavi continued neglecting his work to snuggle in bed with her and watch a mindless action film. They were halfway through it when Carlota called. After chatting with Beth and satisfying herself she'd come off death's doorstep, Beth gave the phone back to Xavi. When he spoke his native language, it was always at a breakneck speed she struggled to keep up with, but she picked up the gist of the conversation.

'Have I translated it right that Carlota's going to Egypt?' she asked when the call was over.

He stretched back out beside her. 'You have—she flies out in a couple of weeks.'

'How long will she be gone this time?'

'It's a big site, so who knows.'

'Is your mum going to do one of her big family meals to see her off with?'

'Probably.'

'Good. I love your mum's big family meals.'

Putting her cheek on his chest, Beth cuddled into him thinking what a great life Carlota had. Blanca, too. Both de la Rosa sisters had always had complete freedom to follow their dreams. Xavi, too.

During the days she'd been in bed with her sickness, she'd spent a lot of time thinking about the past; old memories she'd never given air to in the intervening years had resurfaced, one of them being the time Xavi had told her of his childhood dream to grow up into a man just like his father. She supposed it had stood out because he'd so rarely talked about his father. Back then, she'd found his reluctance mystifying. Pretty much everything she'd learned about Javier de la Rosa had come from Xavi's mother and sisters, who'd had no such reticence.

Back then, Beth had feared death, but she hadn't *known* it, not like Xavi did. She'd been too young and unworldly to understand how some wounds ran too deep to bring to the surface, and as she thought this, an old conversation with Carlota rose. They'd been playing tennis, Beth and Carlota versus Xavi. They'd had to cheat their heads off to beat him. He'd taken his revenge by throwing first Carlota and then Beth—he'd had to chase her round the massive garden to catch her—into the swimming pool, fully dressed. He'd sauntered back into the villa, whistling jauntily. Carlota had wrung the water from her hair and laughingly sighed. 'It's so good to see this side to him again.'

At Beth's puzzlement, she'd smiled sadly. 'He's not been like this since Papi died. Happy, I mean. It's been so long that I thought I'd imagined how he used to be.' She sighed again. 'I think he felt it was his duty to become the man of the house and care for us, especially those months Mami wasn't herself, but…'

'What?' she'd asked into the silence.

Carlota had shaken her head. 'I don't remember seeing him cry, not even at the funeral. I don't think he let himself. I don't think he's let himself feel many things since then, and now you're here…' Eyes bright with emotion, she'd thrown her arms around Beth's neck and kissed her cheek. 'Thank you.'

'Are you okay?'

Xavi's voice cut through the memory, and she undug the nails she'd unwittingly stabbed into his chest and kissed it better.

'Sorry,' she whispered. 'And yes, I'm fine. Just thinking.'

'About what?'

'You and your family.' She kissed the marks made by her nails again. 'I was thinking about your father and how proud he must be of you all.'

The arm holding her tightened.

'You miss him still, don't you.'

He breathed heavily, then slowly said, 'Very much.' His hand groped for hers. 'It is strange, but I've thought about him more in recent weeks than I've done in years.'

'Good thoughts?'

'Always. He was a good man.'

'I know,' she said softly. 'And I know how hard you tried to fill his shoes when he died.' She knew a lot of things; things she'd forgotten.

Deliberately forgotten?

No, she thought painfully. Not deliberate. Necessary.

Painting him as a selfish bastard had made it easier to cope with the pain of living without him.

'I idolised him,' he said simply. 'To me, there was no better man and no better father.'

She pressed her ear tighter to his thumping heart and squeezed his hand. 'You'll be a wonderful father, too,' she whispered, a realisation that made her own thumping heart swell, because at heart, Xavi was a good man. One of the best. He wasn't perfect, but neither was she, and he always did what he thought was for the best. Best of all, he was hers. Would always be hers.

And she would always be his.

The rest of the day was spent nibbling at a variety of food, watching more mindless action films, playing chess—Xavi beat her three games to nil and even pretended to be a magnanimous winner—and even making love. It had been very gentle, but when Beth fell asleep that night wrapped in his arms, it was with a heart full of contentment.

'I have good news for you,' Xavi announced the next evening soon after he arrived home from work.

He'd found his wife—how he loved calling her that in his head—sipping water and catching the last of the sun on the roof terrace. He'd called her a couple of times that day to check on her—it wasn't a breach of his self-determined rules of home and work separation because rules were put aside for sickness. That was basic humanity. Looking at her now, he estimated that she looked 90 per cent better. The 10 per cent was the weight she'd lost. She would never look anything less than beautiful to him, but he hoped she regained the weight soon. There could never be too much of Beth, and with that in mind, he was having dinner brought up to them on the roof.

She raised a curious eyebrow. 'Which is?'

'Probate has been granted.'

He didn't know what kind of response he expected, but the deflating of her shoulders was nowhere near it. 'That doesn't please you?'

She sighed and tilted her head back. 'Not really. It just feels…' She shrugged. 'I don't know how I can feel pleased about an inheritance that my grandfather had to die for me to receive. It feels wrong.' She shook her head with another sigh. 'His death still doesn't feel real to me. I haven't mourned him properly, and I don't know if that's because I wasn't close enough to him or because of everything that's been going on with you and me, but you tell me probate's been granted and all I feel is guilty that he's left me all this money when I didn't love him enough to mourn him.'

'He wasn't an easy man to love,' Xavi admitted. 'I knew him all my life and worked closely with him for many years, but I haven't felt his death on an emotional level, either. He was a brilliant man, but hard and stubborn in mind and heart. I think he loved you as much as he was capable of loving anyone.'

'Do you think…?'

'What?'

She met his stare. 'That he was gay?'

'What makes you think that?'

'Just a feeling. It would make sense of a lot of things. I came close to asking him a couple of times, but lost my nerve.'

'I never knew him to have a partner of either sex,' Xavi said slowly, thinking hard. 'He kept his private life very private. Your grandmother left him before I was old enough to remember her. I don't think even my grandfather knows why. I suppose it's not beyond the realm of possibility that he was a closet homosexual, but that leads to the question of why he felt the need to suppress it. He worked in fashion, after all.'

She smiled. 'There is that. And it is the twenty-first century. Lots of older men of his generation have felt comfortable coming out and embracing their true sexuality.' She closed her eyes briefly and gave her head a little shake. 'Probably it's one of those mysteries that should be left to lie. He was who he was. Wishing can't change the past. I can't wish the truth out of him or wish him into being a grandfather I can properly mourn.'

Their dinner was brought out to them, a gentle lemon chicken dish served with plenty of fresh olives, roasted vegetables and tomatoes. It warmed Xavi's heart to see Beth dive into it with much of her old gusto, even if she didn't feel ready to have a glass of wine with it.

'Are you ready to talk about the implications of what probate means?' he asked.

Her smile was rueful. 'Sure.'

'It means everything is now yours. I didn't want to overload you while you were ill, but it actually went through a couple of days ago. As your grandfather's executor and your appointed representative, I've transferred everything into your name. There are some things, like his properties, that will take a short while longer to be rubber stamped, but the majority is now legally yours.'

Was he imagining that her face had paled a little?

'A couple of days ago?'

'Yes. On Friday. I've got to devote my time to the Grimaldi deal this week—I'm off for an overnight in New York on Wednesday to oversee the finalisation of it, but in the meantime I'll get my legal team to reach out to yours and get the contracts drawn up giving me the power to act on your behalf with the business, and we can get it all signed when I return…' Yes, her face had definitely lost colour. 'Are you still happy for that to happen?'

She had a drink of her water, putting the glass back on the table with a clatter. 'Yes, yes…although I've been thinking about it, and will definitely be getting hands-on with the business at some point soon, but I'll stick to the creative side and leave the running of it to you.'

His relief that she hadn't changed her mind on their deal was tempered by concern at her pallor. 'Are you not feeling well again, *mi vida*?'

'No, I'm… My head's hurting a little.' She drank some more water. There was a tremor in her hand. 'Did you notify my legal team?'

'As soon as probate was granted.' To prevent a conflict of interest, Beth had hired her own legal team to take care of her inherited assets and deal with her side of the legal formalities. 'The shares and everything else that could be were transferred into your name straight away.'

She nodded, almost absently, and got to her feet. 'Excuse me, but I need to lie down for a while.'

His concern growing, he rose, too. 'I'll come with you.'

She held out her hand. 'No, don't. Finish your dinner and enjoy the last of the daylight. I just need to get my head down for a little while. Probably the after-effects of the bug, that's all.'

Seeing she was holding herself well and that her legs showed no sign of giving way, he reluctantly agreed.

The moment Beth was alone in the room, she called Erika, the head of the legal practice she'd hired, a woman who'd given assurance she would take the lead in all of Beth's affairs. For the money she'd be earning from Beth, she could damn well take an evening call.

'Has the share purchase gone through?' she asked as soon as the brief pleasantries were over. God, she could hear her voice shaking.

'It has—the money transferred this afternoon at four p.m. I've been liaising with your finance team, too, and all the smaller shares you were seeking to purchase have also been completed. My congratulations. You are now the majority shareholder of the Rosbel Group. I would have called you to confirm, but your instructions—'

Beth gave a helpless curse.

Wariness came into Erika's voice. 'Is something wrong? We followed your instructions precisely—'

'You've not done anything wrong,' Beth assured her, swallowing back the rising panic. 'All my other instructions, though…forget about them. Destroy all record of them. Right now. Delete them, shred them, whatever you have to do to memory hole them. I'm not taking over the company. The original shares I received as part of my inheritance, I want my husband to keep control of them.'

'But…'

'No buts. Xavi runs the Rosbel Group, not me. I don't want it anymore. His lawyers will be in touch with you very soon. Cooperate with them, but for the time being, say nothing about me owning the other shares…' She swore again. 'I have a lot of thinking to do. I'll be in touch soon.'

Her head now hurting like she'd pretended it was to Xavi, Beth crawled into their bed and concentrated on breathing to drive the panic away.

What was she even panicking for? she wondered as the panic subsided. Surely, it was better that Paul Haldron and his merry band of thieves' shares now belonged to her? They were out of the Rosbel Group. She'd removed one of Xavi's headaches for him, which was a good thing.

That she was the majority shareholder meant nothing. She couldn't run the company, and she'd been mad to ever think otherwise.

No, not mad. Just blinded by hurt and rage from the slashing open of old, unhealed wounds.

She would transfer half the extra shares she'd bought into Xavi's name, she decided. That would be her wedding gift to him. That would keep everything equal between them. She could call her finance team and set the ball rolling…

No. Not yet. Best to wait until she'd spoken to him about it, and with his head and time full of the Grimaldi deal, best to wait for that to be completed before confessing because it would be a confession. To explain how she'd magically become the majority shareholder, she was going to have to explain herself, and to explain herself meant confessing everything. It meant telling him about the baby. It meant opening up about how badly he'd hurt her when he'd jumped into Ellen's bed.

It meant opening her heart to him and trusting him not to break it again.

The last of her panic vanished. She *did* trust him. Xavi

loved her, she knew it in her heart, loved her as much as he would allow himself to love anyone. If she ever doubted it, all she'd need to do was remember the wonderful care he'd given her when she was ill. Given time, he would open his heart fully to her again, too. She was certain of it. He might be angry with her initially, but once she'd explained everything, he would understand, and he would forgive her.

They would forgive each other and put the past behind them.

Feeling immensely better, she was about to get out of bed and set off to find him when the bedroom door opened.

'How are you feeling?' he asked softly, stepping to the bed.

She pulled the bedsheets off to invite him in beside her. 'Better.'

Fully dressed just as she was, he climbed in. 'You are sure?'

She palmed his softly bristled cheek and smiled. 'I've got a bit of a headache still, but I think you've got a cure for that.'

Laughing lightly, he drew her into his arms and proceeded to cure her.

CHAPTER TEN

A FEW DAYS LATER, on the morning of his flight to New York, Xavi quickly showered, shaved his neck, brushed his teeth, dressed and styled his hair. Incredibly early though it was, he should have left the apartment thirty minutes ago, and he left the dressing room fastening his cufflinks…

'Don't tell me you were planning to leave without saying goodbye.'

He stopped short and turned his head.

Beth was sitting on one of the window ledges, the last of the moonlight pouring on her. She was wearing her silk kimono dressing gown, her glorious hair mussed from their night of lovemaking. It was all that lovemaking that had made him oversleep.

'I thought we said goodbye last night.'

She smiled seductively and beckoned him with a finger.

He closed his eyes briefly as he prayed for strength. '*Mi vida*, I'm already running late.' If they had to take a later flight slot, he would be lucky to make it to the meeting with the Grimaldi executives on time. There had been last-minute hitches to the deal he needed to personally fix.

'Too late to give your wife a final kiss goodbye?' she

said in such an innocent voice that he knew before he looked back at her that he was making a mistake.

The smile still playing on her lips, she slowly peeled her kimono open and exposed her naked body to him. Batting her eyelashes, she cupped a weighty breast. 'Sure you won't give me a kiss goodbye?'

He groaned, part with frustration, part with desire. *Dios*, she was irresistible, but he was already late...

She spread her legs and raised her thighs.

Arousal, already fighting his willpower, punched its way through his resistance.

His trousers were undone and he was with her in three strides.

He was freeing himself as their hungry mouths came together, his tongue diving into her mouth as he pressed the tip of his erection between her legs. In moments, he was inside her slick heat, thrusting hard, her wanton moans of pleasure and encouragement feeding him, lost in the exquisite sensation of Beth. He sensed her climax building and drove harder and faster into her, barely holding on to the thick contractions that pulled him deeper into her ecstasy. With a loud shout, he let go, bucking his release furiously into her in one long, drawn-out climax so powerful, white light flickered behind his eyes.

She laughed softly into his neck before her mouth found his again. 'Now you can go.'

Xavi did his best to hold on to his temper. It was rare for him to lose it. Rare for him to even come close to losing it.

It was also rare for him to make such a colossal error. Okay, so the mistake hadn't been directly his, but it was a mistake in the Grimaldi contract he should have picked up on much earlier, not on the day they were due to finally sign it. Heads would have to metaphorically roll, but the responsibility was ultimately his.

Taking a deep breath, he called Beth.

'Hello, you,' she said, her voice filled with joyful surprise. 'To what do I owe this pleasure?'

'I need to stay in New York an extra day. Maybe two.'

Her tone immediately flattened. 'Oh.'

'There's an error in the contract that needs to be rectified.'

'What kind of error?'

'One that, if not fixed, will cost us millions.' An error that would have seen the Rosbel Group forking out tens of millions extra to the Grimaldi brand's founders. Xavi had spotted it an hour earlier when he'd been poised to sign it, but had decided to give the contract one last skim read first. 'It will be simple to rectify the contract itself, but we're all going to work through the night reading and rereading it to ensure nothing else has slipped through the net.'

'Shall I fly out to you?'

'No. You'll only be a distraction. Stay in Madrid with Diego.' Raul's dog had officially moved in with them. Knowing Beth had him for company held back the unnecessary guilt at leaving her behind. 'I'll be back tomorrow or Saturday.'

'Okay.' He could hear the upset she tried to disguise, and tried not to feel resentful of it. If he hadn't been so distracted by his new wife, he'd have spotted the error on his first read of the contract.

For all the vows he'd made to himself and the stakes he'd set out when making his proposal to her, Beth had woven him into her spell all over again, and he, lust-filled fool that he was, despite knowing all the dangers, had allowed it to happen.

Time to reset their marriage to how it should have been from the beginning with immediate effect.

'Do you want me to cancel Gustav's party?' she asked quietly.

He swore under his breath. He'd forgotten about Gustav Blanc's fiftieth birthday party. As the editor of one of the last remaining international high-end fashion magazines to still make a profit, Gus was hugely influential in the fashion world, a man with the power to make or break brands. It didn't matter that the Rosbel Group was sailing so high, keeping Gustav onside was necessary and prudent.

'I'll be back for the party,' he said tiredly. 'I need to go.'

'Call me later?'

'Unlikely. I've got too much on. I'll get Fenella to keep you updated and let you know when we'll be back in Madrid.'

'I can't have video sex with Fenella.'

'Beth...' He sucked in a breath and tempered his tone. She was only trying to lift his mood; he knew that, but it was his constant need to lose himself in Beth that had got him into this mess. 'I can't be distracted with that sort of talk. Keep me in your dreams and I'll be home as soon as I can.'

He ended the call and cursed himself again. Keep him in her dreams? Where the hell had that come from? How was that resetting his marriage to where it was supposed to be? Sweet pillow talk was fine, but talk like that when working?

After stalking to his office door, he yanked it open and barked out an order for coffee.

Then he sat back at his desk, took a deep breath, pushed his beautiful wife far from his mind and reread the offending contract, praying not to find any further errors in it.

Beth paced the living room of the apartment, holding her phone with one hand and rubbing her queasy stomach with the other, trying her hardest not to take Xavi's irritation personally. It was hard not to, and hard not to feel a painful sadness that the cloak of happiness they'd both been shrouded in had been so unceremoniously ripped away.

He was under huge pressure, she reminded herself. This buyout was a big deal. The business press had been reporting on it and were expecting to report its finalisation at any minute. Delays, no matter how small, always fed wild speculation.

She was letting her brain feed on wild speculation, another thing it was hard not to do when the memory of Xavi dumping her after a business trip with nights away from her had never lost its vividness.

History was not going to repeat itself. Xavi's irritation at his situation was perfectly understandable, not a portent of anything bad being about to happen.

She rubbed her belly again. She'd been feeling queasy since she woke up, and it was now mid-afternoon. If Xavi hadn't been so short and irritable, she'd have mentioned it. Mentioned, too, that her period was two days late…

The ringing of her phone made her jump, and made Diego, asleep in the corner of the room, lift his head curiously.

'Hi, Erika, is everything okay?' she asked her lawyer, trying to pull herself together.

'All good here, thank you. Just returning your call.'

Oh, yes. She'd forgotten about that.

Organising her thoughts, she said, 'Thank you for getting back to me so quickly. One thing I promised myself I would do with my inheritance was buy my old company, Miss Amore. I want to approach the owner directly, but I can't find any information on him. The company was bought out not long after I started with them. I remember hearing at the time it had been bought by a businessman as an investment, but my investigative powers are clearly rubbish because I can't find anything about him. Or her. I think it must be a shell company or something like it that owns it.'

'You want me to find the owner for you?'

'Yes, please. And I'd like a contact number so I can call them directly.'

'We can make the approach for you, if you wish.'

'No, thank you, I want to do it myself.' It wasn't like she currently had anything better to do with her time.

'Leave it with me. Do you want me to call when I have news or should I wait for you to make contact?'

'You can call me.' No more cloak-and-dagger behaviour. No more going behind Xavi's back. She would never keep another secret from him. Secrets were corrosive.

When Xavi got home, she would make her confession, drag the past into the present and then put it to bed, for good.

She cuddled up to Diego with the very strong feeling that when Xavi got home, she would be telling him he was going to be a father.

Beth's very strong feeling proved right two mornings later.

Fed up of going to the toilet every five minutes to double-check her period hadn't started and unable to bear the suspense a second longer, she'd taken Diego for a walk to the nearest pharmacy and bought a pregnancy test.

It was unequivocal. She was pregnant.

She'd barely processed it when Xavi messaged to say the deal had gone through and he would be home early evening. He'd even added a kiss to the message, which eased the tightness in her chest a little.

While it seemed that all the ducks lining themselves up were ducks from the past, history wasn't about to repeat itself. This was something she reminded herself every five minutes.

What she didn't like to remind herself was that the main reason history wasn't poised for a repeat was the business. Xavi needed her shares. If only for that, he wasn't going to come home and sever her from his life again.

After running herself a bath, Beth lay in it until the water ran cold. She kept stroking her stomach, her heart veering from wild excitement to wild terror.

When had conception happened? she wondered. It wasn't like before. She hadn't come off the pill this time. Had it been her stomach bug that had caused it, when she'd been too ill to take her pill? Could it have happened that quickly? Or had she just been sloppy?

Had she...had she been sloppy because her subconscious had been seeking a way to tie her to him forever?

She pinched the bridge of her nose and swallowed hard.

On Monday she'd book herself in to see an obstetrician. Xavi would want to come with her. Maybe the doctor could narrow the conception date. It didn't matter. What did matter was reassurance that this baby was going to be fine, and that all the conditions were right so that it could live.

It was an assurance Beth knew in her heart could not be made. Life was too fickle and precarious for assurances like that.

She swallowed back more tears.

Xavi would be home soon. He would give her all the assurance she needed, and by sheer force of his will, make her wishes for their baby come true.

Xavi let himself into the apartment. The door had barely closed when an excited Diego bounded over to run rings around him. And then Beth appeared, ravishing in a halter-neck electric-blue satin dress that plunged in a V to her midriff and fell to her feet. A thin gold belt was wrapped around her waist, hooped gold earrings just visible beneath her loose, gleaming red hair.

He couldn't fail to notice the apprehension on her beautiful face, and knew she was thinking about the last time he'd left her behind when he'd gone away on business. Smiling wanly, he drew her to him. '*Mi vida*, you look beautiful.'

'Thank you.' Her arms looped around his neck, her lips forming the upside-down heart that never failed to make his heart ache. 'You look tired.'

'I'm exhausted.' He hadn't slept in twenty-six hours. A cock-up with the flight slot had seen his plane depart an hour later than it should have done. What should have been a relatively short drive from the airport to his apartment had taken an hour thanks to numerous accidents and roadworks gridlocking the roads.

Her crystal-clear green eyes gazed into his. 'We don't have to go.'

'We do. He's holding it here in Madrid so I can attend.' Though God knew he would give anything to get out of the party and spend the evening losing himself in his beautiful wife, but losing himself in his beautiful wife had already caused enough damage.

He kissed her gently so as not to smudge her lipstick. 'Give me ten minutes to change.'

She nodded and lifted her chin for another kiss. 'Can I get you a drink?'

'A whisky fit for an alcoholic should do the trick.'

Her whole face creased into a smile. 'That bad, is it?'

'It's better now I'm home with you.'

Somehow, her smile broadened. 'Good. And when we get back, I'll show you how much better it is to be home with me and how much I've missed you.'

He went to give her another non-lipstick-smudging kiss, but her lips parted and, with a sigh, her arms tightened around his neck and her tongue slipped into his mouth for a hungry kiss that told him more than any words how much she'd missed him.

For one sweet moment, he returned the hunger because, *Dios*, the nights in the bed of his Manhattan apartment had been excruciating without her.

With great reluctance, he broke the kiss. 'Ten minutes, *mi vida*.'

'I'll bring the drink up to you.'

He put a finger to her lipstick-smudged lips and shook his head. 'We are already late. If you come into the bedroom…'

Her eyes gleamed with knowing, but she stepped back gracefully, laughing. 'Go on, go get ready.'

He swooped in for one more kiss, then bounded to their bedroom, reenergised.

Having showered on the plane, he headed straight to the dressing room and donned a black tuxedo and black bow tie. Polished shoes on, hair swept back, cologne splashed on his neck and cheeks, and he was good to go.

Beth thought it just as well Gustav's party was being held at Madrid's Club Giroud, an uber-exclusive private members' club a short drive from their apartment. Exhaustion was etched on Xavi's face, although he'd certainly livened up since arriving home.

She'd been to Club Giroud only once before, when they'd first been together. Xavi had taken her there for her nineteenth birthday, just weeks before he'd ended it. She thought it best not to mention that to him. There would be enough talk about their break-up when they got home and she made her confession and told him about the pregnancy. Both pregnancies.

For now, she would hug her news to herself and let him circulate and network with his mind where it needed to be—on the business. Because there was no doubt that for Xavi, this party was business to him.

The birthday boy's stare clocked them as soon as they stepped into the club's vast basement. Embracing them both in that non-embracing way the fashion world did so well, he said to Beth in his thick French accent, 'You look well—I do believe you have lost weight since the wedding. Are you taking the injection?'

'I'm afraid an old-fashioned stomach bug is responsible for the weight loss.'

He waved a dismissive hand. 'Whatever achieves the needed results. You should look at taking it for those last ten or fifteen kilos. How is your grandmother?'

Digging her nails into Xavi's palm to get him to loosen

his angry grip at Gustav's thoughtless rudeness, she grinned. Compared to most of the stick insects that inhabited the fashion world, Beth was an elephant. It didn't bother her in the slightest. Xavi loved her curves, and that was good enough for her. 'She's doing well, although I think she's only just recovered from all those shots you and Benoît had her doing.'

His cool face became suddenly animated. 'That we had *her* doing? She drank us both under the table and then did the same at the wedding!' Without a flicker, he re-adopted his usual impervious pose and turned his attention to Xavi. 'I hear the Grimaldi deal has gone through.'

Xavi's tone was as cool as Gustav's, she noted. 'It has, yes.'

'As you are here, some quotes for the magazine?'

His fingers squeezed hers tightly again.

Sensing he was too angry at the slight Gustav had made about her weight to bother schmoozing the arsehole, Beth cut in with a bright, 'Gustav, it's your birthday party! Surely, you're not planning to work? Let the quotes wait for a day or two.'

He considered this through narrowed eyes. 'And you? Will you grant me a short interview?'

'An interview about what?' she asked, confused.

'You are now one-half of the Rosbel Group and one of the richest women in Europe. You are also young and beautiful and married to this beautiful man. My readers—indeed, the world—will be waiting with avid interest to learn about you.'

She dug her nails into Xavi's skin again. Mercifully, he loosened his hold before the blood supply to her fingers cut off. 'Gus…may I call you Gus?'

He looked taken aback at the question, but then gave a short nod.

'Gus,' she said confidingly, 'if I was going to grant an interview to anyone, it would be you, but I'm a very private person. I've not been raised in the spotlight or ever sought it, so I'd rather keep my privacy and stay behind the scenes, and let our relationship remain one of friends.'

He looked even more startled at the notion of friendship, a startlement that increased when a member of the club's security team tapped him on the shoulder and handed him a note.

He read it, his eyes narrowing before his stare darted to them both with barely concealed excitement. 'Excuse me, there's something I need to attend to. I will find you later. Enjoy the party.'

Once he'd disappeared into the throng, Beth met Xavi's tight stare. 'Don't let him get to you—he's not worth it.'

Dark fury was alive in his eyes. 'He's not, but you are.'

'If you're talking about the weight jibe, then don't worry about it. He probably thought he was being complimentary and doing me a favour.'

'Bullshit. And his comment was bullshit, too. You don't need to lose weight.'

'Look around you. Half—more—of the women here are supermodels. They're the women he sees and works with every day. In Gustav's eyes, any woman over eight stone is fat.'

'Then Gustav's eyes need testing. Those women are nothing but clothes horses, and you're not fat.'

'They're the clothes horses who sell the clothes your brands produce to the public. Thin sells. Fact.'

The dark fury faded. With the whisper of a smile playing on his lips, he leaned into her to whisper, 'Thin sells, but curves are priceless, and your curves are the most priceless of all.'

Her smile turned into a beam.

'And it's our brands, not my brands. You're equal majority shareholder.'

If they weren't surrounded by approximately two hundred people, she would have used the opportunity to make part of her confession, but they were and so she let the moment pass and swallowed back her guilt with a sip of the sparkling water she'd swiped from a waitress when they'd walked in, and as she sipped, Xavi noticed what was in her glass.

'Why the water?'

Because she couldn't tell him she was pregnant during a party, either, she smiled and told a partial truth. 'I'm feeling a bit queasy.'

'Still?'

She shrugged to show it didn't matter. 'It'll pass. Oh look, Griselda's over there.'

Griselda was a doyenne of the fashion world, a true original and one of the only creatives whose company Xavi enjoyed rather than pretended to enjoy.

Soon, they were chatting and mingling, and when Beth escaped to the ladies', it was with Xavi fully relaxed and back to his usual charming self.

The club's basement ladies' toilets were as lavish and ornate as the ones she'd used in the club's dining room all those years back. It smelled delicious, one of the many touches that made Club Giroud membership so sought after. Beth touched up her lipstick and eyeliner thinking she'd have to get Xavi to bring her for a meal here again. They could take a trip to Barcelona and try the Club Giroud there, too. Or Athens. Or Paris. Each one had its own distinct style and flavour, and she was keen…

Her thoughts slipped away when she left the ladies' and spotted a bald, rotund man wearing a red cummerbund with his tuxedo approach Xavi. Her blood turned to ice before her brain connected what her eyes were seeing to the online picture she'd seen of him.

It was Paul Haldron.

CHAPTER ELEVEN

XAVI WAS GENERALLY happy to play the schmoozing game at parties like this. It came with the job and was a necessary evil. He might be an apex predator at the top of the fashion food chain, but those lower down needed to eat, too, and if they weren't fed, they died, and then he would be unable to feed. It was an analogy Raul had imparted many years ago. Occasionally at these parties, Xavi would come across a rival apex predator and engage in the mandatory pissing contest, but secure with his place in the world, his heart was rarely in it. It was only with arsehole predators like the shark Paul Haldron that he took enjoyment from metaphorically pissing all over them.

Far from being an actual shark, the Paul Haldrons of the world were more like annoying mosquitoes trying to land on the real apexes with the aim of biting and slowly killing them. Paul Haldron had tried to kill Xavi. He'd led a consortium of investors to overthrow him. It had been a badly misguided effort, mainly because they didn't have the shares, brains or funding to make a success of it. Xavi had taken great pleasure in squashing them all, even if it had been an unwelcome reminder of how vulnerable his position would be without Raul's shares.

Instead of arranging his face into the usual welcoming

smile he gave when being approached, he hardened his stare and drew himself to his full, intimidating height.

'What an unpleasant surprise to see you here,' he said sardonically when Paul stood before him. 'I wasn't aware Gustav knew of your existence.'

'He didn't until twenty minutes ago.'

'Then you shouldn't be here. This is a private members' club. Guests are only allowed if—'

'I know how the guest list works. I got a note to Gustav of my reasons for being here. He read it and added me to the list.'

Xavi followed Paul's gaze. Gustav was watching them from a distance. There was no mistaking his avid interest.

Trepidation snaked up his spine.

He looked back at the American. 'Why are you here?'

'Because I knew you were invited and I wanted to see if you had the balls to turn up given the new state of affairs, and offer my commiserations to you.'

The tension spreading through his veins, Xavi folded his arms across his chest. 'What are you talking about?'

The mosquito smiled a shark's smile. 'Your wife becoming the majority shareholder of the Rosbel Group and kicking you into the dirt. I speak from experience when I say she paid good money for that privilege.'

A pulse was beating loudly in the back of Xavi's head, the tension in his veins turning to ice.

The shark correctly read his expression and bared his teeth. 'So it hasn't happened yet? I did wonder—I've kept my ear *very* close to the grapevine and not even heard white noise.'

His words had barely landed when he nodded over Xavi's shoulders. 'Oh, there she is. She's as ravishing in the flesh as your wedding photos suggested. Still, they do say the most beautiful of the fairer sex are the most deadly. That one is lethal. Enjoy your downfall.'

Beth's feet had rooted to the floor. She knew from Xavi's ramrod stance and the triumphant smile Paul Haldron aimed at her as he sauntered away that he'd told him, and she fought desperately against the hot blood filling her head and the sensation that she was a heartbeat away from her legs collapsing beneath her.

He turned around slowly.

Eyes as glassy and cold as marble fixed on her.

Completely incapable of moving, she fought even harder to keep control of her limbs as he moved towards her with the silent lethality of a tiger about to strike.

He took her clammy hand into his with a smile as cold as his stare and leaned down to brush a cold kiss on her trembling lips and whisper, 'Smile, *mi vida*. This is a party.'

For the next two hours, her hand held tightly in Xavi's, Beth smiled until her face ached. Not a single guest went unspoken to. Xavi laughed and joked as if he was having the best time with the best company, feigning ignorance of the curious eyes darting to them as Paul Haldron spread his poison amongst the party.

Beth did her best to act normally, but with the world spinning wildly around her and the undercurrent of ice flowing out of Xavi through their clasped hands, maintaining her smile was taking everything she had.

It was almost a relief when he murmured, 'Time to go,' before guiding her to Gustav so they could say goodbye.

'Excellent party,' he enthused, clasping Gustav's hand

as he shook it, then slapping him on the shoulder as he added, 'I'll be in touch about those quotes.'

She had no doubt that the moment the basement door closed behind them, the room would erupt. And she had no doubt that Xavi knew it, too. They would be lucky to make it until morning before the news leaked to the press.

She was too frightened to check her phone to see if it had leaked already.

Their car was ready for them. Gentleman that he was, Xavi let her get in first.

'Xavi,' she said as soon as they set off. 'I—'

'Wait until we get home,' he interrupted tonelessly, turning his face out the window.

'I'm sorry,' she whispered. 'I was going to—'

'Stop the car,' he said abruptly into the intercom. 'I want to walk.'

The car stopped.

He faced her.

His expression made her insides shrivel.

'I will meet you at the apartment.'

He'd slipped into the night before she could scramble any form of response.

It could only have taken ten minutes to get back home, but they were the longest ten minutes of Beth's life. The wait for the elevator was excruciating. The fact she had to call it down meant Xavi had beaten her back.

Diego rushed to greet her, but other than his welcome presence, the apartment was silent. She crouched down to stroke him and snatch at the needed comfort he gave, the coldness in her chest increasing with the certainty that Xavi had sent the staff to their quarters.

At first glance, their bedroom was empty. And then she heard noise coming from their dressing room.

The world spun on its axis to find three open suitcases on the long velvet dressing stool, and she pressed her back against the wall to stop herself swaying.

He didn't break his stride at her appearance, pulling a load of summer dresses off a rack and folding them as one and placing them, coat hangers and all, in the nearest case.

'When were you going to tell me?' he asked silkily as he pulled more dresses off the rack.

She could hardly speak through the hammering of her heart. 'Tonight.'

'You don't need to lie anymore, Bethany.'

She didn't know what was worse, the way he was systematically packing her out of his life, that he'd called her by her full name or the normality of his tone.

'I'm not lying.'

'What percentage of the company do you own?'

'Fifty-one. But—'

'I'm impressed. That was quick work. I assume you had everything ready to go as soon as probate was granted?'

'Yes. I—'

'It did cross my mind to increase my shareholding a few times before your grandfather died, but I didn't act on it—it would have felt treacherous.' He zipped the first suitcase shut and lifted it onto the floor. 'Our grandfathers took great pride in their partnership being equal. Neither could benefit without the other benefiting, too. For me to increase my shareholding while Raul was alive would have spat on that fundamental agreement as it would have made me the first amongst equals. When he died, again I could have increased my shareholding, but instead I went to Raul's granddaughter.' Back at the shelves and racks of her clothes, his gaze caught hers for a moment before he gathered a pile of her jumpers into his arms.

That moment was enough for her insides to shrivel all over again. 'I'm sorry. I *was* going to tell you tonight, I swear. Whatever Paul told you about my motives…they changed. I set the wheels in motion to get majority control and kick you off the board the day after you proposed. I was angry and emotional, and I acted rashly, but I swear, I've no intention of going through with it. I would never take the company from you.'

She might as well have spoken to the wind. Xavi continued his monologue as if she hadn't even opened her mouth.

'I thought we could continue that long-established partnership with us both benefiting equally.' He placed an armful of her jeans and trousers into a case. 'I would continue to run the company and you could slot into it in whatever creative capacity you wanted, and we would both reap the rewards, and—'

'And that will still happen,' she promised beseechingly. 'Nothing's changed there, Xavi. Nothing.'

Her words fell on deaf ears, Xavi picking up exactly where he'd left off. 'And if we were going to be partners in business then we should be partners in life, too, and do that thing we'd promised we would do when we were too young to know what we were doing and finally get married.' Crossing the floor to add another pile of jumpers into the suitcase, his stare caught hers again. His lips formed a snarl. 'It never crossed my mind that Raul's granddaughter would be so treacherous as to work directly against me and stab me in the back.'

Although anger had been bubbling beneath his veneer of normality, to witness it rise to the surface made tendrils of her own anger unfurl.

'That is some major revisionist history,' she defended herself shakily. 'You married me first and foremost to keep control. Everything else was secondary, including your wish to marry me.'

His glare was full of contempt. 'I never lied to you, not once, whereas everything you've done has been a lie.'

'Never lied to me?' A sudden burst of fury propelled her from the wall to cross the dressing room floor and wrench the jumpers from his arms. She hurled them to the floor. 'You promised you would love me forever,' she cried. 'What was that if not a lie? You promised there would never be anyone else for you, another lie, and then you threw me away as if I never meant a damn thing to you.'

But this only made his visible anger turn darker. 'So this has all been *revenge*? All these years and you've been harbouring *revenge*?'

'You broke me, Xavi. You didn't just break my heart, you broke *me*. You threw me away like an unwanted toy without any warning, and then days later jumped into bed with Ellen.'

He kicked a jumper so hard it flew through the air and landed on the far wall. 'I told you before, I never slept with her! Nothing ever happened with Ellen.'

'She sent me a time-stamped photo of you asleep in her bed three days after you dumped me!'

'I don't care what she sent you. Nothing happened. She had a party at her house, and I went along and drank a bottle of whisky and passed out. I was so drunk I didn't know it was her bed until I woke up the next morning to find her sharing it.'

'Then why didn't you say that when I asked? Why lie?'

'The question was about sex, not sleeping arrangements. I never had sex with her. I could have told you I'd passed out in her bed, but I was trying to convince you to marry me, not rake over poisonous old ghosts. Hell, Beth, don't you think ending our relationship affected me, too? Ending us almost damned near killed me.'

She threw her hands in the air and laughed bitterly. 'Oh, I've heard everything now. You were like a freaking robot with its humanity wiped out.'

'And why do you think I had to be like that? It's because it was the only way I could do it—I *had* to switch myself off. My brain knew it had to be done but my heart didn't want to let you go, and I only went to that damned party to drink myself into oblivion so I could try and forget you.'

'You didn't need to forget me! I was at my grandfather's praying to every deity in existence for you to come back to me!'

'We were over, Beth! I wasn't going back to you. Ending us hurt us both, but it was necessary, and for you to hold on to your resentment over it for all these years is just warped when you moved on long before I did. Even if I had screwed Ellen that night, that doesn't excuse what you've done. You married me under false pretences for revenge so you could take control of the business for yourself and push me out, and all for something you thought happened that didn't happen eight years ago?' His face twisted with loathing. 'You sicken me. Take your cases and get out of my home, and prepare yourself for a fight because I am not going to let you get away with your treachery.'

'You don't seriously think I did all this because of *Ellen*, do you?' she demanded, angry heat suffusing her from the roots of her hair to the tips of her toes.

'Who knows what goes on in your twisted mind. You brought her up, not me.'

'As an example of what I believed was another of your lies, but it changes nothing else and it doesn't change what you did to me, and all that crap about you drinking yourself into oblivion because of how much you were missing me? Utter bullshit. If you'd felt a fraction for me of what I felt for you, you would never have let me go. You didn't even try to keep us together, just excised me from your life like you were *ripping off a plaster*, and as for that crap about us being too young to know what we were doing before—I'm only three years older now than you were then! You used our ages and the business as an excuse to get rid of me then, just as you're using what Paul told you earlier as an excuse to do the same now. Look at you, packing my stuff for me and telling me to leave and not even attempting to listen to me. You want me gone, just like you did before, except this time you get to pin it all on me.'

'It *is* all on you,' he snarled, leaning his darkly furious face right into hers. 'You married me to destroy me, and I'm not going to listen to another word that comes out of your lying, treacherous mouth, so take your stuff and get the hell out of my home. The next time I see you will be in court because this is war.'

The room was spinning furiously around her, dizzying her as the truth slapped her around the face.

There was no saving them. Xavi had already been

looking for a way out. This was just the excuse he'd been looking for.

All the anger and fight drained out of her as the truth slapped her a second time.

There was nothing left to fight for.

There never had been.

Xavi hadn't played her for a fool. She'd played herself.

Pain gripping her heart in a vise, she stumbled onto the armchair next to her dressing table and hugged her arms tightly.

Her voice was a distant ringing in her ears as she dully said, 'Yes, I wanted to destroy you. I wanted to take your precious company away from you and hurt you the way you hurt me.' Even though her eyes were struggling to focus, she could see the contempt etched on his features, a contempt that tightened the vise until she could hardly breathe. 'I never moved on, Xavi. I never got over you. I tried so hard, but I just couldn't do it. I tried to sleep with other men, but they left me so cold I couldn't go through with it. I've carried you with me every minute of every day since we parted, not just you but our…our…' She had to swallow hard to say it. 'Our baby.'

His head reared back as if she'd slapped him.

The silence that followed was absolute.

Eyes wide, the colour draining from his face, he just stared at her.

'I was pregnant, Xavi,' she whispered, saying the words aloud for the very first time. 'Don't you remember how we were trying for a baby?'

'But…' His voice was hoarse. 'You'd only come off the pill that month. It was too soon…'

She shook her pounding head. 'No. We were one of the lucky ones. It happened straight away for us. I took the test when you were in Milan, and I was the happiest person alive. I was having your baby, the child we both wanted, and that it happened so quickly was, for me, proof that it was meant to be and that we were meant to be.'

He sank onto the dressing stool. 'You didn't tell me.' His voice was barely audible.

'I wanted to see your face when I told you. I imagined your happiness…' Tears were stinging the backs of her eyes, and she fought desperately through their burn. 'I had all these fantasies of how it would play out, but then you came back and you…you…you…'

The tears finally spilt out, splashing down her cheeks in a torrent.

'I thought you would come back to me,' she sobbed, her chest heaving as she drew her knees up to hold herself tightly. 'I didn't—I couldn't—believe you meant it. But you didn't come back, and I lost it five days later.'

He dragged his hands down his face and expelled a long breath. His eyes were shining when he whispered, 'Why didn't you tell me?'

'I would have done, but nature took the decision out of my hands.' After grabbing a handful of tissues from the box beside her on the dressing table, she blew her nose and tried harder than ever to get the rest of her words out. 'When I lost the baby, what could I do but go home to England and try to pick my life up and start again? And I did try, I really did, and I succeeded in many ways, but the pain never left me, and when you made your proposal at my grandfather's wake, it all opened up again. I hated you for asking that of me almost as much as I hated you for excising me from your life the way you did. One minute we were trying for a baby and dreaming of a big white wedding, the next…' She lifted her hands in the air and flicked her fingers. 'Poof. Gone. You threw me away without even checking if our wish had come true.'

'*Dios*…' It was like he'd aged a decade in a stroke. 'I'm so sorry.'

'So am I.' She pulled air into her ragged lungs and wiped her nose. 'So now you know everything. I agreed to marry you so I could destroy you.' A wave of sadness that was close to unbearable rose inside her. She met his stare. 'I knew when we exchanged our vows that I couldn't go through with it, but I'd already set the wheels in motion. I meant to pull the brakes when we got back from our honeymoon, but then I got ill and…' She closed her eyes and sniffed back more tears. 'By the time I knew probate had been granted, everything had happened. If you want to fight me then fight me, but there is nothing to fight about. I've already set the wheels in motion for half the extra shares I bought to be transferred into your name. It should go through on Monday.' She nearly managed a smile as she locked back onto his stare. 'All equal again.'

Lifting his gaze to the ceiling, his chest rose slowly and deeply.

'You know, since you left for New York, I've had the most awful intuition that history was going to repeat itself, and now it has, in all possible ways.' She took a long breath and gathered what remained of her strength. 'Xavi, I'm pregnant.'

CHAPTER TWELVE

Xavi felt every atom in his body petrify into a statue. The red-hot fury that had driven him since that shark Paul Haldron told him his wife had been playing him for a fool had turned to static when Beth told him about the child they'd conceived and lost, and now he couldn't think at all. Couldn't move. He felt like he'd been hit at full speed by a truck.

'We never did discuss contraception, did we?' Her sad whisper was barely audible above the white noise crashing through his head. 'Well, I'm on the pill, but for whatever reason, we've made another baby. I guess we must be the most fertile couple in Europe,' she added, her attempt at levity dying as her voice choked. 'So if you are still planning to go to war with me, know you'll be going to war with your child, too.'

Your child, too...

He lowered his shocked gaze to hers. 'You're pregnant?'

Her usually crystal-clear green eyes were red and puffy from crying, but where there had been disconsolation just moments earlier was now...not hardness, he thought distantly, but clarity.

She jerked a nod. 'I took the test this morning.' Unfolding her legs, she dragged herself unsteadily onto her feet.

'I'll make an appointment to see a doctor on Monday and see what happens from there... Can I use your driver to take me to my grandfather's villa or should I call a taxi?'

With the white noise having only reduced a little, he was sure he'd misheard her. 'What are you talking about?'

'I'm going to the villa. It's not sold yet. I guess I'll take it off the market, at least for now, until I decide what to do.' She tried to laugh but failed miserably. 'I don't think I'm in the right frame of mind to make any long-term plans just yet.'

Surely, she didn't think he still wanted her to leave? 'Beth, there's no need to make any plans, not now. The baby changes everything.'

'No,' she disagreed with a sad smile. 'The baby doesn't change anything. We're over. You just made that very clear.'

Had she taken leave of her senses? 'Of course it changes things. We're going to be parents.'

Dios, he was going to be a father. They were going to have a child together, and suddenly he was thrown back to a time when they'd been cuddled up together in the middle of the night, imagining the names they would choose for their children. Why wait until they were older, they'd figured. They loved each other, were going to spend the rest of their lives together, so why not start trying now, while they were young and had the energy to deal with a football team of children? Money hadn't been and never would be an issue...

'Xavi, you don't want me,' she said, cutting through a memory he'd not allowed himself to remember in eight years.

'I've never *stopped* wanting you.' Not ever. He hadn't ended them because there was something wrong with them, but because it had been the wrong time for them. They'd got carried away on a dream that had to wait to be realised.

'But not enough to try and win me back until you got something out of it.'

There was a twisting in his guts. 'It wasn't like that, as I've explained numerous times.'

'Oh, but it was.' She shook her head, her stare becoming distant. 'I used to think you were the most open and loving man in the world, but you're not. It's just a front. You can only give so much, and then you take it all back. You won't make that final commitment—you're always seeking a way out. You used the cock-ups you made with the business and our ages as your excuse before, and this time you grabbed hold of the first concrete reason to weaponise against me and drive me out.'

'You wilfully and intentionally set out to destroy me,' he said tightly, trying to rein in the re-ignition of his temper at the way she was twisting everything. 'How the hell did you think I would react to that?'

'I wasn't thinking. That's the point. I was impulsive and emotional and put wheels in motion when I wasn't thinking properly that I now bitterly regret, but ultimately, even if I'd agreed to marriage with the purest of intentions, the end result would have been the same—you'd have snatched at the first opportunity to end it.'

He grabbed at his hair and gritted his teeth. 'That's bullshit. I understand you're angry with me threatening war with you, but I was angry that you'd been playing me for a fool and had set out to destroy the one thing you knew mattered most to me. I didn't know you were pregnant. If I had, I would never have taken it that far.'

'For God's sake, Xavi, even after everything I've just

told you, you've just admitted the business matters most to you, and you wonder why I'm not prepared to stay? What happens if I lose this child, too?'

'Don't say that,' he warned, the twisting in his guts spreading. 'Don't ever tempt fate like that.'

'Do you think I *want* to say it?' she cried. 'Don't you think I'm terrified that history will continue to repeat itself? But I'm the one who lived through it and so I have to mentally prepare myself to live it again, and if it does repeat—and God, I pray on my mother's soul to keep our child safe and let it grow into a bouncing baby we will both love and cherish—then I will be on eggshells waiting for the next time opportunity presents itself to you to excise me from your life. Even if the fates keep our baby safe and it survives, I'll still be living on eggshells because I'll know you're only with me *because* of the baby.

'It might be wishful thinking,' she continued, barely pausing for breath, 'but I think you do love me, you just won't let yourself embrace it. You said your father's death cemented Blanca's serious nature, and I think it's done the same to you—your mother falling apart the way she did forced you into survival mode, and the way you survived was by controlling everything, especially yourself. You're *terrified* of losing control of your emotions, a reason why I think you so rarely speak about your father. You never allowed yourself to grieve for him—'

'Do *not* use my father as a weapon against me!' he raged.

'I'm not! But don't you see—his death affected you terribly and it still does. When I came along, you'd spent years burying and controlling your emotions, putting your family and education and the business first, and I was a way for you to cut loose for a while and allow the fun side of yourself out, right until trouble hit. I was a threat to your control, and so I had to go, and I think the same thing's happened now—I got too close again.'

'No, Beth, you set out to stab me in the back and now you're twisting everything to justify your despicable actions.'

'I'm not twisting anything. You control your working and domestic environment with ruthless precision, but emotions? They're messy and uncontrollable, and I'm not controllable, either. Maybe you'd find it easier to deal with your feelings for me if I was meek and mild and compliant, but I'm never going to be that. I'm impulsive and emotional, and life's too short not to love with my whole heart, and it's too short to waste on a marriage with a man whose instinct is to push me away. I'm not a masochist, Xavi, and I've spent too much of my life hating you to want to spend the rest of it living with that on my soul. I need to let go of the past and look to the future, and you need to do that, too, because our child needs a father who can put them first.'

'How dare you insinuate that I won't put my own child first?' he said savagely. Of all the pseudo-nonsense Beth had just spouted, that burned the deepest. 'The very fact I'm prepared to forgive your treachery and make our marriage work proves I'm putting it first.'

Her mouth dropped open. As if in slow motion, angry colour flooded her face. '*You* forgive *me*? Well, thank you very much. I hope your forgiveness keeps you warm at night.' She stalked to the door, only looking back when she turned the handle. 'You're like a rebooted version of my grandfather. He pushed away everyone he loved, too.'

His heart pumping fury through him, Xavi let the treacherous, backstabbing viper go.

* * *

Not until Beth let herself and Diego into her grandfather's villa did the grip on her heart let go, releasing with it a sickening swell of pain that doubled her over and brought her to her knees with a howl.

Xavi was in his home office when his housekeeper knocked on the door and poked her head in. 'Your sister's here.'

He didn't look up from his computer. 'Tell her I'm busy.'

'She said you would say that, and said to remind you that she's flying to Egypt in the morning.'

He swore under his breath. Once Carlota flew off, it would be at least a month until he saw her again, probably much longer. 'Let her in. Take her to the living room and give her refreshments. I'll join her shortly.'

Alone again, he carried on reading through the Rosbel Group's share listing, and then without even thinking, clicked the open tab with the headline from two days ago that screamed, *Beth Granger, granddaughter and heiress of the late business icon Raul Belmonte, breaks her silence!*

His heart had already jumped back into his throat before he read:

Beth Granger has denied reports that she's taken a majority stakeholding in the Rosbel Group and denies sacking her husband and business partner, Xavi de la Rosa, from his dual role of Chairman and CEO. In a short statement, Ms Granger said, 'The rumours are categorically untrue. The extra shares I purchased were a wedding present for my husband. While I can confirm that we have sepa-

rated, the shares remain his and he remains at the helm of our great company and will remain there until a time of his choosing.'

He'd read it so many times and couldn't understand why he kept returning to it.

'Nice smell of alcohol in here,' a voice drawled from behind him.

He whipped his head round and glared at his sister. 'You were told to wait in the living room.'

'Don't take your shitty mood out on me.' Carlota flopped onto the sofa and stretched her long legs out.

'I'm not in a shitty mood and I'm not taking anything out on you.'

'Sure. Can I have one of those?' She nodded at the open bottle of whisky on his desk. There was an empty bottle of the same brand in the bin beneath his desk.

'Did you drive?'

'Not that it's any of your business, but no.'

'It is my business. You're my sister, and if you want a drink, get yourself a glass.'

'I'll have the bottle, and it's nice of you to remember.'

'What does that mean?'

'That you have a sister and family. You forgot to tell us you'd split up with Beth. We had to read about it on social media.' She held her hand out for the bottle.

He thrust it at her with a scowl. 'I've already explained that. The news broke before I had the chance to tell you.' The press must have got wind of the story before they'd left Gustav's party. When Beth had left their apartment in the middle of the night, a photographer had arrived to witness her jumping into a taxi with Diego. A close-up had revealed a blotchy face with red eyes. Social media had been in raptures ever since.

She couldn't have planned her revenge any better. The whole of Spain—and England, their English heiress a paparazzo's wet dream—had taken Beth's side and spent nearly two days fervently cheering on her actions of stealing his company from under his nose.

Her statement had dampened the cheers but set off a flurry of wild speculation as to why their marriage had imploded so suddenly and so quickly.

'Any explanation for why you've been hiding away from your family and the world?'

'I'm not hiding away.'

'Then why aren't you in the office bossing around your workforce?'

'I'm working from home.'

She took a slug of the whisky. 'I thought you didn't believe in working from home?'

'I do when the paparazzi are constantly dogging me.'

Her eyes narrowed slightly. 'Blanca says to tell you that you're an idiot.'

'Why would she say that?'

She took another slug of the whisky with a shrug. 'Probably,' she said, wiping her mouth with the back of her hand, 'because you've sabotaged your relationship with Beth again. She didn't go into detail, so I'm just speculating.'

'There was no sabotage,' he said flatly. 'Beth was actively working against me from the beginning.'

'That's not what her statement said.'

'Her conscience caught up with her.' Every share she'd bought behind his back had been transferred into his name, not just the half she'd said she would give him.

He'd received the notification and felt only betrayal. He'd received her text telling him she'd seen a doctor and that all was well with the baby, and felt such conflicting emotions that he'd opened a litre bottle and buried himself in whisky and spreadsheets.

'Has yours?'

He shook his head in disbelief. 'Don't tell me you're taking her part, too? You don't even know what happened.'

'I don't need to know what happened. I know you, and I know Beth. She thinks with her heart. You think with your brain.'

'And I suppose you think her heart is as pure as the driven snow,' he said icily.

'I didn't say that.' She smiled beatifically. 'So when are you going to prostrate yourself and beg her to take you back?'

He shook his head again. 'That's just great. You take her part and assume I'm the one who needs to apologise.'

'Like I said, I know you both, but if I'm reading things wrong, then I apologise.' She didn't look sorry. Or sound sorry. 'So why are you sat in your study drinking whisky on a Wednesday afternoon?'

'I told you, I'm working from home.'

'Have you tried sleeping at home, too? The bags under your eyes are bigger than Blanca's handbag.'

'Have you only come here to insult me and put me in a bad mood?'

'I came to say goodbye, the insults are free, but if my presence puts you in a bad mood then I'll consider it a bonus.'

'What the hell is wrong with you?' he demanded. Carlota had always been the more aggravating of his sisters, but this was a whole different level.

'Wrong question, Xavi—the question you should be asking is what's wrong with *you*.' Without any warning, she sat up and leaned forward, all playfulness wiped from her face. For a moment, he saw Blanca in her expression. 'Why would you let her go again?'

Wrong-footed, he swore. 'It isn't as... Look, it's none of your business.'

'You're my brother. That makes it my business,' she neatly threw back at him. 'You're my brother, and I love you, and it is my duty as your sister to be honest with you.'

'If I want honesty, I'll ask for it.'

'Like my insults, my honesty comes free.' Dark eyes so like his own softened. 'Xavi, you're a great man, in so many ways, and a great brother, too. If it hadn't been for you, I don't think I'd be who I am today. You're the one who got me through those months after Papi died and Mami got lost in herself. You're the one who let me know it was okay to laugh and be happy again, but I don't remember *you* ever being happy after he died, not until Beth came into your life. Those months you were with her... Xavi, you were the happiest I'd ever seen you, and when you ended it, it was like a part of you died. Outwardly, you were normal, but you became insular and you slipped away from us, and I didn't even realise it, not until you brought her back into your life, and it was like... Oh, Xav, you should have seen your face on your wedding day—you were wearing your heart on it. You love her, and she loves you, and whatever happened to drive you two apart, fix it, please.'

'It isn't that simple,' he whispered hoarsely. His heart had swollen and filled his throat.

She knelt before him and cupped his cheeks, forcing him to meet her earnest stare. 'It *is*. Xavi, it is. I spend my life digging through the past, and when I'm working on ancient human remains, the one question I always ask myself of them is *who loved you*? I'll never know, but they would have known because we always know who loves us.

'Do you remember how Papi was when he was ill? He didn't spend his final days with the business. He spent them with those he loved and who loved him—us, his family. It was *us* he wanted and needed. A business can never embrace you and it can never love you...' Carlota's voice trailed away as water flowed over the hands cupping her brother's cheeks. 'Xavi?'

But he couldn't speak. Couldn't breathe. All these days spent staring at the screen of his computer, veering wildly between despising Beth for her treachery and despising himself for despising her, drinking his conscience to sleep but unable to sleep himself, lying in the bed he'd bought with Beth in the subconscious of his mind and feeling like his heart had been ripped out.

It *had* been ripped out. He'd ripped it out.

He'd broken her again, broken her when she needed him most.

He'd broken them both.

He couldn't contain it any longer. All the emotions he'd spent decades suppressing broke free.

Burying his face in his sister's shoulder, Xavi wept for the first time since he was a little boy.

He wept for the father he'd worshipped and all the years fate had stolen from them, and he wept for Beth and the life she'd lost, the life they'd made together.

He should have been with her.

God help him, he should always have been with her.

CHAPTER THIRTEEN

'ARE YOU SURE?' Beth whispered. Her head was reeling.

'One hundred per cent,' Erika said, sounding almost as dazed as Beth felt. 'Miss Amore is owned by your husband. He bought it eight years ago.'

'But…' It didn't make any sense. How did Xavi own it? *Why* did he own it? And why had he never mentioned it? 'Do you have the date he took ownership of it?'

Erika gave her the date. It was two months after Beth had started her internship there. If she was remembering her dates rightly, it was around the time she'd been offered a permanent contract.

'Do you still want to make contact yourself about buying it?' Erika asked cautiously.

'I don't know what I want.' Her head was reeling too much to think.

Just when she thought she had herself on a vaguely even keel, she was knocked for six again.

The call over, she stroked under Diego's ears in the way he so liked, remembering that morning when she'd walked into the dining room and found Xavi stroking Diego in the same way.

In the four days they'd been apart, she'd received one message from him. It had been a response to her message after she'd seen the doctor and confirmed that all was well with the baby.

Thanks for letting me know—it's appreciated. Please let me know when you book the scan.

And that had been it.

Excised again.

Except this time the excising had come from her. She'd been the one to walk away.

She wished it made her feel better about things, but it didn't. She wished transferring the entirety of the Rosbel Group's shares she'd bought into Xavi's name made her feel better, but it didn't.

Those who said the first cut was the deepest had never lived with the same wound being cut back open with a deeper, sharper blade.

She wished she'd handled it all better from the start. Wished she'd been honest with him about how she felt. If she'd told him all the stuff she'd posted over the years and her bright and happy demeanour whenever she was in his company had been a front, he would have run a mile…

And their baby wouldn't have been conceived, so she retracted that wish.

Who was to say, though, that Xavi would have run a mile? He'd wanted her shares. He would have done anything for them.

He'd wanted her shares, but he'd wanted her, too, and though it hurt her to think it, the more she thought back on their time together, the more certain she was that he loved her, too, which only made her heart hurt even more. She wouldn't have believed there was anything left of her heart to break, but remembering how he'd stayed with her all those days of her illness did it every time.

Feeling tears prickle, she closed her eyes and concentrated on breathing. After eight years of her tear ducts refusing to work, they were making up for lost time with overtime added in. All she seemed to do was cry, and crying was no good when she was trying to plan her and the baby's future.

This pregnancy felt different. She couldn't explain why. It just did. And that made her dare to hope that this time the outcome would be different.

She would stay in Madrid. No running back to England like last time. Her baby deserved to grow up in a city where both its parents lived, even if they couldn't live together. She'd put on a front before around Xavi. Given time, she could do the same again for their baby's sake. After all, she was the queen of fake it till you make it. She just needed time.

Her intercom rang, making her jump.

Bloody paparazzi. They'd been staking out the villa. She'd hoped her statement would be enough to send them on their way, but nope. Thank God for Salma. She'd slipped out and stocked up on food…and here she was, looking troubled.

'What's wrong?' she asked.

'Xavi's at the gate.'

Her heart punched her. She cleared her throat. 'Did he say what he wants?'

'No. Only that he's here to see you.'

Gently pushing Diego off her lap, she got to her feet and nodded. 'Okay. Let him in.'

Somehow, she managed to stagger up to her room. Struggling to breathe, she ran a brush through her lank hair, added a sweep of colour over her wan cheeks and a touch—only a touch; her hands were shaking—of mascara to her lashes.

Looking only a little less like death warmed up, she

gripped the banister tightly as she made her way back down the stairs.

She was three steps from the bottom when the door opened, and a tall, lean figure holding a document folder stepped into the villa.

Her foot stopped mid-air. A moment later, Diego went charging over to him.

Beth used the moment he spent petting the dog to put her foot back on the step. It took a conscious effort to do it.

Their eyes met.

She thought she was going to be sick.

Lifting her chin, she wrapped her cardigan—she couldn't seem to get warm despite the heat—across her chest and said in a voice that hinted at normality, 'Hello, Xavi. To what do I owe the honour?'

He stared at her for a long moment, and in that stare she took him in. The unkempt hair. The unkempt beard. The shirt and trousers that looked like they'd been slept in. The bags under his red eyes and the lines that had deepened into grooves on his face.

And he took her in, too, and she knew he was seeing the lankness of her ineffectually brushed hair and the bruises beneath her red eyes.

Terrified she was going to burst into tears, she reached the floor and turned towards the kitchen. 'Coffee?'

'Please.'

With the excuse of fixing him a coffee and making herself a decaffeinated tea from the supply of English teabags Salma had bought her, Beth kept her back to him and filled the kettle. 'So, why are you here? Is it to do with the business?'

'In a way.' His voice sounded as rough as he looked.

'The shares you gave me... I've transferred them back into your name. I know it's unnecessary, but I've printed them off for—'

'*No!*' Her refutation came out as a wail, and she had to squeeze her eyes shut to better control herself. 'Xavi, I don't want them. I don't even want the shares I've got.'

'Then sell them. Sell them all. Do whatever you want with them, they're yours, but before you make a decision, know I've tendered my resignation from the Rosbel Group. An official press announcement will be released at six p.m.'

She jolted and came within a whisker of spinning around to look at him. Her stare flicked to her watch. It would be 6 p.m. in two minutes.

Her legs trembling as badly as her arms, she leaned her stomach into the counter and added a scoop of fresh coffee beans into the machine, except she missed and the beans went scattering over the surface and floor. Charging over to the cleaning cupboard on the other side of the kitchen for the dustpan, she was on her hands and knees clearing her mess before she was able to clear her constricted throat and ask, 'Why have you done that?'

'Beth, please stop doing that.'

'It needs to be done. Why have you resigned?'

He crouched down in front of her and put his hand on her wrist. 'Please, Beth, stop.'

She snatched her hand away, coffee beans spilling out of the dustpan in the process, and shook her head, terrified to look at him, terrified the tears blinding her were going to fall. 'Please go,' she whispered. 'I'm not ready to pretend to be normal around you.'

'I resigned because I love my wife.'

Her whimper at this was so faint Xavi could have believed he'd imagined it, but the way his heart ripped at the sound… Oh, he deserved to be strung up for what he'd done to her.

'Beth, those shares are yours. I could have bought them when your grandfather died, but the reason I didn't had nothing to do with keeping the de la Rosa and Belmonte partnership going like I said—it was so I had a legitimate reason to bring you back into my life. It wasn't the shares I wanted, it was *you*.'

A truth he'd finally acknowledged on his sister's shoulder when the truth had refused to be hidden away any longer under the flood of decades of suppressed emotion that had poured out of him.

She rocked back onto her bottom and drew her knees to her chin.

'I'm sorry, *mi vida*,' he said starkly. 'I'm sorry for everything. All the pain I've caused you. All the pain I've put us both through. All the wasted years. My feelings for you… I have loved you since the day I met you, and I will love you to the day I die. I've buried myself in work all these years, telling myself I'm continuing my father's legacy when all I was doing was selfishly burying myself from the pain of missing you.'

With a deep sigh, he sank to his backside and looked at her, wishing he could touch her, wishing she would open her eyes.

'Losing my father and seeing my mother lose herself in grief broke something in me,' he said quietly. 'You fixed it without me even noticing. You came into my life, this impulsive, vibrant, affectionate redhead, and you healed me, but when I spent that time away from you in Milan and realised the mistakes I'd been making because of my need to just *be* with you, I pulled away from you and then pushed you away from me because I couldn't handle just how deeply in love with you I'd fallen. I had no control over it, and I *needed* control, Beth. You were right about that, as you were right about so much else. I needed to control everything, and with you, I had none. I never have, and I was a fool to think I could bring you back into my life and not lose my head all over again.

'I don't want a meek, compliant wife,' he continued. 'I want you exactly as you are, because exactly as you are is all I need, and I will never forgive myself for the way I ended it with you all those years ago. I should have guessed you were pregnant.' The burn of tears stabbed the backs of his eyes, and he blinked hard to control it. 'I remember those calls we had and the excitement in your voice… I knew you were keeping something from me, but in my arrogance, I thought you had something special planned for when I got back. That's why I broke things off as soon as I walked in and didn't give you the chance to tell me. My analogy of ripping a plaster off was crude and cruel, but there is no better way to describe it, and because of my cruelty, you were alone when you lost our baby when I should have been with you, and thinking of that kills me.' Throat close to choking, Xavi wiped a tear away. He needed to get through this. Beth deserved everything, not half measures. It was the least he owed her.

'I'd promised you forever and I threw you away, and I want you to know that whatever happens between us now, *mi vida*, know you will never be alone again and I will never, ever, discard you again. I will be there for you, in whatever capacity you need. The business is yours to do as you wish. Appoint whoever you want to run it, run it yourself, whatever you want. You're the majority stakeholder. It's yours. I want nothing to do with it. You and the baby are my only priorities now. I'm yours, however you need me and I will be forever.'

He blew out through his constricted airway and wiped away another tear. 'Please, Beth. Please, find it in your heart to forgive me. I know I don't deserve it, but I swear I will do everything I can to earn it.'

Another blow of air, and he dragged himself back to his knees.

She was still frozen, chin on her knees, eyes closed.

He pressed his mouth to the top of her head and breathed her in. 'I love you, *mi vida*. Always. Call me whenever you need me.'

Beth heard Xavi's footsteps disappear like a receding echo. When the last echo vanished, the tears came. Rolling into a ball on the floor, she sobbed her heart out, wishing harder than she'd ever wished for anything that she could believe him.

She *ached* to believe him, just as she'd ached to believe their marriage could be a real one.

When the tears had finally run dry, she sat herself up and hugged her chest, which felt so bruised. Coffee beans were scattered all over the floor, and the ache in her heart stupidly wrenched even harder to know he'd gone without having his coffee.

She could feel his breath in her hair.

She hugged herself, wishing so hard that he'd wrapped his arms around her so she could still feel his imprint on her.

She wished she didn't love him so much. Her heart, her *amor*...

Amor.

Amore.

Miss Amore.

Her heart punched her again, this one landing like a slap, and suddenly she was filled with the memory of the moment her grandfather had introduced them. That very first look between them. The way Xavi's eyes had widened. The way her heart and her breath had caught.

The memory fast-forwarded into a reel of their time together. Oh, how young and carefree they'd been. How *happy*, always smiling and laughing, always touching each other, drugged on nothing but love and desire...

The reel shifted, flying to their ending and Xavi's words when he'd broken them: *It doesn't have to be forever... I'll always care for you and will always be there for you.*

Through the brutality of his other words, those words had faded into insignificance, but now, through the hot blood pulsing in her brain, Beth realised they'd been the most truthful words of all. He *had* always cared for her, through all the years of their separation. He'd never stopped caring. Never stopped loving her, but she...

Foolish, heartbroken Beth, so recently wounded by the lies of her father about her mother's family and the double life she suspected her grandfather of living, hadn't believed it. Not once Ellen's cruel pictures had pinged into her phone.

But the truth had always been there, as clear as the truth of her love for him that had always lived deep in her heart. She'd just been too frightened and heartsick to see it.

Xavi had never stopped loving her.

Still half-dazed, she scrambled to her feet and yanked her phone out of her back pocket.

Miss Amore.

Xavi had bought Miss Amore for her, so he could always be looking over her. Taking care of her. Loving her.

She scrolled the numbers as she ran to the door.

Miss Amore.

She pressed Xavi's name and ran down the long drive. It went to voice mail as she reached the closed gate. He'd gone.

Ignoring the cameras suddenly flashing in her face as the waiting paparazzi realised their prey had come out to play, she pressed the code to open it and pressed his name on her phone again.

It went straight to voice mail.

Barging her way through the scrum of photographers, she started composing a message to him as she ran, and then her phone rang in her hand.

'Mi vida?'

'Miss Amore,' she burst out.

'Beth?' There was alarm in his voice. 'Are you okay?'

'Miss Amore!' Half laughing, half crying, she said, 'I love you, Xavi. I love, love, love you. I love you to the edges of the universe! I love you, and you love me, and we've lost so many years, and I can't bear to spend another second without you! Please, come back and take me home. Come back and get me, *please*.'

She heard him shout for his driver to turn the car around, and though she knew he would be with her in minutes, still she ran and still she laughed, her heart pounding, overwhelmed with a joy she'd never believed she would feel again, a joy so pure she felt it in the tips of her toes.

A black SUV appeared in the distance.

She ran even faster.

A figure threw himself out and ran towards her.

She threw herself into his arms.

He caught her, just as she knew he would, just as he would be there to catch her, always, for the rest of her life.

EPILOGUE

XAVI ROLLED OVER in his sleep. Instinctively, he reached for Beth and pulled himself awake when he found the bed empty. He craned his ears, even though he knew he wouldn't hear her. She woke in the twilight hours every night and was unable to fall back to sleep until she'd satisfied herself that their children were sleeping safely. She would check on three-year-old Javier first because his room was closest to theirs, and then five-year-old Lorena, and then she would slip back into their bedroom and slide back beneath the sheets, as quiet as a mouse.

The moonlight pouring through their window showed the swell of her pregnant belly as she shrugged her robe off. Moments later, she was back in his arms with her head on his chest and her ear resting right above where his heart beat.

He was just dozing back off when she gently pressed his palm to the spot on her belly their baby was playing football against.

Smiling, he drifted back into sleep.

Life was wonderful.

* * * * *

Did Marriage Made in Revenge
leave you wanting more?
*Then you're certain to love these
other dramatic stories from Michelle Smart!*

Resisting the Bossy Billionaire
Spaniard's Shock Heirs
Forgotten Greek Proposal
His Pregnant Enemy Bride
Greek Boss to Hate

Available now!

BOSS'S BRIDE PRICE

HEIDI RICE

MILLS & BOON

To Natalie, a fabulous author
who is always a pleasure to work with!

CHAPTER ONE

'Tali, a Lorenti Corp helicopter landed in the back paddock five minutes ago!'

Tali Whittaker tugged out her earbuds, the old hip hop anthem still buzzing in her head, and propped the pitchfork against the worn wooden door of the horse stall.

'What? Seriously?' She pushed Gracie, the last of the estate's once impressive array of carriage horses, to one side to join her head groom—well, Westwick's only groom now—outside the stall.

She swallowed the bubble of hope as she dragged off her gloves.

Had she heard George correctly? Lorenti Corp had owned Westwick Hall for the past seven years, ever since the last Lord Westwick's death. But his son Dario Lorenti had never used his title, or even his father's surname, and had consistently refused to ever visit the estate when he was in the UK on business.

In fact, she'd never even received an acknowledgement to the many emails she'd sent to the company's head office in Milan in the past two years to ask for more money—after she'd taken on the job of estate manager when the previous manager had quit.

In the past two years, her skeleton staff had worked their butts off to repair what they could and keep the place running on a shoestring. But the profit they made from the agricultural side of the business, the glamping field they opened during the school holidays and the house tours, tearooms and events they hosted each weekend were not enough to pay for the upkeep of the Hall itself. Six hundred rooms of history and grandeur, the Georgian stately home hadn't seen any significant investment for a decade, and it showed. Her staff were depending on her to make Westwick a success, but she'd felt the weight of that responsibility ever since she'd come to work here as the last estate manager's admin assistant as soon as she'd finished Sixth Form college, age eighteen. And the thought that she was failing them, and failing Westwick, had been keeping her awake at night now for months.

'Yes! Lorenti was in it! He's here, *finally*, Tali!' George's craggy face lit up with excitement. 'I saw him and a number of suits get out of his chopper.'

The bubble of hope expanded and threatened to cut off Tali's air supply.

'He still has a limp,' George said, because like Tali he had met Lorenti once before, when the Lord's son had spent months recuperating at Westwick Hall after a terrible car accident which had nearly killed him. Tali pushed down the memories which still came to her in dreams sometimes. Visions of that surly, moody seventeen-year-old moaning in pain in the huge four-poster bed and shouting at her mother in Italian. Her mother had been responsible for the boy's care as the new housekeeper—and had told Tali not to bother him.

But Tali had been eight and left to her own devices for most of that summer—plus she'd overheard her mother telling one of the maids she thought 'the poor boy' was lonely. So Tali had made it her mission to visit him over the following weeks, even though he'd shouted at her in Italian at first, too—the same way he'd shouted at everyone. He had fascinated her, like the wounded animals she brought into her mum's cottage on the estate and tried to heal... Plus his dad didn't seem to want him. He and his sister hadn't even come to live in England until their mother died in Italy... And they'd never lived at the Hall until he had come to stay that summer.

In all those weeks, Lord Westwick had only visited him once. It gave them something in common, Tali had thought at the time—because her own dad hadn't wanted her either, once he had his 'new' family.

'You should go.' George grabbed the pitchfork, still beaming, as a surge of panic joined the balloon of hope in Tali's chest.

'Crap.' She stared at her jeans and flannel shirt. She was covered in horse manure. Did she have time to change? She wanted to make a good impression—she had so many things she needed to tell Lorenti about the estate.

'You best hurry, Tali. He'll want to talk to you first,' George added, then hesitated, his voice becoming pensive. 'Do you think he'll remember you? You became such friends that summer.'

'I doubt it, George,' she said, not wanting to hope. They hadn't been friends, not really. He'd been a teenager and her just a child. Plus, he'd been a captive audience, because until the very end of the summer he was too broken to even get out of the bed.

She knew he'd seen her as an irritation at first, then a useful distraction, her attempts to befriend him an escape from the pain of his injury—and eventually, a way to relieve the boredom of his long recovery.

Tali had heard the staff and her mother mentioning his only friend had caused the crash and then left him on the roadside to die. When she'd asked Dario if that were really true—because who did something so mean?—he'd growled something in Italian and then sulked for days. So, she hadn't asked again.

That he'd never come to Westwick Hall since his father's death seven years ago though, or replied to her emails, was also a pretty big clue that he didn't remember the little girl who had hovered around him all summer trying to bring him out of his shell. She certainly didn't intend to rely on their past association now to get him to invest in the Hall. Because that would be totally unprofessional.

She rushed out of the stable and raced across the courtyard and around the Hall's main building, heading towards the annexe, which had once been the carriage master's cottage, where the estate office and her tiny flat above were situated.

Finally, she had a chance to pitch all the ideas she had to Dario Lorenti to improve the Hall's revenue and make everyone's job here more secure—which had been her mission since day one.

Lorenti was a billionaire by all accounts. He had money to burn. And it made absolutely no sense to let his greatest asset rot, even if he didn't want to live here.

She skidded to a stop when she rounded the corner, finding a short, older man standing at the office door with a scowl on his face.

'Hi, I'm Tali Whittaker,' she said, realising this must be one of the suits George had mentioned arriving with Lorenti.

'Signora, I am looking for the estate manager. Signor Lorenti is waiting,' he said in perfect if heavily accented English, his tone clipped.

'Right, of course,' Tali began, trying not to feel too disappointed about having to kiss her shower and power suit goodbye.

She'd just have to make a great impression in her muddy jeans.

'I'll come with you...' she started.

The impatient man interrupted her. 'Signor Lorenti only wishes to speak with the estate manager. You must direct me to him immediately.'

Him? Seriously?

So Lorenti had never even *read* her emails.

'You're looking at him. Or rather her. *I'm* the estate manager,' she said.

The man's eyebrows rose as his gaze flicked over her. Heat blitzed her cheeks.

But then he nodded. 'Let us go. Signor Lorenti has been waiting long enough.'

Tali allowed a spurt of irritation to cover the sting of hurt as she followed Lorenti's judgy minion into Westwick Hall and up to the Hall's library on the second floor, where Lorenti had been waiting to speak to her...for all of ten minutes. While she had been waiting for years to *finally* speak to him.

CHAPTER TWO

While Lorenti's assistant knocked on the library door and waited for a reply, Tali brushed off her clothing, tied her long hair into a knot at the back of her head and swallowed the lump of panic.

She was young for her position at twenty-two and not looking her best at the minute. But there was nothing she didn't know about the estate. She'd lived here almost as long as she could remember, ever since her mum had taken the job of housekeeper after her dad had deserted them both—the winter before Lorenti's accident.

She just hoped she didn't have any horse manure on her face.

'Entrare.'

The lump pushed into her throat at the harsh demand delivered from behind the door.

The assistant opened the door and introduced her in Italian.

Tali plastered what she hoped was a professional smile on her face as she stepped into the room.

She inhaled the smell of old leather and lemon polish, comforting and familiar, as the assistant excused himself and closed the door behind him on his way out.

She'd always loved the library—the rows and rows of books, many of them first editions, displayed on shelves that rose two storeys and included a mezzanine level accessed by a wrought iron spiral staircase. At the far end of the room was the old Lord's mahogany desk. Behind it stood Lorenti, with his back to her, as he gazed out of the large, mullioned window, which looked out over Westwick's circular driveway and the fishing lake beyond.

Lorenti's silhouette in the light cast by the mid-morning sunshine made him seem incredibly tall, his muscular shoulders and lean waist displayed to perfection in a steel grey designer suit. His stance was tense, making the usually soothing atmosphere in the library bristle with energy...

The lump of panic expanded. Should she alert him to her presence?

He raked his fingers through his hair, the waves cropped close to his head. His hair was much shorter than she remembered it being that summer, when it had grown long enough to hit his collar.

She shook her head to dispel the distant memory. And gave herself a mental kick.

He's not that wounded, angry teenager anymore. He isn't going to remember you, and you don't want him to. Because you're already at enough of a disadvantage...first-impressions-wise.

In fact, he seemed to have forgotten she was there, transfixed by who-knew-what in the driveway... She hoped it wasn't the potholes they'd been unable to afford to fill in this spring.

The moments ticked past, the grandfather clock by the door keeping time with the hammer thuds of her pulse—and increasing the tension which hovered around him like an aura.

She cleared her throat. 'Mr Lorenti, you wished to speak to me...urgently.'

He stiffened as if he'd been woken from a trance, then

turned. Even in the half-light she could sense his gaze on her. The energy emanating from him seemed to stroke her skin, then sank into her abdomen. The heat in her cheeks blasted to her hairline.

'*Vieni qui*... Come into the light,' he demanded. The brittle tone made her shiver.

She stepped forward with as much courage as she could muster under that penetrating stare—which seemed to look through her without seeing her.

'*Che cosa?*' he murmured.

'I'm sorry, I don't speak Italian,' she managed, wondering if he even realised he'd spoken in his native tongue. She'd been trying to learn Italian on an app over the last two years, in case anyone from Lorenti Corp came to Westwick, but she wasn't confident enough to converse in it yet.

He frowned. 'Who are you?'

'I'm Westwick Hall's estate manager. Your assistant said you wanted to speak with me?'

Now that he was no longer in shadow, she could see his face, and it wasn't helping the swooping sensation in her stomach. His features were sharper and more dramatic now, having lost the softness of youth—but his eyes, that rich dark brown flecked with molten gold which held so many secrets, were exactly the same... The scar on the left side of his face was also still there, slashing across his cheek all the way to his hairline. But where the scar had been disfiguring that summer, the livid bruising and stitching fresh, now it only made him look more striking.

Something else about him, though, was *very* different. Or maybe she simply hadn't noticed it when she was eight—and a child, instead of a woman. The combination of those harsh features, his magnetic eyes and his tall, muscular build made him look incredibly...*hot*...

She dragged in a breath. No, *hot* was too basic—more like *breath-taking*. Her stomach fluttered, annoyingly.

She'd never been the type to swoon over good-looking guys, because they usually turned out to be egotistical arseholes. Not that she'd ever met any who were *as* good-looking as this man.

She mentally kicked herself. Again. *Hard*.

So what if Dario Lorenti's rugged male beauty—accentuated by that designer suit and the dark scowl on his face—was making her light-headed. He was still technically her boss.

Plus, while she'd never been interested in celebrity gossip, Joss and Becca—the Hall's cleaners—had told her all about Lorenti's playboy reputation, because they were celebrity news junkies. So, even if he looked like every woman's fantasy, he really wasn't.

It also became clear he was nowhere near as impressed with her appearance when his eyes narrowed, and his gaze swept over her grubby clothes.

'How old are you?' he demanded, his tone as searing as the inspection.

'I'm twenty-two,' she replied firmly, trying not to sound defensive.

One dark brow lifted. 'How can you have the experience to run a large estate at this age?'

She winced at the judgemental tone and the note of criticism.

The truth was, although she'd worked for two years as the previous estate manager's assistant and taken courses at the local agricultural college in project management, she *didn't* have the experience. But that was hardly her fault.

'When Mr Chambers quit two years ago, no one else would take the job at the reduced salary we could offer,' she said. 'And Lorenti Corp didn't respond to any of my emails outlining the problem.'

She shoved her hands into the back pockets of her jeans, to stop them trembling.

This meeting was not going how she'd hoped. Why was he being so hostile? And why did she get the feeling his harsh expression wasn't just about her lack of qualifications?

'So, I stepped up to the role as an interim arrangement,' she finished.

And maybe if you'd replied to a single one of my emails you would know all this already.

The muscle in his jaw tensed, making the scar on his cheek flex. But then the flecks of gold in his irises shimmered, his gaze intensifying as if he was seeing her properly for the first time. 'What is your name?'

'Tallulah Whittaker,' she blurted out, not sure why she'd given him her full name.

Everyone called her Tali, because she had never felt like a Tallulah. The florid, old-fashioned name had belonged to her father's grandmother, and she'd always considered it just another burden her dad had saddled her with—along with his disinterest, and the crippling bouts of sadness which had dogged her mother for years after he'd walked out on them.

But the formality of her proper name felt like a trusty shield against Lorenti's disapproval.

His eyes narrowed even more as he studied her.

Suddenly, heady recollections of the brooding, unhappy teenager whose enforced solitude she had insisted on disturbing that summer swirled through her consciousness.

Should she tell him they had met before?

Perhaps he hadn't completely forgotten the little girl who had worked so hard to entertain him that summer. But as he continued to stare at her, his inscrutable gaze made her palms start to sweat, still buried in her back pockets. And it occurred to her this meeting was already awkward enough, without bringing up ancient history. Plus, if she had ever known that boy, she certainly did not know the man he had become.

At last, he nodded. 'I suppose your qualifications are of no significance now,' he remarked.

What was that supposed to mean?

The swooping sensation in her stomach went into overdrive when he walked to the desk and lowered himself into the chair. The pronounced limp had sympathy tangling with the knot of anxiety in her stomach.

Was he still in pain? His movements were stiff, unwieldy, but his face no longer had the strained, stoic pallor she remembered from the early weeks after his accident, whenever the painkillers had worn off.

He opened a laptop on the desk, jolting her out of her thoughts.

Stop staring at him and thinking about that boy and start making a better impression on your boss.

Gathering a breath, she launched into the spiel she'd rehearsed a million times in the last two years, during all those sleepless nights, preparing for this exact moment.

'Actually, I'm so glad you're finally here, Mr Lorenti,' she began, determined not to falter when his gaze rose to hers, the blank disdain even more intimidating than the sceptical frown. 'There's so much to discuss about Westwick. I've worked up a detailed investment plan to turn the Estate around. It's got so much potential, and our hiring freeze is only the tip of the iceberg when it comes to problems with staff...'

'Fermare.' He held up his hand.

She stopped talking, intimidated despite herself by the command in his voice. The lump of panic became a boulder. Something was seriously wrong.

'Your plans are not important now, Tallulah Whittaker,' he said, the hollow tone of voice somehow much worse than the earlier hostility. 'As I am here only to end your employment. The land will be parcelled up and sold as soon as possible.' He glanced around the room, his features devoid of emotion, while Tali's stomach went into free fall—and the boulder threatened to crush her ribs.

At last, that searing gaze landed back on her face. 'And the Hall demolished.'

CHAPTER THREE

'But? *Wh-what?* Y-you can't… You can't do that, Mr Lorenti.'

Dario stared at the girl standing in front of his desk, her chest heaving with emotion under the shapeless plaid shirt, her striking blue eyes bright with—were those tears?

He stifled the ripple of something hot and fluid, which had hit him the minute she had stepped out of the shadows and into the light.

She was hardly the sort of woman he would ever consider dating, with her dirty work clothes, her mess of caramel curls tied back in a haphazard knot, her soft, pale skin devoid of make-up. Not only did she look too young for the job she had inherited, clearly by default, she looked too young to date anyone. And certainly too young for a man like him, even if she was telling the truth about her age.

The frustration which had propelled him to this godforsaken place today—thanks to the fallout from his disastrous meeting this morning in London with the Westwick Estate's board of Trustees—swept through him. And resentment blindsided him again.

After seven years of negotiations between Lorenti Corp's legal team and the Westwick Trustees who controlled his mother's old home on Capri—the palazzo he had spent a small fortune renovating and restoring since his father died—those bastards had refused point blank to let him bypass the terms of his father's will to inherit the palazzo outright.

He ground his teeth, furious that he had been unable to circumvent the demands his father had made from beyond the grave—in seven long years of legal wrangling.

It had always struck him as a cruel joke that his father had allowed him to inherit Westwick Hall, a place he had always hated, while keeping the palazzo in trust—until he agreed to marry an Englishwoman. But after trying to force those old fools to see reason through the courts, he wasn't laughing anymore.

But he refused to let his father win.

The bastard had always railed against the fact his only son and heir considered himself an Italian. That Dario had never given a damn about fitting into the mould of an English gentleman so he could inherit the Westwick title and estate. His father had cut him off when he was eighteen to try to force his hand. But instead of capitulating, Dario had borrowed money and built a hugely successful tech business, managing to amass his own fortune without any help from his father.

The terms of his father's will had been Lord James Westwick's last-ditch attempt to bring Dario to heel, by keeping ownership of the palazzo—which contained the only memories he had of his mother—out of Dario's hands unless he married an English debutante.

Seven years ago, when he'd first heard that blasted will, Dario hadn't been concerned. He'd simply set his legal team to work on breaking it… Unfortunately, the ancient aristocratic friends his father had put in place were as entitled, old-fashioned and intractable as the bastard himself, and had stymied every one of Dario's attempts to purchase the palazzo without marrying anyone.

While also spending a large portion of the Westwick trust to fight him in court.

He hadn't cared, because he didn't need or want his father's money. But the irony—that he owned Westwick Hall, a place he didn't want, while he would never own Palazzo di Constanzo now—had only fuelled his fury. That fury had propelled him here for the first time in fifteen years, to decide what to do with the Hall, which he had been ignoring since his father's death.

Receiving an invitation to his sister Mia's wedding while en route here today—she was marrying that Sicilian bastard Sante Trovato, the man who had once abandoned him on a roadside and left him for dead—had added another layer of fury to his frustration.

The fact he would have to attend the wedding only increased his anger. If Mia was foolish enough to fall for that man's dubious charms, so be it. She had made it clear only a few weeks ago she did not value Dario's counsel. She had also refused to accept a penny from him over the years, even though she had been cut off by their father too, her blasted independence so precious she would rather starve than admit she needed his support. But as her older brother, it was his duty to make one last attempt to get her to see Trovato for who he really was. Which meant Dario was going to have to attend the event on the man's private estate in Sicily in two weeks' time. The hasty wedding was also a red flag as far as he was concerned.

If he managed to stop himself from killing his sister's fiancé, it would be a miracle.

But the invitation had helped Dario make a decision about what to do with Westwick Hall. He would sell off the land and raze the house to the ground. Then at least he would have had payback for his father, if not Trovato, for their attempts to destroy him.

Take that, you old bastard!

He hardened his heart against the genuine look of horror in his estate manager's translucent blue gaze.

'There is no need to become hysterical,' he remarked, because she looked as if she were struggling to draw breath. 'You and your staff will be paid six months' severance which you will not have to work for, as I will close the house for good this weekend.'

He wished to find a buyer promptly for the land. Of course, he could have sold the house too. Even in its current state it was probably worth millions. But the resentment that had lived inside him for so long—and had built to a tsunami this morning—meant that demolishing it felt like the perfect revenge for being prevented by his father's Trustees from owning the palazzo.

'Please don't do this!' The girl stepped forward and pressed her palms on the desk. 'You don't know what you're doing. You have no right. Westwick is a part of history, it's a…'

'I assure you I have every right,' he said, as evenly as he could manage while his resentment was threatening to choke him. 'This isn't personal,' he lied.

'But it makes no sense. Why would you destroy something so beautiful?' she asked, the agony in her voice giving him pause.

Apparently, this *was* personal, to her. He let his gaze drift over her again. That strange prickle of memory disturbed him, but not as much as the liquid pull of arousal. Her shirt was open, allowing him to see the tops of her breasts.

'You may think it beautiful.' He levered himself off the chair and walked back to the window, the ache in his bad leg helping to control the spike of lust. 'I, on the other hand, do not.'

'But it's on the English Heritage Registry, you can't just demolish it.'

Dario swung round. 'What does this mean?'

'The Hall's historic significance means it's an important part of the nation's heritage. They could bring charges against you…'

'Puttana!' The full force of Dario's anger and frustration returned in a rush.

Then I will close it up and let it rot…

But as he glared at the girl, who was shaking visibly, her arms wrapped tightly around her midriff, the threat got caught in his throat.

It was what he had felt in his heart ever since inheriting the place seven years ago. A place he hadn't visited since his teens, when he had been locked up here for months, the pain in his leg nowhere near as agonising as the pitying glances of the staff, and the pain in his heart… At his best friend's—his *only* friend's—betrayal.

But he was no longer that damaged boy, vulnerable and alone. Yes, his leg would never be fully healed—the pins used to repair the crushed bones had saved it, but only just. But he'd hardened his heart, not just against Sante, but also against anyone else who might betray him—or pity him—again.

'If you'd just let me outline the plans I have for Westwick,' the girl began, her voice quivering with emotion, 'you'll see it can more than make the money back that needs to be spent on it to restore it to its former glory.'

He frowned at the girl.

Former glory? Was she mad?

Westwick Hall had never been glorious. Not to him. He still remembered the first time he had come here, age thirteen, after his mother's death. It had been cold and miserable that day, the ground muddy underfoot, the clouds cutting out the weak sunlight which had no warmth, even in May. His sister had clung to his hand and looked as lost as he'd felt, while the father they didn't remember, his face contorted with disgust, had shouted at Dario to speak in English—a language he barely understood.

Capri and his mother, and the life he and Mia had lived on the island with her throughout his childhood—free to roam as they wished—had seemed a million miles away that day, as well as in the weeks and months and years afterwards, when they had both been parcelled off to different boarding schools, forced to remain in this dreary country.

There had been no more early mornings scrambling down the path to the palazzo's private lagoon, to go swimming in the sparkling blue waters. No lunchtimes spent begging leftovers from the kitchen staff for him and Mia, while the housemaids cleared up the previous night's mess. No more lazy afternoons spent sailing or fishing, or in the wintertime messing around on his computer, gaming and teaching himself to code. And no evenings spent feasting and dancing and falling asleep under the stars while their mother and her many flamboyant cosmopolitan friends partied until sunrise.

Gabriella Lorenti hadn't believed in rules, and hadn't believed much in schooling either, but she'd loved him and Mia unconditionally.

Their childhood had been precarious at times, scary even, when the men his mother loved to entertain became surly, or possessive. Sometimes, Dario had wished for a little less wildness, a little more sleep, a little more security for Mia—who had quickly become as headstrong and impulsive as her mother. But when he'd come to England, to the cold and the damp, and been forced to live under strict pointless rules, forced to adhere to a punishing school schedule and learn an ugly language, made to spend hours each day reading and writing about old Englishmen when it was the codes and numbers he loved…then he had realised how much more he had lost than just his mother's flamboyant hugs, her endless chatter, the vivacious personality which made it exciting just to be near her.

England was lifeless and tasteless, sterile and suffocating and dull. Much like his father and this godforsaken pile of stone.

But clearly the girl didn't feel the same way, because she was staring at him with desperation in those cornflower-blue eyes.

'Please, Mr Lorenti, if you'll just give me a year. I've itemised everything in my budget. It would mean a small increase in our running costs and some capital investment, to make the necessary repairs and improvements, but we could more than make it back.'

He tuned out the request. But the something he had been trying to ignore ever since she'd stepped into the light spiked in his gut again. And with it came an idea. The same idea he had dismissed seven years ago when he had first heard the terms of his father's will...

He had been determined then not to bow to his father's demands. And not just because he had hated the man's attempt to manipulate him, but also because he had decided never to marry anyone. He simply did not have it in him to trust another person that much. Nor did he wish to care for anyone again the way he had once cared for his mother, and Mia, and even Sante, all of whom had abandoned him.

His advisers, of course, had suggested an arranged marriage early on to satisfy the Trustees. But until this moment he had refused to consider the suggestion. He had never dated a British woman and did not know any members of the English aristocracy, because he had never used his title nor taken up the seat left vacant by his father in the House of Lords. His life was in Italy. But if he couldn't demolish this place to get his revenge on his father, perhaps there *was* another way...

'Are you English?' he asked.

The girl blinked, confused by the question. 'I'm… Yes, I was born near here. But I have British and Irish passports as my mother was born in Dublin.'

The feeling in his gut surged. Even better then—with an Irish passport she could live in Italy with him as long as was necessary to convince the Trustees he had abided by the terms of the will.

To hell with it. He'd been wrestling with this situation for seven years. And the decision to wreak vengeance today on his father, and the stately home he had cared about more than he had ever cared for his children, would have given Dario some satisfaction, but it would not have given him what he truly wanted—his name on the deeds of Palazzo di Constanzo. And frankly, where was the satisfaction in besting a dead man?

'If I save the house from demolition, and consider your proposals for the estate, I will need you to do a job for me in return,' he said. 'One I would pay you handsomely for,' he added, because he required this to be a business transaction first and foremost. He certainly did not want this girl getting any romantic notions about the arrangement. She was young, and clearly not wealthy, and her emotional investment in what was just a job was a sign she was also naïve and sentimental.

'Absolutely, Mr Lorenti, but I really don't need a pay rise. I'd rather put any additional money into the repair budget.' A tentative smile curved her lips, her relief palpable as her pale cheeks took on a rosy glow. 'But you could give *everyone* a pay rise at the *end* of the year, if you're satisfied with the work we've done,' she finished, clearly trying to temper her joy at his sudden turnaround. 'Which I guarantee you will be.'

Yes, she was definitely naïve, he realised, and far too

trusting. She hadn't even heard yet what he was going to ask of her. But her trusting nature only made this arrangement more perfect. A cynic would be more likely to realise their bargaining power.

'The job I am referring to has nothing to do with your work as my estate manager...'

Her eyes widened. The deep blue of her irises shimmered—her confusion tangible. The wary expression reminded him of a young doe he had once had in his sights while hunting with his mother's gamekeeper as a boy many years ago in Amalfi.

'It...it doesn't?' she whispered.

He hadn't been able to pull the trigger and kill the young deer that day. He couldn't, because the creature was so beautiful. And so defenceless. And he'd been less ruthless as a boy. But he had no qualms about pulling the trigger now.

'I require an English wife for a year.' That should be long enough to fool those old bastards into transferring ownership of the palazzo—and while his father had clearly intended for him to marry an aristocrat, there had been no specific reference to his bride's social status in the will. 'If you agree to take the job, I will pay you two million euros as a divorce settlement, in a year's time.'

CHAPTER FOUR

'I… I BEG your pardon, Mr Lorenti?' Tali murmured, sure the emotional roller coaster ride she'd been on since entering the library had just crashed off the rails.

That surge of awareness wasn't helping her keep a grip on her cognitive faculties either. She couldn't possibly have heard the Italian billionaire correctly.

If he needed a wife—for a year—which was peculiar enough, why would he ask *her*? Not only did he not know her from Adam, but she was also so far from being his type she might as well be circling Mars.

She worked on a farm! Her mother had been his father's housekeeper. She'd been literally shovelling horse shit less than fifteen minutes ago, some of which was still decorating her jeans. And she'd never even read about the sort of events and parties and soirees—were soirees even still a thing?—that men like him would attend, let alone been invited to one.

'You heard me correctly, Tallulah Whittaker,' he said, using her full name again, but this time caressing the vowels with that husky Italian accent, almost as if he were mocking her.

Okay, great, now she'd dropped wholesale into another dimension. One in which Dario Lorenti found her amusing, instead of beneath contempt.

Unfortunately, that only made her reaction to him more disturbing.

The heat in her cheeks fired across her collarbone and reached past her aching lungs to tighten her nipples into hard peaks.

She folded her arms more firmly across her chest, attempting to get a grip.

'Are...are you joking?' she asked, not knowing why he was making fun of her, but trying to see it as a good thing. At least with that cynical smile on his lips he didn't look so forbidding.

Whatever was going on with him, she had to negotiate it diplomatically, or he might reiterate his threat to demolish the Hall, which would leave her staff—all of whom she considered to be her friends and her responsibility—out of work and her and, even worse, her mum homeless. Elsa Parker had worked long hours as a housekeeper here ever since Tali's father had abandoned them both. And when she'd decided to take early retirement a year ago after a bout of bursitis, Tali had promised her mother she could remain in the cottage she'd lived in for the past fifteen years. Her mum still helped out in the tearooms at the weekend, so the peppercorn rent she paid was totally justified, in Tali's humble opinion. And losing her home might break her mum again, the way she had been broken after Tali's father had left, which was another reason why Tali would do everything in her power to save Westwick.

'A simple yes or no will do,' he said as he stepped around the desk, his limp doing nothing to make him seem any less intimidating, until he stood in front of Tali. Close enough for her to inhale the scent of clean woodsy soap, blended with the refreshing hint of citrus and sea salt in his cologne.

She tried to step back, aware she probably didn't smell anywhere near as delicious, but he reached out and clasped her wrist to prevent her retreat.

'Are you scared of me, Tallulah?' he asked, those rich brown eyes searching her face. The flare of something in the molten gold was almost as disturbing as the electric sensation sprinting up her arm from his loose grip on her captured wrist.

'No…no, of course not,' she murmured, around the ball of something immoveable in her throat.

He dropped her hand, but she couldn't contain the vicious shudder of response.

'Then stand still,' he demanded, but the note of censure was not matched by the light still dancing in his eyes.

She forced herself not to move and tried not to tremble under that seeking gaze.

'I need a wife, and I am asking you to take the position for a year, at a very generous salary,' he said, his voice so low now it seemed to reverberate in her belly.

'Why do you need a wife for a year?'

And why would you employ me when you've dated tons of much more suitable women who'd do the job for free?

She bit into her lip to stop herself from voicing *that* question, because it felt far too personal.

His brows lowered, his gaze became shuttered and the muscle in his jaw twitched again, signalling his disapproval.

'The purpose of this arrangement is not your concern,' he said. 'Do you understand?' There was that note of command again, and condescension, which was playing havoc with the weightless sensation in her belly.

Was this really happening? Because this whole situation had begun to feel like a weird anxiety dream, which she was hoping she would wake up from soon.

'I… I guess so,' she said, even though she didn't understand at all.

'So, what is your answer, Tallulah? Two million euros for a year of your time.'

'I—I don't want the money,' she said, making his brows snap together. 'For myself…' she added quickly, because she could see he wasn't happy with that response either. 'But if you would consider investing in the Hall as soon as possible, so I could give the staff a pay rise and start putting my plans for the business into action, I'd be happy to consider it... But I'd need a few guarantees first.'

If the Hall could become profitable, instead of just barely sustaining itself, Lorenti would surely want to invest more, and all the people who relied on her for employment—people she cared about—would have their futures secured, too. But she needed to clarify what the position he was offering her entailed before agreeing to more.

What would a man like Dario Lorenti even require in a wife? What exactly was he expecting her to do, and for a whole year? It sounded like a public position. But the way he was looking at her, with that dark intensity in his eyes, was making parts of her ache that had never ached before—and that could not be good...

'What guarantees?' he snapped. The business-like tone, though, helped to stop the hot rock in her chest from vibrating... Unfortunately, it did nothing to shrink the one which had become lodged between her thighs.

'Well, like, what do you want me to do? *Exactly?*' she asked, feeling breathless again.

The cynical smile twisted, but he seemed unfazed by the question when he replied—his tone practical and pragmatic. 'You would marry me, after you sign a pre-nuptial agreement, as soon as possible. Then you would need to do everything I request to make this marriage appear genuine—in public.'

The breath she had been holding released in a rush. So this was a stunt marriage.

He let out a low chuckle. 'There is no need to look so relieved, Tallulah, that I am not proposing a genuine marriage.'

The blush blazed across her chest and blasted into her

cheeks. Was he amused or offended? 'I'm sorry, I didn't mean to imply...' Her heart raced into her throat. 'I mean, I'm sure you're very appealing to women.' The blush burned as one dark eyebrow arched.

For heaven's sake, Tali, shut up!

'But *you* do not find me appealing?' he prompted.

'It's not that, I just, I...' She swallowed, the hot rock between her thighs calling her a liar, but the constriction in her lungs winning. 'I've only just met you... And I work for you. I don't think it would be appropriate for us to...to...'

She trailed off.

Sheesh, why don't you just dig a hole in the carpet and jump into it.

'For us to *what*, Tallulah? Exactly?'

She heard the hint of sarcasm then and saw the renewed spark of amusement in the golden brown.

He was mocking her. The...*bastard*!

She breathed through the flash of temper.

Dario Lorenti was a powerful and ruthless man who held her future and the happiness of the people she loved in the palm of his hand, and who had no scruples about using that power to get what he wanted. Trying to appease him probably wasn't the best strategy, because it was like playing peek-a-boo with a tiger. Eventually, she'd lose.

She had no idea why he needed this fake marriage, or why he had picked her, but she had to ensure she didn't allow him to beguile and belittle her. No easy feat, given she didn't have a lot of experience with men generally.

She wasn't a virgin. She'd dated at school and gone all the way with a boy she'd met at agricultural college... But those pleasant if not particularly memorable encounters hadn't got her anywhere near as hot and bothered as Dario Lorenti had with a single look.

Sexual confidence seemed to ooze from this man's pores,

and he used it as a weapon, without even trying. Because how else had he put her whole body on high alert—every pulse point pounding, each erogenous zone humming—when she was fairly sure she didn't even like the guy? And she certainly did not trust him. He was far too surly, and mercurial, and unreadable. And that was before you factored in that he was proposing they 'pretend' to be man and wife for an entire year...

Stop acting like an airhead then! And talking in silly euphemisms.

'I don't think it would be a good idea for us to sleep together!' she blurted out, seizing the tiger by the tail. 'If I take on the role of your wife, that's all it would be, a role. I just want that understood. In case you were wondering...'

His eyes narrowed, but what she saw in them bolstered her resolve—not amusement anymore, but admiration.

'Duly noted, Tallulah,' he murmured, his ego clearly not dented by her assertion, but at least he wasn't laughing at her anymore. 'What we choose to do in private would not be part of your paid role as my wife,' he continued.

'Okay, good,' she said. His phrasing was a little weird, because they wouldn't be doing *anything* together in private, surely. But English wasn't his first language, and she was glad he wasn't going to press the point, because the hot spot between her thighs had begun to ache.

'You will take the job then?' he asked, although it didn't really sound like a question, his confidence as intimidating as everything else about him.

'I... I suppose so,' she said. His eyes flashed with that exhilarating intensity, forcing her to add, 'But I'd need the money now.'

Westwick was falling apart, and her staff hadn't had a pay rise in years. She couldn't wait any longer to secure the investment they needed.

Irritation doused the fierce glow in his eyes at her counter demand. Clearly, he wasn't used to being bargained with. But she refused to cower or back down. If she was going to spend a year having to appear in public with this man, and dealing with all these bizarre tingles and pulses, not to mention his controlling and volatile personality, she had to make sure it would be worth it. But the truth was, pretending to love, honour and obey him would be a small price to pay to secure the Hall's future—and make all her dreams for her dream job become a reality.

'I will put five hundred thousand euros into the Hall's operating account *once* you have signed the pre-nuptial agreement,' he countered. 'And a further five hundred thousand on the day we are wed. The balance of the investment, though, will be contingent on your ability to adhere to the terms of our agreement—and will *not* be paid until I am entirely satisfied with the outcome of this arrangement.'

Tali blinked, the heat rising in her cheeks—and a few other disconcerting places besides—at the commanding tone, but right alongside that disturbing reaction was the giddy burst of hope.

A million euros! It was more than she could ever have hoped for when she walked in here—and that was before his initial threat to demolish the place. Even if Lorenti wasn't satisfied with the arrangement—which she suspected he wouldn't be, when he discovered she was about as far from being trophy-wife material, even *fake* trophy-wife material, as it was possible to get—the Hall would have a million euros of new investment.

She could repair the holes in the roof and the driveway, give everyone a modest pay rise, fund the tearoom's much-needed makeover and offer their chef Jim a full-time job—so he could give up the night shifts at the local pub she knew he hated. Plus her mum's home would be safe and

Tali could even begin the infrastructure projects that would demonstrate to Dario Lorenti the magnificent potential of the stately home he had inherited.

It was all good. In fact, it was fantastic. And if by some miracle she managed to pull off the role of trophy wife to Lorenti's satisfaction—which was a very big if, but she'd do her best—they would have an additional million euros to play with in a year's time. Of course, it would help if she had some idea of what he was trying to achieve with this fake marriage, why he needed it and why on earth he had chosen her, but that could wait until she knew him better.

The thought of spending more time in his company made the strange reaction in her abdomen pulse and glow, alongside the giddy leap in her heartbeat. She ignored it.

This was a job, he'd said so himself. Lorenti was a fascinating man—and okay, beyond gorgeous. But he was also scarily intense and unknowable, and she suspected that would never change, no matter how much time she got to spend with him over the coming year—which would probably only be a few strategic appearances together, she hoped.

She could still remember the taciturn and angry teenager, whose moody façade she'd only managed to make a few dents in as a little girl. And he'd been a great deal more vulnerable and approachable then—lonely and in pain—than he was now.

She'd been a lot more naïve herself as an eight-year-old, of course, convinced all Dario Lorenti had really needed was a friend, someone to make him smile, someone to care about him, to help him heal. She'd strived to be that person once, but it would be like butting her head against a brick wall now, and she'd done enough of that as a child, trying to get her father to notice her.

What all those ignored texts and emails had taught her, eventually, was that you couldn't change people, and you couldn't make them care about you if they chose not to. So, it was pointless to try.

Even so, her heartbeat thundered in her ears when Dario murmured in a gruff voice, 'Do we have a deal, Tallulah Whittaker?'

She nodded. 'Okay, I'm in,' she replied, trying to focus on the million euros and all the things she could do with it, and not the unreadable expression on his harshly handsome face—which was making her pulse points go haywire.

He held out his hand. 'Let us shake on it.'

She reached out, but as his hand gripped hers, something fierce and shocking leapt up her arm and surged into her sex.

His eyes widened a fraction, as his fingers tightened.

Had he felt it, too—that shocking burst of adrenaline which was even now causing her legs to feel like overcooked noodles and her lungs to contract?

If he had, he controlled it faster than she could, the flecks of gold in his irises mesmerising her as he lifted her hand to his lips in a practiced move. But before his mouth could connect with her knuckles, he sniffed and dropped his gaze to her fingers.

Humiliation engulfed her as she became brutally aware of what he could see, and smell. The dirty, broken fingernails, the rough calluses, the scent of sweat and horses and manure.

His grasp loosened and she tugged her hand free. She closed her grubby, work-roughened fingers into a fist and hid the offending hand behind her back.

She braced herself, the swift kick of vulnerability almost as disturbing as the crippling disappointment. Would he withdraw the job offer, now that he had incontrovertible proof of how unsuitable she was to play his wife?

But instead of breaking their deal, his sensual lips lifted in the first genuine smile she'd seen on his face. The light dancing in his eyes turned the gold flecks to molten magma.

'You have forty-eight hours, Tallulah, to make yourself presentable,' he said, his tone more amused than judgemental. But as the string of orders continued, Tali's relief proved to be short-lived. 'My legal team will arrive today. You must sign the pre-nuptial agreement before we meet in Milan to announce our engagement in two days' time. I will arrange a separate apartment for you there, while we attend events as a couple. But at the end of the following week, we must travel to Sicily for my sister's wedding,' he continued, the dispassionate tone comprehensively obliterated by the purpose in his eyes which seemed to detonate in Tali's sex. *What the hell?* 'I will tell Aldo to make all the necessary arrangements and assist you over the coming days.' He walked back around the desk, but then his gaze skimmed over her. 'He can start by arranging a manicure.'

She wanted to be outraged at his high-handedness and that dictatorial tone. But how could she be, when she'd totally signed up for this? What bothered her more, though, was the schedule he'd outlined so dispassionately.

It was all too much, way too soon.

'But I can't join you in two days. I'll need more time to get my assistant Ellie up to speed here. And I can't spend a fortnight in Milan, especially if you then want me to travel to Sicily with…'

He held up his hand, halting her babbled plea in mid-babble.

'Are you reneging on our deal so soon?' he asked, one brow lifting ominously.

'No, but I'm needed here. Ellie's good, but she's never handled everything on her own. Exactly how long would we be in Sicily…?'

'That is not your concern.' He cut her off, making the panic threaten to choke her. He didn't look amused anymore, his scarred cheek clenching, signalling his irritation.

Unfortunately, he wasn't the only one getting annoyed. 'You will be with me whenever, and wherever, and for as long as I require,' he added.

'But...' she tried again.

'This is not a negotiation, Tallulah. Either you accept these terms, or I close the Hall as planned and investigate how to have it demolished...'

The threat felt like a knife to her gut, but she couldn't quite control her own temper. He was being unreasonable. And she wasn't even sure why. What on earth would she be doing in Milan for close to two weeks?

'But I can't just abandon my staff...' she said, the anxiety making her lungs hurt. 'I've never been away for more than a weekend.' The truth was, she hadn't taken a full day off work in the last two years, and she had never had the chance to travel... She was pretty sure her day trip to Calais at school didn't count. But he didn't need to know any of that, because he had far too much information on how unsophisticated she was already—thanks to broken-nail-gate.

One of the things she loved most about her job at Westwick was the sense of purpose and achievement it gave her. She'd always been industrious and hard-working and, as much as she'd hated seeing the Hall's decline, she'd also adored the challenge of running a place of this size and complexity on a shoestring.

She'd feel utterly useless in Milan twiddling her thumbs, and hideously guilty. Because how on earth were her already beleaguered staff going to manage everything without her?

Lorenti was utterly unmoved by her pleas. His features set in the stony expression of disapproval she had become familiar with in the past twenty minutes. But then, to her surprise, as he stared at her, the muscle in his jaw stopped clenching.

'For this to work, I expect you to be available to me at all times,' he growled, his voice husky with intent.

Tali tensed, the wave of heat which flushed through her shocking in its intensity. 'But I...'

'Hear me out,' he interrupted her again. 'If you wish to continue your work here during the year ahead, I will allow it. Up to a point.'

Allow it!

'I... I do wish,' she managed, feeling like a rabbit in the headlights of an oncoming juggernaut. And not just because he was being such a dictatorial jerk.

She wanted this deal to go ahead, so Westwick would have a future, but the shocking heat flushing through her system like a tsunami made her feel as if her whole life—and everything she had ever known about herself—was being swept away before her eyes.

'Then you may continue your work here in person,' he said. 'When I do not require your presence at my side. Otherwise, you can oversee your responsibilities via the internet. And hire any extra staff you feel appropriate, at my expense. This is my final offer.'

She could see he meant it.

A part of her wanted to tell him she couldn't accept—that she couldn't be his fake wife for a whole year if it meant spending weeks away from the estate. Westwick was more than a job to her. This place made her feel valued and safe, and it always had, ever since she'd first arrived as a child. It was where she'd recovered from her father's rejection, and where she'd helped her mum eventually heal her broken heart.

And while another part of her knew she couldn't throw away this chance to give Westwick the lifeline it so desperately needed... What if saving Westwick Hall and the estate—and looking after all the people who depended on her—wasn't the only reason she wanted to say yes?

Lorenti was demanding and scarily intense, and pretending to be his wife, even in public, was going to be much more of a challenge than she had originally anticipated. But she also knew he had always intrigued her. And agreeing to do this felt weirdly exhilarating as well as intimidating.

While she knew this arrangement wasn't personal for him—despite those devastatingly intense looks, which he probably sent to all women—leaving Westwick, agreeing to see new places, to do new things, would push her way outside her comfort zone. And maybe she needed that, just a little.

Until this moment, she hadn't realised that in many ways she'd been hiding here. Her non-existent love life since college was a case in point…and quite possibly the only reason she was so ridiculously susceptible to those intense looks.

She sucked in a breath and went with her gut instinct, instead of succumbing to the panic making her throat hurt. 'Okay, I guess I can live with that.'

He nodded, then opened his laptop. 'Then I will see you in Milan in two days' time,' he murmured gruffly.

She turned to go, determined not to be hurt by the curt dismissal. But as she walked out of the library on unsteady legs, she felt weirdly like a completely different person than she had when she'd walked in here—could it really have been less than thirty minutes ago?

She was nowhere near as sure of herself and her place in the world, but maybe she was also a bit less artless and gullible and unsophisticated.

Which had to be a good thing. Because handling this dangerous man and his demands, possibly for a whole year, felt fraught with a lot of risks…

Even if it got her the reward she'd hoped for, for so long.

CHAPTER FIVE

Two days later

'SIGNOR LORENTI WILL be here at six to escort you to the opera, Signora Whittaker. The stylist and her team will arrive at four to dress you.'

Another stylist! Seriously?

Tali tried not to scream, or look ungrateful, but after forty-eight hours of being prodded and poked and told what to do, she was utterly exhausted. And frustrated... And closing in on feeling completely overwhelmed.

She'd arrived in Italy less than an hour ago—on Lorenti Corp's private jet, which had been disconcerting enough—and then been taken in a chauffeur-driven car to this penthouse apartment, which Lorenti owned in Milan's Brera district.

As the car had wound its way past the cobbled alleyways flanked by historic terraces built in an eclectic mix of Renaissance and Baroque architectural styles, she'd spotted luxury boutiques side by side with bustling sidewalk cafes and upscale food emporiums. The artsy crowd frequenting them had looked as chic and stylish as their surroundings—and intimidating to a woman who had barely been out of Wiltshire in the past five years.

She hadn't needed Aldo to tell her this area was one of the most exclusive in the city. The luxury furniture and sleek, expensive design of the huge penthouse apartment, which would be her home for the next ten days, and the colonnaded stone balcony beyond, were even more intimidating.

She wished she could be more grateful. But she felt so far out of her depth at this point, and so anxious and stressed, it was hard to appreciate anything—least of all a visit from *another* stylist in less than two hours' time.

The last two days had been endless rounds of appointments with hairdressers, and beauticians, and fashion buyers, and stylists, as well as all the meetings Lorenti had warned her about with his legal team—who had begun to arrive at Westwick Hall less than an hour after she'd made her devil's bargain with Lorenti, and he'd left.

She had been buffed and plucked and waxed and dressed to within an inch of her life while busy being informed about what Lorenti required of her, and reading and signing a ton of legal documents. In between all that, she'd barely had the time to prepare Ellie and the rest of her team for her sudden departure—not to mention to explain to everyone at Westwick, without lying *too* much, exactly what was going on with her and Lorenti. And why she was suddenly leaving for Italy for who knew how long.

Her mum, of course, had refused to buy the love-at-first-sight story which she had hastily concocted—and which had fooled the staff.

'This happened in the space of half an hour? Really Tali, I know he's a handsome man, and you were always fascinated with him as a little girl, but that doesn't sound like a good basis for a relationship, honey.'

Tali had been forced to come clean about the deal she'd struck with the Hall's owner—and then sworn her mum to secrecy. Because the very first form the legal team had insisted she sign, before the sixty-page pre-nuptial agreement even, had been a non-disclosure agreement forbidding her from divulging to anyone that her marriage to Lorenti was not genuine.

'*Grazie*, Aldo,' Tali said as she dropped her bag onto the living area's expensive four-seater sofa. That would be the battered rucksack she had packed with a few clothes of her own, to wear in her downtime, when she wasn't wearing the four suitcases sitting in the hallway full of carefully co-ordinated outfits the London buyer had supplied her with.

'Do you know what opera we're seeing?' she asked, trying to drum up some enthusiasm for the night ahead…and not freak-out completely at the thought of seeing Lorenti again when she already felt overwhelmed.

She'd never been to an actual opera. Surely tonight would be exciting, once she stopped stressing about how everyone at Westwick was going to cope without her, and whether her mother would keep the secret she'd entrusted her with long enough not to get them both sued. And how on earth she was going to persuade any of the glamourous, stylish people Dario Lorenti probably socialised with in Milan that he would choose to marry a farmgirl from Wiltshire?

'I do not, Signora, do you wish me to find out?' Aldo asked, looking apologetic. Lorenti's assistant—who had been so impatient during their first meeting—had turned out to be surprisingly helpful, carefully co-ordinating her many meetings and appointments in the last two days, so she'd had at least some spare time to do her *actual* job.

'Don't bother.' She sighed. Or rather, what *she* considered to be her actual job, even if Lorenti had made it very clear during their one meeting that Westwick Hall was no longer her priority. Because being at his beck and call was her job now…

Buck up, Tali, you're just stressed and confused and hopelessly out of your depth. You'll adapt, you always do. And this is only for a year. Securing Westwick's future is worth it.

Although after forty-eight hours of being at Lorenti's beck and call—without him even being in the same country—she was beginning to realise what an enormous commitment she'd signed up for. Who knew being a fake trophy wife would be this much work? And all of it so utterly vacuous and unfulfilling—because since when was getting your eyebrows threaded or trying on hundreds of designer outfits a viable job?

'It'll be a nice surprise,' she added.

'Shall I request the apartment's chef make you a meal before you leave?'

'There's a chef?' She searched the state-of-the-art kitchen on the other side of the open space—scared a cordon bleu chef was about to jump out and intimidate her even more.

'Yes, Signora. Your staff live in the rooms below.'

My staff? There was more than one person to wait on her. *Oh god!*

The anxiety which had been making it hard to breathe for days contracted around her lungs like a vice.

'I requested they leave you to rest,' Aldo said gently. 'But if you would prefer to eat…'

'No, Aldo, I'm good, really. I'm not hungry.' Because… Nerves! 'I'm just going to crash until the stylist arrives. You've been amazing. I really appreciate all your help over the last few days.'

The man went a dull shade of red. 'It is my job, Signora,' he said, before giving her a stiff bow and leaving.

Good to know one of us has a proper job.

She stared after Aldo as the apartment door closed. Had she embarrassed him? She hadn't intended to. But she guessed this was just another example of how ill-suited she was to the role Lorenti had hired her for. She knew precisely nothing about navigating this level of privilege, even though she'd grown up on the grounds of a stately home.

Chill, Tali. Having a personal chef isn't scary... It's just a bit much. You'll get used to it...eventually.

Kicking off her shoes, she wandered to the balcony and opened the ornate glass door to step onto the cool marble tiles of a huge terrazzo. Propping her elbows on the stone balustrade, she peered across the rooftops towards Milan's Centro Storico nearby—and spied the cloistered splendour of the Palazzo Brera art gallery in the neighbouring square which Aldo had pointed out when they'd arrived. She took a moment to ease her breathing, control the anxiety and absorb the sights and sounds of this beautiful, vibrant city.

This was an adventure. She had never been to Italy before, and while the Milanese were intimidatingly chic, she would need to find a way to relax and enjoy this experience—or she'd end up having a heart attack. Plus, Ellie had her on speed dial if she needed her. She'd managed to hire Ellie an assistant which Lorenti was paying for, *and* she planned to check in with the Hall's new acting estate manager every single morning.

She still had no idea why Lorenti had picked her for this job, and maybe that was what was stressing her out. Unfortunately, thinking of Lorenti brought back the memory of his turbulent gaze, and the sensations which had sprinted up her arm and deep into her belly the first—and only—time he had touched her.

She shivered, despite the warmth of the spring day, and folded her arms around her body, then headed into the apartment, intending to take a shower—a cold one.

This was a fake marriage. He and his legal team had made that very clear. He didn't want more, nor would he, and neither did she. And while the thought of seeing him again in a few hours' time was making the inappropriate heat in her abdomen glow alarmingly and kicking her stress levels back into the danger zone, surely their first public appearance would be a good opportunity to start establishing their working relationship. And stop her fixating on the weird physical response she'd had to him in the library—which had to be a layover from all the other emotions he'd bombarded her with that afternoon. And nothing whatsoever to do with the awareness in his eyes, which she was convinced now had all been in her far-too-vivid imagination.

Dario used his key fob to enter the penthouse apartment he owned across the square from his own residence, annoyed by the buzz of anticipation in his gut, which must surely be a symptom of his unprecedented reaction to Tallulah Whittaker two days ago. It was a reaction he had spent the last forty-eight hours determined to quash.

He tucked his hands into the pockets of his tuxedo pants, aware of his accelerated heartbeat—not to mention the warmth in his abdomen—at the thought of seeing the girl again.

Assurdo!

What on earth was the matter with him? He had hired the girl on a whim, to fix a problem which had been weighing on him for seven years. Nothing more. She had intrigued him—her passion for her job, that sheen of naivete which clung to her, and her obvious awareness of him—more than she should. Perhaps because his encounters with women over the years had become so jaded, her unguarded reactions had been refreshing. But while she was undeniably pretty, her eyes a striking blue which had reminded him of the sea in Amalfi, her figure had been hidden beneath shapeless clothes, and her appearance hardly remarkable.

Two older women appeared, carrying a garment bag and a box of cosmetics. They must be the team Aldo had hired to prepare Tallulah for her debut as his fiancée tonight.

'Signor Lorenti,' one of them said, sending him an enthusiastic smile. 'Your fiancée is waiting for you on the terrazzo. She wished for some air before your arrival,' she added, her gaze skating over him, the appreciative twinkle one Dario had become accustomed to from women, young and old, despite his ruined face.

'Congratulations on your engagement,' the other said. 'You will make a very striking couple tonight.'

He gave them both a curt nod as they let themselves out of the apartment, oddly ambivalent at the news of Tallulah's transformation.

He had told Aldo to hire the best stylists and beauticians in the business in both London and Milan to ensure his 'bride to be' would look the part tonight—so he should be glad to hear they had done their job. The engagement announcement had been released two hours ago—with some concocted story about them becoming acquainted on his non-existent trips to his family estate in the UK over the past two years—so there would be no going back on this arrangement.

Even so, a confusing sensation joined the weight in his gut as he walked towards the apartment's terrazzo—anticipation.

He dismissed the sensation, which reminded him unhelpfully of being a young, untried boy on Capri besotted with the beautiful models and actresses who had frequented his mother's parties.

He stepped onto the terrace and spotted the young woman standing with her back to him, staring into the sunset. The blue satin dress, which stopped far too high up her thigh, seemed to mould to her bottom, displaying it like an offering, while the jewelled heels she wore made her toned legs look about a mile long.

The idea of those legs wrapped around his waist turned the anticipation to harsh, desperate need. He breathed through the intense reaction.

She wore a matching jacket, her hair piled on top of her head and held with an array of jewelled pins. Diamond earrings sparkled in the dying sunlight. No doubt they matched the ring in a box in his jacket pocket which the stylist had sent over that morning, but which he hadn't even looked at.

Just props, to make this engagement appear real.

He coughed, to alert Tallulah to his presence, his throat so dry it felt like sandpaper.

She spun round, clutching a small purse. The jacket had no buttons, revealing the gown's bodice, a concoction of satin and transparent lace which cupped her breasts—drawing his attention to the petal-soft skin of her cleavage, far too much of which was on display.

Che cazzo?

Raw desire burst through his veins—like a river in full flood, swelling the heat in his groin and making him stiffen with a devastating combination of shock, awe and possessive fury.

Although the cocktail gown was undoubtedly stylish, it was nothing short of indecent. Tallulah Whittaker had been transformed from the artless girl he recalled—in muddy jeans and a shapeless shirt—into a sex goddess to rival La Loren herself in her heyday.

What the hell had the stylist been thinking, dressing a woman who belonged to him in an outfit that would display her charms to every other man within a ten-mile radius?

Except she is not yours, Lorenti. This is just for show.

The voice of reason whispered in his head but was drowned out by the thunder of blood in his ears, which was heading south so fast it was making him light-headed.

'Mr Lorenti,' she murmured, her voice unsteady, unsure. 'Is everything okay?'

Her lips glistened in the twilight as she spoke, painted with some kind of gloss. The fierce desire to cover that wide mouth with his and thrust his tongue deep made his temper flare alongside the lust.

He marched across the terrace, only vaguely aware of the stiffness in his leg.

She blinked, the glittering make-up on her lids making her wide eyes look even bigger and more guileless. The deep blue of her irises matched the clinging fabric of her dress, which seemed even more indecent the closer he got.

He paused. The shocked awareness on her face reminded him of that artless girl in battered jeans and a shapeless shirt. Her wide-eyed reaction and the familiar grinding pain in his leg were enough to contain the fire in his gut from burning out of control...*just*.

'You don't like the dress?' she asked, clutching the purse too tightly, then bit into her bottom lip, sending another devastating shaft of heat to his already heavy cock.

He forced himself to breathe, and stop glaring, although he could not be held responsible for the furrow on his brow which was fast becoming a crater.

'It is more revealing than I expected,' he said, on a growl of disapproval.

She tensed as if she'd been struck.

And his anger returned. Although he knew the cause of his displeasure wasn't only disapproval of her attire, or not precisely. That would have been so much easier to handle. No, he was glowering at her because of the dawning realisation that he was going to struggle to keep this relationship professional for a week, let alone a year. The urgent, animalistic desire barely concealed by his tux jacket had already made him lose sight of what this damn arrangement had been supposed to achieve.

'It's not appropriate for the opera?' she asked, her concern obvious as she glanced at the dress and smoothed a trembling hand over the short skirt.

Fuck the opera! I don't wish anyone to see that much of you, except me.

The reply roared in his head, but he managed to prevent it from flying out of his mouth, barely aware not only that it would sound deranged, but that it was also unprecedented. Since when did he give a damn how much skin his dates had on display?

Concern shadowed her wide blue eyes, while her lip trembled.

He ground his teeth to get a grip on his reaction.

This wasn't her fault. She hadn't picked the damn dress— that would have been the stylist he'd paid a small fortune for.

'I'm sorry, I didn't...' she mumbled, looking panicked. 'Madame Rosa said this style is all the rage. Do you want me to change?' she asked. 'There's about a thousand other dresses in my luggage. I'm sure I can find something less revealing.'

But as she went to rush past him, he clamped a hand on her wrist. Raw sensation ricochetted up his arm, reminding him of when he'd touched her before. And the spark of arousal flared. *Terrific.*

'Wait,' he grunted, his tone sharp with demand, as he struggled to control his febrile reaction. 'There is not time.'

He could make time, of course. He owned a corporate box at the opera house, and if they arrived late, it would only make their story more convincing. Everyone would assume he had been availing himself of his fiancée's undeniably spectacular charms. But the violent need coursing through his system made it clear to him that he had to get out of this apartment. Because controlling the yearning to discover exactly what was under that damn dress was already tormenting enough.

'Are you sure? It's no trouble, Mr Lorenti. It's not really my style anyway...'

'Yes, I am positive...' he snapped, his temper fraying, along with his self-control. Then he noticed the pulse pumping against the delicate well of her collarbone.

What would it feel like, to kiss her there? How would she react, if he feasted on the thin skin, and marked her as his for every other man to see?

'And stop calling me Mr Lorenti, Tallulah,' he added.

She stiffened at the harsh tone. He released her wrist and tried to gentle his voice.

'We are supposed to be engaged, the press release went out hours ago,' he managed, trying to contain the burst of temper, and the vision which had popped into his head unbidden and was only making matters in his pants even more pressing, literally. 'You must call me Dario.'

'Right, sorry, Mr Loren... I—I mean Dario.' She dipped her chin to her chest, the blush highlighting her cheeks, making him feel like a brute. 'I'm making a mess of this already.'

The defeated tone and the unnecessary apology finally pierced the haze of lust. His rampaging heartbeat slowed—slightly—as well as the fierce flow of blood charging beneath his belt.

Damn it, Dario. Stop behaving like an arsehole. None of this is her doing.

She did not even appear to realise the effect she was having on him.

'There is no need to apologise,' he managed.

He tucked a knuckle under her chin and raised her gaze to his. The feel of her skin was so soft, he had to force himself to drop his hand, instead of stroking her neck, and tracing a line through her cleavage, to circle the hard bud of her nipple pressing against the satin.

'You have done nothing wrong.'

She nodded, although he could see the wary, guarded expression and knew she did not believe him.

Dio, what was happening to him? He prided himself on always keeping his emotional responses on lockdown, of being sophisticated, cynical and self-reliant. He *never* let anyone see the side of him which had once struggled to contain those emotions. As a boy, he'd been far too needy, far too desperate for friendship and affection after his mother's death. It was why he had attracted people like Sante, who were only too happy to exploit him. But it had always been remarkably easy not to care, not to need anyone after Sante's betrayal...

Until this precise moment.

It is of no importance. This is lust, pure and simple. Something that will be easily contained—once it has been satisfied.

Because it was already obvious that his unprecedented reaction to this woman would have to be satisfied eventually. He'd never experienced such a strong physical connection to a woman. But he had no intention of satisfying it yet, not when he was so on edge—barely clinging onto the cast-iron control he had always relied on during his past relationships.

There was no doubt in his mind, he and Tallulah would sleep together—her lust-blown pupils, engorged nipples and catapulting pulse making it clear she was no more immune to this volatile chemistry than he was.

He had sensed it in Wiltshire but had tried to deny it. Partly because he had no desire to make this arrangement any more complicated than it had to be, but mostly because he had never been led around by his cock before.

He enjoyed sex. A lot. He always had. He was a workaholic and considered it a valuable—and time-efficient—way to relax. As a result, he considered himself a generous and accomplished lover. The women he dated had certainly never complained about the physical aspect of their relationships. Of course, he'd been accused of being cold, and insensitive to their emotional needs, but as soon as that became an issue, he considered it his cue to end the relationship. What some women had failed to believe, once he had dated them more than a few times, was that he genuinely had no desire for any kind of intimacy beyond the physical.

Unfortunately, though, dumping Tallulah once they had satisfied this hunger would not be so easy, because he had employed her to pretend to be madly in love with him… for a year.

Once they had burned out this firestorm of lust, he would end their private relationship, but ending their public one would be impossible—until he had persuaded the Westwick Trustees he had adhered to the terms of his father's will. And knowing how damn contrary those old fools were, he doubted that would happen to his timetable.

All of which meant he would have to manage this situation, so that when he and his fake wife *did* become intimate, Tallulah did not misconstrue their sexual connection for something more.

The possibility that their livewire chemistry might have contributed to his impulsive decision to employ her as his wife in the first place could not be discounted now. The lowering thought was sobering enough to give him some relief from the insistent heat building in his pants.

'The car is waiting downstairs,' he said, determined to get her out of the damn apartment before the respite evaporated.

But when he placed his hand on the small of her back, to direct her out of the apartment, her shiver of reaction echoed viciously in his groin.

As they travelled down in the apartment's private elevator, with her looking subdued, and him straining to recapture his usual control, he grimaced at the thought of the night ahead…when he was going to be forced to watch *La traviata* with her in a private box and persuade everyone that they were already lovers, all while figuring out how to make her his lover for real, without screwing up the whole purpose of this relationship.

The brutal irony did not escape him.

But far worse was the challenge of pretending to be a besotted lover—already a stretch for a man like him, who did not have a romantic or flirtatious bone in his body—while unrequited desire was pounding in his groin like a jackhammer, and the scent of wildflowers which clung to her was threatening to send his senses into another tailspin. And that was without even factoring in the extremely tenuous hold he already had on his temper, as he imagined every single man in the Teatro alla Scala being treated to a virtually uninterrupted view of his new fiancée's breasts.

As he watched the tiny skirt ride up even more of her thigh as she entered the waiting limo, he bit his tongue to contain the renewed wave of possessive fury—and raw hunger—and made himself a promise.

First thing tomorrow morning, Madame Rosa was getting fired.

CHAPTER SIX

Tali settled into the shadowy interior of the chauffeur-driven limousine, aware of Lorenti's forceful—and disapproving—presence as he folded his tall frame into the seat beside her.

Clearly, she'd screwed up with the dress. Or rather, Madame Rosa had, because his reaction to it had been nothing short of disastrous. His gaze had been more searing on the apartment balcony, when she'd turned to find him standing behind her—looking totally devastating in the black tux—than it had been forty-eight hours ago in Wiltshire. But with none of the humour.

The nerves in her stomach tangled. Had she ever felt more hideously out of place in her entire life? She certainly didn't think so. And she wasn't talking about the butt-skimming skirt or the semi-see-through top of her opera outfit.

The truth was, she'd been horrified too, when she'd first seen what Madame Rosa was proposing she wear for the evening. The expensive designer couture was so unlike her usual style—which always leaned towards comfort and practicality. Even on the rare occasions when she took a night off work to go to the local pub she usually just shucked on a clean pair of jeans and a nice shirt. But an opening night at Milan's legendary opera house was hardly quiz night at the Talbot Arms—so she had sucked up her discomfort and agreed to the stylist's suggestion.

But once she'd seen her reflection in the mirror and Madame Rosa and the beautician Clara had complimented her profusely on her appearance, the knot in her belly had dissolved at least a little, despite her nerves.

Maybe she didn't look like herself anymore, or the self she had always known, but the smoky, professionally applied eye make-up, the gleaming lip gloss, the gown's chic style and expert detailing, the diamond drop earrings which dangled against her neck, the elaborate chignon the hairstylist had managed to tease her insane curls into…and those elegant heels! All of it had the wow factor, even she could see that… She'd felt exposed, sure, but also like she might have some chance of persuading Milan's finest that Tali Whittaker had somehow caught the eye of a man as successful and compelling as the city's foremost tech billionaire. So there was that.

But then Lorenti had arrived and instead of being wowed too by the efforts of the designer and the beautician and the hairdresser, he had looked startled and then…well, outraged. His gaze had raked over her, and those rich chocolate eyes had gone dark and stormy with discontent.

She'd been crushed, the anxiety tying her guts back into hard, greasy knots. Not least because his volatile reaction had also made the hot knot in her belly—which seemed to always be there whenever she was in his company—sink even further into her sex.

But as the chauffeur closed the door and the car drove off into the nighttime traffic, the bristling silence that reverberated around the luxury leather interior like a physical force had her crippling embarrassment and confusion giving way to dismay…and irritation.

Lorenti had hired *her* to do this job. He'd even hired the stylist and the beautician and the hairstylist, or at least he was paying for them. In ten minutes—traffic allowing—they were going to have to pretend to be madly in love. And yet he was sitting on the opposite side of the car staring broodily out of the window at the crowds of stylish Italians, refusing to even look at her. Sulking, basically. If he wanted this arrangement to work, he was going to have to meet her halfway. He moved effortlessly through the circles of Europe's elite—the people he was expecting her to impress—people whose lifestyle she knew sod-all about. If he wanted to persuade any of them she was his chosen bride, he was going to have to help. Because no way in hell could she pull this off on her own.

She cleared her throat to dislodge the lump of anxiety and forced herself to take the bull by the horns.

'I'm sorry if you hate the dress, Mr Lorenti. But you're going to have to look at me—and pretend you don't hate it, and me in it—when we get to the opera. Or no one on earth is going to believe you want to touch me, let alone marry me.'

He turned towards her. His eyes flared, the chocolate brown turning to a molten gold. But weirdly what she saw in his gaze wasn't the contempt she'd expected…but something much more confusing—and frankly, dangerous.

'I told you to call me Dario,' he said, but the clipped command was softened by the husky tone. His molten gaze coasted over her exposed skin like a physical caress and turned the weight between her thighs into a boulder. A very hot boulder. 'And the issue is not that I hate the dress, but that I like it far too much.'

Finally, his gaze landed on her face, the heat in it as searing as the sensation now pulsing between her thighs.

'No one will believe I do not wish to touch you, when the problem I currently have is how I am going to stop myself from stripping you out of that damn dress during three solid hours of opera.'

'Oh…' she murmured, shocked not just by his directness, and the harsh appreciation in his expression, but how it made sensation flare across her skin like wildfire. 'Well,

I guess that's a good thing then. That it won't be hard for you to pretend to…'

'I will not be pretending.' His lips twisted in a rueful smile that was almost as exhilarating as the heady leap in her heart rate. 'But it will definitely be hard,' he said, the deliberate double entendre somehow diffusing the tension, while also ramping it up to fever pitch.

Her gaze dropped to his lap entirely of its own accord. And she spotted a bulge in his lap, barely disguised by the loose-fitting suit trousers.

Leaning across the seat, he tucked a knuckle under her chin and lifted her gaze away from the evidence of his reaction. 'Be careful, Tallulah, or I may test my resolve right here in the limousine.'

She blinked, aware of the flush scouring her cheeks. The erotic promise in his eyes was so potent, she crossed her legs instinctively—which instantly made matters worse, when the pulsing between her thighs became catastrophic.

'And that would be bad?' she murmured, the cheeky challenge coming out before she could stop it.

His brows lifted, and she knew she'd surprised him again, which felt oddly empowering. But then his lips curved. The urbane, arrogant smile was matched by the feral light in his eyes—which carried an erotic threat so potent the pulsing in her panties got worse.

'That would be up to you,' he said as his thumb trailed down her neck. The tantalising caress eased over her throat as she gulped, traced her collarbone, then dipped to skim across her breast and tease the tight bud of her nipple.

She gasped, the brutal dart of sensation at the light touch making her swollen clitoris throb so hard she was astonished she didn't pass out.

'Tell me you wish to explore our chemistry, Tallulah, and we can forget about the opera.'

Oh, yes please.

The thought blasted into her brain, but right behind it was the surge of panic when he added, 'But be aware, it would change the terms of our arrangement. As once I have had you, I very much doubt I will want to let you go for a while.'

The dark determination in his eyes, and the way his thumb continued to toy with her nipple, had the urge to say yes getting locked in her throat.

Even through the delicate fabric, his touch felt so sure, so certain, so confident. While her response—the urge to arch her back and offer him more—was so wild and instinctive it scared her.

Sleeping with Dario Lorenti would push her even further out of her comfort zone. What did she know about the sort of sexual liaison he was talking about? Even less than she knew about Europe's cultural elite, frankly.

And that was before she factored in her incendiary response to his slightest touch.

The driving need, the desperate hunger felt far too needy—and completely out of her control. Because she didn't know him. Plus, she was still anxious about being able to fulfil the role he was *actually* paying her for. Adding sex to the mix wouldn't exactly simplify the situation… And it was unlikely to cure her performance anxiety either, given he was clearly a lot more experienced than she was. Despite the enormous bulge in his pants, he didn't seem to be anywhere near as on edge. This would still be just an 'arrangement' to him. And while a part of her knew becoming his stunt wife with benefits would help make their charade more convincing—would she still feel like a stunt wife if she slept with him, given that she was so much less jaded and worldly than him?

She covered her breast with a shaky palm, and his touch dropped away.

'I… I don't think that would be a good idea,' she managed.

Or at least not yet, her needy body qualified. Not until she was sure she could control her emotions, the way he seemed able to control his so effortlessly.

Staying out of Dario Lorenti's bed—especially if he continued to look at her as he was now, as if he wanted to devour her in a few greedy bites—was going to be an even bigger challenge than persuading Italian high society he would pick *her* to be his wife.

Instead of looking annoyed, or even irritated, he simply nodded. 'As you wish, Tallulah.'

That harsh, heady gaze remained on her burning cheeks though, as he reached into his jacket pocket and produced a velvet box.

'But there is something that I want you to understand…' he continued.

He flipped open the box, revealing a beautifully crafted silver ring with a diamond solitaire in the centre. The gemstone glinted in the lights from the passing streetlamps as the car inched through the traffic towards the opera house.

Lifting the ring out of the velvet, he discarded the box.

He took her trembling fingers in his and slid on the exquisite engagement ring. It fit perfectly, because of course it did.

'Whatever you decide, Tallulah, you are mine now, until the conclusion of our arrangement,' he said. 'And I will not allow you to wear something so revealing again…' Those dark eyes met hers, the erotic promise becoming a tantalising erotic threat. 'For anyone but me.'

She shuddered, her throat drying to parchment at the authority in his voice, her nipples so hard now they could probably drill a hole to China.

She should tell him he was only paying for her co-operation in public, that he had no right to dictate what she wore in private—for him or anyone else. But she couldn't seem to unstick the words from her throat. Because no man had ever looked at her like that before. As if the only person he could see in that moment was her.

But when he lifted her fingers to his lips to brush a kiss across her knuckles, the heat in her sex rose to wrap around her heart, and she trembled violently.

As soon as he released her, she buried her fist in her lap, the delicate ring heavy on her finger, her skin burning where his lips had touched.

This wasn't a real engagement any more than it would be a real marriage—whatever they decided to do in private. So why did his possessive statement feel so compelling, as well as completely outrageous?

Tali, get a clue.

As the car stopped on the historic opera house's courtyard, the breath Tali had been holding expelled from her lungs.

She could see the photographers through the tinted glass, crowding around the red carpet laid out on the cobbled stones for the opening night. The Teatro alla Scala's elegant and imposing façade dated back to 1778. All of Italy's greatest composers had presented their work here, from Puccini to Verdi to Toscanini, she'd discovered while investigating what they would be seeing tonight on the internet. But somehow, as she stepped out onto the red carpet, and watched Dario buttoning his tux jacket to disguise the erection she'd caused, the flashes from phone lights and camera lenses, the questions shouted in Italian from the local celebrity hacks eager to ask about their 'engagement' and the thought of seeing her first-ever opera, were nowhere near as overpowering as the feel of Dario's large palm resting on her back. Or the fierce need having a field day in her panties. Or the sparkle of the diamond engagement ring on her finger which was supposed to be a prop for their fake marriage but now felt more like a mark of his ownership.

CHAPTER SEVEN

Ten days later

'THE FEATURE WRITER is with Signor Lorenti, Signora Whittaker,' Aldo announced as Tali stepped from the lift into Dario's palatial apartment.

She smoothed down the demure skirt-and-blouse combo the new stylist had recommended for the interview with Italy's top-selling glossy women's magazine. It didn't do much to control her rampaging heartbeat though. She'd been stressing about this interview ever since Aldo had informed her it had been set up two days ago.

Of course, she had no idea why Dario—who, according to the few things she'd read about him on the internet, had never even given an interview to a tech journalist before now—would agree to something this intrusive. But, as usual, he'd deflected her questions the night before.

She hadn't pressed because she was already struggling with a severe case of sexual frustration, which had kept her awake every night for over a week—becoming more persistent after each evening she had to spend in his company. In the last ten days, since she'd arrived in Italy, she'd only had one night when Dario wasn't escorting her to some new event, or opening, or exclusive party. And annoyingly, that night had been worse than the others, because she'd actually missed the infuriating man. Which was preposterous, because they weren't in a real relationship.

There had been no repeat of his proposition in the limousine on the way to the opera. In fact, he had barely spoken to her on the rare occasions when they had been alone together since. He hadn't set foot inside her apartment since that first night, always waiting in the car now when collecting her. And she'd never visited his apartment, until now.

When they were together for the short drive to whatever event they needed to be 'seen' at, he kept the dividing screen down so the chauffeur could hear every word—almost as if he wanted to ensure nothing could happen between them. But once they stepped into the glare of the public spotlight, his fierce gaze, those possessive, provocative touches that he was a master of—his hand gripping her waist, his palm resting on her back, the light brush of his lips against her neck as he whispered something in her ear like a besotted lover—had begun to drive her insane.

Of course, his behaviour around her in public was all part of the subterfuge they had agreed to. But occasionally, she caught him watching her with that fierce desire in his eyes, and she knew he still wanted her... And unfortunately, whenever he stood too close, and she inhaled the intoxicating scent of sea salt and lemons from his cologne, or felt his gaze on her, she knew their 'chemistry' was still there. And getting worse. Because she wanted him too, desperately.

The thought of sitting through an interview with a journalist, though, filled her with dread. Not only had she never spoken to the press before, she wasn't sure why he had decided to include her. There were so many ways she could screw this up. But when she'd told him about her concerns in the car last night, Dario had simply shrugged and murmured, 'Do not concern yourself, it will be conducted mostly in Italian. All you need to do is look as if you want me.'

She sighed as Aldo led her through the huge penthouse apartment towards the living area. Well, at least *that* wouldn't be a struggle—after the dreams which had been waking her in the dark, hot and sweaty and desperate for those devastating touches in that darkened limo on their first date, which he had denied her since.

Dario stood when she entered the large open-plan living room. He looked tall and gorgeous in a pair of jeans and a black polo-neck sweater which clung to the impressive contours of his chest. Her heart stuttered, the familiar blush rising into her cheeks on cue. How could he be even more devastating in casual clothing than he was in a tux? How was that fair?

'*Ciao*, Tallulah,' he said, lifting her fingers to his lips, his gaze rivetted to her burning cheeks as he pressed his lips to her knuckles.

He introduced her to the journalist, an impeccably dressed older woman called Gianna Lombardi with a shrewd smile on her face. After congratulating them both on their recent engagement, Gianna placed a recording device on the coffee table between them while explaining how much her readers were looking forward to hearing the details of their whirlwind romance.

What details? She didn't have any details, because Dario hadn't briefed her for this interview.

Tali's nerves started to strangle her. Perhaps sensing her distress, Dario laid a steadying hand on her hip and directed her to sit beside him on the sofa. And suddenly it wasn't the prospect of the interview that made her heart reverberate in her chest, but the awareness of him, his arm placed casually across the back of the sofa behind her, the brush of his muscular denim-clad thigh against her bare leg boxing her in and the tantalising scent of citrus and man which engulfed her.

She swallowed, trying to focus on the journalist and look the part of a woman comfortable in her fiancé's presence, and disguise the fact her pulse had kicked up to warp speed and her nipples had begun to throb against her bra.

His fingers skimmed over her hair, and he leaned close to whisper in her ear. 'Relax, *tesoro*.'

Even though she knew his affectionate words were for the journalist's benefit, the husky tone had her giddy heartbeat sinking into her abdomen. She crossed her legs, trying to squeeze the brutal pulse of awareness between her thighs into submission, as the journalist watched them both like a raptor.

'Signora Whittaker is it true that you speak no Italian?' the journalist asked.

'Not much,' Tali replied, caught off guard by the random question. 'But I—I'm taking lessons,' she offered.

Dario's thigh tensed, and his fingers stilled on her hair.

The journalist let out a harsh laugh. 'You did not know this, Signor Lorenti?' the woman asked.

'Of course,' he lied smoothly. 'I suggested it and Tallulah is keen to learn.'

Tali glanced back at him. If he was surprised at the news, it was hard to tell, because his face had gone carefully blank. But his body language suggested he was nowhere near as relaxed as he had been when she'd arrived.

Had she made a mistake? So soon.

She hadn't told him about the lessons she'd arranged through Aldo, because she hadn't thought he'd mind. In fact, she'd hoped he might even be pleased, when she had more than a few basic phrases to rely on… And the truth was she'd enjoyed taking the classes with her tutor, Maria. The app she'd been using had been great for learning vocabulary, but she wanted to learn to speak the language. Plus, it helped fill up the long hours each day after she'd finished her morning session going over all the day's business with Ellie at Westwick and checking in with her mum…and before the stylist and her team arrived in the afternoon to dress her for her next 'date' with Dario.

She'd always been active and busy, and there were only so many books she could read or long walks through the Brera she could go on. Plus, not being able to converse in Italian made her feel at even more of a disadvantage in Dario's world.

'I'm enjoying the lessons, it's a beautiful language,' she added when Dario remained ominously silent.

'This is good, yes,' the journalist said absently, but then her gaze shifted to Dario and sharpened. 'But, still, it is surprising you have fallen in love with a British woman, Signor Lorenti,' the woman said, still speaking in English, the shrewd smile becoming positively sly, the implied criticism of Dario's choice hard for anyone to miss.

'Why would this be a surprise?' Dario replied, his voice calm, but Tali could hear the frigid note of disapproval. His hand swept down her back, to settle on her hip, the intimate touch making her shiver. 'Tallulah is accomplished in many things, and exceptionally beautiful, what man could want more in a wife?'

The journalist's expression became flat and direct. 'And yet, you have never dated an Englishwoman before now. Everyone assumed you would marry an Italian, given your estrangement from your British father, Lord Westwick.'

'My father has been dead for seven years, Signora Lombardi,' Dario shot back, as his hand tightened on Tali's hip, signalling his fury at the line of questioning. 'He has no bearing on my choices, now or ever,' he finished, but the sharp tone couldn't disguise the fact he hadn't denied what she'd said.

While Tallulah had always known about Dario's difficult relationship with his father—given the man's absence from his gravely injured son's bedside during most of that summer and the cruel way he had spoken to him the one time he had visited him—Dario's volatile reaction now felt revealing in a way she hadn't expected.

Was it true? Had he deliberately *avoided* dating British women?

That he didn't want to discuss his dating preferences, or his father though was obvious, but the journalist refused to take the hint. Her eyes gleamed, like a shark's while going in for the kill.

'And yet, it is said he refused to allow you to speak Italian as a boy, after your mother died. That must have been extremely hard, as according to my sources you spoke very little English. But now you will have to speak English again when you wish to converse with your wife?'

Dario sat upright, the relaxed demeanour history, and said something to the woman in rapid Italian. Tali only caught a few words, one of which was the Italian for 'stop'—*fermare*. But she didn't need to fully understand what he was saying to know he was no longer disguising his anger at the line of questioning, especially when the woman's face went red. And she looked visibly shaken.

'*Mi scuso*, Signor Lorenti,' she said, the obsequious tone not doing much to reduce the tension snapping in the air. 'I am sorry, Signora Whittaker,' she added, sending Tali a strained smile, the smug look gone. 'Please accept my apologies.'

'Of course,' Tali replied, trying to smooth over the incident, and figure out what exactly the journalist was apologising for.

'We can continue,' Dario said, but the steel in his voice sounded anything but accommodating when he added, 'But questions about my father are not permitted.'

The rest of the interview was conducted in both Italian and English, the woman's fawning questions making it easy for Tali to stick to the story of their whirlwind romance without having to give the details she didn't have. But Dario's answers remained short, his tone curt, until Gianna mentioned Dario's sister, Mia, and the man she was due to marry—Sante Trovato—during a question in Italian. Tali thought it was an innocuous enquiry about Dario's intention to attend the wedding. At that point, though, his patience evaporated, and he cut the interview short.

The name Trovato sounded vaguely familiar to Tali. Was he one of Lorenti Corp's business rivals? Because Dario seemed almost as unhappy talking about his sister's groom as he had been discussing Lord Westwick.

As the journalist was shown out by Aldo, the woman looked a lot less confident than she had when Tali had first arrived. But as soon as the door to the salon closed behind her, Tali's shoulders sagged with relief. At least showtime was over.

Not that it had been a particularly successful showtime.

Dario strode to the apartment's elaborate terrazzo, his limp more pronounced than usual. Tali stood alone in the salon and watched him. Tension still bristled in the air. She could sense his displeasure in the stiff, unyielding stance, the silence which seemed to throb with anger. Whatever the interview was supposed to have achieved, it hadn't. She hoped she wasn't responsible for that…

She forced herself to swallow the questions she wanted to ask about Dario's impatient replies to the journalist's questions. His difficult relationship with Lord Westwick was none of her business, and neither was his apparent displeasure about the man his sister had chosen to marry. Although perhaps she'd misunderstood that. Because they were going to be attending the wedding. Surely, he would not have agreed to go to Sicily if he had some beef with Trovato?

'Well, that went well,' she murmured.

She turned to leave, feeling like an interloper, but as her heels clicked on the salon's polished wood flooring, a harsh demand echoed across the cavernous space.

'*Aspetta*, wait,' he said, his tone tight with frustration.

He walked towards her, his uneven gait doing nothing to slow his stride. But as his gaze locked on her face, her heartbeat throbbed into her throat.

Had she screwed up again? Because he did not look pleased. When he spoke, though, he said the last thing she had expected. 'There is no need for you to learn Italian, it is not part of our agreement.'

'I—I know,' she said. Why was he looking at her like that, as if she was a puzzle he could not solve?

His brows furrowed. 'Nor will ingratiating yourself with me increase my desire to invest in Westwick Hall.'

She flinched, the cutting remark like a physical blow.

While they had hardly become friends in the past week and a half—because he was even more unknowable now than he had been in Wiltshire—and the tormenting chemistry only added another layer of tension when they were together, which made it even harder to break down the barriers between them, she had believed he at least respected her.

Apparently, she'd been wrong.

The temper she'd been holding on to—during the hours she spent being dressed up like a mannequin, or whenever Aldo delivered another of Dario's demands without an explanation, or every time the hot pulse of awareness became unbearable while he toyed with her in public—exploded in her chest.

'Well, thanks, that's good to know!' she replied, each word dripping with sarcasm. 'You know, this gig would be a whole lot easier if you deigned to tell me what the hell you *actually* want, instead of treating me like an inconvenient accessory you have to pet in public but who you can't stand to even look at in private.'

That damned eyebrow rose, his expression still cynical, still unmoved.

'You know perfectly well why I will not touch you again in private,' he growled. 'Because it is torturous enough having to touch you in public. I have not had a good night's sleep for over a week.'

The edge in his voice, and the suggestion this was all her fault—*again*—had the last thin thread she had on her temper snapping in two.

'Oh, just shut up.' She took a breath, more than ready to let him have it with both barrels. 'You think you're the only one who can't sleep without imagining us together naked? News flash, you're not. And *you* were the one who started it,' she all but howled—not caring anymore if she sounded like a five-year-old having a temper tantrum. 'And FYI, it's not my fault that interview was a disaster, when you wouldn't even tell me what you wanted me to say to that woman. Or why you agreed to an interview in the first place when it's clearly not your happy place to be quizzed about your private life.'

'This marriage must appear real—so speaking to the press was necessary…' he replied, his jaw so tight now she was surprised he didn't crack a tooth. 'And FYI, *you* agreed to do this job. If you no longer want it, perhaps you should say so.'

'Uh-huh.' So, they were back to one of his bloody ultimatums, were they? She threw up her hands, having had enough of those, too. 'Well, FY *another* I, perhaps if you stopped behaving like an entitled arse and told me why you *need* this marriage, I wouldn't feel so out of my depth.'

She swung round, intending to storm out of the apartment, not caring anymore if he called a halt to the whole arrangement. She couldn't live under his constant disapproval any longer. Because it was not only driving her insane—it reminded her of that time in her life when she had felt rudderless and confused, desperate to understand why her father didn't love her the way he loved his other children, while being terrified of the possible answer to that question... That there was something intrinsically wrong with her, which made her less loveable, less worthy than them.

But before she had managed to go two paces, a hard hand clamped around her wrist.

'*Fermare!*' he said, as he hauled her around to face him. And suddenly she was inches from that hard chest, those vivid gold eyes glaring at her, but the expression in them was not anger, or condemnation...but the same furious, untamed hunger which had been torturing her for days.

'My father hated that I did not want his title, or his estate. So, he made it a requirement in his will that I marry an Englishwoman, to inherit the house he owned on Capri where I lived with my mother.' He said the words through gritted teeth. 'For seven years, I have tried to purchase Palazzo di Constanzo from my father's Trustees without succumbing to his blackmail. But I have invested a fortune in the property, and *still* they refuse to let me own it outright. *This* is why I need you as my wife...'

She shuddered, shocked he had confided in her, but even more shocked to see the shadow of hurt beneath the swirl of temper and fierce desire in those molten brown eyes. Because it reminded her of that surly, desperately unhappy teenager—injured and in pain—who had pushed her away so often that summer, like a wild animal caught in a trap.

The sense of connection, of shared pain, made her heart hammer her chest wall. The bite of temper disappeared until all she felt was compassion for the injured boy who still lurked inside the man. Maybe he really believed this marriage was about owning his mother's old home...and defying the man who had tried to keep it from him. But she doubted that was the whole story, however much he might want to believe it. Perhaps his desperation to own the palazzo was also a way of righting the wrongs his father had done to him. All those years ago. She knew how that felt, because she'd spent so long fantasising herself, about making her father regret discarding her, as well.

And to think she had convinced herself in the past two weeks that that boy had become a cold man, who felt nothing.

She pressed her palm to his scarred face, hoping to soothe, desperate to heal.

'Your father sounds like an even bigger prick than mine,' she managed. 'You deserved better, and so did I.'

The muscle in his cheek jumped and flexed against her palm, but then he flinched and let her go. Swearing under his breath, he walked back to the terrace.

He stood with his back to her, staring out at the late-afternoon sun. But his stance lacked the rigid control which had always intimidated her.

She followed him out onto the balcony. 'Is it true? What the journalist said? That he wouldn't allow you to speak Italian?' Maybe she had no right to ask, but suddenly she wanted to know exactly how bad it had been for him. Because while her father had chosen to be absent for much of her life, she had always had her mum. While Dario, it seemed, had had no one to protect him.

He shrugged, but the movement was far too stiff to be nonchalant. 'I do not require your pity,' he said, his tone brusque again.

She sighed. *So that would be a yes, then.*

'All I require is that you do the job I have asked of you,' he continued. 'And I did not ask you to learn Italian.'

Why was he so hung up on her decision to learn the language he obviously loved and preferred to use—especially if his father had used English as a means of punishment when he was a boy? It made no sense. But she forced herself to take a mental step back.

She'd always been too willing to believe the best of people, too desperate to want to heal anything and everything she thought might be wounded, or sad, or need her help. And she had the scars to prove it... All those nicks and scratches caused by the wild animals who had quite literally ended up biting the hand that had tried to feed them... Her mum had called it her Miss Fix-it complex.

Dario Lorenti wasn't that lonely boy now. He was a man who guarded his pain as vehemently as he guarded his privacy. And he'd made it very clear he didn't value her sympathy.

'Do you really want me to stop the lessons?' she asked, carefully.

She didn't want to give them up, for so many reasons—one of which was she didn't want him to resent having to speak to her in English... Which was so screwed up considering he was the one insisting she stop. But Dario was paying for the tutor Aldo had hired, so if he asked her to stop, she would have to.

He turned, and the perplexed frown on his face had the sympathy squeezing her ribs again. Did he even know why this was troubling him so much?

'I have said it is not necessary.'

'I know, but... I'm enjoying the lessons—they're a lot more fun than having to get prodded and poked by the stylist. And I wasn't lying when I told Mrs Lombardi I think it's a beautiful language. Plus, it would totally make our love affair look more convincing...' She shrugged, starting to become wary herself of how much she wanted to continue to learn Italian. 'If I'm making the effort to learn your language, you know...' She stumbled to a halt. Was she making too big a deal of this? Because the yearning to speak to him in his native tongue felt like more than just a way to pass the time. Was she trying to please him without realising it? And to what end, when they both knew this relationship wasn't real?

He stared at her for the longest time, but then his lips curved, the half smile more rueful than amused. He brushed his thumb across her cheek and tucked a lock of hair behind her ear.

She shivered, the automatic response something she couldn't control as the unrequited yearning flared back to life. It was the first time he had touched her when she was alone with him since their charged moment in the limo ten days ago.

'I can think of a much better way to make our love affair more convincing,' he murmured, the low tone reverberating in all her pulse points. The promise in his eyes was as potent and provocative as it had been ten days ago...and just as terrifying.

She pressed a palm to her own cheek, aware of the sizzle of sensation where his thumb had cruised across her skin. She wanted to sleep with him, wanted to find out where this terrifying chemistry would lead, but she felt even more exposed now than she had ten days ago, the tiny glimpse into his past bringing back the fierce sense of connection she'd always felt for that surly, unhappy boy.

She nodded. 'I want you, too,' she admitted, because there was no point in denying it, especially as she'd already broken cover during their argument.

'I know,' he said.

He cradled her face in warm palms, his gaze fixed on hers, and lowered his head to slant his lips across hers.

She sobbed, shocked by the blast of heat and longing, as her mouth moulded to his. He took his own sweet time, tempting, tormenting, swallowing her sighs, absorbing the shimmer of fear. His lips were persuasive, firm, demanding, his tongue even more so as it pressed into her mouth.

She opened for him, her breathing already ragged, her sex already aching, her breasts trapped against his chest as the kiss turned from subtle to scorching in a heartbeat.

His fingers threaded into her hair, angling her head to take more, to take all. His lips commanding, controlling, his tongue delving deep, over and over, exploring, and exploiting each sigh, each sob, each shudder.

She could feel herself falling into the sensual fog, the dazed, dizzying desire, too much and yet not enough.

One hand gripped her bottom, to drag her against the thick ridge in his jeans. Her core melted, as she writhed against it, needing more, but scared to take it, to demand it. Her emotions were still in turmoil from their argument. And that weird sense of connection which felt so real.

She pressed her hands against his chest and pushed him away, more confused and wary than ever, even though the sensations shimmering through her bloodstream still fired her need.

He released her. His breathing was as harsh as her own, his face set in hard lines—his eyes a molten gold.

'I'm... I'm sorry,' she said. 'I'm sending you mixed messages and I don't mean to...' she managed around the desire and panic making her throat feel raw.

Of course, he'd kissed her. She'd told him she wanted him.

But instead of reacting angrily to her rejection, as she had feared, he brushed his thumb across her cheek again, then pressed it to her lips.

'Do not apologise,' he said. 'Are you a virgin, Tallulah?'

Embarrassment scorched her cheeks, at the direct question—and the potent hunger in his gaze.

'No... No, I'm not,' she said.

'But you have little experience, am I correct?' he asked again, the rueful tilt of his lips making the blush explode.

'Well...yes, I suppose so, compared to you,' she answered. What did he expect her to say? And why was he looking at her with indulgence, even affection? Because it was making her feel a whole lot more exposed, while he seemed to be in complete control again.

He let out a rough chuckle. But when he cupped her cheek there was no denying the fierce need in his expression, which matched her own. 'Then we must take this slowly. Because our passion is extraordinary...and I do not wish to hurt you.'

'Ummm, okay,' she said, pretty sure her cheeks were probably visible from outer space by now.

Pulling her closer, he pressed his lips to her burning forehead. 'You may continue with your Italian lessons.'

It took her a moment to figure out what he was talking about, her mind dazed from the endorphin high still powering through her system. 'Okay.'

'I will see you on Friday, for the trip to Sicily.'

She frowned. 'We don't have any other dates in Milan over the next two days?' she asked, pretty sure they were scheduled to attend an embassy party that evening, but her mind was still too fuzzy to remember the details.

Taking her hand, he led her towards the apartment's lift, then kissed her knuckles in that habitual gesture—which should have seemed perfunctory but made the heat rush through her all over again.

'I think it best we do not spend too much time alone together, until you are ready for more.'

'Okay,' she said again, like a dummy.

It wasn't until she'd stepped into the lift though and watched the doors close on him that it occurred to her the yearning in her sex had only got worse. She had agreed there would be more. Although she had no clue what 'more' entailed.

She rubbed her hand across her mouth, feeling the imprint of his lips on hers, the electrifying rasp of his stubble, the harsh demand of his tongue, the press of that huge erection against her belly. The mark of his ownership so much more elemental now than the diamond ring on her finger.

That the realisation was as exhilarating as it was terrifying only made the days ahead seem like more of a minefield… Because she had the sneaking suspicion that as well as having a lot less sexual experience than Dario Lorenti, she was also nowhere near as well versed at ruthlessly controlling her emotions.

CHAPTER EIGHT

Two days later

AS THE LORENTI CORP helicopter circled Sante Trovato's sprawling Palermo estate, the neoclassical grandeur of his home a testament to how high the former Sicilian slum kid had risen, Dario's stomach churned. He rubbed his leg, the muscle cramps triggered by brutal memories of that long-ago summer day when Sante had deserted him—the acrid scent of burnt rubber, the metallic taste of blood, the crushing weight on his thigh, the fear and pain spent drifting in and out of consciousness.

Tension screamed across his shoulder blades. He'd seen Trovato in passing over the years since that day. How could he have avoided the man, after the Sicilian had managed to turn his coding abilities—abilities which Dario had nurtured and encouraged when they were schoolboys together in that godforsaken boarding school in Wiltshire—into the sale of an app that had made him a billionaire several years before Lorenti Corp had begun to corner the European market in a similar field. Since then, Trovato's ambitions had known no bounds, but at least he wasn't heavily involved in the tech business anymore, preferring to invest in property.

Even so, Dario was livid about having to meet the man again and suffer his hospitality. What exactly was Trovato's game? Pretending to love Mia? Asking for her hand in marriage? There had to be an ulterior motive—because Sante Trovato never did anything without one. The man was a user, a betrayer. Dario had discovered that the hard way.

He heard Tallulah gasp through the headphones as the chopper coasted over the citrus and olive groves, the elegant architectural flourishes of fountains and guest houses from a bygone era, the glistening waters of a swimming pool surrounding by exotic blooms which blended in seamlessly with the ornate gardens… Heat eddied in his gut, triggered by his fake fiancée's reaction to Trovato's ostentatious home.

As if it wasn't bad enough he was having to attend this wedding on enemy turf—and quite possibly witness his sister marry a man he despised and who he had already told her she could never trust—he was having to do it while coping with the worst case of blue balls he had ever experienced.

What the hell had he been thinking, kissing Tallulah after that intrusive interview? It had been a mistake of epic proportions. He had slept even less in the nights since, and had to take himself in hand more than once—like a horny teenager instead of a man who could have any woman he desired… Except the one strapped into the helicopter beside him, pretending to be his fiancée—her eyes wide, her cheeks flushed, her breasts pressed enticingly against the soft fabric of the demure designer dress.

The irony did not escape him that when Gianna Lombardi's article had been published yesterday, it had been much more favourable to their cause than he had expected after the journalist's antagonistic questions about his father… Lombardi had declared their whirlwind romance a love for the ages, and Tallulah the woman who had tamed Milan's biggest playboy—mostly because of his unguarded reaction to the news his fake fiancée was learning Italian. The feature writer had been touched by his surprise, apparently. The truth was he had not been surprised, he had been shocked, not just by Tallulah's decision, but by his knee-jerk reaction to it… That fierce yearning to have his fake bride speak to him in his own language—the language his father had once punished him for using—had been swift and sudden, and reminded him of that confused, unhappy, desperately lonely boy. An emotional response he despised…

He glared out of the window, his confused reaction tormenting him all over again. Why should he care if she learned Italian, or what language she spoke to him in? Theirs was no more than a temporary arrangement. Surely that illogical response was simply a result of being unable to feed the hunger which had only got worse since that damn kiss. But instead of coming to him as he had expected—because he knew she yearned for him, too—she had remained wary and aloof.

He had planned to wait until she admitted she wanted to change the terms of their arrangement, too. Pressuring women was not his style, but when had he ever wanted one as much as he wanted her? It was lowering to realise he was starting to become obsessed with her, which was also not something he had ever experienced before either—because he had always known it made you weak to wish for something you did not have.

Now more than ever, he needed the release only good, hard, sweaty sex could give him, to navigate the days ahead. He was already wound too damn tight at the thought of seeing Trovato with his sister. But the prospect of having to treat Tallulah like a lover in public while being unable to touch her in private was an additional torment which threatened to make this trip even more unbearable.

The helicopter settled onto the heliport at the back of the palazzo, once the home of a Sicilian prince. After the blades had powered down, they were greeted by a small army of staff, who would collect their luggage and escort them to the main residence.

As they were led into a huge entrance hall and towards a wide, sweeping marble staircase—already decorated with local blooms and ribbons for the wedding that evening—the grinding pit of resentment in Dario's stomach grew.

He did not wish to be here, forced to socialise with his enemy. But he was doing this for Mia, in one last-ditch attempt to make her see reason.

As they ascended the staircase behind the staff member who had introduced himself as Trovato's *maggiordomo*, he pressed his palm to Tallulah's back.

'I wish to speak to my sister in private, once you have been introduced,' he murmured against her ear. 'Will you be okay alone for an hour?'

'Of course, the estate looks amazing. Maybe I could explore? Is the wedding due to take place tomorrow?' she asked, but the polite smile she sent him only increased his irritation. Why was she treating him like a stranger when the taste of her mouth, the memory of her sobs still tortured him?

'It is scheduled for tonight. It appears to be a fairly modest affair by Sicilian standards as it has been so rushed.' The haste was another warning sign, as far as Dario was concerned, of Trovato's dishonest intentions. 'I certainly do not intend to remain as Trovato's guest for more than one night…' he snapped. Assuming, of course, he could not persuade his sister to see the light and call off this farce at the eleventh hour. But knowing how impulsive and naïve Mia had always been—and how unwilling to accept his advice—he already suspected he was on a fool's mission.

'You're unhappy about the wedding?' Tallulah asked softly, the confusion in her eyes reminding him of her expression when he had questioned her decision to take Italian lessons. Why did that look get to him so much?

'No, I am not happy that my sister has chosen to marry that man,' he said, giving away more than he had intended. Very few people knew of his former connection with Trovato, and he wished it to remain that way. The man no longer had the power to hurt him. He had lived with the consequences of that day ever since, but in some ways, he welcomed the wounds which would never heal. They had made him stronger and more resilient—and would always remind him never to trust anyone the way he had once trusted Trovato.

Because the boy who was supposed to be his best friend had deserted him after the accident, when his father had offered Trovato money to disappear. Trovato had taken the bribe rather than remaining loyal to him. Dario had waited for days in the hospital, in pain, sure his friend would defy his father's version of events and come to see him… But he never had. And then Dario had known everything his father had said was true. Trovato had not gone to get help after the accident, he had run, and he had only befriended Dario in the first place because his father had money… Something Trovato had always yearned for.

He could see the questions in Tallulah's expressive face about his animosity towards his sister's choice of husband, but before she could ask any of them, the *maggiordomo* opened the door to a large drawing room, announced their arrival, and closed the door behind them to give them privacy.

He spotted his sister and Trovato standing together near an impressive fireplace, waiting to greet them. The room's expensive antique furniture and forbidding grandeur did nothing to dim the excitement and expectation on his sister's face. But as Dario's gaze landed on Trovato, the man tensed, and the weight in Dario's stomach twisted, the bitterness so sharp he could taste it.

They looked like a unit, with his sister positioned in front of Trovato. The Sicilian had his hand on Mia's shoulder—his stance both possessive and protective. As if Mia needed protecting from her own brother, instead of the man who was trying to exploit her.

The thought of the difficult conversation he had in his near future with Mia made resentment flare in his gut. Forcing him into this situation was just another of Trovato's betrayals—a way to drive a final wedge between Dario and the only family he had left.

His relationship with Mia had become increasingly difficult ever since they had left Capri and their once carefree childhoods behind. He knew part of that distance was his fault. He'd tried to look out for Mia. She'd been so young and much more vulnerable than him when their lives had been torn apart. And her passionate nature, her stubborn pride, her generous heart and her foolish lack of caution had left her open to exploitation. Her blank refusal to accept his financial help had only made matters worse—frustrating him and forcing her to seek employment with men like Trovato, who would exploit their connection.

But something about the way they stood so close together, the wary look in Trovato's eyes, pricked his memory. He sealed off the thought and gripped Tallulah's hand to walk towards them. Tallulah's telltale shiver of response to his touch felt strangely vindicating. Despite the frustrations their fake relationship had caused, he was grateful in that moment to have her by his side, because facing this bastard and his sister alone would somehow be harder.

'Dario...' Mia whispered, then left Trovato's side to rush to them both. *'Grazie mille, Dario, tu venuto!'* He could see the genuine pleasure to see him in her bright smile and the affection in her eyes as she greeted him.

'I said I would come,' he murmured, switching to English.

The unguarded happiness in her expression dimmed. And he had a sudden recollection of the puppy she'd once brought to Westwick Hall, on one of the rare occasions they'd spent the summer there. It was the summer he had brought Trovato home with him from boarding school because his friend had had nowhere else to go. Mia had adored that puppy and been desperate to keep the pet, but their father—when he arrived—had been furious to see the mongrel dog. Mia had been devastated when their father had the puppy taken from her and returned to the nearby farm where she'd found it.

Of course, Dario was the cause of her sadness today. But he forced himself not to acknowledge the prickle of guilt. Sentimentality would not help this situation. And he had always had Mia's best interests at heart, unlike their father, who had only ever cared about appearances. And unlike Trovato, who had shown his true colours by abandoning Dario to his fate after that accident. Trovato had taken their father's blood money after the crash and used it to build an empire. And now he intended to take Dario's sister from him, too.

To hell with that.

'This must be your fiancée,' Mia declared, the too bright smile back as she turned to Tallulah, no doubt desperate to break the tension between Dario and her fiancé. Reaching out, she grasped Tallulah's free hand, the warmth in her expression making Tallulah's blush brighten. 'It's so wonderful to meet you, Tallulah. I read all about your whirlwind affair with my brother this morning in *Ragazza* magazine. About how you are the beauty who has tamed the playboy… This is indeed a feat.' His sister's delighted laugh pricked at Dario's conscience. He would have mentioned to his sister his marriage was a stunt to gain ownership of their mother's palazzo, but given she was now firmly under Trovato's spell, he could no longer trust her.

'Thank you, I think,' Tallulah said with an uncomfortable laugh, her surprise at Mia's enthusiasm visible when she glanced at Dario.

He cleared his throat, determined to ignore that look, which seemed to be questioning why he had not told Mia the truth. He had explained to his fake bride why he needed this marriage—against his better judgement. His relationship with his sister, and what he chose to confide in her, was certainly no concern of Tallulah's.

'When is your wedding going to be?' Mia asked, apparently oblivious to the subtext. 'I hope Sante and I will be able to attend,' she offered, the olive branch hard to ignore.

But the mention of his ex-friend's first name—a name he had not used to refer to the man, even in his own head, since that summer—had Dario's fury and frustration returning.

'I am not here to discuss my wedding, Mia. But yours. We must speak, alone.'

Mia flinched at his harsh tone, her face falling. He saw the hurt in her eyes, so like their mother's, but when she spoke, he could also hear steel.

'If you've come here to browbeat me into calling off my wedding to the man I love, Dario,' his sister said, switching into Italian, he suspected to save Tallulah any more discomfort, 'you've made a wasted journey.'

It occurred to him in that moment that while he'd always felt his sister had the same flaws as their mother, he could see in her stubborn expression she had an emotional strength their mother had lacked. But right now, he was finding it impossible to appreciate the revelation—because this foolhardy decision was so misguided.

But then Trovato stepped forward and placed that damn

possessive hand back on his sister's shoulder. And it took every ounce of Dario's control not to punch the bastard.

'We need to talk, Dario, all three of us,' he said, also in Italian. 'Because there are many things I should have told you a long time ago. I let my pride get in the way—I refused to defend myself when you believed the worst of me. But I can see now my silence was as much to blame as your gullibility. I should never have let your father's lies about me fester between us all these years.'

Dario's temper sharpened, the words like a slap. The old anger, that miserable sense of betrayal, of being used and then discarded, had the old pain tearing through his insides.

'*My* gullibility?' he snapped. 'You left me on the side of the road to rot and took my father's money. *Bastardo*.' He released Tallulah's hand to pull his clenched fist back. But as he drove it forward, Trovato leaned back, making him punch air. His bad leg buckled, and he stumbled to the ground. Agonising pain shot through his knee and thigh, but the humiliation was worse. He could hear Tallulah's shocked cry, hear his sister's agonised attempts to calm him down. But it was Sante who grabbed him and helped him back onto his feet.

The fury engulfed him, but Sante's arms closed around his shoulders from behind, making it impossible to wrestle free of the bastard and land the punch. The pain in his injured leg spread to his lungs, making it hurt to draw breath, as something brutal rose up his chest, more agonising even than the cramping pain firing across his kneecap. It was as if he were suffocating again, pinned down as he had been for so long that day in the wreckage, terrified and alone and broken.

'Listen to me, Dario,' Sante huffed against his neck, his arms banded tight around Dario's chest, holding him up, holding him close. 'I love your sister with all my heart. This isn't a trick. She is everything I am not. You must let go of the hate. *He* did this to us, because he could. Don't let him win. Not again.'

Dario continued the struggle, but Sante was stronger, not having to battle the pain. His certainty, his compassion were somehow weakening Dario even more than his useless leg.

Suddenly he couldn't hold on to the hurt, the fury anymore, when all he felt was hollowed out. Exhausted.

'I didn't take his money, Dario. Not a cent. And I did not leave you, I went to get help.'

His sister stood before him then, her trembling hands pressing against his cheeks, robbing him of breath, making his throat tighten, his ribs hurt.

'It's true Dario, I saw the terrible wounds on his feet that day. He walked for miles but couldn't flag down a single car. He went to the hospital that night. He was desperate to see you. But our father had told the hospital staff not to let him in.' Tears welled in her eyes, and he felt them leaking into his heart like acid. 'Our father *wanted* to destroy your friendship. Can't you see, Dario? He wanted you to hate Sante, because *he* hated him, a poor Sicilian, a bad influence on his son and heir. He isolated you deliberately that summer.'

The last of his energy seemed to leach away, the words jumbling in his head, but making a horrible, hideous kind of sense as he recalled how his father had referred to Sante as 'the Sicilian guttersnipe.'

The cruel memories of his father's scorn for the boy he'd made his friend came flooding back. Memories he'd pushed to one side during the long, endless days in pain that summer with only the housekeeper's pity and her young daughter—and his own misery—to keep him company.

It felt as if everything were collapsing around him and reshaping itself into something he didn't recognise.

Dio, were they telling him the truth? How could they not be, when he had always known his father hated his Italian heritage, and the bastard had never made any secret of the fact he despised Dario's friendship with Sante, the poor scholarship kid.

He felt his shoulders droop, the exhaustion consuming him, destroying him all over again.

'Let me go,' he murmured.

Sante released him immediately. But when Dario turned, he saw the earnestness, the emotion in his friend's gaze. And all the things he had once loved about that boy—his intelligence, his ambition, his bravery, his fierce loyalty to his country, to his roots, to Dario—came back in a rush of memory so brutal it left him breathless.

Dario stared at the silk rug at his feet, the pain in his leg now nothing compared to the agony in his heart.

All this time, he had believed his father's lies. The lies of a man he knew had never loved him. *Why?* Because somehow it had been easier to have someone to blame for his pain…

Sante was right, he'd been a gullible fool.

'Please believe us, Dario,' Mia said again, the tears streaming down her face now.

He nodded, lifting his head to stare blindly at the lavish frescoes which decorated the room's walls and had been so lovingly restored. Finally, he forced his gaze back to his sister and the man he had once loved as a brother.

'I do…' His voice broke on the words, shaming him even more. But then he caught sight of Tallulah, over Mia's shoulder—all the colour had drained from her face. She could not possibly have understood what was being said. Not only had the whole conversation been conducted in Italian, but no one knew of his feud with Sante except the three of them. The pity in her eyes, though, made it clear she knew…somehow… she *knew* that he had been in the wrong here.

The shame blindsided him, that she had witnessed the terrible mess he had made of his only real friendship. It upset him even more, though, that he had never even slept with this woman and yet somehow her opinion mattered.

The nausea rolled through him. He thrust his fingers through his hair and buttoned his jacket, which had come undone during the struggle. Buying time, desperate to control the emotions he did not want to feel.

At last, he made his gaze connect with Mia's, but he couldn't make himself look at Sante. He owed the man an apology, for believing the lies his father had told him all those years ago. For letting them fester and grow all this time. Sante had tried to take some of the blame for that, but it was on him, and only him. Mia had tried to tell him all this on the phone weeks ago, and he hadn't listened. Because he hadn't wanted to.

Even so, the words he needed to say to Sante wouldn't come, so he forced himself to say the next best thing.

'If you wish, I will give you away tonight,' he said to Mia in English.

His sister's face brightened like the sun. 'Dario, yes, yes, that would mean so much to me.' She glanced at Sante, who seemed taken aback by the offer. 'To us both.'

She lifted on tiptoes and planted a kiss on his scarred cheek, and the scent he recognised from so long ago—when they had been happy together, as children on Capri, when everything had been so simple—crucified him. Somehow it disgusted him even more that he had been forgiven so easily.

How had he let them get so far apart? But how could he allow that closeness back, when it made him feel so weak?

'I love you, Dario,' Mia said softly. 'It feels good to finally have my brother back…'

He gave a stiff nod. 'I should wash up,' he said, desperate for an excuse to get away from the raw emotions battering him.

'We have put you two together in the summer house. It is

secluded and intimate and charming,' Mia said, her words bubbling out, her emotions clearly as close to the surface as his own. 'You have three hours before the wedding. Would you like me to show you the way? And arrange for refreshments for you both?'

'We have already eaten.' He cut off her offer, not sure he could bear to spend a minute longer in her company—or Sante's—contemplating how badly he had fucked up. 'Is it the place on the other side of the orange grove?' he asked stiffly, vaguely remembering the structure from when the chopper had landed, what felt like several lifetimes ago.

'Yes, yes,' Mia said. 'You should let me show you both to…'

'Mia, it's okay. I believe Dario needs some time alone with his fiancée,' Sante announced.

Dario's gaze connected with the man he had once considered his best friend. His only friend, really. He wasn't sure he had it in him to repair the friendship they had lost, wasn't convinced he even wanted to. But he could be grateful the man knew him well enough to understand he needed some time to figure out what to do to quell the emotions making his chest hurt.

But when Sante strode out of the room and appeared with his *maggiordomo*, directing the older man to show him *and* Tallulah to their accommodation, the vice clamped around his chest. Right alongside it, though, was the furious surge of lust as his fake fiancée grasped his hand and squeezed his numb fingers as if trying to reassure him.

He flinched, her pity only making him more disgusted with himself and his loss of control.

The rest of the day was going to be even more torturous if she attempted to talk to him about any of this. He had no desire to confide in her, in anyone—which meant he could not slake this damn lust now. It would have been so simple and uncomplicated to use their chemistry as a means of forgetting all this. But how could he, when his emotions were so unsettled?

But once they were shown into the summer house, she seemed to sense his withdrawal, because she murmured, 'I think I'll go for a run, if you…if you want some alone time.'

He blinked back the sudden urge to ask her not to leave him, shocking him to his core.

But then she murmured, 'Or I could stay? And we could talk.'

He tensed and forced himself to shake his head—despising the moment of weakness but hating even more that she had somehow seen it.

'*Talk?*' he murmured. 'The last damn thing I wish to do with you right now is talk, Tallulah,' he said.

She nodded, the blush blazing across her cheeks a vindication of sorts. 'Right,' she said, then jerked her thumb over her shoulder. 'I'll go for that run, then.'

She dashed off—treating him as if he were an unexploded bomb which she needed to be careful not to trigger. Her reaction would have been ironic, if it didn't make him feel so damn pathetic. What the hell had happened to the man who had always prided himself on being able to control his emotions?

What was far worse though, was that after she had changed into some athletic gear in the house's lavish bathroom, then left him to shower alone…he *felt* like an unexploded bomb. Because the hatred he had fostered for so long towards Sante, even his superior attitude towards his sister's reckless, overemotional behaviour, was no longer there to bolster his sense of self or make him proud of the man he had worked so hard to become. Instead, he felt adrift, in a sea of emotions he could no longer rely on—ashamed that even for a moment he had needed the support of a woman he had paid to pretend to love him.

Desperate to ignore the still throbbing pain in his leg and the brutal recollection of the scene with Sante and Mia, which kept playing on a loop in his head, and his pathetic reaction to the sympathy in Tallulah's eyes when she had offered to *talk* about it, he pressed a hand to the shower's glass tiles and imagined his fake fiancée instead, in the summer house's lavish—and only—bed.

His cock hardened, as he conjured images of her lush body lying naked on the linen sheets, her soft hair fanned out across the pillows, her eyes dark with lust, her turgid nipples begging for his lips, her evocative scent intoxicating his senses—as if she was all his. And *only* his. He grunted as the need crested, and the climax powered from his aching body to splatter against the tiles. The sickening shame returned, though, as he watched his seed wash away.

Damn it, masturbating would never be enough to quell this insistent hunger. Or help him to forget the terrible mistakes he'd made with Sante, and with his sister—and the shame of needing more from his stunt bride than he should, if only for a moment.

As he dressed in the tuxedo his staff must have packed—which he'd never actually considered he would have to wear—he contemplated the prospect of finally getting Tallulah to himself, later tonight. And realised the best way to diffuse this damn bomb had been obvious from the start.

He didn't *need* Tallulah, he merely wanted her, and not taking her had left him on edge this afternoon, magnifying his volatile reaction to Sante and Mia's revelations.

Tallulah was not a part of his past, nor could she ever be part of his future—so any complications sex would add to their fake relationship, and there would be a few, could be managed… And right now, those complications would be worth it if having her meant he could finally satisfy this all-consuming hunger, and control these brutal, untethered emotions once and for all.

Tali rounded the corner of the orchard garden, making her way back towards the summer house…and Dario. It was less than two hours now before Mia's wedding was due to take place. And the stylist and her team would be waiting for her. For once she didn't mind the thought of being 'dressed,' because she really didn't think she could be alone with Dario—not without offering him the sympathy and support he had already made it very clear he didn't want.

But how could she not feel compassion for him after witnessing his reaction to the altercation with his sister's fiancé?

His stance had been rigid with control as they'd been led to the summer house. But when she'd watched him fall to his knees during the fight, the pain which had ripped through his features had been nothing to the agonised expression moments later, when Trovato and then Mia had explained something to him in Italian—which had been too fast for her to understand.

She stopped at the water fountain to scoop a handful of water onto her neck. She'd run for over an hour through the estate—the acres of rolling vines, the groves of orange and lemon trees and the beautifully maintained gardens near the majestic house—unnoticed by the staff rushing to finish setting up the trestle tables in the garden to host the wedding feast. She'd always loved to run when she had a particularly thorny problem to decipher. And was there any problem thornier than her relationship with Dario Lorenti?

She hadn't understood what the passionate argument had been about—her Italian was hardly fluent. But she had been able to make an educated guess that Dario and Trovato had a history which was a great deal more complicated than a simple business rivalry.

But even though she hadn't been sure of the context, seeing the emotions Dario had been unable to mask—sensing how broken he'd been after that confrontation and how alone he'd seemed when they'd got to the summer house—had made the sense of connection she'd been trying to deny that much stronger. Scarily stronger, when you factored in the kiss in his apartment in Milan forty-eight hours ago, which she also couldn't forget.

She sluiced her face with the cool water.

Whatever the deal is with Sante is not your business, Tali.

And trying to make it her business would be a mistake. Because Dario had already made it clear he was only interested in one thing from her.

And having to behave like Dario's devoted fiancée this evening—while knowing there was only one bed in that stunning summer house—was going to make dealing with him tonight hard enough.

Tali made her way along the path to the back of the house, so she could get to the summer house without being spotted by any of the guests who were already arriving on the lavish driveway at the front entrance. But as she went past the outbuildings, she spotted Mia, dressed casually in jean shorts and a T-shirt, chatting to one of her wait staff setting up for the feast that evening.

Tali paused, about to find another way back—because how awkward was it that Dario hadn't mentioned to his sister their so-called 'love for the ages' was a lie—when Mia spotted her and waved.

'Tallulah! Wait, I wanted to talk to you.'

Before Tali could make a dignified retreat or think up an excuse to run, the bride had excused herself and was jogging towards her.

'Hi,' Tali murmured, her already sweaty face probably purple when Mia reached her. 'I… I should head back.' She pointed over her shoulder, the awkward going all the way to eleven. 'I expect the stylist will be waiting for me…and you probably need to get dressed, too.'

'Ha, yes. I'm going to be late, but I had to let Bianca know about a last-minute change to the seating plan… It's the EA in me. I can't help over-organising every detail.' The woman beamed the same sweet, generous smile which had made Tali feel so guilty when they'd been introduced. 'But luckily, it's the bride's prerogative to be late,' she added. 'And Sante is far too used to having me at his beck and call. Now, *finally*, I will get a chance to make *him* wait, which I intend to take full advantage of…' She laughed, her face lighting up at the mention of her groom. Tali's heartbeat slowed at the glow which suffused Mia's features. What must it be like, to know you had found your soulmate? Because from the words Tali had managed to decipher—and the expression on Sante Trovato's face when he had spoken about Mia to Dario during their altercation—that was one thing she had been sure of. The man adored Mia, and Mia adored him right back.

Tali let out a strained chuckle. 'That sounds like a plan…'

'But first…' Mia began, her expression sobering. 'I wanted to apologise for what happened earlier. I hope we didn't make you too uncomfortable?' she continued, looking genuinely concerned. The trickle of guilt became a flood. 'We're so glad you're here with Dario. And I'm so, *so* happy he's found someone who cares about him and wants to support him. He's been alone for so long…' Mia rushed ahead, but the earnest expression only made Tali feel worse about their deception.

Why hadn't he confided in his sister? While it was obvious Dario had been furious with her decision to marry Trovato, none of that was true anymore, was it? Perhaps Dario would tell her tonight?

'I'm sure Dario told you all about Sante, about the things he thought he had done to him—leaving him in the wreckage of that car… But none of that was ever true. And while I'm glad Dario finally knows those lies were all just another way our father tried to manipulate him, it must have been awkward for you to have to witness all that.'

You have no idea.

Tali bit into her lip, the guilt starting to make her feel as if she'd swallowed a rock. This conversation had gone way beyond awkward to just plain awful.

'I just… I want you to know I understand that,' Mia added. 'And if you have any reservations at all, about the truth of what really happened that day, I'd be happy to explain it all to you, in English. Because I'm sure you probably didn't understand a lot of what was being said and knowing my brother. Well…' Mia gave a hefty sigh, but then a rueful smile appeared. 'I very much doubt he has explained any of it to you—because he'd rather cut out his tongue than share and discuss, as I'm sure you're already well aware.'

Tali couldn't help the small smile that curved her lips, because the truth was, even though she wasn't Dario's *real* fiancée, she *did* know exactly how much he disliked sharing anything—his motivations, his secrets and his feelings most of all.

But then Mia launched into an explanation of the poor Sicilian boy who had been Dario's only friend at boarding school in the UK…

And understanding dawned.

So Sante Trovato, the man Mia was about to marry, was the same boy her mother and the rest of the staff had whispered about at Westwick that summer. The boy who had supposedly left Dario on the roadside to die…except he hadn't.

The greasy knot in Tali's stomach became a snake, threatening to gag her as Mia's impassioned explanations continued. And Tali's avid curiosity about Dario's past only ramped up her guilt. She shouldn't be listening to any of this. He wouldn't want her to know… That much had been obvious from the closed-off expression on his face when she'd offered to discuss it with him at the summer house.

'Please, Mia… You have to stop talking!' she finally blurted out.

Mia stopped abruptly. 'What, why?' she asked, utterly confused.

'Because… I'm not… I'm just… Not…' Tali stumbled to a halt, the confession dying on her lips.

She was breaking a confidence, not to mention a binding NDA agreement, by telling Mia the truth about her arrangement with Mia's brother.

'It's okay, Tallulah, whatever it is, you can tell me…' Mia said, confusion giving way to compassion. And suddenly Tali understood. She couldn't lie about this. Even if Dario ended up suing her. Or pulling out of their agreement. She'd never intended for anyone to get hurt. And Mia would be hurt, if she continued to believe Tali *meant* something to Dario, that one day soon Tali would be a genuine part of their family. Mia was so obviously a good person—a kind, sweet, passionately loyal person—who wanted the best for her brother, even though it sounded as if he'd been as distant with her as he had with everyone else… And while a part of Tali desperately wanted to know *why* Dario found it so hard to let anyone in, even his own sister, she couldn't let Mia confide in her. Because Mia would regret it when she learned the truth. That Tali meant nothing to Dario, even if he was starting to mean something to her—which was probably just her delusional Miss Fix-it issues resurfacing.

'I'm not Dario's real fiancée. We're not in love. I only met him a couple of weeks ago...' The truth burst out.

Mia stared at her, her expression going from confused to completely dumbfounded. 'You're not getting married?'

'Well, yes, but... That's not real either. Well, it will be a real marriage, as in a legal one, but I won't be his real wife. He needed to marry an Englishwoman, to inherit his mother's... *Your* mother's palazzo in Capri. Something about the terms of your father's will. I guess the palazzo means a lot to him. Obviously.'

For goodness' sake, stop talking now... You sound like an imbecile.

Mia's eyes narrowed as the truth dawned on her, but the compassion remained. There was no anger, not even irritation in her tone when she spoke again. 'My brother is pretending to love you, so he can inherit Palazzo di Constanzo?'

'Well...yes,' Tali murmured. God, how had she not realised until this moment how crass and manipulative their arrangement sounded?

'And how did he persuade you to do this?' Mia asked, her tone still level, but the spike of irritation there, underneath. Weirdly, though, it did not seem to be aimed at Tali.

'I'm the estate manager at Westwick Hall... I love my job, and the Hall, but it's been in decline for years, and since Dario inherited it, he hasn't wanted to have anything to do with it. He finally came to the estate a few weeks ago to inform me he was demolishing it... But then he agreed to invest two million euros in Westwick, which would secure its future and all our jobs...if I agreed to pose as...his...' Embarrassment gave way to shame as the truth got locked in her throat. 'To pose as his...'

'Shhh, it's okay, Tallulah.' Mia reached out and took Tali's hand, squeezing her fingers. Until that moment, she hadn't realised she was shaking. 'You haven't done anything wrong…'

Except she had. She'd lied to Mia, to Sante, to all the staff at Westwick. She'd even tried to lie to her mother…

Gripping Tali's hand, Mia pulled her to the fountain and encouraged her to sit on the low wall that surrounded it. Tali dropped onto the warm stone, stupidly grateful, because her legs were shaky now, too.

Mia sat down beside her, still holding her hand. The chirps of birds, the buzz of bees, the tinkle of the fountain, the distant rumble of cars as the guests arrived and the hum of activity from the staff nearby faded, until all Tali could hear was the hard thuds of her own heartbeat—telling her what an idiot she'd been.

'Tallulah, is my brother sleeping with you?' Mia asked gently.

'No,' Tali replied. 'God, no!' Because that would make this situation even more sordid. But the rush of heat quickening Tali's heartbeat and flame-grilling her cheeks had Mia's gaze sharpening.

'But he wants to? Am I right? That much is obvious from the way he looks at you, the way he touches you,' Mia said with such confidence, the burning in Tali's cheeks got worse.

'That's all for show,' Tali managed, dying a little more inside. Because she knew it wasn't for show as far as she was concerned. And she had one devastating kiss that she couldn't forget, a whole lot of sleepless nights—not to mention the wettest wet dreams known to woman—to prove it.

'I hate to break it to you, Tallulah,' Mia muttered, 'but my brother is not that good an actor. If he was, he would not have fallen foul of our father so often—and been punished so harshly.'

Harshly how? Tali wanted to ask but stifled the urge—

after all, her curiosity about Dario had only made this conversation more difficult.

'And we also have that gushing article in *Ragazza* as exhibit B,' Mia continued. 'Gianna Lombardi is a very shrewd journalist. She would not have been fooled that yours was a love match if some of what she saw wasn't real.'

'Well, he definitely doesn't love me,' Tali said, feeling oddly deflated. 'We hardly know each other. And he's made it quite clear he doesn't want to get to know me better.'

'But he does want to sleep with you. Tallulah,' Mia reiterated. It wasn't a question.

'Please call me Tali,' she replied. Because really, if she was going to have the most excruciating conversation of her entire life with this woman, it seemed only fitting Mia should address her by the name everyone knew her by, except Dario. 'And in the interests of full disclosure, I want to sleep with him, too,' she blurted out, because it seemed unfair to let Dario take all the blame. After all, she *had* kissed him back two days ago. And if he'd put any real moves on her since, she wasn't sure she would have been able to resist him. Her cheeks became radioactive. 'He's, well... He's very charismatic...' *And beyond hot*. But no way was she about to mention that to his sister. 'And, sometimes, I feel what he really needs is a friend. Which is silly, I know. But I always had a bad habit as a kid of taking in wounded creatures. And Dario seems...well, wounded too, I guess.'

Mia blinked, her expression changing, until a pensive smile brightened her features. 'You have feelings for my brother...'

Again, it wasn't a question, but Tali found herself nodding. What was it about this woman that made it so hard to lie to her?

'I guess I do. Which is nuts... I've known him for precisely two weeks, and he hasn't exactly been easy to deal with. But he fascinates me. He wants to appear cold and in control all the time, but I really don't think that's who he is… But how could I possibly know that? I'm sure it's just a delusion brought about by the sexual tension incinerating my brain cells.' It was Tali's turn to start babbling.

'Except it is *not* your brain which makes these decisions, Tali,' Mia said softly. 'It is your heart. And you are right about my brother…' she added.

'I—I am?' Tali asked.

'Yes,' Mia said, with complete certainty.

And for the first time since Tali had offered to stay with Dario, and he had shut her out, she felt less vulnerable, less insecure. 'How am I right?' Tali pressed, needing to know now if there was really more to the connection she had begun to sense with Dario, or if it had all been in her own head.

'You are right that he is not as cold or controlled as he wants to pretend,' Mia said gently. 'When we were children in Capri, he always protected me. Our mother was beautiful and wild. She loved us, but she did not know how to look after us. When we came to England, our father tried to force all the wildness out of Dario. But to do that, he had to also force out all the joy. And he succeeded, when he turned Dario against Sante. The accident, and the way it crushed Dario's spirit, even more than his body, did the rest. But you are the first person I know who has seen the boy he once was, beneath the surface of that unhappy man. And only in a few weeks. Perhaps…' Mia paused. 'Perhaps if you give in to the desire you both feel, you might discover more of that boy?'

Tali's heart lifted, and the fierce desire surged… But she wasn't sure anymore if it was the hunger which had tormented her for weeks demanding to be satisfied, or the yearning to make that lonely, bedridden boy smile which was driving her desire to know Dario better now.

The only thing she did know was that she wasn't convinced she could resist it any longer.

'*Signora Lorenti...*' A young woman shouted across the courtyard, then rushed towards them, looking flustered. 'You must come. Signora Chiara is concerned there will not be enough time to get your hair styled.'

Mia jumped up and replied in Italian, looking flustered, too, but also incandescently happy, her excitement giving her face a golden glow in the dying sunlight. But before she could follow the young assistant to prepare for her wedding, she turned back to Tali.

'Do not give up on my brother, Tali. He has always needed someone who won't put up with his bullshit… And, although I do not like to think about my brother this way, if nothing else, good sex can be its own reward.'

Before Tali could reply, her unruly heart bobbing into her throat, Mia had disappeared into the palazzo.

But as Tali walked back, through the outdoor kitchen, past trays of delicious hors d'oeuvres being laid out on silver platters, her mind kept snagging on all the things Mia had told her about Dario and his past…

Surely, Mia's input proved one thing at least—that there *was* a fascinatingly complex man lurking behind the façade of the ruthlessly controlled autocrat.

Would it really be so wrong to try to find that man? Especially now she had finally admitted to herself, as well as Mia, she was tired of fighting the hunger which had tormented them both ever since that damn kiss.

CHAPTER NINE

DARIO STOOD AT the edge of the festivities, watching his sister dance with her new husband in the moonlight. The wine had flowed after the ceremony, during the banquet of local delicacies served on white linen and gold-rimmed plates in the open air. And now the two hundred guests were partying into the night, enjoying the fragrant air, redolent with the scent of orange blossom and jasmine.

He'd expected a more formal and extravagant event for a man of Sante's wealth and status, but Mia's influence had been everywhere—her energy, her passion and her lust for life—in all those thoughtful, personalised touches which had made her wedding so relaxed and enjoyable.

For everyone but him…

He'd walked her down the aisle of flowers and fairy lights in the orchard, as he'd promised, aware of his halting steps beside hers and the delighted smile on her face which made him feel like a fraud.

When she'd leapt into Sante's arms after they'd declared their vows, he couldn't quite control the stab of bitterness which remained—towards his old friend. Not because he still believed what his father had told him all those years ago, but because that anger, that resentment had helped sustain him for so long. And now, he felt hollow inside, without the familiar anger to keep the knowledge there was something fundamental missing from his life at bay.

Mia had included many familiar Capresi delicacies in her wedding feast. And watching her dance, getting into the groove of an old disco hit in her flowing ivory silk gown while Sante twirled her in his arms, reminded him of their mother—always wild, always beautiful, but unlike Mia, always searching for a high which had eluded her.

'She looks stunning, and so happy,' Tallulah whispered beside him.

He turned to find her watching him, her blue eyes shiny with emotion—no doubt seeing things he did not wish her to see.

Lust charged through his system though, when his gaze raked over her figure. The satin gown matched the deep turquoise of her irises, its simple lines clinging to her curves, the peaks of her breasts pressing against the fabric. His mouth watered, as the familiar hunger speared into his gut.

What was he waiting for? When giving in to this devastating chemistry would be the perfect way to forget all these pointless memories that were reminding him of the boy he'd once been—naïve and scared because so much of his life was outside his control—and not the man he had worked so hard to become, immune to the flaws that had once made his mother so weak.

Clasping her hip, he tugged her towards him and leaned down to press his lips to her neck. Her vicious shudder was a seductive payback as he whispered in her ear.

'You are stunning too, Tallulah.'

She stiffened, the flare of desire in her transparent expression like a flaming wand igniting his already volatile senses. But when he bit softly into her earlobe, then traced the delicate shell with his tongue, she planted her palms against the cotton of his shirt and gave him a gentle shove.

Her wide-eyed gaze searched his face, the familiar blush turning her pale skin to a burning red.

'Dario, please don't,' she whispered, for his ears alone. 'I know we have to put on a show, but all this play-acting is... It's making it hard for me to tell what's real and what's...'

He pressed his finger to her lips to silence her—strangely touched by her panicked request.

'I am not acting, Tallulah.' He banded his arms around her, to bring her flush against him, until her eyes widened even more—as her belly cradled the hard ridge of his growing erection. 'We must change the terms of our agreement.'

She blinked, the sheen of compassion and understanding in her eyes something he knew he should reject, but he was too desperate to have her to even care about that anymore.

The resentment, the loneliness, the sense he was standing on the edge of a boiling vat of despair and would tumble into if he could not get back his usual control... He wanted all these wayward emotions to fuck off. And the only way to do it was to bury himself inside her at last.

'How?' she whispered.

Was she being coy? Angling for a better offer? His cynicism wanted to believe it, but somehow, he knew that was not who she was.

He forced himself to release her, made himself button his tux jacket over the strident evidence of his desire, aware of the people around them. While the other guests were probably too drunk, and too high on the joy of his sister's wedding, to notice him and Tallulah, he did not wish to continue this conversation in public.

They needed to be alone. Because whatever happened next would not be for show—and was not for anyone's benefit but their own.

'Come.' He clasped her hand, to lead her past the throngs of people clapping and cheering as Sante swung his new wife into a romantic dip. Dario barely glanced their way though, all his focus on the woman whose fingers were clutched in his. 'Let us return to the summer house.'

'But what about your sister and Sante? Shouldn't we say goodbye?' she said, her voice trembling. 'Before they leave on their honeymoon?'

He led her to the edge of the gardens, aware of the summer house on the other side of the citrus orchard, its lights like a beacon as the night closed in.

'It is not necessary, I spoke to them both during the feast,' he said, the tension in his gut building at the recollection of the awkward conversation. He had formally apologised to his old friend, but the distance between them had remained. He'd made sure of it. He could not go back. Whatever lies had been exposed, he would never feel comfortable having the level of trust he had once had in Sante with anyone again. His sister had watched him with a peculiar expression on her face... Not quite pity, but not quite anything else either— which had only made the conversation more excruciating.

But he had done the right thing. And now he wished to forget the events of today, tonight. To live in the moment... and finally feed this driving hunger.

At last, they reached the summer house, the night drawing in around them. He hauled Tallulah through the door, slamming it shut to close off the faint sounds of the festivities from the other side of the estate. He released her, to take off his jacket, and tear off the tie which was starting to strangle him.

His mouth had dried. His breathing was now ragged.

She stood, shivering, despite the warmth of the evening, her breath heaving, too.

He let his gaze coast over that damn gown again, the shimmering satin accentuating the fullness of her breasts. While it was more demure than the gown he had objected to over two weeks ago in Milan, it had the same devastating effect. He'd wanted to rip it off her the minute she had walked out of the dressing room earlier—and been ready to murder every man whose gaze had lingered on her during the wedding.

Surely that was why he felt so on edge?

Tendrils of hair hung down from an elaborate chignon to touch her neck. He fisted his fingers and shoved them into his pants pockets, resisting the urge to thrust his hands into the silky curls and lift those full lips to his, so he could devour them all over again.

First, he must change the terms of their agreement. He had arranged for them to be wed as soon as they returned to Milan—in a simple civil ceremony, witnessed by a small but exclusive gathering of his friends and associates to avoid any unnecessary press scrutiny. But to convince the Westwick Trustees the marriage was real, he had decided to celebrate the union in an extended, month-long honeymoon on Capri at the palazzo. The symbolism had seemed perfect, but he had come to realise—ever since their kiss—that there was no way he would be able to endure weeks of living there with Tallulah without consummating their fake marriage.

She needed to be aware of his intentions before they took this step. Because he also knew one time would not be enough, not now he had become so obsessed with her.

She watched him—the vivid awareness which had crucified him for days, though, ever since the first time he had touched her in the moonlight, was tempered by that brutal sheen of emotion. And concern.

'How do you wish to change the terms of our agreement?' she whispered again.

He stepped close, to cradle her cheek, then slide his hand around the back of her neck, the desperation to touch her impossible to deny any longer. 'I think you know how, Tallulah,' his said. 'As it is not something I can hide.'

He stroked the rabbiting pulse in her neck, tugged her face up and brought his mouth so close to hers he felt her sharp gasp when the brutal erection pressed against her belly again through their clothing.

'If you do not wish to feed this incessant hunger, now is the time to say so,' he murmured against her lips, his voice hoarse, his fear of revealing too much obliterated by the brutal surge of desire. And desperation.

She stared at him, her lust-blown pupils dilating the blue to black, as he continued to stroke her neck... Waiting for her to admit what they both already knew, desperately holding the need in check to bargain with her if he had to. Already aware he would offer her anything she desired right now to have her.

But instead of demanding more or even asking for clarification of where this would leave their artificial relationship once their marriage became legal, she reached out and fisted trembling fingers in his shirt to draw him closer.

'I... I do want to feed it. I want you, so much.'

The whispered declaration snapped the last thin thread on his control and the fierce hunger roared through his system.

He dragged her into his embrace, to capture the thundering pulse in her neck with his lips, sucking the soft skin. Finding the curve of her bottom, he caressed the warm flesh, rocking her against his throbbing cock, to ease the pain.

The need swelled. And hardened.

He boosted her into his arms. 'Wrap your legs around my waist,' he demanded, his voice harsh—his need harsher.

She didn't hesitate, cupping his cheeks, raining kisses over his face as he carried her into the bedroom, the ache in his leg for once obliterated by the throbbing agony in his cock. He ground the turgid length against the juncture of her thighs... Desperate to bury himself so deep inside her, he could make the pain go away.

For tonight, at least.

* * *

Tali sobbed, her lungs seizing, as Dario tossed her onto the huge bed. The fire in her blood became an inferno as he towered over her. His dark eyes remained fixed on her face, making her skin feel tight, and the swelling heat in her sex ache. He threw off his jacket, then ripped open his shirt, making buttons pop.

'Take off the dress, Tallulah,' he demanded as he tore the shirt free of his trousers and tugged it off. His voice was surprisingly calm and controlled, but the feral harsh command had her racing to obey him.

She tugged the zip under her arm, shimmied out of the expensive satin. But her lungs seized again, her gaze devouring the sight before her when he slung the torn shirt away. His naked chest was as magnificent as the rest of him, the muscles bulging and flexing as he bent his head to unhook his trousers. His pecs were contoured with dark hair that trailed down in a thin line past ridged abs, accentuated by the delicious V of his hip flexors.

He grimaced as he transferred his weight to his bad leg to drag off his trousers. Sympathy echoed in her heart as the crisscross of scars on his thigh was revealed. And she recalled the boy she'd known, lying for weeks in the bedroom in Westwick, insisting the drapes remain closed, often refusing to even acknowledge her presence.

She shook off the sentimental thought when he straightened, her gaze fixing on the thick outline of his erection distending the black briefs.

'The dress, Tallulah,' he said, his voice husky with need. She scrambled to finish taking it off, aware of his hot gaze skating over her bared breasts in the half-light. She folded an arm over her chest, suddenly brutally aware of her nakedness. But when she stood, intending to fold the dress, he grasped her wrist.

'Leave it,' he murmured.

The rich satin dropped from her numb fingers as he lifted her chin with his other hand.

'You are beautiful, Tallulah, you must not hide yourself from me.' The words were gruff, and as commanding as always, but somehow also unbearably romantic, the hunger in his eyes making the hot spot between her thighs burn as he eased her arm down, to expose her fully to his gaze.

His thumb skimmed under a rouged nipple, sharpening the ache between her thighs.

'*Bellissima*,' he whispered, scooping the heavy flesh into his palm and bending to capture the tender peak with his lips.

She sobbed, grasping handfuls of his hair, her breath sawing out in ragged pants as he worked the engorged nipple—with his teeth, his tongue—sucking, stroking, nipping, tormenting... The heat rose and twisted, becoming desperate. He pressed the heel of his hand to her vulva, rubbed her through the sodden lace, then found her swollen flesh, to torture her there, too. One finger, then two, stretched her, stroked her, locating a devastating spot which made her buck against his hold, trying to ride that delicious torment, her body no longer her own.

He murmured something in Italian, his tone gruff.

She clung to him, the pants turning to broken sobs, as the storm built, burned, forcing her closer to the abyss. Her body quaked, but he kept her on that brutal edge, sucking her tender nipples in turn, holding her suspended, tormented, as his fingers drove deep, stretching her, possessing her, retreating to tease and circle her swollen clit but not taking her over.

'Please, I need...' she begged. Too close and yet too far.

'Shh, *bella*, I have you,' he soothed, his voice fierce with the same need tearing her apart.

Then he brushed his thumb over the swollen bundle of

nerves. She cried out, breaking into a billion glittering shards of exquisite pain, furious pleasure.

She was still shivering, still shaking, the cloud of afterglow almost as brutal as the titanic orgasm, as he pushed her onto the bed.

She watched him—dazed, dizzy, disorientated—as he dragged off the briefs and freed the massive erection.

She lifted up on her elbows, the desire to stroke him, there, where he was so beautiful, as instinctive as it was unfamiliar. She'd had sex before, but it had never been like this—so stark, so wild, so elemental.

But when she reached for him, he snagged her wrist. 'Do not touch me, Tallulah, I need to be inside you now.'

She swallowed, and nodded, the ache in her throat almost as vicious as the one between her thighs. Why did this feel like so much more than just sex?

'Do I need a condom?' he asked. 'I am clean, I have never taken a woman without one—before you.'

It took her a moment to realise what he was asking—the urgency in his voice an even more powerful aphrodisiac than her recent climax.

'I—I'm clean, too, my only boyfriend was in college, two years ago. And we used a condom, too.'

His eyes flared, the possessive gleam unmistakeable as he hooked his thumbs into her soaked panties and dragged them off. 'And contraceptive?'

'I—I have a coil...' she said, barely able to breathe now, the anticipation building as fast as the emotional storm inside her. And never more grateful in her entire life for the heavy periods which had made the contraceptive device necessary.

'*Grazie a Dio,*' he murmured.

Grasping her hips, he spread her legs to position himself between her thighs. The huge head of his erection butted her sex. She braced, her fingers digging into his broad shoulders as his heavy length slid deep in one devastating thrust.

She groaned, the penetration so huge it was overwhelming. He was wedged to the hilt, stretching her unbearably. But when he pulled out, then rocked back, he went deeper still.

He cradled her cheek, hooked the hair behind her ear from the collapsed chignon. 'It will be okay in a minute,' he coaxed, his tone husky with tension. 'You are very tight.'

She shifted beneath him, trying to ease the pressure, but brutally aware of the licks of pleasure starting to build again, despite the shocking intrusion.

'And y-you're very big,' she moaned.

The erection twitched inside her as he let out a chuckle.

She writhed again, and his hands tightened on her hips, holding her still, her sex throbbing now in time with her heartbeat, the discomfort receding to be replaced by the driving need to take him even deeper, if that were possible.

'Do not move, Tallulah,' he groaned. 'I do not wish to hurt you.'

She clasped his cheeks, the evening stubble abrading her palms as she stared into eyes as dazed with lust as her own.

'I can't be still. I can't stand it…' she gasped. 'I want you to move.'

He grunted, then pressed his lips to hers, the fierce hunger on his face as glorious as the heavy weight inside her. '*Va bene, bella*,' he murmured, the sound rough with relief.

He eased out then back, hitting the spot deep inside her he'd already found with his fingers. But this time, the thick stroke felt hasher, deeper, more devastating, her body's reaction even more powerful, and overwhelming.

'That feels so good,' she moaned.

'*Sì molto buono*,' he groaned back.

Hard hands clasped her hips, the devastating thrusts becoming sharper, stronger, more furious, shooting her towards that desperate peak now with a speed that left her breathless. She clung to his sweat-slicked shoulders, her fingers digging into the muscle to find purchase so she could lift into his thrusts.

She moaned as the brutal orgasm slammed into her at last, her exhausted body shattering, battered by the storm of sensations bursting free. And flew over the edge, as he shouted out his own release, his hot seed pumping into her as he followed her into the abyss.

CHAPTER TEN

DARIO STRUGGLED NOT to collapse on top of Tallulah, his movements clumsy. She let out a staggered moan—her sex still massaging his length through the final throes of her orgasm as he eased out of her body.

He had known their chemistry was extraordinary, but he had never experienced a release so intense, so shattering. He had taken her like a man possessed.

He rolled onto his back, exhausted, even as desire still shimmered through his blood and kept his cock firm.

He had never taken a woman before without protection. Was that it? He tried to rationalise the stunning wave of afterglow. The sense he had just reached a higher plane. Determined it could mean nothing more than sex. But when she shifted next to him, he snagged her arm, not ready for her to leave his side.

'Where are you going?' he asked, his voice groggy as he searched her face for signs of distress.

She had been so tight, but also so wet, so swollen and ready, it had only increased the sense he had never made love to a woman before to whom he was better matched.

Not made love, fucked.

He blinked slowly when she tugged free, desperate to dislodge the haze of pheromones making it hard for him to breathe, let alone think rationally.

'I... I thought I'd take a shower.' She clasped her arm

across her breasts—the pale skin reddened from his attention—as the vivid blush fired across her collarbone.

Damn, had he ever seen anything more arousing?

The polite reply though was contradicted by her panicked expression.

Had she felt it too, the extraordinary strength of their sexual connection? She must have done, although with only one lover before him, she probably had no idea how rare such a connection was. Strangely, the thought of her inexperience helped his frantic heartbeat to slow while his racing thoughts clung to the conviction their connection—however extraordinary—could never be more than sex.

But when she attempted to climb off the bed, he reached for her again.

'Wait, Tallulah… Did I hurt you?' he asked.

The blush brightened, but she shook her head. 'No… I… It felt good.'

He lifted onto his elbow and ran his hand up her arm, to hold her more securely, enjoying her shiver of response.

'Only *good*?' he teased, touched by the way she was blushing so profusely. His heartbeat slowed, the euphoria settling around him when she huffed.

'Okay, very good… I've never had an…' She bit into her lip, clearly not intending to continue.

'You've never had a what, Tallulah?' he asked, smiling, because he could already see the answer in her eyes and feel it in the way her pulse was hammering his thumb. It seemed her only other lover had not been very accomplished.

She tugged her arm free a second time. 'I'm not sure you need a testimonial, Mr Lorenti… I—I mean, Dario,' she stuttered.

He chuckled, he couldn't help it, the combination of indignation and embarrassment only making her more endearing. *Dio*, had he ever met a woman more delightful, or transparent. Her unguarded reactions were almost as enchanting as the way she responded to him with such raw passion.

He'd been concerned about taking this step. Afraid to want her too much. But *why* had he, when their affair had the potential to make the next few weeks and months so much more satisfying—as well as making it impossible for those infuriating Trustees to deny this was a real relationship? It certainly felt real enough now, in the only way that mattered.

He would never be able to trust anyone enough to commit to more than sex. He never wished to be that boy again, so desperate for friendship he had allowed himself to become too needy, too vulnerable. But indulging this hunger with her…that would be a pleasure.

He'd never been so turned on before. There was something about Tallulah that called to his inner caveman, made him want to protect and possess her at one and the same time, unprecedented reactions which he had never had with the other women he'd dated. But then, he had never met anyone as artless as Tallulah, he decided as he watched her scramble off the bed. She grabbed her discarded dress, using it to cover her nakedness as she dashed into the bathroom.

As her naked bottom disappeared behind the bathroom door, he let out a gruff chuckle. Apparently, her lack of guile only made her more appealing.

He flopped back on the bed. Rubbed his hand over his chest, no longer disturbed by the rush of heat returning to his cock as he heard the shower.

He had found his fake fiancée's ability to sense his mood disturbing earlier, but why? This attraction was still only a physical connection. And they had all the time in the world to explore it now.

Climbing from the bed, he massaged the ruined muscles of his thigh as he followed her into the bathroom.

She was standing with her back to him in the shower cubicle.

He noticed the tremor in her slender body as she stood under the steamy spray with her hands braced on the glass tiles—making no move to wash herself...

He could almost hear her brain working overtime, probably trying to rationalise what they had just shared.

Good luck with that. There was no way to rationalise something this elemental. The only thing that made sense was to enjoy it, until it faded.

He cleared his throat. Her head shot round, her eyes widening. 'Dario? What are you doing in here?'

But then her gaze shot down to the reaction he could not hide. And her cheeks blazed anew.

Crossing the room, he opened the glass door and stepped into the spacious stone cubicle.

'I thought I would help you wash...' he said, enjoying the shocked awareness which flashed across her features.

Reaching behind her, he lifted the complementary shampoo off the rainfall shower's shelf and poured the fragrant liquid into his palm.

'It's nice of you to offer...' she said, her voice shaky. 'But I'm not sure it's a good idea. It's... It's been a while since I... And well...' Her gaze—wary and tense—slipped down to assess his engorged cock. 'I'm not sure I can do it again so soon,' she finished. He didn't know whether to laugh or wince, the earnest expression on her face only making her more adorable.

He nodded, the regret—that she was probably a bit sore—tempered by the knowledge she had not rejected him outright.

'I am not an animal, Tallulah,' he said, as he pressed her shoulder to turn her to face the tiles again. 'Ignore the erection. I do not expect to have you again tonight. Let me take care of you now.'

He nudged her chin up. 'You must stop staring at me like that, Tallulah,' he said the wry amusement making the blush race over her whole body. 'Or I will find it even more agonising to keep my hands off you tonight.'

'I—I could sleep on the couch next door, if you like,' she offered, overwhelmed again.

'It is a good thing my ego is so robust.' He chuckled, his eyes twinkling with amusement, which she suspected might be at her expense.

Had she insulted him by implying he couldn't control himself? Before she had a chance to process the thought though, or voice an apology, crippled by indecision and awkwardness, he whipped off her towel and drew back the sheet.

'Climb in,' he said.

She obeyed without question, grateful for the protection of the bed linens on her naked skin. Instead of joining her, he sat on the bed to tug on his boxers over the still-heavy erection. When he crossed the room and pulled a pair of sweatpants out of his luggage, she felt strangely bereft.

'You're…you're not coming to bed, too?' she asked as he put on the pants, and she tried not to fixate on the scarring on his injured leg…or the deep well of sympathy making her throat tighten again.

He sent her an enigmatic smile—as he grabbed a T-shirt and pulled it over his head.

'Not yet,' he said as he returned to sit next to her on the bed. 'I must walk off the stiffness in my leg…'

'Does the injury still hurt?' she mumbled, swallowing down the dryness in her throat as she recalled the agonising pain he had been in that summer in Wiltshire.

'Only occasionally,' he murmured. But she had the feeling she had crossed a line she was not meant to cross, when the wry smile on his lips did not reach his eyes. 'I am more concerned about the stiffness in other parts of my body, which I must walk off too if I am to keep my promise to you…'

'Oh…okay,' she mumbled, aware of the renewed pulsing in her sex at the bold comment.

'Hold that thought,' he murmured, apparently able to read her mind.

He cradled her cheek, the possessive gesture as overpowering as everything else about him.

Her heart pummelled her chest wall. And it occurred to her that sleeping with him—a man who knew his way around a woman's body and had probably had a ton of these types of booty calls before—had put her at a major disadvantage… Because their fake relationship didn't feel as fake as it should anymore.

He planted a kiss on her forehead. 'Go to sleep, Tallulah. I will see you in the morning. Once we are back in Milan we will discuss the new terms of our arrangement.'

She nodded again. But her heart got wedged in her throat as he walked out of the room, the hitch in his stride more obvious than usual.

She lay in the big bed, willing her pulse to slow down and trying not to think about what he meant by 'the new terms of our arrangement'. The scent of their lovemaking permeated the room, stimulating her already hyperaware senses and doing nothing to dissolve the block of concrete which had got lodged in her throat.

But the whirl of the ceiling fan and the dull hum of the wedding DJ's music—still playing bangers on the other side of the estate—eventually lulled her tired mind and her exhausted body into a deep, drugging sleep.

CHAPTER ELEVEN

Two days later

'...*DI AMARTI E ONORARTI tutti i giorni della mia vita*...' Tali fumbled through the wedding vows in Italian, which she'd had less than forty-eight hours to memorise. She hoped she'd said them correctly. What bothered her more, though, was what they meant.

To love you and every day honour you, for the rest of my life.

Had she really just promised before the officiant and the select gathering of Dario's friends and business associates in his penthouse apartment to love and honour this taciturn and overwhelming man forever?

Of course, that's not what their marriage vows *actually* meant—because she also had the pre-nuptial agreement, putting an end date on their marriage, signed and notarised and stuffed into a pocket of her rucksack. Even so, her stomach rose up to butt her tonsils and her pulse went nuts as Dario gripped her left hand and slid the slim gold band on her finger.

The middle-aged female officiant sent them a hopeful smile, and polite applause echoed around the penthouse's living room. But her hand was still shaking as Dario captured her waist to pull her to him.

The desire darkening his eyes made her breath catch, before he framed her face in his hands and lowered his mouth to hers while the officiant declared them man and wife.

The firm, possessive kiss sent the familiar shock waves hurtling through her system, as he claimed her as his wife, for the benefit of the guests. Her breath backed up in her lungs, the desire like a geyser, raw and real and utterly addictive, even though this was the first time he'd held her since leaving her in the summer house bed two nights ago, alone.

When she'd woken the next morning, he'd already been dressed in a business suit, busy barking orders to one of his assistants in the house's living area. She'd felt like an interloper, the only thing that had stopped her from feeling totally ignored, and weirdly bereft, the knowledge he had slept beside her during the night, because she'd seen the indent of his head on the pillow.

She'd barely had a chance to exchange more than pleasantries with him during the trip back to Milan, because he'd been busy fielding calls in Italian on his mobile or talking to one of his business associates over a video link about a US tech deal, the details of which she hadn't been able to understand. He'd been on his smartphone too, when they'd driven back into the city from the airport, giving her a perfunctory kiss goodbye when the car had dropped her off at her old apartment.

And she hadn't seen him since. Not until fifteen minutes ago, after she'd been informed by Aldo at breakfast this morning, the marriage had been arranged for today, four days ahead of the original schedule. Aldo had at least been apologetic when she'd barely been able to contain her shock. Especially after she'd asked to speak to Dario and his assistant had explained that would not be possible.

What had happened to the discussion about 'our new arrangement' he'd promised her two nights ago? She'd been disturbed at the thought of everything changing between them. But this morning—when a designer had arrived with a cream satin dress, and the beautician and the stylist had been prepping her for a wedding she hadn't even realised was happening today until a few hours ago—she'd wondered what on earth she had been so concerned about... Because it turned out *not* having that conversation was a whole lot more anxiety inducing.

She had no idea anymore what was going on between them. Did he still want her? Why had he arranged the ceremony four days early without informing her? And what was supposed to happen next? Because even Aldo didn't seem to know what his boss's plans were, and all her efforts to contact Dario in the last four hours had gone unanswered.

Aldo had mumbled something about Dario being extremely busy. But when she'd arrived in the penthouse's lobby to find her groom waiting, looking devastatingly handsome in a dark grey tailored suit, and then been immediately whisked into the ceremony, she'd started to feel not just dismayed and wary, but frankly, pissed off.

If he didn't want her anymore, all he had to do was say so...instead of giving her the cold shoulder for forty-eight hours and making her feel like an inconvenient accessory again. What had happened to the man who had washed her hair so tenderly, then tucked her into bed as if she were precious two nights ago?

Her fierce reaction now to his kiss—in front of a crowd of people she didn't know—only humiliated her more. Why couldn't she control that instant, instinctive response? The way her body melted into his. The way her heartbeat thundered in her ears. The way arousal coursed into her abdomen—and made her sex ache as if he were still lodged inside her. The way her breathing became harsh and ragged—as if she wasn't already disorientated enough after the whirlwind of events in the past two weeks.

When he ended the kiss, she had to lock her knees to stop her legs from shaking. He clasped her hand and lifted her fingers to his lips, the desire so potent in his eyes she felt as if she'd been branded.

He cupped the back of her neck, to tug her towards him until he could whisper against her earlobe.

'*Complementi*, Tallulah. I did not expect you to say the vows in Italian…but you spoke them well.' His gaze darkened, the approval even more disturbing to her peace of mind than his radio silence over the past forty-eight hours. 'Tonight, we can enjoy each other again on Capri. But first we must suffer this charade a while longer.'

Capri? Tonight? What?

She jolted back, feeling overwhelmed again and not in a good way. Everything was moving so fast. While she'd agreed to this *charade*, as he called it, their relationship had changed since their night together in Sicily. Or at least it had for her. She'd assumed he would be more forthcoming about information. If he considered her his lover now, didn't she deserve to be treated like one, instead of just the fake bride he'd hired?

'But…? I thought I would be able to return to Westwick after the wedding…' she managed, suddenly desperate for a time-out. She needed a chance to get her life back on track after Sicily. Obviously, them sleeping together wasn't a big deal for him. But it was for her, enough that she'd been agonising in the last few days about whether he still wanted her—and whether she'd got any closer to knowing whether the connection they shared was more than just sex. She needed to get her volatile emotions under control. If they were going to make this a convenient marriage with benefits, she didn't want to end up getting any more invested than she was already. But the last forty-eight hours had made her feel as if she had stepped aboard a merry-go-round which was accelerating so fast, she might *never* be able to jump off... And she wanted to get off, at least for a few days, to maintain her sanity, before she gave in to this chemistry again.

Dario was just too intense, too...*much*...for someone with her lack of sexual experience to handle, when she felt so powerless.

He frowned. 'You do not wish to return to my bed?' he asked, so candidly her cheeks ignited.

Her gaze darted around the reception. The guests were keeping a respectable distance, to let the happy couple celebrate their new vows in private. But even so, she was taken aback by the direct question.

'That's not what I meant...' she said, because there was no way she could pretend she didn't want him, when her clitoris was pounding in time with her throbbing heartbeat, and she was beathing so hard she was practically hyperventilating from a simple stunt kiss.

'It's just...no one told me we were going to Capri tonight,' she said, trying not to give away how unsettled she felt. Because she was already at enough of a disadvantage.

His smile widened as he caressed the burning skin on her cheek. 'A honeymoon is expected in such circumstances. Is it not?'

A honeymoon? Seriously?

Couldn't he see how problematic that was now they were intimate? A honeymoon would make this union feel far too much like a real marriage...

'Yes...b-but...' she stammered, with no idea what to say. He looked so sure of himself, so unfazed by all of this. She thought she'd sensed some understanding from him that night. Believed he had understood how out of her depth she was after...after they'd... She swallowed, because recalling that night was not a good way to calm her rampaging heart rate. *At all.*

'You should have told me that was the plan...' she said, because suddenly talking about logistics was the only way to control the panic attack she was about to have, at the thought of their not-so-fake honeymoon.

How on earth could she spend days making love to him and remain objective about what their so-called marriage was actually supposed to achieve?

He pressed his finger to her lips then took her hand. 'Let us discuss this in private.'

He gave Aldo a brief nod and then, his grip tightening on her trembling fingers, marched past the guests milling about in the living area, enjoying the cordon bleu appetisers and refreshments which had been prepared by a Michelin-starred chef, and through the doors of the terrace. He nodded brusquely at the two businessmen already enjoying the view, who offered them their hearty congratulations.

'Gentlemen, could you leave us alone? I wish to celebrate with my wife in private.'

Both men nodded, one blushing, and left immediately, closing the terrace doors behind them.

The word *wife*, though, was still echoing in Tali's psyche when she found herself alone with him for the first time since they had been naked together.

Awkward, much!

The afternoon breeze brushed against her oversensitive skin. She folded her arms around her waist, feeling as if she had just leapt off the high terrace, because her stomach was already in free fall.

He clasped her neck, stroked the pulse point with his thumb, his gaze locked on her burning face. 'Now, tell me what the problem is...'

Where do I even start? Her temper ignited to cover the panic.

'The problem is, I didn't even know we were getting

married today until eleven this morning. And what happened to…to…' She paused, not sure how to word the questions which had been piling up for forty-eight hours without sounding clingy, or worse, as if she was expecting more from this arrangement because they had become lovers. 'You said we would discuss this arrangement, how it's going to work, after we became…' She paused, having to push the word out. '*Intimate*. But I haven't been able to speak to you at all.'

'What is it you wish to discuss?' he asked, so matter-of-factly she suddenly wanted to punch him.

Was he really this clueless? But before she could gather her wits about her enough to come up with a coherent answer to *that* asinine remark, he answered it himself.

'The only thing which has changed in this arrangement, Tallulah, is that we will share a bed. We have a rare chemistry which will enhance our time together. This was very clear two nights ago. Do you not agree?'

'Well, yes but…' She stumbled to a halt. She was being railroaded, but she couldn't seem to control all the emotions which were starting to strangle her now to form a coherent argument. Because she wasn't just annoyed and frustrated with him. What did she do with that terrifying spurt of hope, of expectation, which seemed to go well beyond the physical? 'It's just, this is a lot, for me…' she managed. 'I'm not used to being…well…'

She stumbled to a halt again, more exposed than ever. Especially when his dark eyes flared with something fierce and possessive—which only made the spurt of expectation worse.

'I know this, Tallulah,' he said, the tone patient, and more than a little condescending. 'Which is why I have been avoiding you for the past two days. I wished to give you time to adjust,' he added, the husky tone making the pulse in her abdomen become catastrophic. 'Do not worry. We will take this slowly. There is no rush. I have arranged for us to be at the palazzo for a month. There is much I need to do on the island, especially once I take full ownership of the estate—which should be soon. The Trustees were impressed with Lombardi's article, too, and are already convinced this is a real marriage. Having you in my bed will help with this, too.'

His tone had lowered, the husky words and the awareness in his gaze brushing over her skin like a caress. Until one word jumped out at her.

'A *month*? But I can't stay in Capri for a month. What about Westwick? What about my job?' she said, because thinking about her career was so much easier than thinking about how reckless her stupid, delusional heart had already got about this whole situation. 'The money you promised to invest will be deposited today, and I have to be there to oversee the...'

'You will have the opportunity to contact your staff at the Hall during our stay in the palazzo if you wish,' he cut in. 'There is office space there, and a strong internet connection. But we cannot be apart until the Trustees are satisfied the marriage is valid. Once the ownership has been transferred to me, you will be able to return to Westwick more frequently.'

The pragmatic response had the bubble of hope under her breastbone deflating. This whole thing was still primarily about gaining ownership of the palazzo for him. Because of course it was.

Remember that, Tali. For heaven's sake.

'You have to let me know what's going on, Dario. This isn't just about our... Our...' She swallowed convulsively, feeling hopelessly compromised, even though she knew she shouldn't. 'Our sleeping arrangements. Not anymore. It's also about my work, my life, my choices. I know I signed on to be your stunt wife, but I did that because the Hall is important to me. My work and the people who work there are important to me.' She drew in a heavy breath, not sure she should confide in him, but knowing she wanted to, so he would understand *how* important her work was to her. 'When I was a kid, my father left me and my mum and started another family. For years I tried to get him to see me, to want me, but he wasn't interested. And it crushed me. Moving to Westwick, living there, having a job I loved, working with people I respected, eventually helped me to realise his inability to love me, to even *see* me, was never my fault.'

She blinked, wondering if he could see how that gave them a connection. That they had both been neglected by inadequate men.

But there was one big difference. While she suspected Dario had been determined never to feel too much, her response to that rejection had been to try to make her father come back. And in the process, she'd developed a bad habit of wanting to fix broken things. That's why it had given her so much pleasure making a surly, injured boy smile. But when she'd discovered she was powerless to fix the relationship with her father, no matter how hard she tried, it had destroyed her. Westwick had saved her, eventually. But she couldn't let anyone destroy her confidence again, the way her father had. Not even Dario. *Especially* as she was beginning to sense that despite what Mia had told her in Sicily, Dario had no desire to let her, or anyone else, get too close to him.

Yes, he was a complex and fascinating man, but he also guarded his heart even more fiercely now than he had when he was a teenager.

Perhaps now would be a good time to tell him she'd met him all those years ago. But the fact he didn't know about their history, because he hadn't remembered her, made the confession stick in her throat. Blurting all that out now would only make her feel more exposed, and she was exposed enough already.

He hadn't said anything... But she couldn't tell from his blank expression whether he was shocked or bored or simply dumbfounded by her oversharing... Because his reaction was as inscrutable as always.

Maybe just get to the point then, Tal!

'You *have* to stop ordering me about if we're going to be sleeping together...or it will make me feel...' She sucked in another harsh breath, let it out. 'Powerless again, like I did then.'

He continued to stare at her for the longest time, but when he nodded and then cradled her cheek, to skim his thumb across her skin, his blank expression becoming as tender as it had been that night, the panic finally released its death grip on her chest.

'Your father was *un idiota*,' he said at last.

She huffed out a relieved laugh. '*Absolutamente*,' she murmured, her fledging Italian making his lips curve.

'I apologise for not informing you of my plans sooner,' he added, the tone strained as the smile died. Even so, it felt like a major concession that he'd at least acknowledged she deserved to know what the hell was going on. 'But I want you to come to Capri with me.'

It wasn't really a request, more like a statement of purpose, but it felt vindicating nonetheless—that he had also acknowledged she deserved a choice.

'I... I'll come on one condition,' she countered, determined not to be a total pushover.

She couldn't spend a whole month getting jiggy with Dario Lorenti on Capri without consequences, because that amount of quality time with him was bound to make it next to impossible for her to keep their fling in perspective. He was just so hot and fascinating and demanding, and so unlike any other man she had ever met. Giving herself some time-outs during their not-so-fake honeymoon to visit the team at Westwick and keep abreast of the renovations would help ground her, while also reminding her of the main reason why she had agreed to this arrangement in the first place—to save Westwick, and *not* to indulge in a flaming hot affair with its owner. That was merely a fringe benefit, which she could only come out of unscathed, if she didn't get overinvested in it…and him.

His jaw tensed. He did not look pleased about having to negotiate with her, but instead of attempting to ride roughshod over her wishes for once, which she knew was his default, he simply said, 'And what is this condition?'

She smiled, because it felt like another big win for Team Take-No-Shit Tali.

'I need to return to Westwick for a couple of days each week during our month together on Capri. I want to oversee the new investments being made to the infrastructure in person as well as over the internet,' she rushed on when he frowned, determined to make her request all about Westwick's future and *not* about her insecurities, because it totally was…*mostly*. 'I can do some of that remotely, but my staff also need me to be present.'

The muscle in his jaw hardened. 'You may return once,' he said. 'And for no longer than two days. And not in the first week.'

She sighed, forcing herself to ignore the silly leap in her pulse at how keen he seemed to keep her with him for the whole month.

It's all about fooling the Trustees so he can acquire his palazzo, Tali. It's not you he needs. He just wants to make this marriage look convincing.

She needed to stay focussed now, so she didn't start getting delusional again, and remember her 'marriage' to Dario was a diversion, an adventure, an adrenaline-pumping thrill ride which would end soon enough…

'Okay,' she said. 'I guess I can live with that.' But when she held out her hand for them to shake on it, he grasped her fingers and tugged her into his arms. Cupping her bottom, he caressed her through the satin.

'Our guests are watching, Tallulah,' he said, his gaze fierce with the heated promise which made her pulse bounce, her nipples peak and arousal swell and pound between her thighs.

Then he kissed her so thoroughly, her focus shattered. *Completely.*

Because all she could feel was the insistent erection rising against her belly. And all she could think about was what tonight would hold, once they were finally alone together—and she could climb aboard the adrenaline-pumping thrill ride that was Dario Lorenti…again.

CHAPTER TWELVE

'It's stunning, Dario…'

Pride pushed against Dario's chest at Tallulah's awed comment as the helicopter circled the Palazzo di Constanzo. He tried to catalogue the improvements which had been made since his last visit: the terraces built into the hillside behind the house to create vegetable gardens; the double-level infinity pool which now replaced the old pool which had lain empty and derelict for years; the ornate plastering on the colonnades which had been painstakingly repaired; the recent planting which had come into bloom, the profusion of wisteria and orange blossom adding vibrant splashes of colour to the villa's fanciful frontage.

But his concentration was shot, because his attention was fixed on the woman beside him, and the concerning emotions stirred by the vulnerabilities she had revealed to him on the terrazzo of his Milan penthouse four hours ago.

His heart pulsed, her expression when she had told him about her bastard of a father, was still so vivid—so fierce and yet so open.

The man sounded like even more of a bastard than his own father. How could he have discarded her so easily? But imagining Tallulah as a girl had given him the strange sense that if he could have known her then, he would have wanted to protect her from that rejection, which wasn't just concerning—it was nothing short of ludicrous. Because he had lost the ability to be that man a long time ago, and he had no wish to become that man now.

The flight to Naples had been torture, as he pretended to be engrossed in his cell phone, while being far too aware of his new bride's every sigh, every movement, every breath. Just as he had been forty-eight long hours ago on their return to Milan from Sicily.

Keeping his hands off her until their wedding night had been an exercise in diversion and distraction—and painful denial. It was frustrating to realise starving himself of her company for two days had done nothing to control his addiction.

How could he want her now even more than he had on their night in Sicily?

Especially now he knew how vulnerable she was.

The decision to spend a month at the palazzo had been made after waking up with her lush body wrapped around his in the summer house, his cock so needy it was a miracle he had managed to leave her sleeping. But despite that moment of saintly forbearance, he'd moved the civil ceremony forward as soon as they'd arrived back in Milan, because he'd known he could not wait a whole week to feed this addiction again.

Dio, at least this torture would be over soon.

The helicopter set down on the palazzo's clifftop heliport.

He had wanted to stay at the villa for seven long years but had only had the time for a few cursory site visits—forced to book into a luxury hotel in Ana Capri, the nearby town, while the extensive renovations had been under way. Perhaps seeing the house finally ready was the real cause of this pressure in his chest, as he descended the chopper's steps and held his hand out for Tallulah to follow him—and not the anticipation of a wedding night which only felt real because his new bride looked so perfect.

She wore an elegant pant suit which accentuated her curves, her wild hair tied back with a silk scarf. The new stylist had understood his requirements implicitly—that his wife's wardrobe should not be too revealing. But when the jacket's lapel flicked open in the down draft from the helicopter blades, he got an eyeful of her cleavage, her nipples standing proud against the skimpy camisole beneath, and the familiar pulse of lust blindsided him again.

His hand tightened on hers, touching the gold band he'd placed on her finger that afternoon. Their gazes locked, and the lust swelled when she chewed her bottom lip.

He had requested that the staff prepare an evening meal for them on the main terrace, which overlooked the Bay of Naples, ready for their arrival. With the glow of the approaching sunset reflected in her luminous eyes, he knew he ought to let her eat first, if only to prove he could wait another hour before devouring her. But as the helicopter's blades slowed, he found himself heading instead through the arbour of trees which led to the palazzo's private quarters, charging past the stone walls overflowing with the dark pink blooms of bougainvillea. The subtle honeysuckle scent was one he remembered from the lazy, unstructured days of his childhood, but with her hand clutched tightly in his, and adrenaline pumping through his blood like a drug, the last thing he felt was relaxed.

Finally, they reached the rear entrance. The housekeeper and her staff were waiting for them in the hallway, clearly having assembled to greet his new bride.

But when Tallulah paused to greet them all in Italian, he found himself tensing. Eventually he was forced to interrupt the introductions—and lead his bride away, not wanting to risk scandalising the staff with his condition.

But he could not wait a moment longer to have her.

'Dario, is everything okay?' Tallulah asked as he marched

up the villa's wide sweeping marble staircase to his bedroom suite on the second floor.

As he entered the large sitting room, the salty sea air was tinged with the scent of new paint, but all he could smell was the delicious aroma of her, which had been tantalising his senses ever since he had kissed her on the terrazzo in Milan.

He could still taste her arousal. And he intended to focus on that now, and not the emotions which had made him want to protect that neglected girl.

The terrace doors stood open to let in the evening breeze. The dying daylight added a golden glow to the spectacular view of the Tyrrhenian Sea from the palazzo's enviable position as the lights of Ana Capri twinkled in the distance.

He had waited so long to come here again. To return to the only place he had ever been truly happy. The work he had paid for—hiring the best local craftsmen and artisans to return the palazzo to its former glory, long before the heady days of his mother's endless parties, or his father's deliberate neglect—was finally complete. And it was only a matter of time now before he would own the place outright.

Why then did he feel almost ambivalent about what this marriage had always been supposed to achieve? It was almost as if he couldn't appreciate the beauty of the palazzo and the stunning vista through the terrazzo doors, because the only beauty he could see was Tallulah, her arms wrapped around her midriff, her breasts straining against the silk camisole, the mess of her curls highlighted by the dying sun when she took off the scarf.

His breath clogged in his lungs as the heat surged.

'Do you wish to eat?' he made himself ask. But there was no mistaking the husky desire in his voice.

She shook her head, trembling. 'I don't think I could eat anything at the moment,' she said, her blue eyes shining with that exquisite combination of awareness and sincerity—which he had become obsessed with.

'Are you cold?' he asked, trailing his thumb down her neck to stroke the pulse point hammering her throat.

The muscles jumped as she swallowed, her wary gaze only intensifying the hunger making his cock throb.

'Actually, I think I'm the opposite,' she murmured, her meaning clear.

He chuckled, the sound rough with need. *Dio*, but she was so forthright, her honesty almost as compelling as the colour blooming across her collarbone.

'*Bene*,' he murmured.

Spreading her jacket open, he grasped her waist to draw her into his arms. Capturing her lips, he thrust his tongue deep—to claim her shocked sob. Her nipples thrust against his chest through their clothing as he devoured her mouth, exploring the hidden recesses, capturing each heady sigh, each sweet shudder.

He tore his mouth free, so they could each drag in a shattered breath.

'I cannot wait to have you again, Tallulah. But I promise to be gentle.'

She nodded, the trust in her eyes crucifying him all over again.

Did she have any idea how wild he was for her? He hoped not. But he could not control himself much longer, the tormenting desire to brand her as his fast becoming all-consuming.

Perhaps she was not his real wife—perhaps he had never intended this relationship to be more than a means to an end. But when she allowed him to strip off the jacket, to cup her breasts through the silk, and close his mouth over those yearning peaks, his intentions didn't matter. Her fingers sank into his hair, her back arching instinctively to thrust the engorged nipple into his mouth, and he knew he had never needed anyone the way he needed her. Right now.

He scooped her into his arms, heard her harsh gasp as he strode through the living area, his aching leg nowhere near as painful as his swollen cock.

A new four-poster bed dominated the suite's main bedroom, the other furniture artfully arranged around it, the terrace doors opening onto a dappled view of the coastline and the pure blue sea enhanced by the sunset.

But he couldn't see any of it, because all he could see was her, as he laid her trembling body on the satin bedspread, then proceeded to undress her, the promise to be careful a whole new form of torture.

He tugged off her camisole, her bra, the sleek trousers, her lacy panties with frantic, clumsy fingers… Within seconds she lay naked, her pale skin rosy with heat, the musky scent of her arousal intoxicating him. He stripped off his shirt, and watched her eyes darken as her gaze skated over his chest.

But then she clasped an arm over her breasts.

'*Non*… Do not cover yourself…'

Her eyes widened at the harsh demand, but she let her arm drop.

He swallowed, knowing he had to calm down to make this good for her.

Climbing onto the bed, he took her arm, kissed her fingers, then trailed his tongue along the sensitive skin inside her elbow, across her collarbone, to circle her stiff nipple. Lifting her breast, he fastened his lips on the pouting tip and suckled hard.

She groaned, bowing back, her sobs like a whip to his senses.

He worked one breast, then the other, trapping her tender flesh against the roof of his mouth, entranced by her instant, unguarded response. Had any woman ever been so attuned to his needs, so quick to meet his demands with demands of her own?

He brushed his fingers into the curls covering her sex, and coaxed the slick folds open, to locate the plump nub of her clitoris. He circled it, testing her readiness, aware of the painful erection already threatening to burst out of his pants.

'Dario… Oh… God…' She writhed, each teasing touch making her buck, until she was riding his hand, desperate for relief.

Finally, he gave her the sure solid touch she craved. And watched, enthralled, his own body already on the brink, as she shattered.

She was still trembling, as she opened eyes slumberous with afterglow. He staggered to his feet, to wrestle off the rest of his clothing. Naked, *finally*, he rolled her onto her stomach and dragged her onto her knees until he could probe her glistening sex from behind.

He didn't want to see her face, couldn't let himself get lost in those bright, bliss-shattered eyes, in case he again saw the vulnerability she had shown him that afternoon.

She let out a staggered groan as he drove deep, her recent orgasm allowing him to bury himself to the hilt in a single thrust. He held her hips—to pull out, and pound back—forcing her to take the full measure of him. The tight clasp of her sex massaged him in rhythmic beats as he began to move.

Her cries of fulfilment became rawer and more elemental. Finding her clit, he worked it, ruthlessly, forcing her over again, his own climax building like a tsunami.

The burning heat seared through him, scorching him in brutal waves, the driving need building to a blistering crescendo. His movements became jerky, uncoordinated as the devastating orgasm slammed through him—fast, furious, unstoppable—and he emptied himself inside her at last.

* * *

Tali fell forward onto the mattress, her body shaking with the vicious power of her orgasm... Make that *orgasms*...

Dario's big body collapsed on top of her.

How many orgasms had she had? Because it felt as if each one had layered on the last, until the brutal mindless waves of pleasure had become never-ending.

He was still firm inside her, the penetration still deep. But then he lifted off her. She moaned, the blissful afterglow only intensifying the strong sense of loss.

She'd been looking for a connection with him, but maybe this incendiary connection was all they would ever share.

The rasps of their breathing slowed, and the afterglow faded, but the painful regret remained, snaking around her chest to squeeze her ribs.

He touched her cheek. 'Look at me, Tallulah,' he murmured, the demand softened by the husky tone.

She made herself meet his gaze in the half-light, trying to disguise her reaction.

This is just your first multiple orgasm talking, Tali. That's all.

Lit by the setting sun, his handsome features looked stark, the red glow accentuating the scar on his cheek.

Why did that make her heart squeeze?

'*Bene*?' he asked.

'*Sì, molto bene*,' she said, replying automatically in Italian.

A smile lifted his lips, making his harsh features look almost boyish. The fierce approval in his eyes made her throat close.

She placed her palm on his scarred cheek, needing to acknowledge their connection, however misguided.

'*Amo quando mi fai amore*,' she murmured, hoping she'd said what she'd meant to say, correctly.

I love when you make love to me.

Eager for him to know that much at least.

But she wasn't sure she had said it right, when his cheek tensed and the smile disappeared.

For a moment he looked so much like the surly teenager she remembered, hiding his pain behind a mask of indifference, she almost pulled her hand away. But the desire to reach him was a compulsion she couldn't control either, even though she knew she should.

'This is good,' he said, but the change into English felt like another attempt to create distance. 'It will make our honeymoon more enjoyable.'

He covered her hand and drew it away from his face, destroying the moment of intimacy. But his avoidance only made her more determined to ask the question which had been lodged in her brain for weeks—ever since he'd told her why he needed this marriage.

'Why is owning this house so important to you, Dario?'

His gaze remained fixed on hers. But she could sense him calculating whether or not to give her an answer… It felt like a blow, to know he still didn't trust her with even the most innocuous details of his past, when she had trusted him with some of the most personal details about hers earlier that day.

But she tried not to overreact. He hadn't asked for those confidences, and while their wedding vows had felt oddly real while they had made love—the fierce euphoria reinforcing the elemental connection they shared—that was surely just an illusion caused by the intense endorphin rush of multi-orgasmic sex.

As she waited though, for him to brush away the question, the foolish hope for more turned her stomach to mush.

He flopped onto his back and flung an arm over his eyes. But just when she was sure he was going to shut her out again, he began to speak. The wry monotone was carefully devoid of emotion. But somehow, she sensed that the only way he could reveal even this much to her was by pretending it didn't matter to him anymore.

'I lived here as a boy, with my mother and sister. Mia was so young when my mother died, I'm not sure she remembers much of it… But I do.' He lowered his arm, turned towards her and let out a huff of breath, which was supposed to sound amused, but all Tali could hear was the echo of despair. All she could see was the shadow of the intense emotions he was so desperate to hide in his eyes… 'She was so full of life, but also so volatile, her emotions swinging from elation to desperation, often in a single day. But our life here was always colourful, never dull thanks to the parties she hosted every night because she hated to be alone. The villa was always full of people. And she loved us, very much.'

'That sounds a bit chaotic for a child.' And terrifying. Children might think they loved freedom, but they also needed structure to feel safe. She wondered how a boy—who now maintained such a rigid control over his emotions as an adult—had coped with so much insecurity.

He shrugged. 'Yes, it was precarious at times, but it was also exhilarating.'

'How so?' she probed, touched by his willingness to share something too… But also desperately curious about the glimpse he was giving her of the boy Mia had described, before his father, and his accident, had sucked all the joy out of his personality.

'There were no boundaries, no rules,' he murmured, his features softening with memory. 'She spent all the money he gave her after the divorce on luxury food, the best wines and champagnes, and party drugs. Of course, she frequently forgot to pay the staff—and the electricity bill. Mia and I often wore shoes which didn't fit because practicalities bored her. But we dined on lobster and calamari fritti for breakfast and could stay up all night if we wished.'

'Didn't she ever take a night off?' Tali asked, knowing most children would have struggled to survive such an upbringing.

Did he really remember his childhood with only fondness, when he had created such a rigid structure to his own life since?

He propped himself on an elbow, his gaze intense as it roamed over her face. 'You do not approve?'

'It's just… It sounds a little scary and chaotic.'

He frowned. 'It was, at times, but my life here made me self-sufficient, so I cannot regret it,' he said, but the sadness that remained in his eyes told a different story. Of a boy who had been forced to fend for himself—and his sister—from a very young age. Who had never been nurtured, by either of his parents.

He huffed out a breath. 'What was much harder was being forced to leave Capri, by my father. He closed the house up after my mother's death and left it to rot. Then stuck Mia and me in boarding schools, where they did not want me to think for myself. My father expected obedience and loyalty, while he did nothing to earn it.'

'You still hate him?' she murmured, although she already knew the answer. It had made her sad for him as a little girl to witness his father's lack of interest in him, or his recovery. She recalled the only time Westwick had come to visit his son, the angry words and harsh criticism she had overheard as she hid behind the wardrobe door still burned in her memory. It had made her more determined to become his friend even though he'd shouted at her after his father had left to leave him the hell alone, clearly holding back tears. But it made her even sadder now, to know his hatred of his father had stopped him from allowing that boy to heal the rest of the way.

'I feel nothing for him,' he said dismissively. 'As you

should feel nothing for yours. It is pointless to waste your love on people that will not love you back.'

'I suppose,' she said, aware of the warning note in his voice. But also knowing she didn't agree with him.

She'd eventually had to admit her dad was a lost cause, to protect herself from being hurt any more. But how could love ever be wasted? That she had wanted to repair that relationship wasn't a bad thing, and neither were her attempts to be Dario's friend when he'd so desperately needed one. Even if she now knew she'd failed at that too, because he hadn't even remembered her.

But she was still glad she'd tried.

James Westwick had been an inadequate parent at best, even worse in some ways than her own, because his children hadn't had a mother the way she had... But she wondered if Dario's mother, when she'd been alive, had really been that much better. Maybe she had loved her children in her own way, but it didn't sound as if she had ever put their welfare first.

'How did your mother die?' she asked, recalling the flicker of pain which had crossed his face when he'd mentioned her death.

One sceptical eyebrow arched. The grief ruthlessly quashed.

'Really? You have not done an internet search on me?'

'No,' she murmured, hoping he wouldn't ask her the reason why. Because her desire to find out more about him from *him*, instead of a bunch of news headlines, would probably convince him she was impossibly sentimental, even naïve.

'She overdosed one night, by accident. The staff found her in the morning,' he said so dispassionately, she shivered.

'I'm... I'm so sorry, Dario,' she said, tears stinging her eyes.

He brushed away the single drop which escaped with his thumb. The puzzled expression on his face was worse, though, than the thought of him as a boy, losing his mother so needlessly.

'Do not cry, it was a long time ago.' His gaze became shuttered, before his thumb traced the line of her collarbone. 'This is hardly conversation for our wedding night,' he murmured.

Except it's not really our wedding night, because this isn't supposed to be a real marriage.

It's what she should have said, but then he dipped his thumb under the sheet, to circle her nipple, and she lost her train of thought. Heat arrowed down to her core as the swollen peak hardened.

He leaned closer to place his mouth on the pulse point in her neck. He suckled the sensitive skin, while his hand sank further beneath the sheet to flatten over her belly then drag her to him, until his erection brushed her thigh.

'Can you take me again?' he asked, the gruff demand making her sex clench and release, already desperate to be filled.

'Yes.' She clasped his cheeks, to drag his head up and kiss him. She explored his mouth, as he shifted her weight, until he was wedged between her thighs again, probing at her entrance.

He impaled her in one punishing thrust, taking her breath away, even as her misguided heart battered her rib cage.

Why did this feel like so much more than it should?

But as he established a rhythm, angling her pelvis to drive deeper still, the coil of need clenched tight, thrusting her back towards that vicious edge with startling speed… She gave herself up to the shattering pleasure, desperate to ignore the demands of her eager heart—and the yearning to have him need her, for more than sex.

But as she lay in his arms afterwards, his fingers skimming her breast, his heart thumping against her ear, the bubble of hope expanded again.

Because it wasn't just the sex which felt earth-shattering anymore, it was the knowledge that however wary Dario was of intimacy, however desperate not to let himself care too much for anyone again—after *both* of his parents had hurt him—this demanding, taciturn man had trusted her enough tonight to show her why he guarded his heart so fiercely.

And if he could trust her with that much…was it foolish to think that one day, he might be able to trust her with more?

CHAPTER THIRTEEN

Two weeks later

'THE ROOF REPAIRS will be finished by next week, the slate loss wasn't as bad as they thought. And the interior decorators are starting on Monday. They wanted to run a few things by you about the cornices in the East Wing ballroom.'

'That's fabulous, thanks, Ellie. Send me the details and I'll take a look.' Tali beamed at her acting estate manager through the video link. 'You're doing an amazing job, and I really appreciate the daily updates.'

'And I really enjoy you making sure I'm not mucking anything up.' Ellie grinned. 'How's the honeymoon going? It's all so romantic. I still can't believe you married him so quickly. It's so exciting. And he's so handsome.'

Tali felt her face heat—at the memory of their lovemaking that morning. After two weeks, her sexual connection with Dario had only got hotter. But more than that, Dario had turned out to be a surprisingly attentive and involved fake husband, out of bed, too.

Each day—after they'd both checked in with their work—he had some new excursion to suggest. They'd been snorkelling in the villa's lagoon and taken out his sailboat most days—as he tried, and comprehensively failed, to teach her how to sail. He'd insisted on escorting her on a couple of day trips to Ana Capri, a delightful and surprisingly quiet town less than a mile away, where they had whiled away hours exploring the shops or lunching at the local trattorias, binging on homemade pasta—before they drove home on his motorbike to binge on each other again. He enjoyed her company, as well as the sex. And she adored discovering all the reasons why he loved this place so much. And if her attempts to explain why she felt the same way about Westwick hadn't exactly persuaded him, it was all good, because whenever the subject of the Wiltshire estate came up, he usually insisted on diverting the conversation with mind-blowing sex.

She'd come close a couple of those times to blurting out how long she'd lived at Westwick, because she wanted him to know she understood his reluctance to return to the estate, that she knew how hard those months had been for him after the accident. But she'd stopped herself, deciding it felt like poking at a wound she had no right to poke at.

He hadn't shared more about himself, about his thoughts and feelings, since their conversation on their first night here. In fact, he'd kind of avoided talking about anything deep with the same diligence and determination with which he made love to her… But she refused to worry about it. They were getting on so well, it felt like more than enough—for now.

'Will you guys be living at Westwick once the honeymoon's over?' Ellie's enthusiastic question cut through Tali's latest revelry…

She cleared her throat. It wasn't the first time Ellie had asked the question—no doubt her assistant thought it was beyond odd Tali was still keeping her position as Westwick's estate manager when she was now supposedly married to the owner. But this time the standard reply she'd been giving Ellie, and everyone else—that nothing had been confirmed yet—got stuck in her throat. She hated lying to her staff about the relationship, perhaps because their marriage had begun to feel like more than a fake arrangement to her, too.

Every time Dario touched her with that hot glint in his eyes that told her he needed her. Each time he clasped her hand in his while they were sightseeing, or shopping, or simply lying on the estate's private beach enjoying the sunset. Whenever he praised her faltering Italian or kissed her with enough passion and purpose to make her yearn for the hard drive of his body into hers. Every time he insisted on showing her some new place, or looked at her as if she fascinated him, or pressed his lips to her knuckles while teasing her, the tender gesture in sharp contrast to the fierce intensity with which they always ended up making love... She became that little bit more invested, that little bit more convinced that something real was happening between them.

But how did she make him acknowledge that this was more than either of them had intended, if their relationship still had an end date...and she didn't even have the guts to have a conversation with him about returning to Westwick for a few days, like they'd agreed?

She was beginning to realise she needed to soon, more than ever. Because as much as she'd loved the past two weeks, which had flown by in a haze of pheromones and intimacy, how could this be more when the marriage—and her life here—was still effectively a stunt to fool the Trustees? She had to bring herself back down to earth to figure out if her growing attachment to Dario was more than just the adrenaline rush of great sex and having his undivided attention. Because there was no doubt about it, the man was intoxicating, especially now she was getting more tantalising glimpses of the boy he had been before his mother's death—wild and free, his spirit undimmed by his father's neglect and judgement.

But he was still so unwilling to even think about Westwick, her updates on the Hall's progress always instantly dismissed. And he still hadn't contacted Mia and Sante, to heal the rift with his best friend the rest of the way...

She sighed. 'Honestly, Ellie. I'm not sure where we'll be living in the long term. But I'm heading back to Westwick on Monday.' She pushed the words out, knowing that if she made it official, it would force her to talk to Dario. It was past time for her to call in that promise.

'Oh wow, really? That would be amazing. Will Mr Lorenti be coming with you?'

'Ummm...' The left-field question had the bubble of hope pushing against her breastbone again. It would be amazing if Dario came with her. Not only would it show a commitment to the Hall, but it would also be a commitment to her. To *them*... Whatever *they* were.

But then she got a clue. Dario hated Westwick... The priority now was to stop letting Dario have everything his own way. And to give herself space to figure out what was really going on between them.

Because she was afraid she was already more than halfway in love with her fake husband... And she still didn't really have a solid idea how he felt about her.

Going back to her real life, regrouping, rebooting, giving herself a purpose again—beyond the pursuit of endless pleasure—if only for a few days, would give her that much-needed perspective.

And standing up to Dario might finally give her the courage and the confidence to tell him about the past they shared...and how much their fake marriage was starting to mean to her.

'The Trustees signed the papers necessary to give you full ownership of the property and the estate two hours ago, as per the terms of your father's will. Congratulations, Mr Lorenti. The palazzo should be yours officially by this time tomorrow when all the necessary documents have been filed with the court.'

Dario nodded, as the head of his legal team in London smiled at him as if he had just won the lotto. But the euphoria he should be feeling eluded him.

'There is no chance they will renege on this position?' he asked.

The solicitor frowned. 'They can try if they want, but the property is yours now, not much they can do about it. I guess they could sue, but it would be a lengthy process, and costly. And I doubt they'd want to risk their own money on any further legal action against you. Why do you ask?'

Because the marriage is not real.

It felt too easy, after seven years of legal wrangling, to have the Trustees release their stranglehold on the palazzo after only a month. The deception had given him what he had wanted. But the very first thought that came into his head was not how easily he had bested those old fools in the end—it was disappointment at the thought he would now be able to release Tallulah from the terms of their agreement sooner than planned.

He would not divorce her until the end of the year. He might own the palazzo, but he did not want to encourage a lawsuit, if the Trustees realised they had been duped into signing over the property.

But there was no tangible reason to remain here, pretending to have a honeymoon. No reason why his 'wife' could not return to her life in England, and he to his home in Milan in the next few weeks.

The only problem was, every single cell in his body rebelled against the idea of letting her go...

It's the sex. It has to be.

He still had not had his fill of her. That was all. Even though they had been making love every morning and night and so many snatched moments in between for two weeks now, he still wanted her, incessantly—to the extent that even when they were not making love, he enjoyed being with her. She fascinated him and enchanted him. He felt like a teenager again, the boy who had been starved of affection, and now he wished to gorge on it to his heart's content. Because Tallulah was just so *kind*…

He swallowed, the thought of how artless and engaging and delightful she was, both in and out of bed, even more disturbing than the thought of letting her go.

She was so open. So tender. So compassionate. So genuine. He'd never before met a woman so positive and honest and undemanding. And because of that, she had become a fire in his blood.

Of course, this fire would burn out eventually. He already suspected sometimes when she looked at him, she wished for more from him. And a part of him understood, as he held her late at night, while she slept beside him, her open and tender heart would become bruised eventually when she fully accepted there could never be more between them.

But this fire had not burnt out yet. Plus, she had agreed to remain on Capri for at least a month, so why end this arrangement prematurely, when they were both enjoying it? It had been years since he'd taken a genuine break from work… And now the estate was his, why should he not enjoy the fruits of the labours to bring it back to life?

'Good work, Carstairs,' he said.

'By the way, our real estate department has a buyer for Westwick,' the man said. 'It's a Saudi investment conglomerate. They want to turn the place into a resort hotel, which would probably mean some substantial remodelling. We've looked at the building's status on the heritage registry, and apparently it's only the frontage that's listed, the rest of it can be demolished and rebuilt. Anyway, it's a great offer. You want me to set that in motion?'

Again, the news should have been like having all his birthdays come at once. The Hall still held so many unpleasant memories for him, those long days spent festering in the bed after his accident. It represented everything about his childhood he had always hated—his father's searing contempt, the loss of his mother, the loss of his life on Capri, the loss of his freedom... But in the past two weeks, every time Tallulah mentioned the Hall, which she did quite often, he had begun to understand a little more how much the place really meant to her. And there had been other memories that had tickled the back of his consciousness. The little girl who had been so determined to coax him out of his shell, whose presence and bright, lively friendship had eventually made that long, unhappy summer bearable.

It made him feel weak and foolish to remember that girl now, and how much he had come to depend on her daily visits to his sickbed. And in some ways, Tallulah's love of Westwick made him hate the place more too—because he knew she would want to return there once their time together was over. But could he bring himself to take the one thing away from her that he knew she cared for so passionately?

He had turned himself into a cold and ruthless man over the years, deliberately. So he would never be that scared, lonely boy again. But sometimes, late at night, with her beside him, he had allowed his mind to wander, enough to even question how happy the isolation he had imposed on himself since that summer had made him. After all, letting his resentments, his anger fester, had allowed him to believe his father's lies about Sante for too long. So long in fact, he now found it impossible to return the calls and messages from both him and Mia, inviting him to return to Sicily.

Similarly, how could he take the one thing away from Tallulah she had wanted out of this whole arrangement, when they parted? And what if he did not wish to cut ties entirely?

Having her working for him would give him an excuse to see her again, should he wish.

'Hold fire on that for now,' he said, suddenly feeling almost sentimental about Westwick.

'Are you sure?' Carstairs looked astonished. 'I don't know how long the deal will be on the table, Mr Lorenti.'

'I'm sure there will be other interested buyers if I decide I still wish to sell,' he heard himself say before ending the call abruptly.

He could never live in the Hall, but Tallulah seemed devoted to the place and the people she worked with there. And surely, he owed her that much, for helping him secure ownership of the palazzo.

Although strangely, since he'd been here with her, he'd also become aware that the idyllic memories he had of Capri had always been overshadowed by other emotions he'd been careful to lock away since. As a boy he'd adored the freedom, but hadn't he also been in constant fear that his mother's dark moods would come back, that Mia would not have enough to eat? The staff had come and gone with alarming regularity because his mother squandered the money to pay their salaries on her endless pursuit of pleasure at all costs. And the house and its grounds had been in a deteriorating state long before her death, the wild parties often becoming scary when the adults were all either drunk or drugged up to their eyeballs.

His money had repaired the property, but Tallulah's presence had added a layer of something more… Companionship, friendship, stability even, that he hadn't realised he had yearned for then, until these past two weeks.

He blinked, the sentimental thoughts somehow lowering his guard.

Dio, when had he become so soft?

The light knock had him turning to find Tallulah standing on the threshold of his office. Something swift and sharp rushed through him.

Why was he so overjoyed to see her, when they had made love less than two hours ago?

'Dario, I need to speak with you,' she said.

He strode towards her and grasped her around the waist, deciding that fierce rush could only be the desire to have her again. To feed this damn addiction. She wore a simple summer dress, making it easy for him to lift the skirt and palm her lush flesh, even as he dragged her the rest of the way into the room and slammed the door closed with his foot.

'How about we talk later?' he said, sinking his hands into her panties to cup her naked bottom.

She gasped, but if she was shocked by the demand, the scent of her arousal that filled his senses told him her answer. He clasped her hand, strode to the desk, and pushed the laptop and papers to one side to lift her onto the surface… and inhaled the sultry scent which told him she wanted him with the same intensity.

He covered her mouth with his, to swallow her sob of surrender and found the hot flesh between her legs with insistent fingers. She moaned, lifting her arms to rope around his neck, while he worked the swollen erection free of his pants.

'Yes?' he asked, even though her eyes were already dazed with need.

She nodded, and he clasped her hips to thrust his straining cock into her, the penetration impossibly deep.

They rode the sharp, swift wave to completion in a matter of seconds, her orgasm massaging him to his own fierce release, their ragged breathing reverberating around the quiet room. The heady mix of need and desperation disturbed him as he felt his heartbeat start to slow and her hands shaking where she gripped his shoulders.

He buried his face in her hair, suddenly ashamed of the vicious hunger he hadn't even attempted to control.

What was wrong with him? She wasn't just a fire in his blood now—she had become someone he couldn't seem to live without for more than a few hours at a time.

She shifted slightly, still impaled on the rigid length. He pulled free of her body and felt her flinch. The shame twisted in his gut like a blade.

He raised his gaze to hers, cradled her cheek to press a kiss to her temple.

'I apologise, Tallulah, that lacked finesse,' he managed, which had to be the understatement of the century. He had treated her as if he were a rutting bull.

Her face was flushed, her lips trembling, and yet the smile which crossed her face was unbearably sweet. 'Don't apologise, Dario. I—I love it when you need me like that.'

He stepped back to repair his clothing. How could she be so artless, so innocent and yet affect him so deeply?

She climbed off the desk and lifted her torn panties from the floor, before shoving them into the pocket of her dress.

Dio, had he ripped her underwear from her? How had this need become so wild, so elemental?

'What did you wish to talk about?' he asked, forcing his mind to engage again through the fog of pheromones and panic.

She stared at him blankly, her lust-blown pupils hazy with confusion.

Good to know he wasn't the only one blindsided by this hunger.

She blinked. 'Oh, yes... I wanted to return to Westwick tomorrow—just for a few days.' For a moment the information would not compute in his endorphin-addled brain. 'The decorators are arriving on Monday, and I need to be there to oversee the work.' She hesitated then rambled on, making no sense. 'I've arranged a flight from Naples. I was wondering if I could borrow one of your cars and park it at the airport...'

She continued to babble about her travel arrangements as frustration rose up inside him.

'No...' He barked the word more harshly than intended, making her jumbled information slam to a halt. 'You cannot leave Capri yet.'

Because I still want you, all the damn time.

Thank god he managed to bite off that confession before it could tumble out of his mouth. But the fear continued to claw at his chest. He could not let her go, not yet. He wasn't ready.

Her eyes widened. But then her chin firmed, and he saw the stubbornness which had been absent for the last two weeks... It was annoying to realise he'd missed it.

'We agreed, Dario, in Milan, on the day we exchanged vows,' she said, with a patience that infuriated him. Did she think him an imbecile, that he didn't remember that? 'And you...you promised.'

He let his frustration build, to control the panic. He didn't want her to go. What if she did not come back? He needed her.

Even as the thought struck him, the walls of the study, bright with the mid-morning sun, seemed to close in around him. His leg throbbed, alongside the scar on his face... And he was suddenly that boy again, trapped in the wreckage of an overturned car, waiting forever for his only friend to return to him.

He stalked across the room, turning his back to her, to stare at the rocky coastline, the shimmering blue of the sea, the glint of the cliffs, the rambling pinks and purples of the bougainvillea, his body still humming with afterglow, his stomach hollowing out.

He thrust his fingers through his hair, trying to buy himself time, to control the fear, the emotion, that hideous feeling of being abandoned, of being alone.

'I'll be back in a few days...' she murmured.

He swung round. 'No, I will accompany you,' he managed, his throat still raw with panic, the sweat pooling to run down his spine. 'We will take the helicopter to Naples, and the jet from there to Heathrow. Then we can transfer by car to the estate.'

Even as he suggested the hasty travel plan, he knew he sounded deranged. The last damn thing he wanted, the last damn thing he had *ever* wanted, was to spend time at Westwick. But how could he force her to stay? Not only had he promised to let her return to Wiltshire during the month, but worse, it would make him seem weak and too needy to refuse her request.

Her face softened with surprise and then a brilliant smile crossed her features.

'Really? You'll come to Westwick with me?'

'Yes, of course. We must not separate yet, the Trustees still need to be convinced this marriage is real,' he said, the white lie coming easily.

'Oh Dario, that's wonderful.' She rushed towards him and wrapped her arms around his waist. He clasped her shoulders, stupidly touched by her transparent, and uncomplicated reaction. And ignored the prickle of guilt that she had accepted his lie so readily. Because her blind faith in him, and her trust, however undeserved, was somehow even more intoxicating than the furious lovemaking, the effects of which still echoed in his groin. As she began to reel off a list of things she wanted to show him—to do with the renovations—he didn't have the heart to tell her the truth, that he had no interest in the Hall. But as she continued to babble, the brutal thunder of his own heart, crashing against his ribs, started to ease.

He would take her to that godforsaken place, and then bring her back here with him… And keep her here, until he could lock the fear away again for good.

Then, at last, he would be able to let her go.

CHAPTER FOURTEEN

DARIO STARED OUT of the window of the chauffeur-driven limousine, which had picked them up at Heathrow two hours ago, as it drove through the gates of Westwick Hall. The last time he'd been here, he'd only had to stay for a matter of minutes. But now he would have to remain for several days. The thought did not appeal to him, the hollow sensation he had been running away from for years making his stomach drop to his toes.

But as the large Palladian frontage came into view—the twin staircases which led to the front entrance obscured by scaffolding—he found himself glancing at the woman asleep beside him.

She had been talking non-stop when they had boarded the jet that morning in Naples, keen to apprise him of all the different infrastructure projects she had put in motion with the investment he'd given her... How had that simple bribe—to get her to marry him—become so damn complicated in the weeks since? He'd started kissing her—mostly so he could shut her up about Westwick. But of course, as soon as he'd touched her, tempted her, she'd responded with the artless enthusiasm he found so intoxicating... And before either of them could say 'mile-high club' they'd been tearing each other's clothes off in the jet's bedroom. He could see now he'd exhausted her, because she'd fallen asleep as soon as they'd driven away from the airport.

Her enthusiasm about this place had only deepened the chasm in his stomach which had been growing ever since he had agreed to this trip. With her scent filling the car, though, and the thought of what lay ahead when they arrived at the Hall, it was impossible for him to switch off his brain...or the memories which continued to torment him.

The chauffeur braked on the newly laid driveway in front of the towering edifice of his father's house. Even with the May sunlight glinting off the recently sand-blasted stonework, the place loomed over him—oppressive and judgemental—a miserable reminder of the grieving child, and the broken teenager he'd tried so hard to destroy. Why did this place always yank him back to those times in his life when he'd felt so powerless and alone?

Except he wasn't alone now, he thought, as he glanced at Tallulah, her head nestled on his chest. He pressed a kiss to her hair, knowing he should control the pleasure which welled inside him like a drug—but not quite able to today, while the shadow of his past lay over him like a shroud.

'Wake up, bella,' he murmured to Tallulah as a young woman bounded out of the house, a smile of welcome on her face, followed by an old man whom he vaguely recognised.

George, the groom. Was he still here?

Then an older woman appeared, and every muscle in his body tensed. He recognised her immediately, despite the greying hair. Elsa Parker—the housekeeper at Westwick the summer he'd been brought here after the accident.

He could still remember the pity shadowing her eyes that day which had made him feel so weak, so pathetic.

What the hell was she doing here? Hadn't she left years ago? She was one of the reasons he hadn't had any intention of returning before this year. She had been kind to him that summer, but he hated that she had known him as that broken boy. And she was also the mother of the girl whose company he'd come to rely on far too much that summer.

The chasm in his stomach widened. Apparently, this damn trip was going to be even more excruciating than he had anticipated.

Tallulah stirred against him, her cornflower-blue eyes blinking open. Then she stretched and yawned. 'We're here.'

He found himself smiling despite the weight in his gut.

Dio, but even her misguided love for this miserable place enchanted him...

At least he would not have to suffer it on his own, not this time. And while Elsa Parker might remember him from that summer, she would not recognise the man he had become. He had exorcised that boy a long time ago. And he doubted she knew of his friendship with her daughter, Tali, as she had been so busy with her new responsibilities. He would have to be sure to keep the housekeeper well away from Tallulah. He didn't want his fake wife seeing that weakness or even knowing about it. The less she knew about that messed-up kid, the better.

'Come, your staff are already waiting to greet you...' he said, his voice gruff as he threaded his fingers with hers, reassured by her presence again.

How had he become so reliant on her company in such a short space of time?

She looked past him, then grinned, as the chauffeur opened the door. '*Your* staff, you mean.'

But when he climbed out of the car, and helped her out, the strangest thing happened. Elsa Parker rushed up to Tallulah and threw her arms around her.

'Tali, you're back! How are you, love?'

Tali? The name reverberated through his consciousness. That was *her* name, the name of the child who had snuck into his room, and talked to him about everything and nothing, taking his mind off the pain, the loneliness... But who had also been there, hiding in the wardrobe, the one time his father had come to visit him. And berated him for being foolish enough to befriend a Sicilian guttersnipe—and detailed all Sante's crimes, crimes which had turned out to be lies.

He watched, in horrified slow motion, as Tallulah hugged the woman back. 'Mum, you didn't have to come and meet me. I told you I'd come to the cottage to visit this evening.'

Mum? Elsa Parker was Tallulah Whittaker's mother?

The woman he had married, the woman who had somehow broken through the barriers he had spent so long building since that summer...was also *Tali*. He remembered the girl's name. The little girl who had once seen him at his very worst, before he had been able to put those barriers in place.

The weight in his stomach plummeted, his mind reeling, the shock and anger making his heart pump so hard it felt as if it would smash through his ribs.

Suddenly, it all made a hideous kind of sense. The way he'd gravitated towards her. The way he'd come to rely on her. The way he'd trusted her so easily, *too* easily. Because it was the same thing he had done all those years ago, when he'd spent a summer in darkness and agony and had come to depend on that cheerful, cheeky child to drag him back into the light.

There had been something about her, that first day, in the library, something familiar which he had ruthlessly ignored, because it had made him feel weak. But now it was staring him in the face, impossible to ignore.

Nausea gathered in his gut, threatening to rise up his throat like bile.

He could still see her childish face, so bright, so earnest, so sweet, telling him not to be sad, that she would be his friend, while tears of humiliation stung his eyes. And the pain in his leg had been nothing compared to the agony in his heart.

Because his best friend had betrayed him and left him to die. Because his mother had been so reckless and impulsive she'd put her addictions above the needs of her own children. Because his father saw him as nothing more than a means of continuing his own sterile, pointless legacy.

They'd *all* betrayed him, but somehow, in this agonising moment, the fact Tallulah, no, *Tali*, had remained silent about who she really was, for a month, felt like the biggest betrayal of all.

She glanced over her shoulder now. But those beautiful eyes, which still had the power to destroy him, immediately saw his anguish. 'Dario, is everything okay…? I—I want to introduce you to my mum.'

He gave a stiff nod, letting his anger build to hide his panic. What a fool he'd been, to trust her. To *let* her trick him.

'We've met,' he mumbled, unable to look at the older woman.

Tallulah's eyes widened, her face flushing.

He saw the flicker of distress cross her face, but the fear was too huge, that she would see the hurt, the anguish churning in his stomach.

If only he could get back into the car, and leave, arrange to sell this place as soon as possible. He owed her nothing. She had deceived him, wormed her way into his affections, when he didn't want her there. When he'd *never* wanted *anyone* there. Ever again.

But somehow, he couldn't seem to make himself walk away. Even now, he couldn't make the clean break that would take him back to being the man he wanted to be, instead of the broken boy.

He grasped Tallulah's upper arm—acting on impulse now—and walked past her mother and the others. The varying levels of surprise and shock on their faces was nothing compared to the guilt he saw shadowing Tallulah's face... no, *Tali's* face.

'We need to talk,' he said, grinding out the words past the fury and pain as he escorted her into the house. 'About why you lied to me, *Tali*.'

'Dario, stop, you're scaring me...' Tali tried to dig her heels into the carpet as Dario marched through the house, past the salon, where the crew of decorators had already set up. Down the hallway, then up the main staircase.

She had to jog to keep up with his long strides, the limp not slowing him down much.

She hadn't expected him to even remember her mum, had convinced herself he'd forgotten them both. Because he'd never mentioned it...

But what should have pleased her, had devastation welling in her chest. Because she had seen the devastation on his face when he'd recognised her mother...and then her.

He hauled her into the library, slammed the door behind them, then grasped her other arm to force her face to his.

'You lied to me,' he said, the tone of his voice vibrating with anger, but beneath it she could hear the panic. 'You let me marry you, let me come to rely on you, let me fuck you like my life depended on it...without ever telling me who you really were.'

She struggled out of his hold, clasping her hands over the place where his fingers had dug in, her whole body shaking with all the emotions bombarding her at once—shock, panic and anguish at his visceral reaction to discovering her identity, but topping them all was confusion.

What had she done that was so terrible? So unforgiveable?

But one thing she did know was that she hadn't lied to him.

'You never asked,' she said. 'I—I thought you'd forgotten all about me… If you must know, I was embarrassed to remind you, because it made me realise that while our friendship back then had been so important to me, it never had been to you.'

She'd loved being with him that summer. Because she'd been lonely, too. Her father had disappeared that spring, she'd had to leave all her friends behind in Dorset to live at Westwick, and every night for weeks she'd listened to her mum's wrenching sobs through the bedroom wall, not knowing what to do to make her happy again.

But then she'd discovered Dario. And every time she had made that surly boy smile, even laugh, it had felt like she had achieved a miracle. And it had helped to convince her, long after he'd gone back to boarding school, that she'd be able to fix not just her mother's sadness, but that somehow she might have fixed him, too.

He swore, in both English and Italian, then turned away from her to march to the tall, mullioned window which looked out onto the grounds.

He growled something else in Italian…the words thick with anger. But she grasped the meaning. He was accusing her of deceiving him. Of knowing who he was, of knowing all about his dysfunctional relationship with his father, because she'd witnessed it, and pretending not to know.

'What exactly was I tricking you into doing, Dario?' she asked, her voice shaking as she approached him, knowing she had to find the courage to confront him—and to stand up for herself. Because she wasn't the only one who had wanted to change the terms of their arrangement.

Perhaps she was a naïve idiot to have fallen in love with him. And yes, maybe that *was* because she had known the damaged, victimised boy, as well as the man he had made himself become. But why was he so upset that she'd been able to see past the ruthless, controlled autocrat to the caring, tender, protective, possessive man he could be...if he had ever allowed himself to need her the way she needed him.

She hadn't tricked him—not intentionally. Because *he* was the one who had always held all the power in this relationship. And *she* was the one who had fallen hopelessly in love. Yet she had *never* demanded more from him than he was willing to give her, because in some neglected part of her heart, she'd convinced herself she didn't have the right to ask.

Yes, she should have told him who she was, but the reason she hadn't was she had been scared he would look at her with the same blank expression on his face her father had given her the last time she'd seen him, before he'd walked out on her and her mother.

But whose fault was it really that she loved Dario so much now, when he had never even attempted to disguise his desire for her? Not once.

When he swung back round, his gaze was harsh, fierce, still furious.

'You tricked me into caring about you. Into needing you. More than I should. Much more than I ever wanted to.' He glanced around the library, then swore again. '*Dio*, I even considered keeping this estate that I hate, just so I could keep you...'

He spat the words at her, as if that was the greatest insult of all. And worse, as if she had been angling for that all along...as if the feelings she had tried so hard not to burden him with had been nothing more than a scheme to make him keep Westwick.

Her eyes burned with all the tears she'd never shed for that little girl, who had wanted her daddy to love her but had never understood why he couldn't. And the grown woman who had wanted to tell this man that she cared for him deeply, that she wanted more than a fake marriage but had been scared of asking too much of him, too soon.

How had she allowed herself to be so vulnerable? *Again*.

'I didn't trick you...' she said, the tears scalding her throat now as she fought like hell to hold them back. She wouldn't cry—she wouldn't *let* him make her cry. 'Do you really think I care about Westwick or my job more than I care about you? About us?'

He reared back as if she'd slapped him. The flash of panic and fear in his eyes only confirmed what he'd already told her though. He didn't *want* her to care about him. Which only made it so much harder to admit that she always had.

'I did not ask that of you. Nor do I require it.'

And there it was, the rejection she'd feared all along.

But as she tried to gather herself, to guard what was left of her already battered heart from more pain, he added, 'This relationship can never be real.'

'Why not?' she asked, but she could see the answer she'd feared in his eyes.

'Because that is not what I want. And it never was. Not even as a boy.'

It wasn't true. She *knew* it wasn't. She had seen how lonely he had been that summer, the way he'd softened towards her over the weeks, even when he'd tried to disguise it. Even as an eight-year-old, she'd understood—he'd needed her.

But she couldn't reach this man the way she'd once been able to reach the boy.

And she would only hurt herself more now if she tried.

'You know that day your father came to visit you, I hated him so much. The awful things he said to you, the way he talked to you as if you were nothing. It was so obvious he didn't know you, that he didn't care about you...'

He stepped forward, his face rigid with rejection now.

'Don't talk about that day. I don't ever want to hear you talk about it again.'

'He hurt you, and you were already so broken...' she carried on, despite his warning tone, refusing to be silenced again. 'But you know why I recognised how broken you were?'

He didn't respond, his gaze fierce with fury.

'Because my father had already abandoned me, too.'

He flinched, and she saw a moment of regret cross his features. But that too was ruthlessly controlled. 'This has no bearing on your deception now.'

She shook her head, feeling sick inside.

'When did you become *him*, Dario?' she whispered. 'When did you close yourself off from your emotions so completely, that you believed the lies he told you about Sante? When did you convince yourself that it's better to feel nothing than to let yourself get hurt?' She gulped, because he was staring at her now as if she'd lost her mind.

She didn't care. She wasn't going to let him gaslight her and make out like she was the coward here.

'I didn't tell you I was Tali because I was convinced you didn't remember me, and you know why I was convinced about that? Because for a moment, I didn't recognise you either that day in the library.' She glanced at his scar, which flexed as he clenched his teeth. 'Oh, I knew who you were, the scars, your injured leg, but I didn't recognise the boy who could smile, who could laugh, who I'd managed to draw out of his shell... Until we were in Sicily and then Capri... But that was all just an illusion, wasn't it? You were on an endorphin high that I'd supplied.' She gulped in a painful breath, the sickness, the regret, the devastation almost more than she could bear. 'I get it now... It wasn't *me* you wanted. It was just some great recreational sex, and to get your mother's palazzo back.'

'I never promised you more...' he began, his words so terse and defensive she wanted to scream.

'No, you never did. And that's on me. But you knew every time I reached for you, every time you reached for me, that I wanted more... And on some level, you let me believe there *could* be more. You know, my dad made me think I had no value because he didn't want me. I won't let you do the same...' she declared, even though she knew in many ways she already had. Because it was going to take a very long time to repair her heart.

She threw up her hands, looking round the library she'd always loved. The place where she'd agreed to his bargain, in order to save it... The place that was tarnished now... Because it was a symbol of how stupid she'd been to think a pile of stone and mortar, however grand, however beautiful, however important to her, and the people she loved, could *ever* mean more to her than her pride and confidence and self-respect.

She'd allowed herself to fall in love with a man who'd closed off his heart a long time ago—and she'd been too starry-eyed and optimistic to truly have known she couldn't fix him too, the way she'd had the tiles on the roof repaired, or the potholes in the driveway filled.

'If you want to sell Westwick, to demolish it, I can't stop you...' she said, utterly defeated. She'd failed her colleagues, her mum, and that hurt, but she'd failed herself more. 'Because our bargain is done.'

She turned and walked away from him. He didn't say anything to stop her, the silence deafening... Somehow, she managed to keep the tears inside her, until she walked down the stairs, past the workmen, then through the hallways smelling of fresh paint. She broke into a run, though, as she passed the carriage house, where her old office was, and the flat that was no longer her home, and rounded the stables until she reached the path through the fields leading towards the woods and her mother's cottage.

She'd have to tell her mum and Ellie and George and everyone else how badly she'd fucked up, soon. But somehow losing Westwick, and everything she'd worked so hard to save by making that stupid deal with him, didn't feel as painful as losing the dreams she'd nurtured for the last few weeks—god, maybe even years—that she could be the one to scale the walls Dario Lorenti had built around his heart.

CHAPTER FIFTEEN

'I—I have to talk to everyone, tell them they're losing their j-jobs,' Tali murmured, her voice jerking through the gulping sobs she hadn't been able to contain since her mother had arrived at the cottage ten minutes ago.

'Honey, don't worry about any of that yet…' her mum said, her voice soothing, her arms tightening around her as Tali knelt by the old armchair and hugged her mum's knees, trying to gather the strength to stop crying and start planning. 'You're distraught, Tali. There's no need to…'

'There's e-every need, M-Mum.' She raised her head, forced herself to stop burying her face in her mother's lap like a child instead of a grown woman. 'Don't you see, it's all my f-fault. I've lost everyone their jobs, and you your home, because I c-couldn't get it into my stupid head that this relationship was always fake.'

Her lungs tightened with panic.

'I don't even know if he'll give them severance pay,' she said, starting to feel nauseous again. 'He was so angry with…'

'Stop!' Her mother's voice became firm, and less sympathetic. 'If it comes to that, it's out of your hands. We are all adults, and you've always taken far too much responsibility onto your shoulders for everyone here, not to mention for this estate.'

'But Mum, you'll lose this p-place and…'

'And I'll be okay. I'll find somewhere else to live, we both will,' she interrupted again. Then pressed warm hands—roughened by years of hard work—to Tali's cheeks. 'You have to stop worrying about me, sweetheart, I'm not fragile the way I was that summer. Let me look after you now, okay? Because that's *my* job, not yours.'

Tali nodded, feeling even worse. 'Okay, Mum, you're… Y-you're right. And I'm sorry.'

Why had she tried to hold everything together so tightly? Wasn't this just another example of how she had let her tendency to want to fix everyone but herself become a weakness instead of a strength?

'You have nothing to be sorry for, Tali,' her mum continued, her tone softening as she wiped away the tears still streaking down Tali's face. 'That little girl was so fierce, and so determined to make me happy again. And it worked, you know. Because I finally realised, that even though he walked away from us, he left me with you.'

Tali bowed her head, blindsided by her overwrought emotions again.

'But you know, Tali, I'm not sure all this guilt over Westwick is even warranted anyway.'

'How so?' Tali asked.

'From the look on Mr Lorenti's face before he realised who you were, I don't think it was fake for him either…'

'Please don't, Mum.' Tali stood up to get away from her mum's misguided attempts to make her feel better.

She swiped the last of the tears off her raw cheeks as she walked to the window that looked out on the woods. The thunderous rainstorm, which had begun not long after she'd got to the cottage two hours ago, was somehow a perfect refection of her misery. Her ribs started to ache, alongside her heart, because that blasted bubble of hope hadn't entirely died and she needed it to now. Whatever her mum had thought she'd seen in Dario's expression, she'd been wrong. Just like Tali had.

God, what was it about them both that they still had the ability to romanticise a man's reaction after they'd both been so comprehensively slam-dunked by love?

'I expect he's halfway back to London by now,' she said, trying not to imagine him in the limo alone, with that blank look on his face—which had been worse than his fury. 'Busy ordering his real estate division to find a buyer...' she added. *Or figuring out if he can have Westwick demolished*, she thought miserably, the sickening feeling—of how badly she'd messed things up by falling in love with her fake husband—working its way up her chest again to strangle her. She didn't try to swallow it down this time, though, because she needed to feel the pain if she was ever going to get over him.

'He didn't leave, you know. He was still in the library looking morose. I found him there twenty minutes ago after searching the place for you both.'

Tali swung around, shocked at the news. It had been nearly two hours since she'd left the Hall... And she knew he hated to spend any time here—it had been obvious as soon as he'd agreed to accompany her here that he hadn't wanted to come back. Just another reason why she'd started to convince herself he might actually care for her...

But then she forced herself to breathe through her latest delusion.

It was pissing down outside. He had probably just decided to stay put until the weather cleared. Knowing he was still so close, though, was a whole new form of torture.

She was about to say as much to her mother when a loud rap on the front door made them both jump.

'Who could that be in this weather?' her mother asked, heading past her to the front door.

But when she flung it open, and Tali saw Dario standing on the doorstep, his designer suit soaked through, his eyes as dark as the storm clouds outside, her heart went into free fall... As it plunged to earth, about to crash and burn all over again, he stepped over the threshold, dripping onto the doormat and asked her mother, in a low voice, 'Signora Parker, please may I speak with your daughter alone?'

Before Tali could detach her gaze long enough to tell her mum she couldn't speak to Dario, not again, because she wasn't sure she could keep hold of the few morsels of pride she had left and not throw herself at him this time—when he looked so sad, so tortured, so alone—her mum closed the door behind him and said, 'I'll go and fold the laundry upstairs and leave you two, but you need to understand one thing, Mr Lorenti.'

He blinked as if he were trying to wake himself from a coma, his gaze raking over Tali with an intensity that was making her skin heat despite the pain.

But then he turned, to address her mother. '*Sì*, Signora Parker.'

'If you hurt her again, I'll have to murder you, even if it means Westwick is lost forever.'

He nodded, slowly. 'Understood.'

And then her mother was gone. Tali's heart was in pieces, but she wasn't sure anymore whether it was still broken or about to mend. Because Dario didn't look furious with her anymore, and he didn't look indifferent either... He looked shattered, too.

Was it possible that by finally standing her ground, finally telling him what she needed, he'd realised that he needed it, too?

Dario limped across the small room, his head nearly butting the exposed beams, towards Tallulah. His leg was killing him, the vicious spring storm and the trudge through the muddy fields as he'd searched for the cottage having cramped the ruined muscles—but something about the pain and the grim weather suited his mood perfectly.

He deserved to be in agony. He deserved to be punished. After the things he'd said, the things he'd threatened to do. All simply to protect himself, from this woman who...as soon as she had stood up to him and called him out on all his bullshit, he had finally understood he couldn't live without.

How had he managed to lie to himself for weeks?

She stepped away from him as he got closer, tearing his heart right out of his chest.

He had done this. He had hurt her so badly she did not love him anymore. But maybe he could still salvage this situation. Maybe he could still keep her, make her love him again...if he begged. Funny to think that begging someone to care for him—letting them see all his weaknesses and vulnerabilities—had always been the thing he had been most terrified of, but it wasn't anymore... Because not doing so would mean losing Tallulah.

'Dario, why are you here?' she finally whispered, her face a picture of...*what*? Was that panic, disgust, shock? Why could he not read her expression anymore?

She stared at him, those luminous blue eyes making the regret and guilt slice through him like a knife, because he could see no hate in her eyes when there should have been— only compassion. Was this good? Or was she just too kind a person to hate anyone—even him?

He clung to the thought, though, desperate to believe he hadn't destroyed his chance completely.

'I came to say I'm sorry,' he said, his voice breaking on the inadequate word. 'I want another chance.'

'A ch-chance for what?' she said, but then her eyes grew round, and the hurt shadowing them had the knife twisting in his gut. 'If you need this marriage to get ownership of your palazzo, y-you don't have to divorce me yet, but I can't be with you, not anymore, you must understand that… It's too painful for me.'

Hope swelled against his ribs, hope he didn't deserve but would grab with both hands.

He brushed his thumb over the reddened skin of her cheek, disgusted with himself when she flinched.

'I already own the palazzo,' he said. 'The legal transfer of ownership was completed yesterday.'

'You…wh-what?' she asked, the transparent expression—confusion and concern—almost as beautiful as she was to him.

'I didn't tell you because I did not want you to leave me.'

'But…'

He cupped her cheeks in his palms, grateful that she did not flinch again. Pressing his fingers into her silky curls, he drew her into his body. He held her, stroking the soft skin, needing to breath in her ragged breaths, needing to share this connection, which had always felt so visceral, so right, so perfect, even though he had tried so hard never to acknowledge how much it meant to him.

He must confess everything now and place himself at her mercy.

'I see now, what I should have realised the first time we made love…' He swore softly when she shuddered. He was doing this wrong. 'No, the first time I kissed you.' He lifted his forehead from hers, stared into those bright, luminous, honest eyes and forced himself to be honest, too. 'No, the first time I touched you… That I wanted more from you, too.'

Her brow furrowed, but her hands flattened against his waist, her fingers curling into his wet shirt. 'Do you really mean that, Dario? Please don't lie to me again.'

'I have been so lonely, for so long. I thought…' He swallowed, controlling the familiar panic, forcing himself to tell her the truth. 'I thought if I owned the palazzo, it would be enough. But I don't want to be there without you,' he replied, without hesitation this time, without anger, without cowardice. 'I know now, it was never my safe place, that was always you. Even when you were Tali, and not Tallulah, you were the only person who ever made me feel unbroken. I'm sorry it took me so long to admit the truth to myself as well as you.'

'Dario...' she whispered, but the sadness remained in her eyes when she pressed a trembling palm to his scarred cheek. 'I want to believe that so much. But I'm scared... You shut me out. And that hurt. I want to be with you too, to see if we can make this a real relationship but I can't...'

'Shhh...' He held her face up to his. Pressed his lips to hers. 'It is already real, Tallulah.' Taking her palm from his cheek, he pressed it against his wet shirt. 'Do you feel how hard my heart is beating?'

She nodded, her eyes widening, the love in them so transparent he felt humbled.

'That is because I am scared, too,' he said, finally forced to admit his greatest fear. 'In fact, I am terrified, that I have messed this up so badly—by not trusting you, by accusing you of things you did not do to protect myself—you will decide you do not love me after all.'

'Don't be scared, because I do,' she said with such courage it humbled him even more.

How could it be so easy? he thought. All he had had to do was trust his feelings, to trust her love, and she'd let him back in.

The pain in his heart lifted as he clasped her head and covered her mouth with his, devouring her sweet lips, feeding the surge of desire and letting himself be swept away on the wave of love.

When they were finally forced to break apart, to breathe, she whispered, 'Does this mean we're really married?'

'*Absolutamente*,' he said, and then sealed their deal with another kiss.

EPILOGUE

Two years later

'BRACE YOURSELF, here comes chaos,' Dario murmured in Tali's ear, his arm tightening around her shoulders as she waved enthusiastically while they watched Sante and Mia's large black SUV drive into the palazzo's forecourt—three hours late.

She laughed, delighted by his stern expression and the heat in his eyes. 'Oh, shut up, and stop pretending you don't enjoy the chaos when they're here,' she whispered out of the corner of her mouth.

'And yet, I am also equally delighted when they are gone again!' he said, but she could hear the amusement in his voice.

Mia popped out of the passenger seat, followed by two dogs who bounded up to them in a melee of delighted yips and barks and wagging tales. Mia's round belly made the fierce hugs she gave them both—amid a tumble of profuse apologies for the delay—almost as chaotic as the dogs' excited welcome.

Sante meanwhile jumped out from the driver's side, to lift his baby daughter, Ariana, out of her car seat in the back and carry her over to join the welcoming party—the baby apparently totally unflustered by all the noise and activity.

'Oh wow, she's grown so much!' Tali remarked, reaching out to take the blinking toddler into her arms. 'How old is she now?' she asked, even though she already knew the answer.

Sante's chest puffed up with pride as he stroked his daughter's fluffball of hair. 'Thirteen months and *finally* sleeping through the night!' he said with mock exasperation. 'Mostly.'

'Just in time for this one to arrive in two months' time and keep us up all night instead,' announced Mia as she stroked her stomach.

'And whose fault is that?' demanded Dario, going into big-brother mode. 'What were you two thinking getting pregnant again so soon after Ariana was born?'

Mia sent him a cheeky grin. 'It wasn't exactly planned, Dario,' she said, at the same time as her husband murmured, 'It is certainly not my fault your sister is irresistible, Dario.'

'*Dio*, Sante!' Dario said, covering his ears, while the dogs continued to prance around them and Ariana started to cry. 'Do not talk to me about my sister like that...'

'Hey, you're the one that started it,' Sante replied, the smile on his face one that made Tali smile, too.

She jostled Ariana on her hip until the baby stopped crying, while the staff arrived to transport the insane amount of luggage from the car to the apartment Tali and Dario had had decorated over a year ago, so Mia and her family could visit the palazzo whenever they wished.

The two men continued to talk on the patio, while she and Mia headed into the house.

It was so good to hear them joking with each other. After a shaky start, Dario and Sante had become good friends again. Buddies even. And she loved to see it. For Dario most of all... After having no one close in his life, he now had three people—four if you counted the niece she knew he adored—who would always be there for him.

'Here, let me take her, she's tired, I should put her down for a nap,' Mia suggested, because Ariana was still niggling.

'It's okay, I've got her,' Tali said, loving the warm weight of the little girl in her arms, and the smell of baby shampoo that clung to her. The pang of longing in her chest was hard to deny. 'Let's take her to her room,' she said.

It didn't take the two of them long to get Ariana ready for her nap. Tali changed her and gave her a bottle while her mother directed the staff where to put all the luggage.

After burping her, Tali placed her into the crib and watched with tears stinging her eyes as the baby rolled over and dropped into sleep almost instantly.

'She's so gorgeous,' she murmured, the wave of raw emotion making her lungs hurt.

She blinked furiously, to stop the ridiculous tears from falling. She thought she'd got away with it, but as soon as they had tiptoed out of the room and Mia had closed the door softly, her sister-in-law's eyes narrowed.

'Okay, spill it, what's going on? You look exhausted, Tali. And as adorable as I find my daughter, she doesn't usually make people look as if they're about to burst into tears.'

Tali choked out a laugh. She couldn't help it, even as she felt the twinge of panic.

She should have spoken to Dario about this a week ago. She'd bought the pregnancy test five days ago now, and hadn't had the guts to use it, convinced her period was bound to happen any moment. She'd had her coil removed, a month ago, and the doctor had mentioned they should wait seven days or use other forms of contraceptive after she'd starting using a contraceptive patch, just to be on the safe side. But they hadn't…*quite*…and now she was more than a week late. And she still didn't know how to bring up the conversation.

They'd talked about having children—of course they had. But only in a vague, we're-both-on-board-with-the-concept-eventually kind of way. While she knew Dario had been joking with Mia and Sante when they arrived, she also knew he was a man who liked to plan things out. So did she, really.

But they'd been so busy over the last few days, finishing up their work commitments to make time for this two-week visit... And this morning, when she'd planned to tell him she was a bit late, and probably should take a test, before she could mention it, he'd started kissing her and well...they'd got sidetracked, completely.

Seriously, who am I kidding?

The truth was she was a total coward. She didn't want to tell Dario, in case he wasn't as overjoyed about the prospect of a pregnancy as she was.

'I think I might be pregnant...' she blurted, as the words she should have said to Dario first popped out without warning.

Mia's eyebrows shot up her forehead, but then a smile beamed across her face. 'Oh. My. God. This is wonderful. Why didn't you two tell us when...'

'Because Dario doesn't know, yet,' Tali interrupted Mia's excited response. 'And neither do I, really,' she added, the guilt starting to cripple her now. 'I haven't taken the test yet. It's still in my bedside drawer. In fact, I haven't even got up the guts to tell him I'm a week late. I feel like such a...'

'Whoa, whoa, whoa...' Mia grasped her hands, then slung an arm around her shoulders to pull her into a tight hug. 'Breathe, Tali. It's okay.'

She drew in a careful breath and let Mia hold her, the hug comforting, and somehow reassuring.

'I don't know what's wrong with me. I'm probably not even pregnant,' she started to babble. 'It's just...as soon as I realised I *might* be pregnant, I wanted to be, *so much*. But what if Dario doesn't feel the same way? What if he's not ready yet...'

'Shush, it's okay…' Mia placed warm palms on Tali's cheeks and smiled at her, managing to calm her rampaging heartbeat, at least a little. 'Really, Tali, the only way to find that out is to ask him.'

'I know it's silly, but…'

'And honestly, I think he'll be overjoyed at the prospect.'

'You do?' Tali said, still unsure, still not wanting to hope too much.

The last two years had been like a dream—a dream she never wanted to wake up from. Of course, they'd had their disagreements. Dario was bossy and demanding, and he liked to have things all his own way. So, she'd had to discover her kickass side, and fast—particularly when he'd suggested she give up her job and move full-time to Italy. It hadn't always been easy to make their marriage work, but after some heated arguments, and lots of debate—and no small amount of make-up sex—they'd found a compromise. They divided their time now between Wiltshire and Milan and Capri, both of them working remotely when required. And she loved their life. She wasn't sure how a baby was going to fit into that, if there was one. The only thing she was absolutely sure of was that her mum would be overjoyed to be a granny. But she wanted to face the challenge of starting a family with Dario. She knew he would be a wonderful dad—just watching him with Ariana had proved that. But what if he wasn't as sure?

He'd let his guard down with her. And she knew he trusted her. But she also knew he still found it hard sometimes to be open about his feelings, to share and discuss—after a lifetime of being scared to show a weakness. And she was even more scared that if he didn't want this 'possible' baby, he wouldn't want to tell her how he really felt, for fear of losing her. Even though she'd told him so many times that would never happen.

'Yes, I do,' Mia said, with a confidence Tali wanted to feel, too. 'He adores you, Tali. And he'd make a great dad... Probably way too overprotective of course, but I'm afraid you'll have to deal with that. Then again, I've managed to stop Sante from freaking out over every minor hiccup, usually on very little sleep, so I'm sure you can do the same for my big brother.'

Tali laughed, the first genuine laugh she'd managed in over a week.

Mia was right. Of course she was. She was working herself into a tizzy for no reason.

'Listen,' Mia murmured, rubbing Tali's arms. 'Why don't I go downstairs and send him up so you can take that test together? Sante and I have to get unpacked anyway, and settle Romulus and Remus, before Dario has them both evicted,' she added, rolling her eyes comically because they could still hear the dogs barking intermittently downstairs.

'Okay,' Tali managed, but she could still feel her stomach going into free fall as Mia headed off with an encouraging smile on her face.

'Mia said you needed to talk to me in private.' Dario walked into the bedroom suite, his stomach flipping over and his heart hammering his chest wall.

Something was wrong. He'd known it for days. And when Mia had arrived on the terrazzo and told him—with no small amount of drama—his wife needed to speak to him, it had started to scare him.

Why the hell hadn't he said something sooner? Discovered what the problem was? He'd noticed her silences, those far-off looks, the strange expression he had been unable to decipher because he hadn't seen it before. Not exactly panic, but not the sweet, uncomplicated happiness he was used to seeing. And she'd been so tired in the past few days. Most mornings she rose before he did—but not in the past week. And while he'd enjoyed the extra time to snuggle with her, now he was questioning that, too.

He had no idea what this something was. But when she turned towards him, her hands clasped so tightly the knuckles had whitened, it didn't just scare him anymore—it terrified him.

He crossed the room in a few strides, gripped her hands until they stopped shaking, then laid his palm on her cheek.

'What is it, Tallulah? Whatever it is, we can fix it,' he said, the panic starting to consume him, because he could see the sheen of tears in her eyes now, too.

He watched her throat contract as she swallowed, bracing for the worst, when she whispered, 'I need to take a pregnancy test.'

He stilled—the sudden rush of joy so strong, it was almost impossible to contain.

He had wanted to speak of babies for months now. Especially when she had had the coil removed. The suggestion that she not get the contraceptive patch had been on the tip of his tongue. He wanted to see her round with his child, to see her become a mother, to see her blossom and shine, to see her nurture his baby at her breast. God, he wanted all of it. He'd even been jealous of Sante, for having a beautiful daughter and another baby on the way…

But he knew his wife loved her job—in fact, they'd had more than a few arguments about her keeping the position at Westwick in the early days of their real marriage. Once he'd realised how important it was to her, though, he knew he couldn't pressure her into starting a family too soon.

So, he forced his features to remain impassive now. It was harder than he thought, even though he had had a lifetime of practice at keeping his emotions on lockdown, until he had met Tallulah.

'Okay?' he said. 'Do you want me to get Angelo to acquire one from *la farmacia*?'

'I already have one, I've had it for a week. Because I'm a week late.'

He nodded, not sure what that meant. But then she blinked, and a tear rolled down her cheek—which felt like a knife to his gut.

'You are not happy to have my baby?' he asked, his usually fluent English deserting him.

She shook her head. But then a watery smile spread across her lips. 'You—you're not unhappy at the prospect of us having an unplanned pregnancy?'

He placed his hand on her flat stomach. '*Dio*, no,' he said, the joy rushing through him as the smile in her eyes made the tears sparkle and glow. 'There's nothing I want more in this world than to see you have my child.'

She laughed, the sound echoing joyously in his heart, as she threw herself into his arms and he caught her. Then she whispered against his neck. 'Ditto.'

Ten minutes later, when the extra line appeared on the test stick, he swung her around, then kissed her senseless.

It was a long while later before they managed to make it downstairs to tell Mia and Sante the good news—and ring Tallulah's mother in Wiltshire. Dario was so overjoyed at the prospect of becoming a father, he didn't even mind that Sante spent the rest of the evening mocking him for failing to properly plan his *own* family.

'Sometimes, brother, planning is overrated,' Dario declared, slapping his old friend on the shoulder. 'And now, I can't wait for the chaos to begin!'

* * * * *

*If you just couldn't get enough of
Boss's Bride Price,
then be sure to check out the
previous instalment in the Enemy Tycoons duet,
Enemies Until After Hours
by Natalie Anderson!*

*And why not explore these other stories
by Heidi Rice?*

Queen's Winter Wedding Charade
Princess for the Headlines
Billionaire's Wedlocked Wife
The Heir Affair
Greek's Kidnapped Princess

Available now!

MILLS & BOON®

Coming next month

HIS FORCED SICILIAN BRIDE
Jackie Ashenden

'That's why you took me, isn't it?'

Caterina's pointed chin lifts, her expression half defiant, half imperious. 'So you could finish the job you started twenty years ago?'

So, the little *gattina* remembers me. I wasn't sure if she did.

'If I wanted to do that, you'd be dead already,' I observe. 'But you were right back there in the cathedral.'

Her long, thick black lashes flutter as she blinks rapidly. 'You kidnapping me, you mean? Oh...' Understanding dawns. 'I'm a hostage.'

I give her a slow smile, because I do like an intelligent woman. 'Excellent answer. Ten points to you.'

'My father will—'

'Your father,' I interrupt, 'is irrelevant, no matter what he will or won't do. I'm afraid, *gattina*, no one is going to save you this time.'

The delicate bow of her mouth, highlighted by some kind of shimmery, pink lipstick, compresses into a line, and fear flickers briefly in her eyes.

I expect her to cower in her seat, but she doesn't.

Instead, she stares back at me, undaunted despite her fear. 'So? I'm going to be your prisoner?'

'No, *gattina,*' I correct her gently. 'You're going to be my wife.'

Continue reading

HIS FORCED SICILIAN BRIDE
Jackie Ashenden

Available next month
millsandboon.co.uk

Copyright ©2026 Jackie Ashenden

COMING SOON!

We really hope you enjoyed reading this book. If you're looking for more romance be sure to head to the shops when new books are available on

Thursday 23rd April

To see which titles are coming soon, please visit
millsandboon.co.uk/nextmonth

MILLS & BOON

FOUR BRAND NEW BOOKS FROM
MILLS & BOON MODERN

Indulge in desire, drama, and breathtaking romance – where passion knows no bounds!

OUT NOW

Eight Modern stories published every month, find them all at:

millsandboon.co.uk

TWO BRAND NEW BOOKS FROM

Love Always

Be prepared to be swept away to incredible worldwide destinations along with our strong, relatable heroines and intensely desirable heroes.

OUT NOW

Four Love Always stories published every month, find them all at:

millsandboon.co.uk

OUT NOW!

Available at
millsandboon.co.uk

MILLS & BOON

LET'S TALK
Romance

For exclusive extracts, competitions and special offers, find us online:

- **f** MillsandBoon
- **X** @MillsandBoon
- **◉** @MillsandBoonUK
- **♪** @MillsandBoonUK

Get in touch on 01413 063 232

For all the latest titles coming soon, visit
millsandboon.co.uk/nextmonth

Made in the USA
San Bernardino, CA
14 March 2017